ABOVE

THE UNIVERSE

BELOW

ELIAS BARTON

Iron Glass Press

Above the Universe Below is a work of fiction. Names, characters, places, and incidents are the products of the author's imagination or are used fictitiously. Any resemblance to actual events, locales, or persons living, dead or undead, is entirely coincidental.

Copyright © 2012 Elias Barton

Iron Glass Press
ISBN-10: 0615660746
ISBN-13: 978-0615660745

Originally published in the United States by Iron Glass Press.

For Peter

CONTENTS

ABOVE
THE UNIVERSE
BELOW

"This was unlike the story it was written to be
I was riding its back when it used to ride me"
— Joanna Newsom

.

1

SALMON BELLY

Time passes like a kidney stone whenever leaving home and this ride is no exception. Carder Quevedo's experience on the subway is maze-like and assaulting, colors too bright, voices too loud. He only rides when necessary, and is just this side of finishing his yearly pilgrimage to his barber, Vinnie DiMeo, who brought his wild mane back to cropped civilization. Over the course of three decades, Vinnie has failed to persuade Carder to try a crew cut, and this time, when Vinnie informed him that he was moving shop to Lower Manhattan, Carder reflexively grabbed the old man's wrist even while scissors sat in his hand like a small, metal acrobat swinging her legs.

"Sorry, Card, I'm moving," Vinnie said with tender eyes, shaking free from Carder's grasp.

Now standing on the rocking train, Carder sadly considers never seeing Vinnie again. Then again, it provides one less reason to leave the house. Carder avoids venturing into Manhattan, keeping all underground experiences to Brooklyn and Queens. Even the thought makes him nauseous. Get home—he tells himself. The lives of fellow commuters press against him on all sides: this one's brittle hair brushes his hand, that one's lingering stare, another's insecurity or macho swagger, this one's untied shoelace. An old woman stares at him until he turns away. Concentrating on familiar sensations for distraction, Carder notes the renegade hairs leftover from the haircut sticking to his neck.

When a seat opens up, Carder sits only to face the crotch of a fifty-year-old man wearing sweat pants but no underwear. *These people.* Molecules of their sweat find him. Remnants of their morning arguments fill his ears. Their collective exhaustion is fruitful, multiplied, filling the car, the city, the earth. When they crowd his world too much, he goes to another, to the World of the Dying—but he hasn't been there in a long time and pushes those thoughts away.

Carder armored himself for his journey with a stocking cap, aviator sunglasses, gloves and an air of detachment. He's lost the music-player he'd received as a gift last Christmas, so while headphones plug his ears, their wire leads only to lint and loose change in his pocket. While the borders of his body graze other people, Carder pretends otherwise, staring into infinity.

Starting conversation on the subway is like talking to the grieving during a funeral service. During millions of rides each day, commuters have an eerie, unspoken knowledge that they're far from natural light and further underground than the dead.

A woman scrambles into the seat adjacent to him, wearing a mauve business jacket, a matching skirt and a pair of bright white sneakers. A canvas bag sits at her feet with an apricot peeking out. Her lap holds an issue of Chic Chick Magazine.

"Excuse me, is this train headed uptown?" she asks, attempting to engage Carder before the doors close.

"Yup," he affirms, but as he suspects of most sneakered business women, she knows exactly where she's going.

Chance had taken the altogether average looks of Carder's parents and rearranged them appealingly on their son, where sharp cheeks drop below lush lashes. Carder isn't simply male, he's a guy, a lug, a pair of muddy, oversized boots when it rains. His expressions vacillate between brooding contemplation and a serial killer grin, fascinating but alarming. If that doesn't send women running, they're won over by the sweet shyness rare among men of his stature. One of his few ex-girlfriends said that sex with Carder is like being stabbed with sincerity. If life hadn't cast him in the roles it has, he might have been a surfer, a playboy, the man whose girlfriend wears his t-shirt as a nightgown, or the vacation lover one hooks-up with for two incredible weeks. But Carder didn't get those roles. His role is darker. And lonelier.

"I like your jacket," says the woman.

When Carder looks at his jacket, he sees a miniature circus tent unsuccessfully housing a mastodon—too small in the sleeves, too big in the body. The yard sale windbreaker barely breaks enough wind to be worthy of the name. Carder mumbles thanks, pushing a headphone ear bud deeper into one ear. He rummages through his empty pocket, feigning adjustments to the imaginary music-player to stop the woman's verbal assault.

"What brand is your player? It looks like a…?" She acts as though she might peek into Carder's pocket and discover its mute lint and missing player.

Taking a deep breath, he looks at her iridescent nylons as she bites a peppermint in two.

"It works great." He squarely lobs the answer onto her to discourage further banter.

"Tiffany," she answers to an unasked question.

She smiles, flipping through her magazine until they reach the next stop, 7th Avenue, where she leans in, pointing to a shining page in her magazine. "This contest is great: *What super power would you choose and why?*"

Carder has considered that question many times over the years and doesn't sugarcoat the truth: "If I could have any superpower?" He knots his lips in false thought. "If I could, I'd choose the power to make a person crap their pants instantaneously. But they couldn't know that I made it happen, or that I even *knew* it happened. Imagine the power."

Tiffany looks as if she'd been a flying duck that now lie shot. Zipping up her canvas bag, she shields her apricot and closes the magazine.

"Are you going to enter the contest?" Carder asks. Tiffany may not interest him, but the subject does. "Wait! What's *your* superpower?"

"Enter the contest yourself," she says. "My superpower is… disappearing."

She does exactly that, moving to the other end of the train.

Back to the ride. Close your eyes. Listen.

Whimperings catch Carder's attention. He can't stand knowing an animal is distraught. Where is it? There it is. It's not even caged, which is an improper act if not an outright train crime. The colors of broken shadows and scattered molasses dapple its fur. The animal constantly shifts as the train gyrates, alternating between burying its head in its owner's lap and attempting to glimpse the crowded subway.

The dog shouldn't be here. Carder whispers, "You're gonna be okay, girl."

"Boy."

"Boy?"

"Boy," is a human's reply. "Male."

That's when he sees the dog's owner.

Those eyes. He cut out a pair in the same brilliant green only two days prior. Blues and browns become forgettable, but greens come in endless variety and saturation: green apple, safari, Heineken, frog. Her particular green is mossy and hypnotic. He assesses the woman's age as close to his own: early thirties, not old, but by this time she's lived. Crowned with short, ginger, pixie hair, her ruddy complexion advertises sun. Long legs emerge from beneath a wrinkled skirt of linen and meet flip-flops in a familiar hue: Salmon Belly Pink. He knows the color from plastics. Twenty years ago it was highly popular, the color of excitement, and is now highlighted by toenails painted with Sky-7. Carder wouldn't mind being the flip-flops between her toes.

He starts sweating. The train car grows fuller though no additional passengers have gotten on. Does this woman have the very superpower he discussed with Tiffany? *Please no.*

"I stand corrected. You're gonna be okay, *boy*," he says, confused that he's continuing to speak of his own volition. "What a sweet little guy."

"He was an adorable pup, but more of a pain in the ass nowadays. Much too smart for his own good. But we must care for our own, right?" she asks with a weary smile.

"It's worth it, isn't it?"

"Does it matter?" She pauses. "Listen, do you have a dog? Because if you do, never go to the East Run Veterinary Clinic on President Street. The guy's a quack. Rocco here has been incontinent ever since the operation."

The mottled mutt doesn't move his head, but looks at Carder, his bulging eyes pop with awareness that he's become the conversation's subject. They prompt a thought that slides over Carder's tongue faster than he can wrestle it back. "He looks like a little zombie."

"A zombie? How's that?"

"The ice-blue eyes."

She laughs—a disarmed laugh that holds lilies and softens metals. "A little zombie. I can see that. He's had problems from the beginning. At four months old, he had a run-in with a car. Thought it was livestock or something. Chased it for an entire block."

"He caught it?"

"Sort of. The car stopped. Rocco didn't. He should be dead."

"So he's *un*dead. That makes him a zombie."

"Zombies are passé. Overplayed."

"Tell them that while they're chasing you. Maybe it seems overplayed because life *is* a zombie movie. You're trying to get through all this without becoming one—most of us fail miserably. Look around."

She does. The faces of fellow passengers are expressionless, sleeping, disconnected. Cogs begin turning in Salmon Belly's face, the expression of a verdict en utero. In the city, the line between harmless stranger and avid criminal is razor thin. Is it worth speaking with Carder any further? He's grown accustomed to the usual decision. Myra Bean, who dated him for a week in the 11th grade, summed it up while setting her corsage on her plate at Marco's Ristorante. *I'm sorry. You're hot. You are. But man, you're weird!* Carder doesn't want to wait for the same judgment from Salmon Belly.

Instead of being logical and getting up to move to another part of the train, Carder starts babbling: he doesn't currently have a dog, but loves them and he'll make note of her suggestion. He whips out his trusty pad and pen to write it down. What's the veterinarian's name again? He cringes at the awkwardness of his conversational improv.

But Salmon Belly doesn't seem to notice Carder's ramblings. "The Vet's name is Carl Kirkin or Gherklin or something, I can't remember, but you'll know him by his red nose and coughing fits."

Despite sweat surfacing on Carder's back, which should stop him, he asks the woman her name, though he already finds her unforgettable. Her flip-flops are embedded in his mind, stuck in his brain like an ax to a zombie's head. Salmon Belly has the sleekness of a praying mantis, the poise of a princess stolen by elves and raised by gypsies.

She looks Carder in the eye and raises her chin. "My name's Haika... like *Haiku* but with an 'uh.'" The explanation runs like one she's played on repeat her entire life.

"Haika." He tries on the name. "Haika. Unusual."

"It's German. It supposedly means *soul of an Indian warrior*. Isn't that hilarious?"

That's it! Salmon Belly-Haika reminds him of an Indian warrior housed in the body of a svelte German-American girl. Carder follows suit by clarifying his own name, even though it makes him feel like they're at a freshman dance with punch bowls and pink streamers. If it plays out as things did in ninth grade, Haika will vomit on his shoes. His birth certificate reads *C-a-r-t-e-r*, but he'd been an obsessive child, and changed the 't' for a 'd' in an effort to align the spelling with phonetics.

"In that case, how do you spell 'sweater' and 'water'? I'm kidding. You're Latino? You can't be!"

"No one in my family marries within their own ethnicity. You name it, I've got some in me: Swiss. Spanish. Dutch. French... Latvian. I'm not sure if I got the best or the worst of each."

High school classmates had claimed Carder was too bottled up to be Latino, but not ambitious enough to be white. The school counselor once told him he needed to be more aggressive. Even as an adult, job searches would have improved if Human Resources saw his skin-color instead of a resumé topped with his last name:

Carder Quevedo
672 Paylow Avenue, Brooklyn, New York 11231
email: throw.me.away.immediately@loser.com

Carder fishes for anything to keep the conversation going. "Are you from Germany?"

"I'm as German as Wiener schnitzel. I was born in Berlin. But my parents hated walls and didn't want us growing up with a guilt complex, so we moved to Mexico when I was little. Before the Berlin wall fell. The Germans *love* remodeling. Iris and I went from making our beds so tight you could bounce a quarter off them, to jumping on our own unmade beds. Throughout the rest of my childhood, I was batted between the U.S. and Mexico, so I suppose you can throw some chorizo in with the wiener schnitzel."

"I love Mexico," Carder says despite speaking no Spanish and having never been further south than Washington, D.C. His idea of Mexican culture is folded within tortillas, piñatas, margaritas and ponchos. He immediately feels guilty he hadn't investigated any place producing a creature as interesting as Haika.

"I grew up in Puerto Vallarta... close to it anyway," she clarifies.

"I love Puerto Vallarta. And the surrounding towns." Again, not a lie. Carder loves the sound of the name, its spiciness on his tongue. He loves any city Haika's set foot in.

"What's your gig?" She pauses and restates, "Your story?"

Carder stares into the eye of a hurricane. His attraction to Haika shakes up feelings of ignorance and shelter, worsened by the knowledge that she's traversed continents while he's barely left his home, his block, his city, his head. Still, he wants to conjure an offering before he and Haika wash away in the city's web. He searches for anything to latch onto. A detail he rarely reveals now gleams. It could be impressive when used on the right person, so he closes his eyes and throws it out there.

"I'm a toy designer." When the words hit air they sound lame, like a lie, so he quickly ends with, "...who just got a haircut."

A fart might have gotten more recognition than Carder's revelation. The one time he offers up his sordid, cringe-worthy history into the light, there's none shining.

"Leaving the haircut a little wild suits you," Haika says. "Anyway, I work at an art gallery in Manhattan, but ducked out to take zombie-dog here to the vet. It's been exhausting. He's lethargic, sleeps all the time, stays inside—I'd even say he's depressed. I don't know whether to diaper him or put him to sleep."

They agree that it's one tough decision.

The dog leans its head on Haika's legs as if considering the dilemma, reaching its tongue to the warmth of her hand, then to the cool of her metal bracelet. However, it keeps a steady eye on Carder, which Carder takes as a desire to live. He meets the dog's hope by changing to the adjacent seat and offering it a taste of his hand.

Haika tilts her head, assessing Carder. "Where are you going now?"

"Home. To shower and wash my hair. I'm itchy."

She stares. Something twists and turns inside her before diving out. "I know this is a ridiculous question, but would you like to get a cup of coffee before you move on? I live in Brooklyn Heights. We could just stop off. No pressure."

The train stops and the doors slide open, demanding immediate decision—inside or out?

Carder agrees to the invitation of this beautiful stranger before fear can wrestle away the steering wheel. All he has to do is play a character other than himself. Salmon Belly-Haika doesn't even know he rarely ventures away from home. Plus, it's been ages since he's gotten laid, so while his heart pounds at the endless possibilities, a pang for exploration erupts below his belt.

Brooklyn Heights is the neighborhood adjacent to his own, a mere fifteen or twenty minute walk. Though it's an uncomfortable distance, Carder can't say no. He agrees to coffee, and clumsily carries Zombie up and out of the subway for her, realizing that while they were talking the dog had lived up to the claims of incontinence.

2

DRAWING HIM IN

People have abandoned their homes for bright streets, hoping to seduce summer prematurely with sunglasses and ice cream cones. They mill about on sun-warmed sidewalks and chat in parks. A skateboarder whizzes by in gym shorts, legs exposed, pale and gangly, while a senior citizen stands on the opposite side of the street, waiting to cross.

The zombie-dog seems content above ground, flopping around on the warm cement before Haika produces a leash with which the mutt pulls them through the streets. They pass a Coffee-Star without going in. Women stand in packs outside, infants draped over their shoulders or sitting in pouches. One mother excitedly tells her group that *Dominic won't sleep in the afternoon! I've tried everything! Does your Bella have that problem?*

"We just passed the Coffee-Star," Carder tells Haika, confused.

"I know. I asked you to coffee. Is that what you think I meant? That place? Is *that* what you think coffee is? I won't even say that name." To clarify she mouths 'Coffee-Star' soundlessly. Its shape is pointy—a small explosion. "No, no, I'd never do that to you. I meant real coffee—there's a blend my sister Iris sends from Mexico... *es muy rico.*"

Though he's certain that C***eeS**r has a Mexican blend, Carder is also inexplicably sure that Haika is a connoisseur. He follows her several more blocks to an imposing three-story brownstone home. It dwarfs anything in Carder's neighborhood including the modest carriage house that served as the only fulfillment of his mother's dreams. Haika explains it's the garden level on which they enter where she works, relaxes and gets away from things. Carder doesn't ask about the levels above. He wants

Haika's.

Once inside, he conducts a quiet investigation. Photographs, drawings and paintings sit propped against hallway walls. Empty frames tilt for support—some broken, some black, some silver, a few gaudy gold. Panes of glass are piled at the far end. He and Haika cross into a musty sitting room with white walls much like an art gallery. However, unlike a gallery, Haika's walls teem with a mosaic of art hanging in no apparent theme. Colors clash. Genres battle each other as though wall space is virgin countryside of which to stake claim. A painting of a sour-mouthed man staring at the ocean borders another with nothing but two overlapping geometric shapes. Next to that, hangs a canvas with threads of drizzled paint. Then, a pubescent girl in a linen gown walks across a dim Irish moor, holding a glowing lantern. Below these scenes, a floor once painted black is scratched and worn.

Carder sits down in one of two sun-bleached armchairs while Haika brews coffee. He picks up a blank book which is two-thirds *un*-blank. The latest entry is a handwritten poem:

Set Death Down

Remove it from your mouth
don't bite it with teeth
unready to be broken.
Never again
offer your head as sky waiting
for cannonball lightning.
Set death down
take it to a dumpster
blocks away
Don't cradle flavors of steely sin.
Don't french it
Don't tongue its barrel
One taste, a last meal
One kiss, a handshake.

Haika's shuffling from the kitchen prompts Carder to return the book to its spot. He hasn't read much poetry since the well-earned 'C' he'd received in high school for his term paper: *Street Thugs & The Canterbury Tales*, but it doesn't take a literature major to see that

Haika's not only too gorgeous for him but too educated. Carder hates poetry—its riddle and the obtuse meanings that cloak themselves in word. Still, despite his inability to instantly dissect the poem, he thinks he understands Haika on some far-off level. He wants to believe that. Aside from Tiffany on the train earlier that day, it's been ages since he's had a conversation with a girl who wasn't bagging his groceries. Girls spook easy. Not Haika.

"Here you go, Carder. An authentic café con leche."

"Oh. Could I get this without the leche? I'm somewhat leche-intolerant."

"Of course." The mug hovering over the tabletop is gone before it can land.

In a few moments, Haika returns with a real, authentic, leche-less coffee and sits down. Carder enjoys the drink's bitterness, and warms his nervous hands with the mug while listening to his host.

"I came here escaping my family's business—running the Come Stay Inn. It's a cute hilltop inn with a five-star view and one-star accommodations. And even that *one* star is only the sun."

Carder sighs, fascinated.

"I'm kidding about the one star, but the Inn's nothing fancy. My parents opened it in Mismaloya to catch the growing number of gringos many years ago. It's a charming little neighborhood…"

"Wonderful."

"…with lots of gays too. We courted their arrival. It's a free-wheeling, live-and-let-live kind of barrio."

Knowing nothing about Puerto Vallarta, Carder nods his head and says *wonderful* again.

It's impossible for Haika's beauty to hide behind the steaming cup of coffee. And pouring the same liquid down their throats makes Carder jittery. The zombie-dog wanders by carrying a ratty stuffed lizard in his mouth. His nails click-clack across the floor.

"Are you bi, Carder?" Haika turns her head, as though asking a common question. She pokes his shoulder with her index finger, melting him in the soft oils of her fingerprint.

"Am I bi? Do you mean sexual or polar?" He stammers, then the words careen out in one breath. "Both have been suggested—I mean—neither has been diagnosed—or explored—but—well, okay—I guess I'd kiss a guy—I'm open—I once had a friend who told me it's like kissing a girl with whiskers—which isn't alluring in the least—and I've not been told I'm bipolar either—I get depressed sometimes—but the late great Kurt Vonnegut said you can't be a good writer if you're not depressed—and not that I'm a writer—but I relate—my best paintings come when I'm depressed—and I paint a lot." He stops and looks at the dog, wishing he could collect and swallow his spilled words. He pauses, acting as though he's said none of it, but eventually breaks the silence. "I don't know. Maybe?"

"Paintings?"

Carder's stomach drops. Paintings? Why had he said that?

"Honey, relax. I don't care. Bisexuality is the next social frontier, that's all." She tops off his coffee. "What do you mean by your *paintings*? You paint?"

"I've done it for years. It got me into toy design."

"I'd love to see them."

"No." He motions to the surrounding walls overwrought with lofty paintings, prints, and photos. "They're not... like this stuff."

"I wouldn't want them to be like this stuff... but obviously," she mimics his motion to the walls, "...you appreciate." Leaving a flip-flop on the floor, she pushes her bare toe against Carder's knee as though the pressure gives support.

"Yeah..." Haika's foot is disturbingly warm.

"...and you love animals too," she says, acknowledging the slobbery dog toy dropped on Carder's shoe.

"Yeah..." Haika's toenails are each small painting themselves. Blue paintings, five small windows to the sky outside.

"Then, go around the corner there and look at the painting. You'll like it."

He gets up and heads through a hallway, until he stands in a bedroom. Printed sheets of faded flowers twist a cotton tornado on an unmade bed. At its head, hangs a large painting, an ink-splotch in the shape of a swan.

Carder ignores the knee-high platform boots sitting akimbo on the floor, and the invisible woman who's wearing them—legs wide open. He overlooks a wire jewelry tree with one necklace hanging like a sparkling noose, disregards the magazine atop a dresser opened to a story called *Soon* and looks past the paper lantern hanging from the ceiling like a giant saffron-colored tick. No, he concentrates on the painted black swan, a creature of which he's never heard. "Are there really black swans?" he asks.

"I bet so." Haika's half-whispered reply is closer than expected, delivering the nutty scent of coffee. Carder senses a disturbance in the Force. The energy shifts. A pulsing awakens within his pants. He turns from the black swan to Haika. She's already removed her shirt and drops her bra as soon their eyes meet. She extends her arm as though reaching. Or begging. The tiny nodules of her spine need tracing with Carder's fingers, but a realization pries him back: she's not reaching for him at all, but rather giving him something. Something small. Something black. Something charcoal.

Upon taking it, the charcoal transfers soot onto Carder's hand. Haika brings a large pad of paper out from behind a bookshelf. Her melancholy smile commands Carder not to make wisecracks, and as she plops onto the bed her legs curl into question marks asking him to draw.

And he does.

Why not press a facsimile of Haika onto paper if reality won't press her to him in the flesh? His initial trepidation flips into an artist's unbreakable right-brained concentration. Carder takes his time, spends too much of it concentrating on his subject's beautiful, perfectly placed bush: a slight, grassy knoll far below the moon of her navel, unlike his own patch of unruly pubic hair stamped flat against his body like a crop circle.

Halfway through drawing her halo, Carder concludes with certainty that they won't be having sex. It was never Haika's goal. While a knife might cut the sexual tension, he hasn't been given one. Instead of trying to manipulate the situation, Carder soaks in it, no longer wondering why things have happened this way. He simply sinks into creative waters, allowing the charcoal to do what it will without attempting to impress, think, explain or guess.

Art = Emptiness^2.

Back in the seventh grade, his alcoholic art teacher posted that phrase on the blackboard throughout an entire semester. It still hangs inside Carder. Art expresses and accentuates the isolation stewing inside everyone. The representation of Haika draining from his hand serves as a testament to their distance from one another. It isn't Haika's image at all. It's only the costume of their moment together. The result lacks shading and gravity—a confused line-drawing with Haika floating in white space like a nude astronaut.

Once finished, they don't discuss the drawing. Thought and anxiety rush back into the room, but their experience doesn't need commentary. Carder is cringingly reminded of his least favorite movie—*Titanic*—replete with contrived drawings and romantic love that cannot be. He won't be left as a human ice cube, he won't surrender to desire that can never be realized. If embarrassment weren't preventing it, he would crumple the drawing into the trash it is.

Either Haika doesn't notice Carder's worry or pretends so. She's relaxed and unbothered, as if nothing's happened.

"Would you like a carrot?" she asks. "I eat more of them since I quit smoking."

When he shakes his head *no*, she puts on a short silk robe and heads to the kitchen, all the while telling him how detrimental cigarette smoke is for art. Over the years, she's learned the hard way. In her absence, Carder sits down on the bed, spent.

Haika returns to the bed, her mouth plugged cigar-like with a carrot, and sits next to him.

It's time for the Confession Game.

The rules of the Confession Game, as Carder knows them, are: each person tries topping the other's divulged secret, piling them up, laughing at their ridiculousness, musing over their collective sins. Carder tells Haika about his deceased mother—he wanted her to live forever. She didn't. He divulges his hatred of his father. He wished he'd died instead, but "Evil lives forever," he says and smiles.

Haika doesn't laugh. "He'll pass on at some point. Both of mine already have."

Though such disclosures are too big for their small intimacy, Carder confesses to having lost some hearing in one ear.

"How?"

"Evil lives forever," he repeats. "Anyway, it's a good thing—helps me choose where a chatty person should sit."

"I hope I got your good ear," she says and tussles Carder's hair, the first time they touch post-drawing.

Carder brusquely sits up.

Haika quickly adds her own confessions, "All my travels during youth made me feel like I was neither American, nor Mexican, nor German—not even some deformed combination. The concept of home evaporated. But *not* belonging to any country can be liberating. *Expats*—that's where it's at!" Her laugh rolls into a sigh, before making another admission: "I may as well tell you... I don't like my dog. Never have. Isn't that horrible? I do like him more as Zombie than Rocco though. By the way, I didn't name him." She reaches for a framed photo on the nightstand. "This is the dog I love. This mangy mutt is Klaus."

"Where is he?"

"In Mexico. With my sister." She reaches for another photo. The subject looks like Haika, but with long, tragically fried hair. "That's my sister, Iris. My twin. You'd love her."

"An identical twin? Then, you've never been alone."

"I wouldn't say that. She stayed in Puerto Vallarta to run The Come Stay Inn while I settled here, as much as anyone *can* settle in this city."

For a while, they simply breathe together as Haika strokes the base of Carder's back. His neck still itches from that morning's haircut, but there's definitely no reason for him to shower here. A clock ticks. The swan on the wall sits stationary on its paper pond, unable to move or fly away. Haika dresses, putting her shirt back on. Braless, her nipples jut against cotton.

"God, I hate carrots. Anyway, you should meet my husband. You'd like him."

"Your—your husband?"

"You'd like him. His name's Mike and he... Oh! Okay, maybe you *wouldn't* like him. Listen, either way, you should come over for dinner sometime this week. The Zombie already misses you."

The Zombie is nowhere to be seen.

Carder leaves, pondering. Marriage has plucked away any prospects with the woman whose pubic hair he'd so meticulously drawn. Does he really want to meet Haika's *husband*? What more hasn't she revealed? Were her neglected toddlers ransacking the levels above them? Still, he knows how his week looks: sitting at home, adding another mac'n'cheese-encrusted bowl to the dirty dishes, and if he's lucky, the stretch will be broken by a visit from

Darren. Yawning Monday will morph into Insomniac Wednesday into Listless Saturday, with Carder combating the passage of time by hunching over another painting while Rachmaninov plays.

3

A REAPING: TOLL UNCOUNTED
Carder at 4 years old

It's a fall. It has trajectory, but it's a fall. There's no time to catch himself, no time to right his tiny body to save the masses from his gravity. He's a bomb, a flash flood. And they will never see him coming. One second, he's standing at the top of the stairs. The next, his back has extinguished a city. His hands, a village. He can't tell what his elbow's crushed. The victims remain unseen, but he feels their liquefaction, hears their nano-screams before they become nothing. And just as soon, he's no longer a grim reaper, but back in his own world. From below, he watches the figure of a man still trembling in anger. The door at the top of the stairs slam shut.

4

EVERYDAY DEMONS

The hum of Brooklyn Kingston hospital has Carder counting his footsteps, focusing only on his destination. *Eleven. Twelve. Thirteen.* Going from home to job is always jarring. Outside, ambulance sirens met him in the parking lot. Inside, a mechanical voice endlessly pages Dr. Wheeler. Techs misguide hospital gurneys, hitting people and equipment, with no apologies.

Nineteen. Twenty.

Carder needs protection, an exoskeleton. Shaky and frenetic, the rhythm of his steps drum faster. He wants to get this over with.

Forty-two steps will bring him to the nurse's station. He's memorized the number of steps to that desk at every hospital he's ever worked at—at least eight. Once there, he'll get the paperwork and the direction he needs to find his donor and complete his assignment.

Twenty-four. Twenty-five.

At step twenty-six, an obstacle arises: Nurse Grey. Nurse Grey is the same at every hospital, no matter her age, breath, the color of her eyes or the body she inhabits. He knows this one's cornrows before seeing them, their tight braids pulling at her scalp. That one's got tattoos. And here's the cat-loving lesbian. Here's the pageant queen who had to get a real job. Here's the single nurse who works here solely to meet a doctor to marry. Here's the cheerleader. The misplaced librarian.

"Don't tell me: you're mute again today, right?" asks the current Nurse Grey as he passes. Her lips wrinkle like origami, folding out the words.

Carder smiles faintly, attempting to move on. He'd rather not stop her from dumping the bed pans she's collected.

"Uh-huh, I thought so," she yawns and stops what she's doing. This one is chomping gum. Pale and blonde, she's probably Swedish, and definitely imagining rhinestone manicures and terry cloth sweat suits awaiting her at home.

Twenty-seven. Twenty-eight. Twenty-nine.

Carder's invisible blinders never faze Nurse Grey; they magnetize her. Like Pandora in medical scrubs, she's never seen a box she doesn't want to open—and he's shut tight. *How's your mom?*—versions of her used to ask—but that stopped when Carder's answer became *'Dead.'* Still, Nurse Grey pops out at every hospital to dip her toe in his world.

"Carder Quevedo!" she calls. She's one of the more attractive ones: young and Italian, with bouncy black hair like winding telephone cords.

It means nothing. Anyone can see the name on his identification badge. He keeps walking. *Thirty. Thirty-one.*

"Carder Quevedo! You stop right there! If you're headed to the nurse's station, you may as well know that I'm the Charge, so you're going to have to talk to me at some point." Her words are harsh but they pour out with therapeutic care. This one's good. A true nurse through and through.

He stops, but almost without turning to her. Still, he doesn't have to make eye contact. *Eleven? Yes, eleven more steps.* Only, now she's also going to be a part of them since he needs her direction.

"Doing anything tomorrow for Valentine's day?" she asks.

"Not really."

"Isn't it charming that holidays are the ER's busiest times? Valentine's Day means poisonings and after last year Halloween will always be head injuries. Tonight we've already had more drunk drivers than usual, some old lady who claims she was hit by a car, and two suicides. Two." She says it as though she's surprised. "Don't worry, neither were donors—not that it would've mattered for one of them. Let's see, you'll find your subject in…" she checks a chart, "…Trauma Room 4."

He looks up, waiting for her to hand over the information.

"You're looking a bit tired tonight," says Nurse Grey. "You sure you're up for this?"

"Of course." Grabbing the clipboard from her, Carder heads to the Trauma Room. It's imperative to respond promptly since corneas only remain viable for extraction for six hours after death.

Working with the deceased makes sense to Carder. Unbothered by gore and corpses, he immediately becomes more comfortable with people after they've taken their last breath. This time, the corpse of a newly deceased man in his late 40's lays behind the curtain. He's dead but the machines still have his lungs pumping and his blood making laps so all the organs can be removed for donation. The eyes were covered with moistened gauze to keep them fresh for cornea retrieval. Extraction isn't a lengthy process. It takes Carder less than an hour from start to finish, including paperwork, even less if the entire eyeball can be suctioned from its orbit instead of excising the cornea alone. What he wouldn't give for something that easy tonight.

People often grimace when Carder tells them about his job. Of course, they don't know that his other job, the one in another world is much worse. Still, to most people, cutting eyes from the dead at local hospitals is hard to stomach. Mentioning it stops most conversations, but every once in a while the curious dig for details.

"How can you do that?" a candy striper once asked. "The eyes are the window of the soul!"

"I don't pretend to know what happens when we die," Carder responded, "but once a person's dead, there's no soul inside the windows. It's an empty house—no longer mesmerizing or sad, or beautiful—just parts."

Familiar with the body's mechanics and unaffected by sentimental leanings, Carder thrives in his hospital job, at least in the actual work. But today, this particular subject is only a few years younger than Carder, kept in limbo by a machine that breathes her breaths and won't let her go. Her body hasn't been properly covered. Almost nothing should be exposed. The sloppiness peeves Carder, but allows him to note her satiny hair, the type used in shampoo commercials. She's different. At first, Carder can't figure out why. He's excised many corneas from dead youth. It's not the flawless skin or shampoo-fresh hair that's diverting his attention. Something bothers him. What is it? He wants to latch this feeling onto something.

Oh.

It isn't the woman at all.

They've come.

As he slips the blade into the white of the woman's eye with utmost care, one of Carder's creations catches his eye from across the room.

It's one of the Pups.

Again? Here? At Kingston Hospital where the rules of sterility and antisepticism are touted as ironclad? Mother Nature could never have produced the beast he sees. The closest approximation might be a nuclear accident's mutant offspring. He tells himself that he's overreacting, that this mutant is only a figurine with a cheap plastic body and rooted, combable fur. But to Carder, the Pup's a green firecracker in a black sky, a black sky over a white boat, a white boat afloat in toxic waste—impossible to neglect even when Carder's full attention should be on organizing his tools.

The toy sits on a heating unit in the corner. Pushed far back, it would've gone unnoticed by any other person, a child's misplaced trinket left behind. Not to Carder. The rubbery dog watching him is Chalkdust. The fur on its head, once white, frizzes out like electrified serpents, matching a garish finger-in-a-light-socket grin. Blammo Toys introduced Chalkdust as part of the Pick-Me-Pups' Schooldaze line decades ago. Had Chalkdust, who'd gotten Carder through the endless, friendless days of third grade, done the same for—he checks the chart again—*Wilburn, Tanya*? Or had she given it to her own small daughter who inadvertently left it behind? Is that little girl now at home in bed, begging God to bring back both mommy and Chalkdust?

Nurse Grey enters the room, wearing scrubs printed with winged cartoon pigs. She's not supposed be here. She's supposed to leave Carder alone to complete the procedure.

"Did you see the toy too?" she asks. "I hate it when stuff like isn't removed. Don't worry, Jonathan will be written up." She's heads to the heating unit to retrieve the Pup.

"Let it be. It's fine." Carder stops with gloved hands raised, holding a blade.

"You sure? I just can't help thinking about this patient—outlived by some non-biodegradable toy. Seriously, it'll exist in some form, probably for thousands of years after this woman is long forgotten."

"I thought you said this was a busy night?"

"Are you kidding? It's only noon and slower than rush hour traffic in here. Anyway, Tuesdays are *always* slow. What I wouldn't give for a bus accident."

Wasn't this Saturday? "Listen, you've got to let me do my thing here."

"Fine by me." She leaves, taking a wounded look and the flying cartoon pigs with her.

Carder hates cartoons. Cartoons are childhood. Childhood was isolation. Isolation poured the mistakes of Carder's youth into a mold, solidified and multiplied them into countless vinyl monstrosities. The Pick-Me-Pups. The popular little beasts were strewn worldwide over the last three decades. Ignorant children now ride Carder's embarrassment on carousels at carnivals. The handles of their toothbrushes are shaped like his nightmares. Brush, brush, brush, rinse, spit—and then set his terrors back in the cup on the sink and tell daddy you have to wee-wee. Children walk to school carrying backpacks emblazoned with decals of Carder's naive hopes, grinning disappointments and flustered desires. Everywhere he turns he meets these shrines of each scraped knee and adolescent pimple he had. Now, even though he's long since left behind injuries and acne, he can't make the dogs disappear. They're his scars, craters into which he falls.

Everyone knows the Pick-Me-Pups. Introduced during early childhood, toddlers suck, teeth, and *goo* at them. The sucking and *goo'ing* allows parents to concentrate on other things. The chewing is fine, because the Pups are blobs of plastic too large to swallow, sticking out from kids' mouths like safety flags. Besides, introducing the Pups during formative years assured Blammo Toys a lifetime of brand recognition. Tiny souls become aware of them before they're even aware of themselves, providing imaginary friends prior to human companions. Babies can identify the brightly-colored characters before they're able to recognize their own reflection in a mirror. An underlying message assures small hands: no matter how life kicks them, no matter who lies, cheats or steals from them, no matter who breaks their hearts, they'll be fine. The Holy Grail of unconditional love dangles before their chubby faces—and it's a frolicking cartoon canine.

For decades, people in every continent but one had known the Pups. Even that changed when a small but wiry girl named Kimberly Pearson became the twenty-third woman to set foot on Antarctica's frigid tundra. She arrived during an icy -24°F summer with the image of a husky white Pup named Frost lodged in her psyche. While bracing against vicious winds with her backpack, an accidental girlhood memory surfaced: snow was falling as her seven-year-old hands held the plastic dog, its paw pointed toward the forest behind her family's home, directing her to explore the great beyond. She only recounted that memory once before, under the influence of peach schnapps and a bad break-up.

You.

You know The Pick-Me-Pups.

Maybe they hid at the bottom of your toy box, were abducted from your sister for ransom, or their Saturday morning TV show kept you from building a diorama of the solar system for the Science Fair, but you know them. You bought them on discount for your niece's birthday. You kissed them, thrashed them, whispered secrets to them when no one else cared, stuck steak knives into their bodies and bubblegum in their fur before hacking it off. Perhaps you were one of those precious kids, the kind who never touched them, but only admired them standing on their designated shelf next to your AYSO soccer trophies. You were happy to own something so clean. For years, when you squeezed a Pup during church sermons, you imagined heaven having the same chemical smell.

They'll be there when you're on your deathbed, floundering in visions laced with pain-killers and regret, sallying forth nonsensically in front of your adult children and their children: *Where's Dazzledrop? Bring me Dazzledrop!*

They were your guardians.

They were your Rosebud.

They're Carder Quevedo's hell.

Carder's hands begin to shake, which is distressing in itself. He prides himself on commanding every thought and movement during cornea retrieval. Pausing to regroup, he reviews the deceased's chart for the third time while talking himself through the situation. He can do this. He's the best. *Wilburn, Tanya* and the recipient of her soon-to-be harvested corneas deserve nothing short of the best.

A shadowy figure with a kinky red hairdo and orthopedic shoes appears in the doorway. Nurse Grey again with her flying piggies. "You trying to bring her back to life? You're usually faster than this."

He maintains silent concentration, hastening her departure.

There was a time when Carder spoke to Nurse Grey. There was a time when he thought he was required talk to anyone who said anything, that he was obligated to answer every question posed. That's what happens when you're raised with manners. Nurse Grey's candy-lips and caring eyes made him divulge secrets he should've kept, her freckles searched to fill the space between them with information—*his* information.

"I find it tragic…" the first Grey once said, pushing the glasses back on her nose while Carder organized his paperwork. She was nervous and new, trying to keep him close as long as possible. "…tragic to have never owned an actual dog. You're telling me that not one has set foot inside your house? Not ever?"

No. Aside from his father, the only physical evidence linking Carder to anything canine are the paintings bearing his original Pup designs, one character per painting. In reality, each painting represents a reaping Carder had made in the universe below, a foreign death to be commemorated. But he'd kept that mum.

Having painted obsessively since childhood to keep himself company, he knows he'll only be able to stop when he gives up his own corneas. Long ago, when his mother sat sorrowfully in the front room built for company that never came, her small shoulder blades pressed against an overstuffed recliner, Carder's new paintings were often the only thing forging her smiles. His art drove her to the station closest to happiness, and even if she never boarded the train, she had admired its slick sheen. Even still, Carder lives in rose water memories of the times she'd held his latest plate to her bosom, embracing it like the newborns she no longer had, losing herself in the tiny brushstrokes. It was a small favor Carder had provided—serving up hope on a porcelain plate. Hope that lied.

The hospital room grows too hot too fast. Despite Carder's trembling hand, he manages to saw with precision. Despite the plastic canine gawking from across the room, he's careful not to damage *Wilburn, Tanya's* eyelids. The face must remain as intact as that of a cheerleader, a bride, a first crush or proud mother.

Chalkdust. How can the figurine of a dog be so unnerving? He places the second cornea into the receptacle. In order to finish the extraction process, Carder does something never before necessary: he gives himself the *what a wonderful gift, the gift of sight* spiel. *Wilburn, Tanya—you're giving someone the blessing of a visual world!* He sighs. What a mess. He's become a public service announcement.

Done. Carder covers the body and its glossy hair, then swipes the figurine, placing it in his tool case, and smuggles it past Nurse Grey at the nurses' station.

"Wait!" a voice says. "Wait, dammit!"

Returning to his car, Carder settles into the bucket seat and turns on the radio. [*CarFreaks with Casey Meeks*]. He pulls the smuggled dog from his tool case, setting it on his lap. [*A '93 Honda Accord with 240,000 miles? Before I replaced the battery, I'd think about keeping it and replacing the car instead.*] Smart-ass. Carder retrieves one of his extra blades from a plastic case, while the caller explains their situation. [*It's driving me crazy! After about four or five miles the lights fade, the engine feels like it's on one cylinder and the car finally dies!*] He examines the knife. In milliseconds, it can part a sea of skin into an ocean of blood. He then inspects the smuggled Pup. Aside from matted fur, it's in good shape for being nearly thirty years old. [*That's noted in older Honda Accords especially in UFO reports. Seen any funny blinking lights overhead?*] He takes a breath, and raises the blade. Using the same care he'd given *Wilburn, Tanya*, he lands the blade, slicing the green plastic. Separating eye from doll is more difficult than harvesting a human cornea. The material is tough, but Carder doesn't have to be careful. One eye is out. The dog's days of sprinkling sugar on life's ugly side are over. And now, the second. He peers into the gaping holes in the artificial dog's head. Empty. [*Don't get nostalgic on me. Every car finds its way to the junkyard eventually. Maybe you should drive it there while you still can.*]

A shape fills the corner of his eye: outside the car window, a woman with curly black hair is bent over, looking in. Her gloved hand is positioned to knock, but stops before touching glass. Nurse Grey. Without making eye contact, she backs away, carrying a small basket of chocolate Easter eggs on one arm, and returns inside the sliding hospital doors from whence she came.

Carder waits a few minutes. Then, he opens the car door, sets the synthetic carcass in front of one of his tires and drives off.

5

A REAPING: 'BIS

Carder at 7 years old

A small figure wades through the hill's dusky grass. Suddenly, the beast knows he's no longer alone. Alert, his ears mushroom up from a pelt of nocturnal green, dominating the fiendish creature's head like satellites reaching through distance to filter sound. Bloodfrogs chirp, while cicadas and pitchfeathers call.

Veils fall over the sky as two suns fade and evening arrives. The crouching demon's bleached eyes open blankly. In the distance, creeps the slip of a shadow, almost imperceptibly. It's only an unskilled human. They always betray themselves. At first, the beast pays no mind to the slug of a boy, at least not obviously. There are other concerns.

Walking on two legs, then running on four, it bolts forward in a brutish manner, stopping, searching, bolting again, viciously protecting a perimeter of land that stretches miles taut enough to snap.

This is 'Bis—the guardian.

Never hesitant to drive teeth into challenger or prey, his fangs were worn on punctured lives. Even before reaching the boy, 'Bis realizes the human lacks the scent of war but carries fresh wounds, the blood-odor of fear and desolation. Something or someone had maimed the child but left him uneaten. An instinctive gurgle climbs inside the animal's stomach. Saliva coats his tongue.

The child stops, maybe too hurt to move further. 'Bis approaches without care but changes posture, walking seamlessly on two legs without breaking stride. Upon meeting, he leans into the trembling human, resisting urges to gorge himself. The child is too young, too helpless. 'Bis's musty breath holds odors of raw meat and blood. The stench drenches his words.

"See the moons overhead? They're merely crescents."

The child nods, peering up at the double-coupling of suns and moons: four celestial bodies pinned to the sky in short-lived conjunction before night is fully decided.

"They're smiling tonight," says 'Bis. "And I don't eat humans. They make me ill." It's a lie, but there's something about this one. Something different. "Thus, Creeping thing, you'll remain free from harm."

The creature sees the child shaking and continues. "Creeping thing, crawl into this night any day, and into this day any night. Don't fear me—I promise you, a promise that goes up and down, to and fro, that in one form or another, I'll roam to find you as often as you roam to find me."

The Creep tests the demon's vow of safety, touching the beast's claws. They're sharper and longer than any needle, but no longer seem to scare him. If anything, they probably distract the boy from his pain. He touches 'Bis's fangs, measuring their varying length with his fingers - stalagmites and stalactites in a cavern of death. It would make sense for him to be frightened, to be devoured, to be taken inside that cave, yet he fully explores them.

"Only teeth," 'Bis says.

"Only teeth," Creep repeats in the way children play with adult words.

"Only teeth can be the monuments we need."

The Creep appears puzzled. Is 'Bis speaking of the fangs he's been allowed to touch? At the child's young age, the meaning of a word like 'monument' is malleable, and can be shaped into a variety of meanings. The boy searches his mind for its worth.

"What do you mean?" he asks. Using his fingertips, he traces the ridges on the monster's black cheeks, up the front of its forehead, and down the rippling, armor-like texture of its spine.

"I'll show you. Come."

As they trudge the grasses to the hill's peak, the demon gently holds back speed until there's a new view: two living, ivory stones protrude up from the ground as of Stonehenge. They give shade even in the disappearing light.

While the child ponders the smooth white stone and the sanguine grasses hugging their bases, he puts his finger to his mouth, tracing his tender, pillowed gums. Pressing the tip of his tongue through the gaping hole, he tastes his bloodstained lips from the inside. He'll now have to wait for two adult teeth to emerge. But the aching expression in the boy's face has been replaced by curiosity.

"Tombstones?" Creep asks, trying to understand the formations.

"No. Not yours anyway. Monuments."

The demon and the Creep settle into their mutual presence, no longer communicating with unnecessary words. Before the boy discovers more of that world, they enjoy a small universe made of sunset, one that contains only two heartbeats, two rhythms, two drums. Creep sits while 'Bis grows colder, his breaths shorter, weaker. Eventually, only one heart beats—and the boy moves on.

6

SQUID INK & GAS MASKS

Though finished with his hospital shift, Darren is still in his medical scrubs, taking a moment to liberate his afro in Carder's Trans Am. Years of church-Sundays have transformed Darren into a self-proclaimed TIE-fighter, walking a path where formalwear isn't an option. Sure, he may don a uniform for his hospital job, but it's not a three-piece suit—and being a TIE-fighter involves more than avoiding suits and neckties. It means living a fully organic, cosmic lifestyle—one in which Darren's decompressed 'fro bounces like a DJ grooving to his own licks.

"You can't have just one date," He tells Carder once they sit at their usual table in The Fuller Diner. "It's like potato chips, man. You've gotta have a bunch."

"Possibly. But also like potato chips, they cause heart attacks. I only agreed to date her in the first place because I lost our bet."

"You know, Card, sometime you and I need to have a serious conversation about you and gambling. I knew you'd lose long before you even agreed to it. No more bets for you." Darren motions to the waitress. "Magda?"

Zombie applies tepid tongue to Carder. The little beast was only allowed inside the diner after they'd promised Magda nobody would notice. Its lick-lick-licks remind him to *be here now-now-now*.

Allowing the dog inside isn't the wisest choice, but when Magda crossed the wires of decision, rebellion's acidic taste smoldered in her throat: rebellion against FDA regulations, rebellion against a customer who ordered four chocolate malts while brushing his hand against her leg, rebellion against the crotchety boss who always gets her schedule wrong. Magda's rebellion is an arrow shot at cheap napkins and watery ketchup, at the high rents of New York City, the hairy backs of horny men—at cockroaches, lint and cheap ballpoint pens. At serving. Rebellion isn't freedom, but it sometimes tastes like a replica. It proves to Magda that she's still alive. And though she'd be happy never to see Carder or Darren again, there are a few times a week when they're the people for whom she feels the least disdain.

"Okay. But the dog goes below the table," she directs, "between you and the wall... and make it worth my while."

"I'll make sure of that," Darren says.

"You do that, Doc." She stuffs a pad of paper behind her apron strings and walks away.

For years, Carder and Darren have eaten at the Fuller Diner, watching Magda blossom from a disillusioned unibrowed teen into a perpetually disappointed, full-figured waitress. Adulthood had replaced her unibrow with two inky lines, giving her the distinct look of a cartoon princess trapped in a greasy world. Darren and Carder are her punching bags. On the other hand, Magda reminds them that life could be worse. Twenty minutes later, she slides them their meals, tossing silverware and napkins on the side.

Over the years, Carder has watched Darren eat hundreds of the never-changing *Chef's Choice*: chicken parmesan. The aroma is comforting.

"Tell me about your date already!" Darren demands before shoving a heaping fork into his mouth.

One thing was responsible for Carder's online dating profile: hairless cats. Darren had claimed he'd recently awoken in a booty-call's bed with one bald feline sitting on his chest and another's razor-claws kneading his crotch. *These cats would scare Satan!* Darren never saw the woman again, but the cats still prey on him in nightmares. Carder hadn't believed any of it, so the bet was made. Carder would go on one date if hairless cats were real. The bet was lost. Thus, Carder created an online dating profile.

When he received online messages from *3toedLuvr*, they were from Mimi Manchester, a pear-shaped woman whose photo flaunted more teeth than a mouth can comfortably fit. During a Costa Rican vacation, Mimi had fallen in love with the three-toed sloth. Their moon-pie faces and casual life philosophy had won her over. Since that time, she embarked on living the three-toed life: moving in a slower, more deliberate manner, and keeping an ever-present pokerface so as not to scare passersby. On *3toedLuvr*'s profile, the section starting *"I'm passionate about…"* was completed with *"…vintage doll collecting."* Carder shouldn't have shut his eyes to that, but she lived close by, making their potential meeting less dreadful. When Mimi invited him up for a drink at the end of their quiet date at the Fuller Diner, the doll collection couldn't be ignored. Case after case of Pick-Me-Pups merchandise lined her living room walls. Dolls, a lamp, blankets, dog-shaped backpacks and thigh-high tube socks peered out, silently beseeching him for help. Carder didn't admit his responsibility for her fetish. Nevertheless, Mimi Manchester did have a rare honor: hearing the bloody details of cornea retrieval. Carder offered to demonstrate if she provided a knife and a cherry tomato. Her jaw unhinged in a ruined pokerface. She escorted him out of her toy mausoleum at lightning speed. *3toedLuvr's* online profile promptly disappeared.

"It didn't have to play out like that!" Darren says, smacking the table. His plate jumps, causing the brief appearance of a dog nose. "This whole thing's unbelievable, man! Situations like these provide multiple doors to go through, but you choose the wrong one every time, always the safest route. Isn't it obvious you should've told this chick about your role in the creation of her favorite toy? She would've gotten on her knees and worshipped you, man! You'd have been Jesus and Santa Claus mixed into one!"

"I don't want to have sex with anyone wearing a pink sweater they've knitted themselves."

"That's why you rip it off!"

"Listen, it looked like she'd sat down to knit the sweater and didn't get up again until it was finished three months later."

"What does that mean?"

"Everything you think it could."

That shut Darren up.

Carder wishes to choose the right door, not the merely the safest one. After thinking about one particular door for four days, he accepts Haika's dinner invitation—even if he would prefer her husband remained faceless. The meal is to be at their home, no doubt on a level holding more than dusty art. Carder considers the event a natural disaster with advanced warning, wondering whether he'll be swallowed up by the ground or will have to wait to the end before assessing damage.

While brushing his teeth, he decides he won't slap her husband's face with sexiness. He won't wear anything conveying, "Hey, I've enjoyed your naked wife and now your quiche! Both are delicious!" He throws on a pair of old khakis, a t-shirt with a smattering of holes near the neck, and his windbreaker, hoping the overall nonchalance might create a disarming fog, dismantling high expectations and lulling any perceived threat—victory won by playing the loser.

"Dollface, come in!" Haika says, opening the door. Her night-colored dress has simple, angular cuts. A shimmering moonstone necklace blinks silver-blue layers. Classy and deliberate. She pulls him by the hand into the entry eight stairs above the street, one floor above the garden level where she'd posed nude.

Those eight stairs separate two universes. Devoid of the musty, stunning chaos of Haika's level, the upper-world is impossibly clean, as though passing through its threshold breaks a hermetic seal. Carder brings a dearth of germs which he assumes a maid will extinguish the next day. Once Haika assures him that bare feet don't repulse her, he removes his shoes.

"I was in bare feet through my entire youth," she says, and in an act of solidarity, removes her satin slippers. "Mike's in the kitchen cooking the pasta."

Oddly, there are hairline differences from the Haika he'd previously met: a scratch here, a loss of focus there. She plots every word, every movement, carefully placing her steps in an almost ritualistic pattern. Curious images pop into Carder's mind: forgotten memories of a hornet's nest humming on his uncle Trenton's property during Carder's sole visit years before. The nest fascinated Carder. Something had to be done to keep the whizzing hornets from torturing Aunt Vera while she tilled the soil. Hence, Carder awoke to his uncle's nudge in the middle of the night, and they snuck out to the tree in the moonlit yard, quickly throwing a plastic bag over the nest and clipping the branch from which it hung. After it had spent a night in a freezer, Uncle Trenton pulled out the silent nest and cut out a subsection. They peered in, searching the papery nest for any signs of movement. The dead hornets were motionless, flipped on their backs this way and that, with pointless wings that had become little more than crystal costumes on miniature mannequins. It was astounding—something buzzing with life so easily stripped into an inanimate object. A second is all it takes. One dead hornet remained on her feet: the queen. Still and graceful, her eyes shined like panoramic, burned-out bulbs. Carder never knew whether it was wind or remaining life that moved the queen's antenna, but for years, he imagined she staged her frozen death in order to spring forth at the first opportunity for escape. Startled, he'd dropped the hive and sprinted away.

Haika and Carder are drinking a blood-colored cabernet when her husband, Mike Fiore, comes into the parlor from the kitchen. The fragrance of homemade red sauce fills the room with tomatoey reassurance. At the very least, the evening will result in good food.

Mike is a tall, pale ghost with slick black hair which evolved through centuries to become shiny, laminate and American. His nose had either once been broken or had readjusted its angle during growth. He looks like a man of the 1960's, a kool kat, slick as a saxophone, confident as the winner of a Nobel Prize or someone who's spending their year as Mister Universe. Having lived with aristocracy embroidered into his life, Mike is royalty that knows it's royalty, never experiencing anything different.

"It's nice to meet the famous Carder," he says, gripping Carder's hand until it throbs within their handshake. "You made quite an impression on Haika. From what she's said, you're a man of many talents." Mike lifts a glass of wine. "To talent."

To which talent do they drink? To the talent of leaving one's own home to survive another's? To Haika's talent for luring strangers to her bedroom for artistic endeavors? To the talent of drawing pubic hair in a realistic manner?

"Haika didn't get a chance to tell me what it is *you* do, Mike," Carder says.

"Can't blame her. Aside from my investments, I'm a professional bridge player. I'll tell you right now, it's boring."

Mike is right, yet that doesn't prevent him from explaining

Bridge and its subculture in detail through an entire glass of wine. Apparently, much like hairless cats and black swans, old women who play Bridge do exist. Not only that, but they pay dashing young men to join them. The description of Mike's drab career leads Carder to study his empty goblet against chandelier light. He finds a flaw—the hardened film of dishwasher residue around the rim of the glass. Maybe the defects of Mike and Haika are slight, almost invisible, but they're there.

Over the next ten minutes, Mike details his financial philosophy [...*looking into transferring a couple of smaller amounts into a 451. It provides flexibility for the investor, where after a certain period of time...*]. The jargon translates into Mike having secured enough wealth to avoid going up or down subway stairs unless he wants to ride the train as a venture among groundlings.

Spanning the following five minutes, Mike apprises Carder that he'd given up his law career after investments paid off. He then discovered a flair for card-playing and geriatric women.

For three more minutes Mike praises the wristwatch Haika gave him for their last anniversary. "Isn't it superb? Real secret agent stuff!"

He takes off the watch, pointing out the edging around the face. Waterproof up to 50 meters and connected to a satellite, it can be located in an avalanche, a shipwreck, or a hike through the Amazon.

"Here, try it on! Feel its weight."

Carder puts it on.

It's heavy—and its weight spells out Mike's ownership. Now all Carder needs is the Swiss Alps, a white squall, or malaria so he could die, get lost or become ill—anything to escape listening. "May I use your washroom?" he asks.

Under the fuzzy light of a decadent bathroom, the burden of the wristwatch has Carder using his other hand to unzip his pants and manipulate his junk. Mirrors show the slate walls behind him. Carder already knows all he needs to about Haika's husband. Mike contains no code, no hieroglyphics to decipher. Mike is the type of guy that reads pink business newspapers, carries a comb in his back pocket, has a glass case displaying cufflinks, and dips into a humidor for perfect cigars. Washing his hands, Carder pictures Mike standing before the sink in a monogrammed bathrobe, splashing his square jaw with aftershave. He has visions of Mike's weekly visits to a Wall Street men's spa, placing his hairless feet in the hands of Korean women for the Deluxe Executive Pedicure. Meeting Mike in an elevator would lead to an understanding by the third floor that he's an all-around hero of good stock. And he parades Haika around like the champion shitzu at the Westminster Dog Show. Bravo Mike, fine specimen.

When Carder wanders back to the sounds of the dining room, he arrives to another glass of wine and a steaming pot of pasta. The dining room is peppered with ten chairs, the backs so rigid that they could easily dump their occupants. A giant potted jade plant, thick with branches and rubbery leaves, stretches for shuttered windows. Haika tells him they call that plant the Old Lady: she'd replaced Robert Plant, who'd met his demise when smashed by a fallen Mark Ryden painting. If the Old Lady is like most senior citizens, she might be aghast at the hefty art hanging above her: a group of entangled men and women wear gasmasks—some are sexually posed, others are merely contorted uncomfortably. Except for the gasmasks and one man in long black dress socks, they're all nude, wearing their genitalia like sliced peaches and lazy sausage links. Carder hears his dead mother gasp.

Aside from sitting as if she has a metal rod in her spine, Haika seems comfortable, her legs crossed beneath her chair. Carder prays she rarely opens them to Mike, or that perhaps Mike's sterile or too selfish for children. A mix of Mike and Haika would seal two separate universes into a malformed mass of excellence.

"Her husband's got me yawning and I wasn't even there. But man, anybody or anything getting you out of your house has some intrinsic merit. What you need is to drop this Haika and go on another date ASAP." Darren has reached the halfway point in his chicken parmesan, but not in his efforts to force Carder's progression.

"You know, it's not polite to take someone to dinner and then give them indigestion during the meal," Carder says.

"Man, you're in your thirties."

"Early thirties, and who cares? You're not married either."

"Maybe Stephy and I never got the certificate, but we went

through the same hell as any other married schmucks. After that, anyone would need a break. You, on the contrary... " He raises friendly but frustrated hands to his temples.

Acid fills Carder's stomach. "If I meet the right person..."

"Right now every person is the right person for you. Hear that? Get out there. Outdoors. Outside the home. There's a world beyond your house and the hospitals. Try looking into someone's eyes without a blade in your hand. Someone breathing!" Darren sighs, crumpling his napkin.

Carder contorts a pained expression. "Can we *not* talk about this right now?"

Zombie shifts under the table, leaning against Carder's legs, his fur like paintbrushes and the interior worlds within their bristles.

Lick. Lick. Lick.

Here. Here. Here.

Be here.

Carder envies the dog's natural Buddhist take on life. Zombie is a guru by default, giving everything his fullest consideration. If it isn't happening *now*, the dog isn't concerned. Zombie's simple philosophy: pay attention to the crap lying at your feet and ignore the rest. Carder tries adopting this outlook, but constantly fails at being in the now. Still, the dog's dogness calms the whirring storm of Carder's mind. Aside from his paintings, Zombie comes closest to stopping thoughts of property taxes, the laundry, news reports and of avoiding social interaction. When Zombie catches Carder contemplating the afterlife while they walk, the mutt lurches against the leash toward a fire hydrant. *Pee here now.* Carder finds simple satisfaction in prying a discarded styrofoam cup from the gutter out of the dog's jaws. Together, they're merely a simple thing: a man and his dog.

"Isn't the squid-ink pasta gorgeous?" asks Haika.

The pasta is strange. And black. A bit al dente. It's taken Carder years to solve the riddle: pasta is pasta no matter the shape. Spiraling rigatoni, tiny couscous and stringy angel hair are all clever ways of repackaging the perfect meal. Nonetheless, this flat black noodle infused with squid ink tastes like all kinds of wrong, the textured noodles turn too easily into suctioned arms holding onto his teeth.

Haika Onassis-Kennedy restates her question with her bowl

tipped forward, displaying its contents. "Carder, have you ever seen such beautiful food?"

Carder spins his fork into a whirlpool of black noodles. Flickering candles wink as Mike admires Carder's t-shirt despite, or perhaps because of, its holes.

"Isn't it amazing how much we'll pay for something just so it looks as if we paid nothing?"

"I did pay almost nothing—seventy-five cents—several years ago at a stoop sale. The holes are mine though. I earned them." Carder loves this shirt. So much good television has been watched in it. Upon his admission, he knows Mike's image of him and the shirt flips upside-down, changing from chic to strange. Darren will have a field day with this experience—thinks Carder, as the slurping of noodles becomes the only sound in the room.

Mike clears his throat and dishes prosciutto-wrapped asparagus onto his plate. "So Carder, Haika tells me you're good with dogs."

Haika diverts her eyes, surmising the state of everyone's wine glasses

Yes, Carder is so good with dogs that Haika and her mirror-image twin probably fought over the dogs he created while they grew up in Germany, Mexico and America. He visualizes two girls with copper-colored hair walloping one another for the chance to brush Cherry Burst's nylon coat. He relishes this new sight: Haika, uncomfortable. She won't look at him. She's rearranging the dark noodles in her bowl.

Eventually, she meekly says, "I told Mike you're going to help us with little Rocco. He laughed so hard when I told him you call him Zombie. I like the new name. I've been calling him that ever since."

Mike groans. "That dog's been nothing but trouble. I'd rather not have to get rid of him, but I have to be honest, at this point I'm in no way opposed. Haika's the one that has issues with it... as you obviously know. You definitely intercepted her on the train at the right time. It takes guts to persuade a stranger on their way to having a pet put to sleep *not* to do it! Still, I hate this dog dropping loaf-bombs everywhere. Until that changes we're keeping him on the garden level."

Carder is confused. "I didn't convince Haika of anything. If she made that decision, it was her own." Why hadn't Haika told him she'd meant to dispose of Zombie? He senses her shame as she shrinks close to her bowl.

"Why you want to take on that little crapper is beyond me," Mike says, "but we certainly appreciate the help."

Carder has no intention of taking on the little crapper. It would be absurd: he doesn't clean his own bathroom, has never changed a diaper and the only dogs he's been around at length are inanimate.

Haika's nostrils flare in anticipation of Carder's answer, and he knows their future depends on his response. He wants to draw her again, to see her again, to ring the doorbell and have her answer, to taste the coffee of every pot she brews. She chews her food slowly, forcing herself to swallow. Mike's oblivious. It all makes lopsided sense. Carder is, after all, playing a role—though not of a recovering shut-in but of a dog-trainer in demand.

"The dog's not so bad," Carder tells Mike. "Your wife had me eating out of her hand when I met her. I'd have done anything. I'll tell you what: there's a long list of dogs waiting for my handling, but for Haika and Zombie… and for you, Mike—I'll bump you to the front of the line. One condition: I'm refusing the usual fee."

"You're what!?"

Carder might as well have said he was going to grate an infant over the pasta.

"We made a deal: I refuse to take any money since Haika's helping me with my niece in return. Mandy's from Pennsylvania, and will be visiting soon. She'll probably stay for a month or more. I have to make sure she has a blast but don't know exactly how to accomplish it. She's seventeen and I'm a geek in his thirties. She's a Jehovah's Witness and I'm a heathen. Haika's insight is far more valuable than my helping your dog."

Mike shoots a hearty laugh across the table. "It must be a good deal if she's helping you with your niece. Haika hates kids."

"Hate is the wrong word," she interjects. "Hating your sister's kids is not the same as hating all children."

"Mandy doesn't consider herself a child," says Carder. "She's graduating from high school, so she's probably into boys and make-up—she's probably fully menstruating by now, right? When did that all start for you, Haika?" Carder swallows his laughter. He's now enjoying steering this odd conversation.

Haika rolls her eyes. "Oh, that makes her an adult all right! Is she at least on Ritalin? According to the moms I've talked to around here, that's the miraculous solution. It is! Mike's sister says that Zoey's actually become religious since taking it: kneels, prays, sits still, begs and rolls over. You know what? When I look at that type of child, hate *is* the right word."

"Haika," is all Mike says.

She clears her throat, folding her hands and draping her face with a grin. "I'm joking! Of course, I'll do my best with your niece, Carder. Her being a Jehovah's Witness is intriguing. Not celebrating holidays and all that, right?" More wine disappears from her glass. "And I was thirteen. I thought I was dying. But I'm sure Mandy's been accustomed to having her period for a long time now." She sops up the remaining red sauce from her bowl with a bit of bread. "You're right though, it sounds like she's no longer a child. She may be tolerable."

Looking down at his bowl, Mike pushes it away. "What a meal, eh Carder? Incontinent animals and the monthly flow of womanly blood!"

"And gas masks." Carder points to the painting on the wall.

"And gas masks," Mike repeats with clear agitation.

"And dress socks."

"And dress socks! See, Haika, I told you! Listen to me next time. Can you imagine if we'd had someone else over and they had to eat across from that image?" He rises up from his chair, plucks the painting from the wall, and sets it on the floor, facing away. He briefly turns back before leaving. "A pleasure meeting you, Carder. Thanks for helping with the dog. I'd rather not get rid of it… but whatever." He slips out, his voice trailing from the next room. "And pay him, Haika. Work it out."

Magic exists: Mike leaves them for the remaining moments of their night. The idea of going out for dessert has either been erased or forgotten. Besides, he has to work early tomorrow. Carder is content with Mike's absence, and resists asking what professional bridge players work on in early morning.

A gentle silence saturates the room. They begin clearing dishes.

"You're different with Mike," Carder says.

"That's because you're different *than* Mike."

"I meant *you're* different when you're with him. Why did you lie like that?"

Haika's cheeks flush red. "I'm not a liar. Are you going to help me with Zombie or not?"

"I guess so."

"Then I didn't lie. I made it happen. Big difference." They clear the rest of the table without speaking. She stacks the porcelain, placing silverware in the highest bowl. Once Haika's cheeks return to their normal color, she continues, "Do you want to see the dog before you go?"

"As I'm apparently taking him on as my apprentice, I guess a word before I leave makes sense."

"Okay, let's go down. Here, let me take that painting. I guess it's sentenced to forever leaning against the downstairs wall."

"I didn't have a problem with the gasmasks," says Carder.

"I know. It's the dress socks, right?"

The Fuller Diner bustles. Carder smears raspberry jam across his toast. He didn't have to ask for toast burnt to coal, Magda just knows. He places the knife on his plate, leaving a glob of jam to walk the plank.

"Tell me about your newest screenplay, Darren," Carder requests while Magda refreshes their water.

Darren leans forward to shield his ideas from lurking writers that eavesdrop, jotting down others' ideas. They're everywhere in Brooklyn. In a low voice, he says, "It's gold. Picture this: In a dark, gotham world, a panty-raider strikes across the city, breaking into homes, from the smallest railroad apartments in 'Billyburg to the highest security doorman buildings of the Upper West Side. He scales fire escapes and elevator shafts. He crawls through basement windows. Class and culture have no bearing—this guy loves diversity—filling his bag with peach lace garters, paper-thin Hanes-Her-Ways, granny panties and thongs so small they have the black hole effect. There's no explanation, no evidence except missing underwear. Thing is, he takes nothing but panties. Eventually, he causes a shortage throughout the city."

"What's it called?"

"*The Undertaker.*"

Magda overhears and chimes in, "All for underpants? Dumbest plot I've ever heard." She rips the bill from her pad, setting it down. A whimper sounds from below the table: a dog clearly tired of hanging in the shadows of the blue plate special.

"I'd see it," Carder says, countering Magda's insult. "And you know I only see serious film."

Darren smiles. "I see a serious film on these drinking glasses."

"What's serious is that you gotta get that dog out of here," Magda says. "This isn't a kennel, okay?"

"Then why do you always act trapped? Give us a second, will you?" Darren says it in a way that translates *what do you know about film anyway?* "So, Carder, you gonna keep walking that bitch's dog?"

"For now. But neither Haika nor Zombie are bitches. Please stop using that term."

"You're at least getting to check Haika's oil, right?"

The question's rhetorical. Darren knows the answer and Carder isn't going to dignify it with a response. Carder bites into the toast, a welcome obstacle to speech.

"She must be damn hot if you're walking her ugly dog."

"I enjoy Zombie. He's a better person than most people I know. It's taken me two days, but I've taught him to sit up and beg."

"All dogs beg. And it sounds like Haika's taught you the same things."

Carder's posture stiffens. "I'm not like you! I don't need thirteen booty calls a week!"

Darren has always sparred Carder into new experiences, but carefully. Pushing his empty plate to the table's edge, he leans back with arms crossed behind his head, settling deeper into the booth with a full stomach. "Don't make me get brutal on you. You know I can and will. Wasn't one shiner enough?"

One shiner was enough. Nowadays, Darren's threats of black eyes are playful peace offerings. With the build of a tank, Darren could easily hurt Carder but never would. They got that out of the way when they met in 8th grade's summer school History class. A fictional journey on the Oregon Trail had ignited their friendship, though Darren might've survived the Trail had he joined Carder's group. The teacher tried interspersing misfits equally into each group, but an unusual number of losers were in summer school that year after staff shortages required gym teachers to teach History and Geometry. Too exhausted to argue for Darren to join Carder's group, the teacher gave in. Darren chose the group containing Jasmine Williams, forgoing a covered wagon so he could walk next to the smooth-skinned beauty through Nebraska, Wyoming and Idaho. The trail was a gauntlet of freezing rain, broken wagon wheels, starvation, accidents and lightning strikes. Food was scarce, dysentery was not. Only two of the six groups in the classroom survived to Oregon. When Darren's group refused joining a protective wagon circle, Carder laughed so hard his cap fell off. Marauding Indians scalped not only Darren, but his wife Jasmine, and their two children: Joe Forlini, a breasted boy with yellowed armpits, and Claudia Beard who proclaimed her virginity to convince herself and everyone else that it was by choice. Carder gloated. If Darren had agreed to join his fictional family, generations of Darren's imaginary offspring might have lined the western United States like 24-hour convenience stores. Being scalped infuriated Jasmine—tears of humiliation welled up. She couldn't afford to flunk out of summer school. If she did, she'd be sent to live with her father in Nowhere, New Jersey. Her disregard for Darren turned to hatred.

When the seventh period bell rang, Darren followed Carder out of class, kicking at his shoes, chiding that since Carder could barely survive day-to-day life, how in the world could he have survived the Oregon Trail?

"Cooperation. Cooperation and determination. That's what it…"

Darren lunged forward from behind. "Let me ask you a question…" he hissed, grabbing Carder by his collar. Carder didn't need to see him. Darren's hot spittle had found his bad ear. Carder couldn't make out the words, but felt their violence. "…you ever get a black eye from a black guy?"

By the time Carder's shiner healed, they'd become fast friends. All of Darren's anger had dissipated in one whack. They quickly found they had one important thing in common: Star Wars. That, and that neither of them were accepted, celebrated nor noticed among their classmates no matter how they tried. Reality had never given Carder and Darren a trail to follow. Yet, clinging together in life's harsh surf at least meant they clung to something. Over the next decade and a half, they fashioned a raft of friendship, warning each other of sharks and coral, and helping one another keep their heads above water. Together, they searched for land on which their lost feet could settle. And this time, Darren survived.

7

CLOSE TO THE GATE

The keys to Haika's home are soon in Carder's pockets, on his keychain and opening her front door. The bleats of the alarm clock become obsolete. Excitement wakes him. Morning sun becomes a magnet pulling him to his feet. He hasn't been relied upon in any significant way for years; it pushes blood through his veins. He wouldn't dare risk running late only to find that Zombie shat beside the bookcase. The dog leash tethers Carder to Haika's world. Sidewalks were laid only to connect their two homes and provide pause between fire hydrants. The dog's progress is whispering, almost invisible, but *outside* becomes easier for his agoraphobic trainer.

Library visits provide many books on canine behavior: *Tough Dogs, Gentle Hands*, the insightful *Stop Treating Your D-o-g Like a G-o-d (You've Got it Backwards!)*, and *Who's a Good Boy, Who's a Good Dog?* Several hundred pages establish concepts basic to any relationship in which both parties breathe: regular exercise, discipline and affection. For weeks, Carder follows their suggestions, trying this and that, but the books train him more than he trains the dog. Soon, Zombie gives notice at the front door or squats on newspaper. Mike and Haika learn not to leave The Times on the floor if they're still reading it.

Attempts to ignore his feelings for Haika are unsuccessful, but Carder wraps them within concern for Zombie's training. Carder's longings are irrelevant, frivolous thrills to enjoy for their own sake.

Mike's mandate relegating Zombie to Haika's level prevents the rest of the home from stinking. The brownstone's upper floors hold nothing but vacuum tracks and a lemony-fresh smell. Carder prefers the garden level's disarray of damaged objects, where a cracked mirror splits reflections in two, and stuffing pokes out from a chair cushion, where the faucet leaks and floors creak. The pendulum of a faded grandfather clock swings too fast and slow, measuring time in jagged, irregular pieces. Haika's space is a museum of imperfection, where mismatched items arrive as relics the instant a flaw appears. Everything there seems saved from death—a feat Carder was never able to accomplish in any world. The art quickly grows comfortable with him, hanging with less gravity each day that he and Zombie laze about, trading contented sighs. The dog gnaws rawhide while the man watches superclusters of dust suspended in the fat of noon. Carder's mother always advised against leaving home, but the slide into another's culture—a culture free of other worlds—is shockingly easy. Its borders seem thicker, more distinct.

Carder enjoys the cool of Haika's place before setting out to walk the dog. He plays Haika's stereo, flipping through worn photo albums as plinking Bossa Nova songs wash the walls. A smooth-lilting voice orders him to *imagine your dream as an ice cream.*

The sticky cellophane-lined pages of his favorite photo albums advertise the decadent 80's. One album is shaped like a pie-eyed owl with twine eyes serving as frames. One eye holds a tiny photographic version of either Haika or her sister, but the other is blank, as though offering an interior view of the owl's white skull. This album is childhood, its old odors pungent with what Carder imagines are Mexican spices and—is that glue? Many aged photos capture the two sisters like identical nymphs, imprisoning them in moments of sisterly affection. In one, each girl pushes blackberry-stained hands into the other's mouth. The dark juices explore their white sleeveless t-shirts. Their smiles and embraces make Carder's stomach churn. Snapshots of his own childhood are so different, containing his lock-jaw smiles, his older sister Lucy painfully displaying the metal tracks of braces, and his unsmiling mother in polyester pants. His pictures are always the same—family excursions were almost nonexistent—taken at in-home destinations, in front of the couch or curtains, or at the kitchen table. What his own life lacked has found easy documentation in Haika's pictures. Even a photo in which one troubled girl wails with closed eyes while the other mocks her, holds wisps of camaraderie. Neighboring shots show them embracing again.

Shuffling outside, usually denoting the mail's arrival, mingles with Haika's unexpected voice. It's impossible to hear what she's saying, but she purrs sympathy for the postman. Carder quickly pushes the photo album back onto the bookshelf, using the remaining time to slide back in the leather arm chair, not intending to appear frozen instead of relaxed. He folds his arms behind his head as though he lay in the arms of a daydream. Except for the sweet exhilaration-laced shame of having entered Haika's private past, he hopes he appears calm when she enters.

"Hey Bubb," Haika says, setting a grocery bag on her living room floor. "Why so edgy?"

She crosses to the desk, picks up a tiny turtle-shaped box, and pops off its shell. "This isn't ivory," she assures as though concern is thick between them. "I got rid of all Mike's ivory. He was swimming in death. When I told him it had to go, he wanted to sell it. Imagine that! This is a nut from the Amazon: *Tacqua*. It looks and feels just like ivory. I tried to interest Mike in distributing it." A green odor wafts up from the open box. Marijuana. "Problem is, people want giant objects as trophies. And this nut isn't big or majestic. I told Mike to prove he has a dick and money some way other than killing giant, beautiful creatures, you know?"

The contents of the turtle box further augment the satisfaction that Haika's arrival brought. His former days of smoking, which Darren wrenched away years ago, rush back with the dank, candied aroma. Carder decides that despite his excitement, actually because of it, he'll take only one toke.

This is the Haika that Carder loves. Earthy-Mother-Goddess-in-Paisley-Herb-Garden-Love. He promises himself that he won't confess to thumbing through her photos.

"I thumbed through your photos."

"You *didn't* just tell me that!" She holds the unshelled turtle to her nose, inhaling the scent of vacation. Rolling a joint, she sprinkles ground plant along the length of rectangular paper. "Let this be a moment, will you? The day's so beautiful that I snuck out of the gallery. Tino is delighted. He loves when it's under *his* jurisdiction." Haika holds the white stick between them. "This is ours." She says it like they've made a baby.

Carder reminds her that smoke destroys art, but she only tilts her head, informing him that this type of smoke *seasons* it. Still, she turns on a fan. "I bought a greeting card for Mandy, one that isn't too… anything."

"Why'd you do that?"

"I don't want her clamming up when she meets me. If she's going to know who I am, she's going to know me before she comes."

"You're a stranger."

"I won't be by the time she arrives. Besides I'm not a stranger. Carder, I'm a Gemini."

Whatever that means.

She hands him the joint and a lighter. He pulls smoke into his lungs until a spark nearly walks the paper bridge to his lips. Instantly, the high takes him to inner-lands (too much so, Darren always insisted) but Carder stuffs the feeling. For once, he wants to be right where he is. The pair's eyes meet while they sigh plumes of smoke that curling like white hair of a maidenly spirit.

His last encounter with weed was so long ago that one puff packs power. The higher Carder feels, the more sense it makes that Haika would establish a friendship with Mandy—another rope pulling him and Haika together. Despite the absence of sex, Carder and Haika are sliding into permanence, as permanent as anything ever gets. But what does she gain from this? Why did she so readily trust some guy from the subway, letting him rummage through her belongings and care for her dog? Carder wants to know, but can't ask—it lives in the land of things unsaid, things existing as surely as any turtle box or photo album, but which can't be painted or held— even if their weight is heavy and colors bright, even if they're as strong as ivory. Besides, he prefers simply watching Haika sway in the rhythm of Brazilian songs. Her jade necklace swings like a jungle vine.

Zombie whimpers, wanting to be taken out, his skinny tail points at the door.

Haika jangles keys. "Come on. We're going to walk Zombie.

We're going to *your* place to look through *your* photos."

Carder stops breathing. He makes sure he can feel his heartbeat before starting again. "But wait, I thought I'd surprise you by washing your dishes first. Cornflakes calcify, and I bet your cleaning lady would appreciate it."

"Oh, get off it! You're not a cleaning lady and she doesn't wash my dishes anyway. Like I said, let this be a moment, will you?" She takes the dog's leash in one hand and drags Carder by the other.

Whatever groceries are in the bag on the floor will be there for the next few hours.

Under the influence of cannabis, Haika notices the buttery nature of her own skin. She often falls into poetic musings in this state, waxing on her life and now on this new friendship. Carder, she thinks, possesses a bridled brilliance, the same way the sun's trapped heat radiates in city steel and concrete. In other settings, the same sun is astonishing instead of nauseating, and draws worshippers to the seaside, displaying their bodies to stretching sky. Here, that same sun is blistering, scorching everyone into running for shelter and escaping into shops solely for air conditioning. Haika loves sun, but not what this metropolis does with it. Enjoying natural things in the city can be challenging. Carder is like that, she thinks—a natural thing in an unnatural place. Still, his core is there even if largely unrecognized, regardless of life trapping and sedating it.

They walk on.

"We should go to the beach soon!" she says, "I've always loved getting slightly cooked." What would Carder look like in a swimsuit? The image is clumsy.

Carder grunts, lost in the trajectory of stoned thought. Realizing this, Haika wanders over the cobble stones of her own mind wherever auto-pilot takes her. She knows exactly what Carder's home will be like: a clammy cave with curtained windows and the stench of locker-room socks. He's probably never gotten over dorm room living.

Haika gloats to herself while they cross Atlantic Avenue: having chiseled away at Carder, mining opinions and information, building a complicated mosaic, she feels she sees a richer, more precise picture of him. Recently, after they'd walked the Brooklyn Promenade while discussing news of a naked body found at the base of the bridge, Carder told her that he'd once extracted corneas from a dead man who'd lived in the neighborhood. Haika smiled at that discovery. Finally, she knew what he did! She never believed his claims of being a toy designer. He never said one thing to make her believe it. He seems to prefer animals to children, and he doesn't have a pulse on the toy market like Mike's friend, Gavin, does.

Carder's shuffles are a perfect match for Zombie's micro-steps. The contempt Haika once would've felt for someone so opposite her husband, now prompts affection. Mike is strong, forceful and articulate, but their giddy chance meeting at a holiday party years ago turned into harsh married years. Mike's high-gloss personality no longer blinds Haika, but has given her vision, allowing her to find interest in a person whose cloudy exterior seems scratched, but teems with color beneath. She's willing to apply the slow wax that Carder's shell requires. Mike, on the other hand, lives life on the surface, much like the way they'd once skimmed the Everglades on pontoon, barely touching water, aware only of the sun above and alligators below. Even then, the inclusion of a client during their ride removed both danger and pleasure—only security had been small enough to board. The power of speed had supplanted less obvious things, erasing mudskippers, cockles, fairy wasps, pollen in the air, flying bats, and the ink-blooded horseshoe crabs surrounding them. Mike couldn't find the egret Haika pointed out, but had noticed seagulls trying to steal their food. Of the different roads Haika's life might've taken, she never would've imagined her foot on this one, sharing nights with a man who, after long card games with old women, drunkenly spills himself inside her to prove he's still young. If there are a billion parallel universes— thinks Haika—I'm in the wrong one.

A red light staves traffic off for a century while they cross the street. Traffic morphs with their cannabis high, singing instead of screeching, but Carder's lips still won't curl. Smiles are rare—one of the main reasons Haika wants to see his photo albums. Looking through childhood photos will tell her when things changed. Children instinctively run around with gap-toothed grins. If they don't, something is amiss. She wants to pinpoint when happiness disappeared. Then again, Carder doesn't seem especially tortured or angst-ridden; he hardly ever complains. With Haika, he'd quickly shed the detached film which separates him from the rest of the world. The absence of amusement from his face feels truthful, and truth calms Haika. There's typically so little of it. Looking at him, Carder's gentle soul is knotted up in his thoughtful eyebrows, in the hands he uses to comfort her dog.

"Haika? Haika!" calls a voice approaching from the opposite direction. The sniveling tone can only be one person, which an extended hand confirms.

"Gavin Daguerré! What are you up to today?" Haika asks.

"A little grocery shopping at Granola Lola's. Isn't it nice to have a high-end store in the neighborhood? Try the blueberry soda. Sounds off-putting as shit, but you'll be addicted. And the wine! Anyway, who's your friend?" Gavin looks refined, yet his accent is hard—old school Brooklyn.

After introductions, Carder discretely wipes the handshake onto his pants.

The man before them has hairless legs that meet sockless feet in penny loafers. He isn't merely wearing plaid shorts, they look *placed* on his body below a mint green polo shirt turning his belly into a rolling hill. If his round eyeglasses could speak, they would ask to be called spectacles. Gavin Daguerré is a weird mish-mash of a man, the sort which fate might have thrown toward mob life, but with bad aim, landed him in a soft-bellied life among high society ass-kissers.

"Hello Mr. Quevedo. Let's see, 'Quevedo' roughly translates to... 'obstacle,' correct?"

"It means I have ancestors from Quevedo, a city in Spain."

"No need to impress me with your Spanish. Haika would best us both!" He motions to Haika. "What are you two up to this fine day?"

"Carder and I just smoked up and are trying to get this dog to drop a load." Haika's words are deliberately uncouth. They bite.

Gavin redistributes grocery bags to his other arm and sniffs, distracting from the buoyant arrogance on his face. "Well, don't let me keep you. Haika, give Mike my regards, and perhaps you'd consider returning Doe's calls so she stops mentioning it to me? I think I'm more entitled to ignoring my wife than you are! And don't forget about the party at Café Beryr. You *are* coming?"

"Do I have a choice?"

"Bring Mr. Quevedo here with you." He then turns to Carder to explain, "Café Beryr is a little restaurant I'm opening—a small, inconsequential café of Spanish-French fusion. Thus, the name reflects as much."

"Wait," Haika says, "Isn't the café the girls' project?"

"My wife is my project, so her projects are my projects. Do you think any of it would've happened without me?" His face is smug. "Okay, I must be off. Enjoy your day."

As their intersecting paths draw further away, Haika and Carder laugh. Haika pledges that she doesn't regret her coarse demeanor. If truth is insulting, so be it. She explains that the friendship of Mike and Gavin developed when Gavin mentored him in college. It's taken Gavin years to remember Haika's name despite being Mike's best friend and best man at their wedding. He even paid for their honeymoon.

"He hangs around with these twins, the Vivienne girls—he's married to one, but no one knows which. One looks like an updated version of Dolly Parton, and the other like a drag queen *impersonating* Dolly Parton. As far as I can tell, they alternate between which is the real Dolly. But I suppose you'll soon see for yourself. I'm so happy there's someone else to suffer through the party with. You've already improved that experience by three thousand percent."

"What about Mike?"

"Mike gorges on parties like that."

They soon reach the speeding white noise of the Brooklyn Queens Expressway. Decades before Carder's birth, the city constructed the six-lane highway along his street, but out of consideration, dropped it below ground-level to minimize disturbance. Regardless, it remains difficult to veil. Residents concerned enough with smog, and who had the means to do so, had already left. The Quevedo family did what they do well: they stayed.

"Look at this! Zombie's pissing on fire hydrants instead of at home on my purse!" Haika exclaims. "He's responding so well to training."

"He's not such a bad dog. His problems, I think…" Carder looks away to the cars below, "…are probably due to his owners. Dogs need affection."

Haika shrinks back. "I don't hate him, Carder. I just don't have the time…"

"Then why did you get him? Why get a dog you can't take care of?"

"Our first anniversary. A gift from Mike."

"That's not the dog's fault."

"There's no fault, Carder. And I don't hate Zombie. If it weren't for me he'd be dead. Not everyone wants a dog that craps all over the house."

"You know what? Sometimes not being dead isn't good enough."

Rather than arguing, Haika decides she loves what Carder said. Mike would've been happy if she'd come home having dropped their pet off the Brooklyn Bridge. Not Carder. What world did Carder grow up in? What microcosm, what field?

Still high, Haika's mind runs down memory's winding path until she's a girl back in Puerto Vallarta: she sees a tiny boy who appeared in the barrio of the Come Stay Inn. With shredded clothes and cracked feet, he lived on rooftops, climbing from window to window, begging for food when someone appeared, doing who-knows-what when no one did. Depending on the season, living on the street was likely less agonizing than an orphanage. Haika gave the boy many of her desserts in exchange for tiny drawings of the things he didn't have: pictures depicting his father and mother as a warrior and saint searching for him. The visits occurred with regularity until Haika walked to school one morning along a bayside street. She and Iris were arguing about the frosted jean-shorts that Iris hogged, practically wearing the thinning denim until it was gone. The girls walked in unison, quarrelling with their arms around one another so that affection could easily turn to pinches and slaps. They came upon a circle of people standing around the barrio boy who lay sprawled in the street. His eyes were closed, his arms spread over his head to a halo of blood. He's sleeping—Haika had told herself. Concerned whispers grew silent, and people left upon realizing nothing could be done. Haika stayed, telling herself that if he woke up, she'd take him home, give him her bed. He could have her meals. That never happened. Before the boy's body was taken away, Haika stole a drawing from his pocket, a drawing of a family. She'd kept it for years, before Iris ruined it with scribbled notes.

Haika returned to reality with Zombie winding his leash around her legs. They'd walked many blocks, away from the movie set feel of Brooklyn Heights and into the neighborhood of the unadorned Columbia Street waterfront. She unwraps herself from the leash, walks a few steps, and then stops. Then Zombie stops. Then Carder. Haika bends down to the dog.

"Do you ever carry Zombie?" she asks.

"There are limits. He's way too big for that. I only carried him on the first day we met because..." he leaves the statement unfinished.

Haika removes Zombie's leash and tries to look as though lifting him isn't difficult, like it happens often. The dog licks her chin, its eyes agog. Funny that Haika stopped, because when she tries walking with the dog in her arms, Carder doesn't follow. He raises his eyebrows, waiting for Haika to turn around. Zombie's tail whips wildly. It motions to a dirty brick, two-story carriage house. The building is as plain as the rest of the neighborhood—no plants, no flowers. Years are stacked upon its thin mortar.

"So this is it, huh?" asks Haika.

"Thirty-three years housed and stored."

A wrought iron fence meanders around the building; depressed in its middle as if someone heavy left a permanent imprint. The paint on the front door has become a snakeskin shedding dusty browns and graying purples. The carriage house is a reminder of the days when owning a building in the city didn't automatically imply wealth.

Carder's keys chime his befuddlement. Haika hadn't previously noticed his resistance to bringing her over, though upon reflection it was always there. Early on, he'd dismissed suggestions to pay him to dog-sit at his place.

"It's not a doggie daycare," he'd said.

When she'd wanted to drop off keys, Carder rushed right over to intercept them at her house. Therefore, standing outside his home produces a tingle of glee—the same feeling she gets unveiling a painting or curating a show. She stands at the entrance of a mystery about to be solved.

The lock clicks and Carder turns the knob, slamming the door open in a bang, revealing a hallway and stairs leading to a second floor. They enter antique air: a symphony of moth balls, privacy, old books and oil paint. Under normal circumstances, Haika would've noticed she'd traveled back twenty or thirty years, viewing a bite of lower-middle-class New York so perfectly preserved it might've been in formaldehyde. Orange orb lamps hang like rusted moons over a plastic-covered sofa and loveseat. She would've marveled at the flimsy wood paneling accenting one wall since the days of disco mirror balls and white polyester. She would've seen kept things kept the same, kept forever.

Haika doesn't notice those things. Her view is stolen by something more interesting. Paintings. Everywhere. Painted plates hang on the walls, hiding the wood-paneling along the staircase and pulling her view into the living room they dominate. Haika immediately understands: it's a blueprint of Carder's life in a galaxy of shapes and sizes, settling around every corner, hanging on every wall from chair rail to the eleven-foot ceiling.

"Oh my God, Carder…" She sets down Zombie, who dives into a history of scents.

"I know. I don't clean much and it's stale. I'll open windows."

Still only a few feet inside the home, Haika looks up and around. She's been transported. Transfixed on this wonderland. "No. Your paintings. They're…"

Carder sees Haika judging his sprawling weirdness. "They're ridiculous," he says.

"…amazing. They're amazing."

The paintings can't be avoided, so despite his reluctance Carder gets explanation out of the way. "You're at the beginning. See that one behind you, centered right above the door, below that small window? That's the firstborn."

The plate is 'Bis—showing Carder's first encounter with a named being in another world. All previous instances were nameless and blurry. The picture shows a frayed coat of fur silhouetted on hill slope.

"When was it done?"

"I was six. Mom hung it there to hide a crack I'd gouged. I thought my iron airplane would fly if I could just get it to the window. Crazed, she found an entire stack of plates that I'd painted down in the cellar. I spent a lot of time there. Anyway, she hung it, promising me Dad wouldn't have a clue. And she was right."

"That's the starting point? Hmm. So, all the earlier ones were painted on plates? Where did your mother get them? Some of these are giant!"

"It was my grandfather Quist's dream—the Swiss one on mom's side—to open a Swedish restaurant in America. Over the decades, he collected enough plates to feed an army, but not enough New Yorkers have a taste for pickled herring and blood pancakes. There were so many plates and platters—I still have more in the cellar. Mom had a hard time letting things go."

Haika's visit is a horror: Carder is frozen, shriveled, balls-out naked and being inspected by this beautiful woman. She breezes nonchalantly through his stagnant world, disturbing the atmosphere.

Haika scrutinizes the plates as if she's found artifacts on an archeological dig in Transylvania. At first she makes offhand comments, "really imaginative, Carder," and "the storm of lines on this one..." but she soon falls to murmuring while Carder pours himself some Jack to burn away his embarrassment. She walks slowly, winding around the room, starting at the earliest work, touching some, craning her neck to see those near the ceiling. Since his mother's death, few have seen Carder's paintings: Darren, a plumber who'd come to make repairs, and Carder's sister Lucy who had visited to attend their mother's funeral. She described the paintings to the neighbor, Mrs. Gunderson, as *very Carder.*

Haika spins around. "Would you mind if I have some time with these?"

Leaving her to assume his silence means permission, Carder takes Zombie into the kitchen for a drink of water. He watches from the doorway, as Haika pours her gaze over the plates, spilling it slowly from one to the other. Up. Down. Over. She seems to have forgotten about him while her trained eye picks apart his spawn with artistic vivisection. The stiff lessons of Art History radiate in her posture, the knowing swagger of Advanced Art Criticism I & II. The Principles of Design fill the bowls formed where her neck and shoulders meet. Carder winces and fetches Zombie's favorite chew toy, a squeaky rubber steak the dog plays like a crack addict on a two-note accordion.

Haika circles the living room in a measured, whirlpool walk. "Is this one dying?" she murmurs to herself.

Sweat crawls through Carder's hair while he tries focusing on the chimes of an ice cream truck outside. Smooth-voiced Bossa Nova lyrics replay in his mind: *imagine your dream as an ice cream.* Carder's hands have nothing to do, but they eventually find more whiskey and the telephone, the latter of which he loathes using, but he's desperate for a lifeline.

He dials Darren.

Nothing.

Lucy is next. Chances are good that she's home—someone has to be watching the children. Carder hates talking to his sister, but needs time, and it's amazing how long it can take for two people to justify a phone call.

A lazy teenage voice answers.

Carder almost calls her Rabbit but catches himself. "Mandy?"

"Hey. Is this..." Mandy places his voice, "...Uncle Carder! S'up?"

"Where's your mom?"

"You wanna talk to her? She's..."

"No! I, uh, wanted to talk to you. About your trip here."

"What about it? It's not like you're going to have to watch me or anything. I'm chill. And who's the chick that sent the Hallmark? Tell her not to write again, okay? If Mom or Dad had seen that, I'd have gotten in a lot of trouble. Lucky I caught it before they did."

"Why's that?"

"Never mind. Can you just tell her not to write? I didn't even know you had a girlfriend."

"I don't. Haika's a friend who's excited to meet you. She knows all the cool places to take you while you're here. Wait until you see her gallery."

"Her gallery?" she asks as though it's a nascent concept. "An art gallery? Do they serve wine? Mom and Dad won't be down with that at all. *But* I can deal without their knowing."

"I don't know if there's wine. Probably during parties. How are your mom and dad?"

"Okay. The usual—fighting, Bible reading, blah, blah, blah. Dad's not home much with peach season starting. Anyway, when are you coming to pick me up? I'm ready for New York. My bags are packed. Actually, I don't even need bags. It's not like I'm naked or there's a clothes shortage."

"Then talk to your parents and..."

"Uh-huh, I see. I'll talk to my parents about it." Her silence is clearly disappointment. "Listen, Unc, I gotta go. Should I tell Mom you called? She's out going door-to-door."

"Naah. I really only wanted to talk to you. Your mom goes preaching during the week too?"

Carder hears a squeak of laughter from Haika in the background. She says something difficult to make out. He doesn't want to know.

"What reality are you living in?" Mandy asks as though he's daft. "Mom preaches in her sleep. Don't you read the Watchtower rags she sends?"

"Sorry, no." He'd called the Watchtower headquarters earlier that year and asked they stop sending them. Why waste paper?

"Okay, but whatever you do, don't say that you don't read them! Promise?"

"Why would I promise that?"

"Because," she says in a tone close to whining, "she won't let me visit you if she knows that. Can you just not say it? "

He doesn't like this. *Teenagers.* "Yeah, probably."

"Thanks. Okay, Uncle Carder, I better go. Bye."

"Goodbye..." he starts saying, but she's already hung up, "...Rabbit."

Carder first held Rabbit when her fingers were the size of macaroni noodles. She'd winked up at him in Morse code, wanting to say something, but being a newborn stuck in a miniature body, unable to talk, she couldn't give him insight. Back then, conversations with Mandy transcended words. He spent the few hours he could holding her, watching her look out at the world as she lay on his chest, rising and falling with his breaths. Like a rabbit, she sensed the world with her nose. Thus, Carder applied the label.

In her early years, Rabbit presented him with the possibility of coolness. She worshipped him—or a mythology of him since he lived 300 miles away. Through the years, her drawings of butterflies and bats, favorite trees and Bible characters transformed into letters about her newborn brother, Mordecai, and stories of her dead cat,

String Cheese.

Mom told me Jehovah won't resurrect String Cheese 'cause animals don't have souls like people. I told her that I hate God if he doesn't love String Cheese like I do. String Cheese = the best! Mom grounded me for questioning God's justice—but that means now I can write you!

Like noon or midnight, when Rabbit's clock struck twelve years, her bond with Carder instantly disintegrated, twisting the little girl he loved into something new and impossible to keep up with: Mandy Sutcliffe. She even had a last name! Carder wasn't fast enough to adjust to Mandy's constant changes. With every passing year, now seventeen of them, she grew more alien, pointing out the ways her uncle was out of style—solely from photographic evidence—and quoting Bible verses on minor matters. Recently, even that communication waned. He was left to being out of style without even being told why.

While Carder stands ruminating over Mandy, the phone clicks to a screaming off-the-hook pulse.

"You little bugger!" Haika shouts from upstairs. Carder's phone call to Mandy had successfully distracted from Haika's ascent to the second floor. He hadn't even heard the stairs creak. A wave of whiskey jumps from his glass as he rushes to prevent her from wandering too deep.

Haika continues, "Who was on the telephone?"

"Mandy."

"Mandy? You could've at least let me talk to her. Did she get my card?"

"She got it." Carder bumps Haika's elbow to usher her back downstairs. She shrugs it off, still threading her eyes from piece to piece.

"Carder." She waits for him to look at her. "I didn't know."

"It's just a hobby."

"This *isn't* a hobby."

She's right. Normal adults aren't like this. Men don't spend weekends painting in lieu of getting laid. Men make money, returning home from the office to accompany alluring wives to parties. They pop corks from champagne bottles while discussing baseball and concerts. They slide their hands into panties and under door handles of Land Rovers or Mercedes. They slide *themselves* into investments and hot tubs. But this! This is no hobby. This is an illness.

The rift between Carder's and Haika's perspective is a wide one. Haika interprets the breathtaking surroundings as a sort of small-town museum showcasing the junkyard of Carder's past and present. The orgy of imagery is so prolific that Haika can see his future—many different futures—in an array of outcomes. Carder's art is his life unfolding. The blueprint. If Haika still had the naïve thirst with which she'd launched into her own career, she might believe she's been preparing for this moment for years. The months spent coming to know Carder, as rewarding as they were, have somehow earned her the privilege of diving into a shadowed, bestial world with its own ecosystem.

Familiar with the various movements and genres of art, Haika knows Art Brut, Naïve, so-called Low-brow and Outsider Art. Carder's work shares many of their leanings. Often, untrained artists' work retains a callow amateurish quality, refined in imagination but remaining aesthetically primitive throughout the artist's life. That isn't the case here. True, Carder's early depictions are crude, missing the great lessons formal education would have thrust upon them, but they exude life that commerciality often strips out. Carder's paintings aren't appealing in obvious ways but they mesmerize. Its colors are reluctance and seclusion. And the paintings flourish with skill. He'd clearly explored, challenged, and expanded his perception on every level as the visual narrative continues around the room. What a puzzling travesty that no one has recognized his talent! How many other artists, singers, inventors and engineers have faded into oblivion with untapped genius? How many diplomats are shoe salesmen? How many maids are sleeping scientists?

The paintings play with Haika, futzing with her understanding and wiggling out from under expectation so that she has to constantly reorganize. A scintillating tug of war pulls her between their lace of beauty and their vicious loneliness. Haika is careful. She suspects any emotion other than *pleasant* might make Carder recoil. But, if only she can, she wants to spend time among the fangs and claws, to stretch her arms within this drunken maze. She doesn't understand the paintings, but wants to allow them to explain.

"Come on. Let's go," Carder says. "Let's get some ice cream! There's a Mister Softee coasting somewhere around the neighborhood. Hear the ice cream song? I bet it's two blocks away."

"I live with Mister Softee and that's enough. I want to stay, Carder."

"No." His panic dashes out of reach whenever he tries extinguishing it.

"I love the progression your work makes. They start out so wide-eyed and... and innocent, but steadily become darker. This one, so ominous, and yet it maintains fragility..."

"Yep. Right. It's encased in it like sausage."

Carder isn't sure about the new labels pinned on his work, but the art now hangs uncomfortably askew. The ominous, fragile one she points to is *Tymbolt*, painted during Carder's freshman year. He had grown weary of propping up his dad's failed toy designs with his imagination only to see the paintings transformed into saccharine dolls for three-year-olds. After years of his father coaxing Carder's interior world from him, then gutting, deboning and regurgitating it into the appealing line of Pick-Me-Pups, Carder rebelled. By that time, Gordan Quevedo was close to leaving Carder and his mother. It had made Carder sick knowing *that* money turned into a new wardrobe for Agnes Pye instead of bunion surgery or a vacation for his mother—even if she never left the house. Tymbolt was far from the tribe of previous dogs: hunting in a wild, crouching pose, poised to pounce and kill, but the beast remains suspended in paint strokes and canvas, as safe as the doily under Sylvia's Bible.

Haika pivots to face a closed door to the left of the painting. A woman's red leather bag dangles from the door knob. Carder hopes she'll overlook it among the paintings. There was blood on his hands when he'd placed it there years ago. Thankfully, she seems to, even while gently touching the doorknob, as though testing its temperature.

"May I?"

"No."

"Surely it's only fair, seeing as you rummaged through my private photo albums."

"You know what? Zombie just took a *monster* dump downstairs and I'm not cleaning up his crap while his owner stands by. Paper towels are in the kitchen."

"Don't be an asshole." She knows he's lying and moves forward with her hand resting on the knob, turning it. A breeze whooshes forth from between door and doorframe. "It's only fair," she whispers, then laughs.

Haika's chuckle rattles Carder. Why is she laughing her way through his idiotic imagination? Is this funny? They're not in an art gallery, and he isn't trying to sell anything. His father's words, spoken in Haika's exact spot almost twenty years prior, repeat in Carder's ear as they stand before the entrance: "Ah, Planet Carder—must be hard without gravity, son."

Carder has to make a choice: stop Haika now or risk her diving deeper into his neuroses.

He clasps her elbow—not gently, but definitely. They struggle.

"*Stop!*" Again, she laughs as though he's teasing. "*Stop it!*"

Carder doesn't mean to tackle her. Especially not *into* the room he's been trying to keep her from. If the door had remained closed they would've fallen against it, but in a mess of elbows and knees, they stagger, flopping onto the floor in a room as dark as Carder's mood. Neither of them make efforts to get up. They just lie, looking up, letting dust fill their lungs, then coughing, then clearing their throats, reorienting to their surroundings.

Beasts are everywhere, but no longer only on the walls. Some have left two-dimensional existence, coming into the world via sculptured clay, wire, wood and fur. They're deformed creatures—dismembered, bleeding, snarling. Dead, dying beasts. Some yowl alone. Others fight together. A mother carries a bleeding pup in her mouth, too late to save it from danger. Some are vampiric, leeching blood from other beings, though it's hard to tell who the victims are. In the corner, stands a sculpture in progress - a tall, wolfish monstrosity on hind legs, with albino white fur and eight red, opalescent eyes.

"Carder..."

Haika's voice reorients him. He sits up with his head buried in his hands, his eyes shut to block everything out. He doesn't need to see his own work. He knows what's there.

"Carder, I'm sorry..."

Raging electricity crackles through him, but he tries calming his trembling voice. It doesn't work. "Get out."

The heat of Haika's hand hovers off his shoulder. "I'm sorry,

Carder. That was wrong of me. I didn't know."

His jaw clenches, his hands ball into fists. "Get the fuck out, would you!? Leave! Go-Now-Get-Out!"

Carder stays put, digging his fingernails into the palms of his hands while Haika collects herself and quietly leaves.

Eventually, she closes the door of the desecrated room, but it creaks back open. Time, the ever-present voyeur, stands still.

In a chaotic heap, Carder is immobile for what feels like hours. He doesn't have the energy to move. With the aim of conserving himself, he sits white-knuckled at the crossroads of the world he wanted and the one he got.

Much, much later, when the fire inside Carder simply smolders, small, familiar steps pad across the floor and a few small licks paint his hand.

8

A REAPING: CLOVE
Carder at 10 years old

He raises his leg from the bubbling river's flow, but Creep's foot is gone. The left pant leg ends abruptly mid-calf, having disappeared along with the foot. Trying not to panic, Creep stretches the remainder of his leg, unintentionally pointing it to the opposite riverbank. There, sits an iridescent red being directly across from him.

The oozing mutant has six crablike legs and sideways movements, but definite canine qualities rest within her alien appearance. If he were closer, Creep would see that her shimmering ruby coloring results from a lack of skin. She wears moist, striated muscle like blood-soaked bandaging. Long, thin horns protrude from her head, reflecting sun in their golden spirals. During growth, the horns had wobbled, warped into corkscrews of varying degrees. Except for a gaze of awareness, the red creature makes no adjustments to Creep's presence.

The confounded boy is careful not to lower his leg into the stream again. He doesn't want his body separating from him any further.

"What did you expect?" The beast calls from across the water. Faraway, her controlled tone is scant but soothing. "The river Vanishment was aptly named. You might've considered that before dipping in." She moves forward a couple of feet. "Regardless, don't worry. You'll be fine if you keep your wits. And don't look at what isn't there. It's wasted sight."

Creep looks again at what isn't there. Will he ever be able to walk again? Where is his missing foot?

"Boy!" she yells, "Did you hear me? Resist giving it your attention."

When Creep looks up, the beast is no longer there. The rapids of Vanishment might easily have devoured her. Kneeling, he searches the waters until his eyes sting, but sees nothing. He stands on one leg to get a better view.

"You're the one they call Creep?"

The boy breathes upon hearing her voice behind him, relieved she hasn't evaporated. Before he can turn to face her, she reaches her cold muzzle to his existing foot, inspecting it with a frothy, bubbling mouth. She's not as miniscule as she appeared from far off, and though strange her features aren't frightening. She maneuvers herself to stand under the stump of Creep's leg, sliding the pulled flesh of her backside flush against it, massaging her body with it, or it with her body, or both. This produces a milky sky-blue substance from nipple-like nodules trailing down her flanks. It's sticky, producing cool-burning tingles.

"Has your tongue also disappeared?" she asks.

He shakes his head.

"Then... you're the Creep? Speak up, will you?"

"I am."

She patters out from under him into the flowing river until her immersed legs dissolve in the streaming waters. "I'm Clove. Half-Clove now. Come, I've a task for you."

The growing disappearance of her body is disturbing, discouraging Creep from heeding her instructions. He doesn't budge.

Clove turns to him. "Don't you want to see your foot again? Plunge in. It's the only way out." With that, she pitches herself below the surface, leaving him behind.

Creep takes a moment to scan the landscape. Except for the river, it seems devoid of anything other than moss-drowned rocks for miles.

He dives in.

It seems they're submerged for days, swimming to the river's deepest parts. The fuzz of a red shadow swims with him, guiding him below the surface: Clove. Syrupy blue threads billow behind as rippling muscles propel her. Creep's lungs burn for fresh oxygen, but as the two swimmers are about to touch the deepest point of the riverbed something happens: the floor is no longer the floor, the bottom isn't bottom—it's another face of another river of another land—and they shift, reoriented, peering up like fish into a green-sulfur sky. A creaking, shifting, crack suddenly breaks. It's deafening even underwater. Boy and beast burst forth from the river.

Seconds or weeks drip from Creep's body, he can't tell which.

Sprawled on the dark shore of a new land, Creep is gasping and numb. He can barely feel the thrill of his foot's reappearance. Once again there are two smooth, pink feet, but he only has the energy to wiggle the toes on the foot he hadn't lost. Surely, that's due to the icy waters, and once warmed, he'll command both feet.

"The disappearance is only permanent if you don't cross. Many never do." Clove then scrambles sideways with feral excitement. "We're here!" Unbridled, she abandons the boy, winding circles toward a large willow tree surrounded by a dark swath of King's Robe flowers with long violet petals draped to the ground.

Spurred to action, Creep walks awkwardly, eventually catching up. Standing next to one another, he and Clove peer into a pit twenty feet wide, sucking light into its bleak void.

"Follow!" she commands, leaping into the abyss.

Clumps of soil fall over the edge as Creep approaches. It isn't an abyss but a hole. Nevertheless, if he jumps in, he won't be able to climb out. Far below, the faint shape of the little red mutant is pacing at the pit's bottom. Something squirms next to Clove: four trembling objects—smaller creatures—faint, pale and fleshy. They're identical, each with their newborn eyes closed. Like their mother, they wear the same striped, skinless musculature more delicately.

"They're ready, but I can't get them out alone."

Unable to resolve the best method of retrieving Clove's newborn offspring, Creep breaks off a weeping willow branch to retrieve them. He spends time mastering movement, steadying his reach, but at last, one little Clove-ling bites into the branch, securing itself, and he pulls it up from the pit.

The first…

Then another…

After a time, three pink yowling blobs wriggle helpless on Creep's chest. Exhausted and sore, he plucks their hooks from his shirt. For safety, he places the cubs among a circle of King's Robe flowers. They blindly gorge themselves on deep purple bleeding from the flower petals into the soil, leaving the blossoms like discarded ghosts haunting indigo grounds.

Creep returns to the remaining Clove-ling whimpering in the nest.

With its mother's assistance, the fourth of Clove's brood clamps onto the soft willow branch. Lacking the ground to stabilize her, she writhes frantically while being raised. When she's close enough, Creep transfers the cub into his palm. Her weight, little more than a shadow, won't settle in his hand as the others had. She's agitated, wriggling, shivering, unable to comprehend what's happening. She shakes and sways in fearful fits. The boy tries adjusting the cradle of his hand forward in support, but she moves back in a scattered, irrational manner. Each of them moves in opposite directions, jostling her from side to side.

Like a heartbeat, she's lost.

The quick struggle drops her. She descends into the dark.

While falling back into the mouth of the hole, her body already seems lifeless. If it's not, gravity soon snuffs it out.

Creep looks for Clove, but there's only a large spot of bubbling blue liquid in the soil below.

He calls.

He looks.

Nothing.

No one.

9

RESUSCITATION

Carder wondered at his own craziness for decades, having discovered that his interior galaxies are more immeasurable and fantastic than anything exterior, or at least he has more access to their vastness. As a child, all was easily dismissed as pretend play: imaginary friends, monsters, doppelgangers, fairytales. As far as he can tell, the only world people knew of was represented by the globe high atop a bookshelf in his father's den. Though inspired by space travel, his little fingers couldn't locate Cape Canaveral on the globe, so Carder ignited rockets of exploration inward.

Weeks pass before he sees Haika again. She hasn't asked for her dog. Zombie does better in his care anyway. Of course, in time she would notice that Carder's an odd cookie - made with thumbtacks and spiced with jalapeños—but he wasn't prepared for Haika's tough taste buds. Couldn't she have allowed their friendship to relax for a longer time, let it sip mojitos and gaze skyward, before throwing its suitcase back on the luggage carousel of reality? Haika had violated him more than Dr. Donaldson does during physical exams, more than inserting a couple fingers. Both she and Dr. Donaldson are now familiar with parts unintended for exposure. Because of this, time with Haika has mutated into impossibility.

Zombie doesn't feel the same angst. Training regresses when Carder designs new walking routes circumventing the possibility of running into Haika. Nonetheless, as soon as Zombie sets one paw outdoors, he tugs at his metal chain, pulling Carder toward old stomping grounds as if his old home were a magnet. Carder resists the dog's tow for the first week. Zombie stops and starts in spasms, leaning so far against the leash, he might asphyxiate. If the animal wants something that badly, then it's beyond Carder to withhold it. And so their radius becomes uncontrollable, their path organic and unplanned. There's no use counting footsteps any longer.

Haika never shows up. And Carder doesn't want to see her. He doesn't *want* to see her when he and Zombie round the corner from Pacific to Henry Street, nor when they circle her block, or when he sits on the Promenade with her popeyed pooch on what had been their usual bench.

Another week passes. Zombie has a new black studded-leather collar but holds fast to old habits, herding Carder through the streets near the Fiore-Haus home. Carder's resistance has all but disappeared. At times, Zombie carries the leash in his own mouth while the human follows.

Another week. Carder ignores all calls and texts unrelated to work. He eats microwavable dinners while Zombie chomps through store-bought organic meatloaf. They're miserable losers satisfied with one another's company. By the end of the third week, Carder accepts Zombie as the spoils of an interesting time with a beautiful woman.

When not painting, Carder sits on the living room's hardwood floor for hours at a time. Sleep left with Haika. He's hardly had any for six days, finding naps whenever and wherever they lay. There are questions without answers: Why am I a graveyard? Why are my interior coffins shut so tight their ghosts can't emerge? In the mirror he sees a bearded version of exhaustion, of hollow, twisted stories which would kill his life if shared. He can't tell anyone about them, about where he's gone, what he's done. As a child, he'd collected enough worried looks from his parents and a teacher that instinct threaded a needle, sewing his mouth shut. He'd been taught firsthand what happens to anyone out of the ordinary: basement walls and the universe contained therein, meal plans and medication, bruises and knots, homework assignments sent home and immobilized healing. Even Darren isn't privy to Carder's deepest secrets—not even when Carder is drunk or high or depressed or raging.

Fliers and phone directories have piled up outside. Today, Zombie is bored, chewing on the legs of the desk.

Who am I when no one is around—Carder asks—what am I?

Where? There's no answer. There are multiple answers. A shut-in. A deathworker. A sight-giver.

Only I could make Death uncool.

He's awake in the dim morning, ignoring hunger pangs as well as knocks on the door, ignoring a shadow cupping its hands to look through his windows. Today is a free-for-all for thieves. Come and get it! Take whatever you want.

The raps on the window are too firm for the thin glass. In a moment it will crack. So what? Let it shatter. He's experienced far worse. He's seen things that don't exist, watched skin and muscle dry on strange skulls, skulls which wouldn't fit in any head he'd previously seen. He's heard songs sung in a wordless language, observed the mating dance of two dying creatures ripping themselves in half to create a third.

The raps at the window are now interspersed with yelling, but Carder is lost in thought.

What's real and what has his mind contrived? He'd never knowingly chosen to create alien worlds. Years ago, he'd realized that questioning his sanity was pointless. Yet, here he is again.

Rolling over, Carder looks at a new painting he's been lost in. From afar it appears to be a solid black canvas, but a closer eye would see layers of shadowed darkness materializing into beastly form. So much time has passed in its jaws.

Something is shimmied under the window and the frame slides up. Carder's house is being broken into. A foot appears, a leg, a torso.

"You're done with that painting. Right now. It's finished, goddammit, you hear me?"

It's Darren and he drags Carder to a mirror to see how filthy heartache becomes when wallowed in.

"Now, I'm gonna wait here while you get off your raggedy ass, shave this gnome-beard, and..." Darren starts pulling at Carder's clothes, as if he's going to strip him, but stops. "Is the cell phone that you haven't been answering *out* of your pocket?"

Carder nods.

"And your wallet?"

Another nod.

"You haven't eaten anything, have you, bro?"

Shirtless, Carder shakes his head and Darren drags him to the bathroom, turns the shower on and boots Carder, half-dressed, into the cold water. If he hadn't, Carder would've eventually ended up a skeleton with a paintbrush clenched in its fist. But Carder meets Darren's demands—and doesn't add another stroke of paint. He's grateful to be shaken out of the carbon world and its layers of black and black and black.

"I'm never picking up after this dog no matter what," Darren stipulates before walking with the grizzly man and his dog. Once that's agreed, he accepts the leash in hand. The animal struggles much less against him.

According to Darren, they're headed to the Farmers Market at Grand Army Plaza at the request of Darren's Aunt Mildred, who swears by their corn. *Corn that sweet don't need no butter*—which means she's also saving three dollars not buying butter. By the time Darren finishes imitating his aunt's shrill voice, things relax enough to place Zombie's leash in the envelope of the dog's own mouth. As his own warden, Zombie walks next to them as though a higher canine mind now guides wilder inclinations.

Walking and talking lubricates Carder's nerves. Though by force, he's back in the world above the universe below. Zombie weaves in and out of their legs until they arrive at a giant memorial arch initially created as the gateway to Prospect Park. It now stands on a small concrete island caught in a swarming circle of constant traffic. Carder is adamant they enter through the arch as it was originally intended.

At the park, thousands of residents share their relationship with nature—a sort of amusement park of plants for city-dwellers. The Farmers Market, which sticks to the park's true entrance like a barnacle on the hull of an aircraft carrier, bustles with young families and beaming locals who either sell or search for fruits, vegetables, flowers and homemade preserves.

Before scouting for the needs-no-butter corn, Carder and Darren are distracted by a lavender van, its side emblazoned with hand-painted lettering: *BEST SMOOTHIES ON MOTHER EARTH*. Carder insists on buying a drink for an unwilling Darren. The Lean Green Machine is a mucky concoction of apples, strawberries, cilantro, orange juice and celery. Darren soon wears a scowling smoothie mustache while yucks shiver through his body.

"Every time I take a sip, my tongue says '*Huh?*' and then, '*Why?*' The stuff's undrinkable! Your taste buds shouldn't have to figure things out. Put cilantro in my enchiladas and celery in my salad, but don't blend them and charge me for the results."

"You didn't pay. And at least you were open to it."

"That's right, Carder, at least I was open to it. I'm open... unlike someone else we know. And you know what? You're a total paranoid, because I've seen your drawings and painting for years—and not once have I gotten the heebie jeebies... at least not for the reasons you mention."

"Some people might think my new work sadistic. I want to say they'd be wrong. The subjects deal with death and pain and... heartbreak."

"Big deal, man—we deal with those things every day—we work at hospitals! Seriously, you've got to get over this. You're so stuck in the pit you've dug your life into that you think others are paying attention to the hole. Fact: most people are in their own pits, they aren't going to notice yours. Remember when I was dating C.O.M.T and I was so worried about..." he mutters under his breath, "my birth mark? Well, you were right, she didn't even mention it. Didn't freak out."

"If that's the case, where's Ms. Cum-On-My-Tits nowadays?"

"Dude, that's like four hundred girls back. She probably drives her kids to soccer games in a mini-van with images of us running through her mind." Darren chucks the mostly full Lean Green Machine drink into a garbage can while mimicking the dizzying swoons which probably trip up Ms. C.O.M.T.

A few feet in front of them, stands a small Asian boy fingering the straps on his overalls, close to tears. He sucks his lips against bursting wails. Zombie pads softly over to the boy and drops the leash at his feet.

"Darren, look at this," says Carder.

"Well, hello there, little guy," Darren says.

The boy's lips give way to sobs.

"What if he's been abandoned?"

"Carder, this isn't a movie," Darren says as though such things are only fictional. He turns to the child. "Are you lost?"

The child whimpers 'no' while shaking his head 'yes.' He's facing the conundrum that the strangers he's not supposed to talk to are now all he has, learning that fears can be actualized, parents can disappear and loss often sweeps in suddenly and uninvited. The boy's body fills with terror like popping corn. He covers his mouth with his hands to keep breath from escaping. Or to keep from throwing up.

"Hey, little guy. What's your name?" Darren asks.

The boy hesitates, turning a soft shade of olive green, and burps out, "Anthony."

"Look at me, Anthony. You're going to be okay. Your mom or dad's probably over there looking at the corn. Don't worry, we'll stay with you and find them. Where did you last see them? And when?"

The child points toward a long row of produce stands.

"Hang in there," Carder says, "You'll soon be home with them, eating corn on the cobb."

The child won't stop crying, which alarms a female official from the Local Farmers Organization. It's the same internal alarm that rings when a lone man walks through a toy store, watches a carousel spin or peruses children's books. She wrings her red smock as she hurries toward them. With nervous courage, she rubs a name badge engraved with *BRENDA—FRIEND TO THE ENVIRONMENT! ASK ME HOW TO TURN GREEN!*

While Carder may not come across as a father, he could've adopted. How dare she make assumptions! Yet, he doesn't want to encounter this woman in order to make that point. The closer she gets the more butch she becomes, wearing a wife-beater t-shirt under a smock, her black bra straps show defiantly on her shoulders.

Carder is bracing himself when he realizes that Zombie is gone.

Oh God! Haika will kill him. Though if the dog isn't found, he'll do it *himself.* He spins around searching the grounds for the undead dog—nothing except the bawling child who now has a small group of bystanders surrounding him, all vowing vigilance, protecting him as they would the produce from prying hands and pesticides. Darren seems to notice Carder's rising dread.

"You go look for the dog, Card. I'll take care of the human."

Carder darts from stand to stand, through melons and chili peppers, calling out to Zombie, pushing, scuttling through the crowd, spilling a grey-haired woman's snow peas, not stopping to hear her curses. He gulps down thoughts of losing the only being that relies on him, pushes aside knowledge of speeding cars and images of the furry beast skidding across the street. Carder wouldn't survive the loss. If Zombie isn't in the market, he can only be inside the park or herding traffic. Carder heads toward the park's mouth, entering where hordes of trees and grass fight for dominance, and frisbees, joggers, bicycles and birds intersect from every direction.

He springs forth to run, but hits a large white object that groans. There's no time to worry who it is—it's probably Randy of *Randy's Red, Raw & Delicious*.

As Carder turns to make quick apologies, he meets something unexpected: the familiar figure of Mike Fiore—Haika's Mike. He stands like a monument to himself, calm, flawless, with his chiseled chin and taut skin, and holds the slobbery handle of Zombie's leash on the other side of his grip. At the leash's other end, Zombie sits thumping his tail against a bushel of pearly onions, munching a rawhide bone.

The dog is found.

Carder accidentally hugs Mike for a split second. "Mike, you don't know how happy I am to see you! I thought I'd lost him."

"I wish you had, but he's too smart for that."

Interaction with Mike is always spotty. Early on, he and Carder had quickly settled into the numbness of occasional greetings. Handshakes are offered when their paths cross, but deeper communication would be a never-ending fruitless journey. They've both added their invisible signatures to a silent agreement, signing away any need for conversation. Thus, there they stand: two traffic cones on a road paved by mistake.

Still feeling funny about the situation, Carder launches into a long, lying explanation of why he's kept Zombie at his place—to ensure the dog stops chewing the legs off furniture—and promises that it will give up its beaver-like addiction. Already, the dog avoids certain chairs constructed of specific types of wood, mostly anything Mid-Century Modern. Zombie has taste.

Mike and the dog look through Carder, beyond him, so he stops talking.

"Huh. I figured Haika had finally gotten the courage to put him down. She hasn't mentioned any of that. But she *did* tell me about your art. How protective of it you are. Says she intruded *on something important.* Something private. You gotta hand it to her, the girl knows art. Exactly how did you get into gargoyles?"

Mike's question confuses *and* clarifies. Gargoyles?

Gargoyles.

Carder begins, "Well, I... " but he's interrupted by Mike again who's scanning the crowd.

"Haika says your place is positively crawling with them. From what I've heard, you've got a lot going on in that head. Honestly, I'd like to see these gargoyles."

The blood which had returned to Carder's face upon finding Zombie drains once again at mention of his artwork. The only thing worse than Haika surveying his inner-world would be Mike wandering through with a clipboard, guiding bulldozers to clear land. The suggestion alone could cause months of diarrhea. But Carder knows Mike is only half-present and a quarter interested. The idea evaporates faster than the words, forgotten as Mike sets his sights on a distant object coming closer, closer, closer.

Two warm, familiar hands come from behind and cover Carder's eyes.

10

PECULIAR FEAST

Beneath a pale sky, Café Beryr's doors open into cave-like darkness. Inside, pinpricks of light hang randomly like glitter in zero gravity. Adorned in the dulcet magic of the Vivienne girls' decorative skill, the restaurant could've easily been a cutting edge discotheque from the Neolithic Age. Carder is glad that enough time has passed for him to forgive and accompany Haika to this strange destination.

Café Beryr was created as more of a trifle than a restaurant, a token, a mute acknowledgement that something *must* be done with one's time. Some people take up creating latch hook rugs, others attend monster truck rallies, knit socks or collect lawn ornaments. The fabulously wealthy might spend a few months in Paris taking up smoking at cafés before moving on to Tuscany to quit. Or they might open a restaurant.

Gavin Daguerré resents having a wife named after an animal that carries ticks. Doe. The name lacks a sense of status and civility. The woman he loves should possess a name reflecting sophistication, something along the lines of 'Claudette.' In fact, Doe would've been named Claudette had she been born fifteen minutes earlier, but her twin sister's spot in the womb held more gravity. Or, as Gavin suspects more probable, Claudette fervidly poked and prodded at a dot of light until she fell out onto the hospital table while Doe waited behind.

"Really then, wifey, you were born as an afterthought," Gavin occasionally chided.

"We're androids, fembots, my dear, sweet Love," Doe once

replied. "We came off an assembly line. I'd think someone like you would appreciate that more than most. I wasn't an afterthought. I'm something perfect—multiplied. When I'm gone, you can move on to Vivienne girls 3, 4 and 5, simultaneously if you like."

Unlike her twin sister, Doe's voyage from embryo to grown woman was plotted according to whatever Claudette *didn't* take first. She's happy in the periphery of Claudette's leftovers. In fact, Café Beryr would never have entered Doe's mind had Claudette not yawned over a watercress sandwich one afternoon, saying, "Sis, let's say we open a restaurant? How fun would that be?"

At first, Gavin hadn't been able to tell the twins apart. The only noticeable difference was that one sister thought meals were bad habits to be broken by soy chips. The other didn't. By now, his view of the Vivienne girls is divided by more than rice cakes and orange veggie snacks, but Gavin remains convinced that he married the wrong twin. He's spent several years having imaginary sex with Claudette during actual intercourse with Doe, and when occasion asks he delay his own huffing orgasms so his wife can meander to climax, he does so by returning to the reality of being inside exactly who he *is* inside. Thus, the internal tug-of-war between hard and soft, repulsion and delight.

The Vivienne girls share, not only identical DNA, but a penchant for speaking to one another in Elvish, a fictional language used by fictional elves of a fictional world. Gavin tolerates the whispering elf-speak, though he worries the girls shared a prenatal brain. Perhaps they were Siamese twins who successfully rejected one another before their earthly debut, each taking only half the good stuff.

Except for the tits.

The Vivienne girls' breasts explain everything. They're Gavin's downfall, his prize, his achievement. The ripe fruit hanging from their torsos must be why nature chose to duplicate their genetic material. Theirs are powerful busts, the type placed on bows of pirate ships, chests thrust forever forward, or on ancient chiseled statues of headless women. If they could, infants would battle to the death for a chance to latch on to Vivienne nipples, to taste what nectar came. Gavin hit the jackpot, not only dwelling in the presence of two perfect breasts, but four identical supple human mammaries: two to dive between and two to ogle at close range.

When the Vivienne girls presented their ideas for Café Beryr to Gavin, he asked, "And exactly what kind of cuisine will we be serving?"

The girls smiled, whispering back and forth in an Elvish tongue that trades magic spells and foolishness, while Gavin pulls at the tassels on his penny loafers.

"We want the food to be a fusion," Claudette said. "It's so post-modern."

Doe agreed and added, "We want to reflect a melting pot of sorts. Something now-ish, very zeitgeist, you know, finger-on-the-pulse and all that?"

"But, my dears," Gavin asked, "What in *hell* will we melt in the pot besides rice cakes and celery sticks?"

The Vivienne girls hadn't thought that far ahead.

Time passed—the type known to cause death in lab rats and seeds to become thick trees—but Café Beryr was eventually ready. When the menu and décor were flawless, they planned an opening party celebrating their opulent accomplishment. Gavin was almost proud of their collaboration. They brought in vases sick with twisting twigs and inflamed blossoms burgeoning toward the ceiling. The food prepared for the party could've fed some small countries for a year. That night, large Agarwood doors opened to their nauseatingly wealthy friends (what other kinds are there?), each curious to see, scoff and celebrate whatever lavishly creepy mayhem the Vivienne girls have brought.

With Carder thrown into the mix, what might have been a lonely excursion to the Café among the ennui of affluence becomes a delightful spectacle for Haika. The entire scenario has to be seen to be believed, and she knows Carder possesses the unique sight to recognize the moneyed tedium to which she's grown accustomed. His promise to attend helps both of them move beyond the mishap among the art in his house. When they arrive, Carder begins marveling at the café's strange interior, only to be ambushed by Claudette or Doe—who knows which?

"Well, if it isn't the better half of the Vivs," Haika jokes, squeezing Carder's arm upon seeing one of the Vivienne girls. As a twin herself, Haika knows that the differences between the girls could cram a landfill but refuses acknowledging their individuality on principle. She walks a social tightrope above them and doesn't want their daftness throwing her off balance.

The Vivienne girl sets down a parrot-colored cocktail, flits for a moment to guide a waiter, and then returns. She and Haika join in momentary embrace.

"Dear Vivs," Haika says, "What cuisine is the Café again? I was trying to explain the dining experience to Carder."

Carder extends his hand, admiring a large nest of platinum blonde hair topping a slight but chesty woman. Due to the sheer number of sequins, it's difficult to see any silk on her kimono. A small satellite dish in the form of a flowering orchid perches purple on one ear.

She gasps as though the type of cuisine should be obvious. "We hoped the name of the café would provide a clue. It's a fusion!"

"A fusion of what?" Carder asks.

"We like to think of it as Mediterranean ghetto spliced with Spanish... seasonings... like chorizo... which is fattening but delicious... though I won't touch the stuff and..." Pursed lips tell them that she's quite aware of her failing description.

When Carder's brow furrows, she sums it up. "There's cheese. If you indulge in that. And wine. And you two need drinks! I'll get you a menu to better explain the fare." She steps away to flag down a server.

Haika and Carder partake of the inevitable cocktails with vigor. The drinks all have baffling birdlike labels. Haika has the Robin's Egg and Carder has the Sandpiper—which they chase with waves of cheeses spiraling on a plate.

"She eyed me," Carder says.

"Don't gloat," Haika replies, monotone.

"You think maybe she finds me all right?"

"Carder, putting on ignorance is beyond annoying. You look a hell of a lot more than all right and you know it."

"Then, I'd say she's hot for me."

"Well, there's a fifty percent chance she's married, and a 100% chance she's stupid. They..."

Their conversation is interrupted by the Vivienne girl's menu-less return. Her glistening, interested eyes and purring pussy push Haika into leaving to find her twin. As much as Haika doesn't want to discuss Pilates, she's less drawn to watching a messy mating dance between a Viv and Carder. Besides, Carder is dealing unusually well with the crowd.

Walking only a few steps, Haika momentarily turns around and straightens Carder's rumpled collar, then pulls his chin until his eyes meet hers. "Dollface, don't dive into pools without first surmising their depth. You could break your neck." She then sneaks away into the growing crowd.

This Vivienne girl's awkwardness is alluring. She doesn't just speak, she chatters. Doesn't just move, she flutters. Usually, conversation with a fellow bumbler is more difficult for Carder as there's shaky ground to be staked out and built upon together and without a plan. But as often as Jupiter orbits the sun, Carder meets a person whose social puzzlement gels with his own. The gin further softens his clumsiness, allowing the two to stick together comfortably like chalky marshmallows in a cellophane bag. The pieces of their conversation slide simply and succinctly into one another. Even the pauses relax. The more he drinks the more her charm sparkles through any veil of pleasantries.

"You never told me your name," says Carder.

She closes her eyes halfway, sizing him up. "Call me Vivienne. Haika calls us 'the Vivs.'"

"I only see one of you in front of me. What's *your* name?" He's past caring if he slurs words. The rules are: ask someone's name, they give it. Withholding something that simple keeps everything at square one. There's playfulness in her which could easily be mistaken for vapid, but it's purposeful. She's fishing for someone who sees past first impressions.

She unfolds a napkin sitting on the table next to them, studying it as though writing might appear, then returns it to its spot. Her name remains a mystery.

"Come with me," she orders. He follows her into the kitchen, providing obstacles to the wait staff, dividing the aroma of steaming noodles and fried dumplings, delving through hot-grease-humidity until they reach a sweaty dessert chef standing at a stainless steel counter, chopping pineberries. The chef argues that too much heat will turn the berries to mush.

"It's okay," says the Vivienne girl. "Nobody even knows what pineberries are. Besides this is an emergency. Take the chopping board with you. Please. Now. Please. Right now." She takes two napkins from a nearby pile. With one, she wipes clean the stainless steel, but she keeps the other and shoves herself up to sit on the countertop.

She waits.

"What?!" Carder asks. "Why are you looking at me like that?"

She picks up a discarded paring knife, gesturing with it as she speaks. "Tell me something—Ugh, I hate all this frying grease—tell me something you don't tell everyone else. God, please cut through this evening already. Please. Divide it into something more interesting." She slides the blade's tip across the countertop as if it will cleave it in two. Even among the kitchen sounds, metal sings on metal.

Carder searches his mind's attic for interesting artifacts. No way will he buzzkill their conversation with the Pups. He pulls forth one of his heavier mental boxes, one rarely opened, one he's kept hidden, even to Haika. Only Darren knows its contents. Carder runs both hands through his hair, wishing it were long enough to cover his face. Looking her straight in the eye, he says, "I watched my mother die on the edge of Times Square."

She gasps with flickering fascination. "I'm so sorry!" she says. Apparently, sorrow realigns her posture, leaning her closer, with sparkling eyes. "Tell me what happened!"

Why is Carder telling her this? Is it the cocktailization of his mind? Is it her body wrapped in a kimono like wet butcher paper on a filet mignon, begging to have the heat turned up so it can be removed and she devoured? Perhaps it's the timid slope of her nose and the strands of white-blonde hair curling like wood shavings. If not for the hefty, breasty speed bumps on her upper-torso, the Vivienne Girl might have disappeared. Then again, maybe the fact that Carder doesn't even know her real name makes him feel safe. Whether she's petrified or terrified is irrelevant. She's not a person and doesn't matter. She'll never matter.

Carder continues. "I took mom to see her favorite Broadway show: Les Misérables. She used to polish the furniture at home while singing the soundtrack all day. It was nauseating. But it made her happy. She wouldn't even obey Dad's orders to stop. It was the one time she flipped him the bird. Maybe that's what finally drove him away: *Master of the House.* He'd come back from a frustrating day thinking up toy designs and…"

"Wait, your father designed toys?"

"But that's not the point…"

"Of course, go on." She bunches up the napkin in her hand as if it's a bird she's protecting from kitchen heat.

"Mom didn't go to Manhattan much. I don't recall her setting foot on it once, though she'd been watching the New Year's Eve ball drop since, well, since my own balls dropped. Her tales of dating my father—the shows, the dinners—it was magical. The lights weren't advertisements to her but blooms in an electric garden. She said they were like the flowers of Sweden on fire, though she'd never set foot outside America." Carder lifts the sweet, leaden memories into the open with all his strength. "…so, we were walking down 8th Avenue to get some coffee and crumb pie, but Mom first wanted to walk back to the lights of Broadway. You should've seen her face."

Pots clang, a waiter argues with the chef. The Vivienne girl shifts in her seat, her eyes wet with impatient understanding.

"Mom asked me to hold her purse. But the night was crowded, and I was immediately heckled with compliments on the big red bag, as if it were my thing. I got so exasperated I didn't notice Mom starting to cross 42nd street. I didn't notice… until."

"Until?"

"Until…"

"Until?"

"A taxi." It's all Carder can muster, but his gesture makes the outcome clear.

"Oh my god! I'm so sorry."

The memory is as ugly in full light as Carder remembers.

"Funny thing is, I got to identify the body the moment it became one." He chokes tears into a coughing laugh. Reflecting aloud on the experience feels rough, crass, sacrilegious, beautiful. Carder was the last thing his mother had seen—him and a blinking sign advertising a better telephone plan. His mother was happy with both just as they were, and told her son so with bloody words and broken teeth. *Don't let me go*. But she went. Her son could only watch as her soul faded, her sticky blood seeping into his dress shirt. The most private woman in the world's death was a show, a billboard on display advertising mortality to a crowd only there because they had free tickets. Carder could live in that moment eternally, but the Vivienne Girl's penetrating stare pulls him back.

"Okay!" Carder says, "We better go back out there to the dining room. We've got people to see. Drinks to drink. And they'll wonder what we've been up to."

"Card, I'm sorry about your mother. It wasn't fair."

"Yeah, well…" He won't continue tattering the evening with the dinner story of death. This night is meant for celebration not vulnerable admissions.

"Wait," Carder says. The Vivienne girl perks up, leaning in, forcing his mumblings to become intimate whispers.

"Yes?" She stiffens again, her hair now an egg penetrated by Carder's head.

"Why did you call this restaurant Café Beryr?"

She takes on a confident but confessional countenance, "Promise not to tell? Promise? It's Elvish. We named it 'Beryr' after my sister's husband."

"Beryr means 'Gavin?'"

"No…" She paints secrecy, raising a finger to her lips, "…it means 'nutjob,' more or less."

With that, she hoists herself, her hair and her kimono, now saturated with sugar and fruit juices, down from the table. Removing an ornate pen stuck in her hair as decoration, she writes something on the napkin and presses her lips into Carder's hair, leaving a bit of tacky lip gloss on his ear. Was this woman flipping the somber memory of a dead loved one into kink? She gently pushes the napkin into his hand and leaves the kitchen. Carder uncrumples it. Bloated, bubbled handwriting flirts with him in purple ink, specifying her telephone number and the words: *I'm Claudette. Call me!*

"I see you brought your friend!" It's Gavin Daguerré, standing beside Mike Fiore. 'Heys' and hands are thrown back and forth, then a showboat kiss between Mike and Haika. According to Haika, they'd arrived separately and haven't seen much of each other lately. Heavy week in Bridge.

"Gavin, how 'bout we bring the beauts through this fine establishment?" Mike suggests. "Haika, wait 'til you see the V.I.P. room. He bought a painting by... whassis name? That artist from Mexico."

"Mikey, you're already getting sloshed!?" Haika protests. "You know there are oodles of Mexican artists. It's a big country. I'll be there in a bit to see it. You go on. I'll keep the Vivs company. They may need some help. I was hostess at Gayle's Pancake Shack for three years, so I'll have this place stacked and buttered before you know it."

If Haika hadn't declined following, Carder would've done so himself. Nevertheless, he trails Mike and Gavin deeper into the café, by default becoming part of a trinity ruling the V.I.P. room. Gavin wears the V-est of the I.P. slots like a headdress, standing against the lavish wood lining the walls of a former storage closet. While space is a luxury in New York City, Gavin wants it known that in his life luxury is a necessity—a necessity he can both afford and create. Consequently, what once held very important buckets, brooms and bags of rice in its last incarnation now holds three cramped people, twenty thousand dollars' worth of wood, and a painting from a Mexican artist whose name no one remembers.

Gavin Daguerré's wealth trumps common reality. When a hung-over cashier once mistakenly charged Doe $4,853.35 for a cranberry scone, Gavin was bothered, not by any damage to his bank account or the headache of rectifying the oversight, but by Doe's lack of awareness. His lineage keeps him from worry, and is the reason money is of no meaningful concept or consequence to him. Decades prior, 1922 saw—or since the common television was yet to be invented, *didn't* see—a shortage of television repairmen,. Eventually, much like knights became baseball players, ogres became meter maids and vampires became authors—box makers, radio repairmen and engineers became entwined in the concept of television. Gavin's grandfather was an engineer who helped push the new-fangled moving pictures into every house in America, and wrapped millions of dollars around the trunk of their family tree.

Carder clears his throat and looks around. The room holds the privileged secrecy of a speakeasy. But Carder has never spoken easily. On the other hand, Gavin and Mike banter back and forth in the smooth volley of a conversational tennis match, occasionally allowing Carder to pass through like a ball boy retrieving an errant ball. Gavin leans casually against the wood panels, blowing cigar smoke into the air while reflecting on the days when Mike interned for him at Princeton. Younger by twenty-some years, Mike soon found pizza replaced with pâté, partying among the wealthy. He repaid Gavin by yanking him back to youth. They were soon competing to bag chicks, sometimes bagging the same ones. Everything was a game won with the most money.

Gavin yawns and stretches. "Tonight I feel like a czar. The Godfather! I have two gorgeous women, now a restaurant. There's no telling what I'll chew on next. What a life, eh?"

Carder is too large to hide behind his cocktail's plumage of stirrers and straws. "I can't imagine," he says.

"You can't imagine it? He can't imagine it, Mike! If you can't imagine it, it'll never happen. I imagined. It became."

Carder bristles at the rank smugness. "Gavin, there are infinite things in my imagination that never become reality, but if you stepped inside it for six seconds, you'd run away squealing like a piglet."

The room inflates with silence until Gavin's sharp laughter pops it. "I like this guy, Mike! He's the real deal—and has a bit of pluck after all. They could make stuffed animals of Carder and sell them to every amusement park in the world!"

"At the funhouse!" Mike jokes.

If they only knew.

"You need another drink," Gavin says, grasping at Carder's glass now drained of everything but blurring ice cubes. "Your last name's Quevedo, correct? I remembered that. 'Quevedo.'" He rolls it around on his tongue to decipher its oddly familiar flavor. "Yes, 'Quevedo.' It's easy to remember that one…it means 'obstacle.'"

Haika's experience at Café Beryr is something akin to being fed chocolates while tortured. Initially repelled by the Vivienne girls, she's grown to view them as a weird study on the type of twins she *doesn't* want to be: wearing similar clothes, speaking a secret language, trumpeting their intimacy before everyone as though the only way into their club would require being their triplet. Haika spent her life working against exactly those things. She craves autonomy and relishes her own tastes, vastly different than her sister's, perhaps even developing some tastes *because* they're different. At gatherings, Haika is a distant satellite to the Vivienne girls, observing their strange stupidity from afar, afraid that if she told them of her own twin sister, they'd pull her into their atmosphere. No, her current distance is the right one.

At the bar, she and the twins form three points of an invisible triangle. Haika sits in front of the bar like a customer, while the Vivienne girls each stand behind, clipping the annoyed bartender's wings, relaying each drink order despite the fact that he'd heard it the first time.

"Two Blue-footed Boobies over here," Doe calls out.

"Two Blue-footed Boobies over here!" Claudette mimics to the bartender already making them.

"How do you like the decor, Haika? Isn't it heaven?" asks Doe.

"How do you like the barstools? They cost fuckloads," Claudette adds.

Sitting atop one, Haika thinks they look like tiny vases designed to hold a single bloom. "They're definitely compact. However, if the seat were any smaller, customers would become unwilling subjects of anal probing. Oh, don't get me wrong—in a good way, Vivs, in a good way!"

The Vivienne girls skid laughter across the surfaces of their drinks, losing some of the liquid over the sides of the glasses. Both are tipsy, Doe even more so as her body is tinier and more lean. It's a wonder she can stomach any more alcohol than the glass holds.

Haika continues, "What's your plan with the café from here on out?"

The girls join arms, one leaning her head into the crook of the other's neck, both justifiably resting on the bar as if they own the place. One dangles a maraschino cherry before Haika's lips, but Haika doesn't bite.

"*This* was our plan. Now that it's been fulfilled... we don't know. We've so many interests and I think one restaurant's enough.

Sis?"

"Greece. Ibiza. Maybe Mexico."

"Oh, Haika! Let's go to Mexico and hang out at your resort!"

"It's an inn, and compared with what you're used to it looks like something out of a horror movie."

"But with you it'd be fun. We could see what it's like to be regular people."

"Sis is right! No matter how bad things are, you entertain us. After months of nothing but café, we're bored! And the kitchen in here is too hot. And bad for the skin!"

"Thing is," Haika teases with a hair of meanness—especially since what she's going to say isn't true, "there's no such thing as non-fat food in Mexico. They smother everything with melted cheese, sour cream, every sauce you can imagine. I recommend the chimichanga, it's deep fried and…"

It doesn't matter. Doe has moved on, saying, "But we must think of something. Sis has been talking about producing movies, small independent films. Can you imagine the parties? Either way, there's not a chance in the world we're going to stay in this café, wearing hairnets. Kiss that thought goodbye. After tonight, we don't foresee coming back often."

Upon hearing this, the bartender who's spent the last few hours preparing every existent bird species into cocktails, wipes out an empty glass with a rag, and decides he might continue working a little while longer at Café Beryr.

11

SKYSCRAPERS SET DOWN

The golden capsule of Carder's Trans AM speeds toward Gettysburg, Pennsylvania, home of his sister, Lucy, and her family. To Carder, leaving the city highlights how knotted up in it he's become. Brooklyn is a ball of yarn and he fights his way out from the center until it unravels into highway. For years, he's ventured no further from home than necessary: fulfilling hospital assignments, meeting Darren at the diner, buying groceries or getting his yearly haircut. Carder is comfortable in the heart of the city, not the capillaries, not in the frozen toes of endless legs. Sky should be pinned back by skyscrapers, broken by bridges. Every inch of every foot of every mile of passing road stings.

Haika nods off in the passenger seat, wearing the sun like a mask covering half her face while the stereo plays songs from a mix she's made specifically for the trip. She would've acquiesced to classical music or a New Age soundtrack if it had been needed to lubricate Carder's journey, but he's assured her that he wants what *she* wants— and she doesn't want whale song muffled by crashing cosmic oceans, or the antiquated orchestrations of Beethoven or Braham. *Pretend I'm not going*—Carder had directed—*put on music you'd listen to without me.* His passivity disappointed her. Determined that Carder and rock & roll are long lost siblings, Haika only needs the catalyst to reunite them. She chose the Beatles as the first brick in Carder's musical wall.

"Hang tight, Doll. You'll love the Beatles. Nowadays, babies are born with an innate love for them. It's in their blood. The Beatles are *that* great. We're just catching you up."

Carder knows it means a lot to Haika, and wants to care more than he actually does. He tries showing it by commenting on songs he recalls as part of *other* peoples' childhoods. He occasionally senses Haika's watching eyes circling his experience for epiphany, wandering around his face, spinning in the dip above his lips, hoping for signs of sudden delight, which still wouldn't quench her. The more she prods the more Carder fails, sluggishly lobbing quips and critiques.

When he declares *Lucy in the Sky with Diamonds* simplistic and nonsensical, Haika resists the urge to chop off his head. Instead, she uses a tissue to wipe the sweat from his brow, way too comfortable with him. He hates it, loves it, is made sick by it and wants more.

Carder imagines reality reversed—with the car sitting still as trees speed by, poking at them, reaching to join branches from both sides of the highway. Trees aren't this abundant in the neighborhood where he'd grown up. As a child, Carder was disconcerted upon learning that trees, in their gnarled sculpture, are living, breathing creatures with thick hides of bark and bodies continuing underground like the subway.

"How's Mike?" Carder asks.

"I don't know. I haven't spoken with him since we left. Have you?"

"We talk all the time!" Carder says with wise-ass detachment. "Mike's fine. He's always fine."

The music and conversation help distract Carder from the glum highway and the unfamiliar wilds surrounding them. Haika embarks on a confusing explanation of The Beatles' *Yellow Submarine* and the psychedelic stylings of the Meanies and Pepperlanders while she bangs a rhythm on the dashboard. It's lost on Carder—she may as well be speaking another language.

Conversation roams for several hours. Carder recounts his observations of Claudette—she doesn't seem as bereft of positive qualities as Haika seems to think, but Haika's blind to it. Carder ventures that perhaps Haika's social circle is commentary on Haika herself.

She's aghast at this. "You've got to be kidding me! It's called being married. Hell, it's called life. The Vivs are warts. Gavin is slimy.

I'm not going to transform them into something clean and pretty just because I have to be in their company!"

"You may be right about Gavin, but you're wrong about the Vivienne girls. Definitely wrong about Claudette. They're far more intelligent than you think."

"The Vivs are the type of women who make little girls hate their bodies and decide that being pretty is their sole mission in life."

"You're wrong. They've opened a café and Claudette's looking into film production. If anything, they *are* little girls who were taught they've nothing to offer. But doesn't the way you treat them reinforce that? You don't even use their first names!"

"I see they've worked their magic on you. They're adults. The statute of limitations has run out."

"Why? Everyone is a kid! No one *ever* grows up, no matter the clothes they wear or the money they make. Whether I look at Gavin, Mike or at my own reflection in the mirror, I only see older, uglier children."

"A perpetual Never Never Land? That's sad… and somewhat pathetic."

"Possibly, but sad or pathetic, it's true. So, perhaps a little compassion for the other children on the playground is in order? Compassion is one of your most attractive qualities, Haika. When you *don't* have it the contrast is blinding."

"Not everyone can hole up in a tower away from society. My life isn't exactly how I'd like it to be, okay? "

"I know. Maybe no one's life is." Carder can't make out the problem. Maybe it's a fight cut down the middle by gender: men feel one way, women the other, leaving mistranslation in its wake.

"Here's the thing: I'm not going to pretend! I'm recognizing reality, even if it sucks."

"Sorry. Can we just listen to the music?"

"We'd better." She reaches over and cranks the volume higher as *We Can Work it Out* plays.

"I like this one, it's kind of…" Carder trails off. He doesn't know what it's *kind of.*

Haika swallows her ire as countryside flows by. Carder almost provoked a regrettable statement from her granting him permission to sleep with Claudette. Almost. As if he needs Haika's permission.

She rolls down the window. Puffs of air hit one side of her face. The gusts allow her to sigh without detection. Stewing and unsure of her view, she looks at grassy hills out the window. What was once green in her life has been replaced with grays, blacks and browns. The miles pile, foot upon foot, minute upon minute, hour upon hour. Four hours later, they roll into Gettysburg, the pancreas of America and crotch to the Civil War, with a wax museum to prove it.

For the month preceding the trip, Carder has tried soaking his mind in what Sunday's mean to his sister's family. It was discussed with his niece at length. Apparently, Lucy doesn't monitor Mandy's conversations with him, and she made clear that whichever haphazard ways the other days of the week might land, stalwart Sunday always stands the same.

"The only way they're going to let me go with you, Unc, is if you come to Kingdom Hall for Sunday Meeting while you're here," Mandy informed him over the telephone.

"So essentially, in order to do *you* a favor, I have to do you *another* favor." Carder was trying to tease, but Mandy wouldn't play the game.

"Look, Uncle Carder, if you don't want me there, don't have me."

Carder had sensed a dejection he'd never heard before. Desperation leaked into Mandy's must-be-cool tone, betraying her words. Of course, Carder had no problems with her coming to Brooklyn, she could move in for all he cared, except in order to make it happen he had to leave Brooklyn to pick her. Lucy and Stan wouldn't put her on a bus or train alone to get robbed and raped. After their eye-opening New York City trip a decade prior, where they observed not only the miraculous printing of Bible literature at the Watchtower factory but the hurried, empty lives of New Yorkers, Stan decided they'd only leave Gettysburg for their yearly religious conventions in Philadelphia. Thus, Carder saw that Mandy was like him—stuck—and he wanted to help her set foot on a new road, or any road different from his or his sister's. In order to help, he resolved to become *un*like himself, *un*stuck, for a while at least, so that his niece might become so as well.

Once Carder confirmed he would pick her up, Mandy tried to

mask her excitement, but it lined her breath with an enchantment which teenage angst can't mummify. She started a rambling list of acceptable attire for Sunday worship at the Kingdom Hall of Jehovah's Witnesses.

"Unc, you gotta shave, okay? Beards aren't cool…I don't mean they're uncool, but they're not allowed. They're considered a sign of rebellion."

"Didn't Jesus, wait, didn't every man in the Bible have a Rasputin-length beard?"

"Uncle…"

Apparently, logic didn't matter. "Settle down, I shave every four or five days. I'll plan. And anyway," he said, trying to be funny, "Isn't there just an instructional handbook you can send me, listing all that I can't do and one sentence explaining what I can? Right now, I assume your church can't take part in almost any activity."

The statement contained too much truth to be funny. The color immediately left Mandy's voice. "Unc, this situation has to happen perfectly. If it doesn't, I won't get to go with you, and I'll never get to see anything but the Civil War. Do you want me to die of boredom and missed opportunity?"

He didn't—even more so as he hears a television talk show buzzing in the background of Mandy's call. No, he didn't.

One time, when Carder asked Lucy if her religion had taught that 1975 would bring the end of the world, she explained that God provides more understanding as time continues "like a light that keeps getting lighter and lighter." Carder is suspicious of a god who plays with a dimmer switch—he'd been left alone in the dark too many times. However, this time the light got brighter via the email Mandy promised:

Hey Unc,

S'up? I'm mailing you the books for Sunday meeting at Kingdom Hall, so you'll already have them when you arrive. Please don't mention where you got them. Oh, and I know you asked, but please don't let your friend bring her dog. I don't have a prob with it, but M and D would. Sorry!

Mandy

PS. The list below might help you dress for Sunday.

4 U:

business suit, collared shirt and tie. ←*important!*
black dress shoes—make sure they shine. Dad notices dull shoes (dull shoes = disrespectful). No black sneakers!

4 the chick:

A dress/skirt falling below the knees
A blouse buttoning to the top = safe. Modesty is key!
No crazy jewelry, maybe simple earrings in good taste.

The male attire was easy enough. After all, *generic* was the theme. Carder ransacked his closet for a business suit he'd bought years before for job interviews which never happened. It was there, stiff and navy, as interesting as a night sky without stars. He tried the suit on and looked in the mirror. He'd become the universal symbol for the *men's bathroom.* The necktie didn't matter as much, so he grabbed whatever met his hand: a long band of solid silver-mirror silk printed with a pattern of abstract rabbits or airplanes—were they ears or wings? With fastidious care, he polished the same Dr. Martens shoes he had the last time he'd seen Mandy. They would have to do.

The concept of Haika's costume was more worrisome. He'd never seen her in anything approaching Rabbit's description. He visualized Haika belly-dancing into the Kingdom Hall, walking barefoot on the seats of the chairs, lying across laps of stern, Christian men. Thoughts like these prompted his trips to women's clothing stores: Dress Ranch, Clott's and Lacy Space, where he nervously told the clerks he was purchasing a gift. Everything they suggested was too trendy, shiny or low-cut. Still, Carder had to settle on something.

When presented with three gift-wrapped boxes, Haika was surprised. "You're so thoughtful!" she said, sliding her thumbnail through tape to undress the first box of its wrapping while Carder explained Mandy's emailed instructions and the entire reason behind the gifts.

The swoop of Haika's finger stopped abruptly and she handed the box back unopened. "You've *got* to be kidding. There's no freakin' way anyone's dictating what I wear. No man! No church! No way! I'm serious. I understand what you're trying to do. It's kind of twistedly thoughtful in a deformed way, but I can't. Dollface, I wouldn't even set foot in a Dress Ranch. I'm not cattle... or a cowgirl."

"But there are guidelines." Carder produced the printed list from his back pocket.

"Then those guidelines will guide me."

Upon reading the guidelines, Haika declared their visit to Gettysburg would be even more fun than she'd originally thought. Could she wear a bonnet and a gingham dress? No, she could not. They weren't Amish. In fact, the Amish might be the one group with *more* restrictions than Lucy's church if such existed. To further guide her, he provided recent photos of his sister and her family, the last being a family snapshot. In it, Lucy's eyes looked trapped despite a grin. No one in the snapshot touched except for Mandy holding Miriam, whose jaw was unhinged with wailing. The picture had cropped off the crowns of both Stan's and Lucy's heads, turning them into columns supporting the photograph's frame. Haika was mesmerized.

"This is the best guideline you could've given. Can I take these?"
"Sure."

"And can I use the red purse hanging on the doorknob upstairs? Or is that off limits?"

That bag was last used on the night of his mother's death, when she'd hailed a taxi to the afterlife. In her last moments, Sylvia had admired its perfect condition, perhaps in an effort to convince herself and her son that she wasn't dying. Carder acquiesced to Haika's request without telling the tale of how the purse had matched his mother's blood.

Carder wasn't allowed to pre-approve Haika's outfit. She didn't show it to him ahead of time. Though not fully trusting her judgment, Carder settled in for the show.

A fairy hangs sloth-like from a Ginkgo tree. It's not a fairy, it's a boy pitching his head back. His pudgy four-year-old face fills with blood and his battered wings look like they want nothing more than to separate from his small body and soar into the sky. Their bent wire resembles Italy's borders more than wings, and reach in the wrong direction to a worn patch of ground below.

"I'm a fairy!" says the little boy.

"You sure are, Sweetie-babes," Haika calls up to the fairy, who in reality is Carder's nephew, Mordecai. "You're Mordy in the sky with glitter!"

"Glitter!" he yells before flopping back to Earth, grounded. His delayed groan makes it seem the wind was knocked out of him, but no one runs to him, nor does he appear to expect they would.

The backyard is huge, spotted with trees, tricycles and half-naked dolls. An inflatable swimming pool is half-filled with stagnant water and littered with dead moths. A child's shoe lays on its bottom. Carder is nearby, finishing up a bowl of cold oatmeal at a plastic picnic table in primary colors. Haika aimlessly wonders around the yard, inspecting objects and the plants bordering the perimeter.

"We're trying to get him off of his fairy kick," Carder's brother-in-law Stan explains. He's as red-faced right side up as his son was upside down. "He's obsessed. Tries inserting them into Bible stories. It's embarrassing, but he's a kid. A few weeks ago during Family Bible Study, he said it was fairies who rejoiced at Jesus's birth. Replacing angels with fairies—he can't seem to remember the difference—which ones are pagan, which are Christian. Which ones are real."

"That's adorable!" Haika says.

"It's stupid," says Mandy, looking at the grass as though it's far more interesting than anyone around her. She's been caught in a teenage pout since Carder and Haika arrived, and has said no more than 'hello.' To Carder's further dismay, her baby face has evaporated into a taut, thin-lipped mask. Her poker face is occasionally severed with longing eyes and a petulant mouth, with teeth that could open bottles. As she argues with her father about Mordecai's stupidity, she pulls at caramel braids, parted and tied with white ribbons behind her head. A denim dress hides the girl inside from neck to ankle, giving the appearance of a grounded blue kite with white streamers. "Dumb," she adds redundantly, matching her father's level of exasperation. She grits her teeth and blows back inside the house.

"Yeah?" Stan screams so Mandy will hear. "Well, it would help if you stopped buying him those Wonder Woman comics. It confuses him with Greek mythology! If I see any more of them, I'm burning them." He softens his tone. "I'm sorry, Ms. Haus. Mandy's in *that* stage."

"Please, call me Haika. And Mandy is a beautiful girl. Carder tells me she's got *brains*. That's atypical of most—"

"—girls. I know."

"I was going to say *people*, but I suppose girls are people."

"Sometimes I wish she had a little less brains."

Stanley Sutcliffe is a curious man. When he was twenty-five, his girlfriend of three years aborted her pregnancy and moved to Prague. Heartbroken, Stan was enraptured by the comfort of his co-worker, Lucy Quevedo. But he was thwarted. Lucy would only date him on one condition: he must convert to the Jehovah's Witnesses as she had. He was assured she'd never consider an abortion, a resolve made easier since she refused sex until marriage. Flustered with sexual frustration and willing to take his mind off of it with scripture, Stan soon wrote letters to the Catholic Church, the Elks club and Playboy magazine, divorcing himself from all three institutions to please Lucy and her God. Every morning since their simple wedding, he has worn the clothes set on the bed for him. During rare times when Mandy earns it, Stan chauffeurs her and a friend to the mall, but stays in the car, studying the Watchtower magazine or preparing his next sermon. He allows Mandy small purchases, a book or a trinket, but make-up is out of the question and earrings aren't allowed. Satan's world paints girls like porcelain dolls then twists their heads off. That isn't going to happen to his daughter.

Carder hasn't seen Stan or Lucy in more than ten years. Mandy was six, maybe seven years old, when they'd come to New York City to tour the nearby Bible Factory. At that time, the other two children were yet to be conceived.

"It's called *Bethel*, not the Bible Factory," Stan corrects Carder. "But isn't it funny that the headquarters of God's house and the capitol of Satan's system are in the same city?"

Upon his arrival in Gettysburg, Carder hoped a wave of familial bliss would crash over him. It's the first time he's seen Mordy and his diapered sister Miriam in the flesh, and he hasn't seen his sister Lucy since their mother's funeral. Their mutual absence from one another's lives causes no bad blood—Lucy wants to stay out of the city as much as Carder wants to stay in it. Any guilt cancels itself out on both sides. Despite their lack of physical proximity, Carder still receives the requisite drawings, cards, and awkward moments on the telephone, and he faithfully sends each child one hundred dollars a year, usually in August as it's far enough from any birthdays and holidays, which they don't celebrate. He's written Mandy letters throughout the past thirteen years, ever since she could realize who they were from. As far as uncles who never see their relatives go, Carder is as good as it gets.

Like a puppet, Lucy comes into view in the second floor window of their home. She's tying back her hair with what looks like scrunched up underwear while blowing her bangs from her face. She calls out in one long breath, "Mordy-pie, it's time to get ready for Meeting, that goes for all of you, we have to leave in half-an-hour, Stan, have you seen Miriam's ducky?"

Sitting on the overstuffed couch with Miriam wriggling on his lap, Carder hears the muffled rustlings of Haika getting ready down the hall in Lucy's miniscule bathroom.

They'd talked Mordecai out of his fairy wings. Like a sullen super-hero, Mordy easily wrestles Stan's attempts to put a necktie on him, while still throwing dominoes at the wall. Lucy and Mandy are primping in the bathroom upstairs, the ceiling creaks with their footsteps, open cabinet doors slam shut—the whole process seems slowed—as if a pageant of hesitation will stall them into staying home from Worship. Looking around the room at framed school photos hanging between two wooden signs reading *Faith* and *Truth,* Carder knows that even if he were turned to stone this isn't where he'd want to plop his rock. The living room has only enough space for a sofa and a huge television on an oak entertainment stand. A football game plays: New York versus Philadelphia. The crowd hisses in support or mockery. Lucy plays a Kingdom Melodies cassette in protest and competition: sports versus spirituality. The ballgame becomes a haphazard dance to light orchestral arrangements about Christian life.

"Here I am." Haika announces before entering. By the time she takes the few steps into the living room, Miriam has urped up a multi-colored flower of half-digested Fruit Loops onto Carder's lapel. However, concern over the personalized corsage is supplanted by Haika's entrance. It appears she not only used the photos he'd given as guidance but had replicated one of the outfits exactly.

Lucy clasps her hands together when she comes into the room and sees Haika. "Don't you look delightful! I've a blouse just like that in lilac. Isn't it wonderful? So delicate and soft against your skin? Here, let me re-tie the ascot for you. I've gotten quite good."

"Thank you, Lucy. It's hard to tie a bow under the chin from this angle. Do you think the blouse looks all right tucked into the skirt?"

"Absolutely. But don't get near Miriam with this silk. Or Mordecai. Carder, where did you find this woman? She's so put together."

"On the train."

"How brave of you to talk to strange men," Lucy says, adjusting Haika's collar from behind. When she sees the familiar red purse Haika carries, her dead mother's purse, she puckers her mouth in decision: is carrying the purse immoral? Is it immoral but forgivable? Perhaps even fascinating under the circumstances? No, Lucy swiftly decides she's *not* fascinated. Still, perhaps it pushes her brother one step closer to the remote possibility of having a wife. She mouths silently to him, "I like her."

Haika catches the communication. "What?"

Lucy is swift. "Carder always hogged the Strawberry Quik. That awful red powder you stir into milk? Always hogged it."

"Do you have any?" Carder hopes.

"If I did, you couldn't have it," Lucy says, sashaying away.

From the outside, the Kingdom Hall of Jehovah's Witnesses is a large shoebox made of brick, an upscale barn. It's windowless, with few flourishes or architectural adornments. Spacious enough to hold a couple hundred people, the congregants amount to far less—a range of senior citizens and young families. A shriveled woman stands against the mauve walls adorned with printed scripture, the lettering imposing enough for use as a highway billboard:

"Love endures all things. Love never fails."—*1 Cor. 13:8*

Carder, Haika and Mandy sit one row behind the rest of the family. To the congregation, Stan and Lucy are known as Brother and Sister Sutcliffe. The implication sends shivers down Carder's spine—neutering Stan and Lucy into siblings. Then again, they fight like such, so perhaps it's fitting.

Without the natural light of windows, Carder slips into a familiar daze that has occurred in every church he's ever entered. It transcends religious creed, even creeping into classrooms at times, but he's sure people around the world typically gather in places of worship to float and soak inside their own minds. Carder's head swirls and mingles with the minister's statements, blurring into a free-floating world of acrobatic thought and feeling. A vapor of images from Carder's life arises: the aroma of his mother's perfume, the sounds of morning bacon crackling in a skillet and the scrape of the spatula, child-Carder lying in bed, having reaped another soul the night before. He's waking up to sunlight fighting through drapes printed with smiling Indians fighting happy cowboys. The taste of maple-syrup-breakfast is still in his mouth. Carder knows better than this. He knows what daydreaming might lead to.

Carder meditates on his sister while maintaining the appearance of being captivated by the sermon. It's a stretch that he and she entered the world through the same portal. Every part of Lucy, from her long face to her costume of heightened femininity fooling no one, from her frail feet wearing clunky pumps with clip-on bows, to the lipstick resembling a small stop sign—all *that* is unremarkable. What amazes Carder are the pieces of his mom that inhabit Lucy. Strands of Sylvia wind through, lighting Lucy up, giving her determination to weather a sour world, and the willingness to sedate her way through a husband she no longer loves. Though Carder hasn't seen it in years, Lucy behaves with Stan as she had with past boyfriends who were on the verge being cut loose. Only, she treats Stan worse, keeping him on the edge while at the same time letting him know that they're *forever*. It perturbs Carder that Lucy's desire to live forever on earth means an eternity with someone she'd given up on long ago. Again, the flavor of maple-syrup-breakfast is still in Carder's mouth. Again, he tastes it. He knows better than this, knows what daydreaming might lead to…

12

A REAPING: CRUSH
Carder at 9 years old

That smell. Maple syrup. Sweet. He looks around at the rubble from the fallen tower. Worn stone bricks lay everywhere, denting the ground. Many are as large as him. Hurriedly, he searches among the rocks for anything, anything. He listens but hears nothing: and realizes that he's arrived among that pause of silence just after tragedy has struck, when everything is still in shock.

Ah, but were Creep one of the angels his mother always talks of, the guardian angels that push people to safety, that undo accident and emergency. No, Creep brings only one thing.

There.

Its eyes are wide and open. The creature is pinned beneath the tower brick. Its wings are splayed up, fractured feathers spread, and its foxlike face holds half-closed eyes. Having no way out from under the rock, it's as if the arms that tried pushing it off, have given up, now embracing it. An overturned pail lies next to the poor animal. The sticky syrup he was collecting is spilled, and the tree he was collecting it from, obliterated.

"You won't remember this," Creep promises. "You won't remember this."

He bends down and kisses the creature's forehead—it's gone.

"But I will never forget."

It's gone.

13

THE BATTLEFIELD

Haika flounders in the church setting, as if trying to swim in an ocean of flour. Wielding a borrowed New World Translation Bible on her lap, Haika flips through the onion-skin pages furiously as the minister directs the congregation to various scriptures. She searches for a verse in a book called Obadiah.

"Where's Obladi-bla-da?" she asks quietly, hoping the Bible book will shriek at her when she gets there.

Mandy leans back to whisper the name phonetically, "O-bah-DIE-ah—comes after Amos. Toward the middle. He's a minor prophet."

Haika wonders what *minor prophet* means. Did Obadiah work in mines while prophesying? Was he not yet eighteen? Were his prophesies small? Things that everyone knows will happen anyway? *You'll soon be thirsty? Tired? Feeling trapped?*

The sermon is delivered by a frog of a man who, when pausing, looks as though his tongue will catapult out to catch an insect. Preaching that *a successful marriage has God as its head*, he admonishes Sisters of the congregation to subject themselves to their husband and his decisions, *even if they don't always make sense*. Before the Brothers can get too cocky, the speaker bulges his eyes and tells them not to be mistaken: *husbands may be the head but wives are the neck that turns that head*. The audience provides a collective chuckle. Marital tips proceed in a tit-for-tat manner, giving both parties an arsenal of scriptural texts for their next family argument.

During the second hour's question-answer study of the Watchtower magazine, Carder shushes Haika's playful attempts to raise her hand and insert her own comments, but eventually the session of worship comes to a close. Tired butts leave exhausted seats and members chit-chat their way to the exit.

"How did you like Brother Carlisle's sermon?" Lucy asks.

It was long. It was boring. It was important to her.

"It was good," Carder replies.

"The way he stressed the differences between man and woman, how men are like a heavy beer stein and women are more delicate and fragile like crystal goblets—isn't that true?"

"I don't know. I'm probably more like one of those cheap Charlie Brown glasses sold at the McDee's when we were kids..." Carder says. A beer stein he's *not*.

"Oh, Carder," Haika swoops in, "you're too much. If we compared ourselves to drinking vessels, I'd be afraid to know what I am. But I get the point: we need to treat others as unique vessels, whether goblets, steins, fast-food glasses, or...or a bucket! Lucy, it was an interesting sermon, and on more levels than I could possibly explain."

"I'm glad you liked it. Brother Carlisle will be coming to picnic with us on the Battlefield if you don't mind. It's our family's turn for Hospitality."

"Will his wife be coming as well?"

"He's not married. He brought his brother though."

The prospect of spending more time in costume blows Haika's smile out like a candle.

Lucy sees the change in her face and offers reassurance. "Don't you worry, Haika, you'll have a tremendous time. I made my marshmallow pie just for you. And you can't rightfully come to Gettysburg without seeing the Battlefield."

Almost a century-and-a-half has passed since blood and death marred the soil of the Gettysburg Battlefield. In time, its scars were bandaged with costume-soldiers, reenactors carrying mute muskets, and cannons with no balls. Monuments were erected marking what was lost and what was gained. Tourists mill about, sensing or ignoring the sorrow-permeated air rushing their lungs like gun powder. Time couldn't erase the energy. Even vats of potpourri would never be able to remove the loss still hanging in the atmosphere, sewn into the grasses, stained invisibly into the landscape. Memorials weren't built high enough to reach what transpired there. Sculpture can't recreate or convey the possibilities and paths erased during three grisly days of battle in July, 1863. Futures were stopped short. Other futures, and futures of futures, were extinguished before they could bubble up. Death tore marriages asunder and countless sperm would never meet wasted eggs. Inventions and technologies-to-be vanished before they were even inklings. Such is war for both sides. However, the present is its own monument built on the fractured spines that came to dust.

The Sunday worshippers and the tag-along, bookend heathens of Brooklyn set their picnic blanket near Devil's Den. Lucy hands out turkey sandwiches, brown guacamole, tortilla chips, mayonnaise, mustard and spray-on cheese. Stan goes googly-eyed over pork rinds, and the kids deflate silver-foil drink pouches. Carder looks over at Brother Carlisle who seems younger in sunlight, perhaps in his late twenties, with acne scars chiseled into his cheeks like cryptic code. Seeming as relieved as the rest of them that he finished the sermon, he concentrates on his sandwich as though sharing secrets with it telepathically. His brother Charlie smiles, showing his teeth like bathroom tiles, staring at Mandy. Being about a decade or so younger, Charlie's bloom of pus and blackheads haven't yet settled into scars.

Stan sits on a tangerine blanket printed with strawberries and jars of marmalade, while Miriam lies silently on his lap, staring up at the sky as if through a kaleidoscope, reaching for things to put in her mouth or with which to soil her clothes. Apparently, wearing a dress the size of a hand towel makes one want to wipe things on it.

"Mordecai," Stan instructs, "tell Brother Carlisle what your favorite Bible story is."

Mordecai stops skipping around in circles and mumbles, "Noah's ark. 'Cept for he missed saving the unicorns. They drowned."

"I never said they drowned," Stan corrects, shaking his head free from the ideas of foolish children.

Brother Carlisle is shocked. "Unicorns are satanic, boy. Their horn was used to deflower virgins. That's called bestiality, and it's vile. You'll understand what it means one day."

"I know what it means," Mordecai says, verbally sticking out his tongue at the man though keeping it inside his mouth.

"What?"

"It's when you get licked by cat butt." He points as though the *you* he speaks of is Brother Carlisle.

Stan blushes at the notion of bestiality and turns four shades deeper upon Mordecai's stab at explanation. "Go play, son." Once Mordecai skips off, Stan lowers his voice, "We don't know why he came out kind of ...slower than most. My little brother, Brody, used to say stupid things like that. On the other hand, Mandy wasn't like that at all. She memorized the order of all sixty-six Bible books before she was four! Mordy has a wild imagination though—like his Uncle Carder."

Haika's mouth is obscured behind an empty styrofoam cup riddled with repeating arches of gentle teeth-marks she's bitten into it like colorless rainbows perforating white sky. She meets Carder's gaze with a mischievous smile, enjoying the role of spectator and anthropologist. She's relaxed, as if sitting in a bubble bath with a goblet of wine in hand, reading this all in a novel someone lent her.

Love.

That's what Haika is: love. Not just love for Mike or art or New York. Haika is love in every moment. She's loving to Carder, to his relatives, to the Carlisle boys. But she's more. She's love in the cloudless sky above, in the honey she brought for tea, in the music she tries to soundtrack Carder's life with, in the thrift-store clothes she's wearing, in the ascot knotted at her chin, in her bare feet sliding through what would once have been war-torn grass, in the sadness sometimes hiding in the corners of her lips. She brings love to every moment... something Carder has never seen in another person. Ever. He obsesses over every detail, and gulps down the harrowing thought that he'll one day lose her. He tries to be love like Haika is, to laze on the hammock of friendship hanging from her eyes *right now*. He fills with gratitude. This has actually happened. She had actually been in his life, and no one can take that away. Carder could live off it for decades and fully plans to.

Mordecai whizzes to and fro, over and under the spaces between the boulders of Devil's Den. Everything in Gettysburg is the inverse of New York City, as if turned inside out. Instead of Central Park, fenced in by the city on all sides, it's as though one giant park barricades and dominates this small Pennsylvanian burg. The air is crisp, unfettered by billboards or overblown architecture. It brags of its own luxurious space. Wide-open spaces are disconcerting, but Carder tries using the giant stones to conjure the same sense of shelter that skyscrapers give. It's clear why soldiers holed themselves up in rocks where sunlight and death were less likely to penetrate.

Haika makes the mistake of asking Stan why Jehovah's Witnesses don't celebrate Christmas, Easter or birthdays.

Stan's happy to provide answers. "All holidays have pagan origins, so anyone partaking in them is essentially worshipping false gods, gods of fertility, sex, orgies and human sacrifice. Even worse, in the case of celebrating one's birthday, you end up worshipping yourself."

Haika puzzles over this. "You mean, God, omnipotent, all-knowing God, can't figure out that you're not celebrating the ancient pagan aspects? Or that you're not worshipping yourself? Wouldn't he know? Wouldn't he be able to tell? *I* can tell that."

"Look at it this way: If I offered you something to drink, but you knew it contained a tiny bit of poison, would you still drink it?" He's used this reasoning in his ministry a million times before. Stan doesn't require response—it was a rhetorical illumination. Turning to his wife, he says, "Lucy, pass me another Diet Coke, will you?"

Pfft!

While Stan and Haika are deep in conversation, Lucy takes her opportunity. "Carder, let's walk." She wipes crumbs from her lap. "Do you want to take more lemonade with you?"

"It's too sweet."

"There's no such thing as too sweet." She sets the thermos down and grabs leaflets from her purse.

Sitting by Charlie Carlisle and his acne, Mandy sees them leaving and starts squirming for escape as well. Charlie's talking about a job he's recently secured in Mechanicsburg cleaning out rooftop gutters. *Pay's good. 'Spect I'll soon be buying a place.* Mandy leans toward Carder and Lucy as if they had invited her to join.

"You stay here," Lucy commands stonily. "This way, Carder. We'll walk towards Little Round Top." She gestures toward a hill topped with a castle-like memorial.

Carder hasn't been alone with his sister since they'd eaten the neighbor's, Mrs. Gunderson's, apple pie together after their mother's funeral. They ate it without speaking, plugging their pie-holes to make conversation impossible, allowing their scraping forks to make distant calls to one another. But now, Carder can tell by the way Lucy stomps that this walk has a purpose. To keep her high heels from sinking into the ground and giving the impression of someone shrinking, she avoids the grass when possible.

"Nuts! I should've changed into sneakers," she says, dumping a rock from her shoe. "You know, you shouldn't be driving alone with that Haika woman. You need a chaperone. It's inappropriate. She's nice though and, aside from the short hair, seems somewhat modest and respectful. You two should study the Bible together. I'll find a way to contact Brothers and Sisters in Brooklyn for you."

"Haika isn't interested in religion, or at least not the Bible."

"Not true. I saw her looking up the scriptures during Brother Carlisle's talk. That's a good sign—most people take for granted that whatever the preacher says is in scripture, but Haika validated it, making sure it was there. Like the Boreans."

"The Boreans? I don't know them, but Haika's not the type to try keeping up with the Joneses if that's what you mean. That's against the Bible too, right?"

Lucy rolls her eyes at her biblically ignorant brother. "The Boreans were a first century congregation. They didn't take anyone's word for it, but made sure everything taught was right there in God's word. Anyway, Haika clearly has a spiritual hunger and I ask you don't stand in the way. Promise me that."

"Lucy, I assure you I won't provide obstacles to Haika's spiritual yearnings."

"Okay. Then, on to other matters." She blocks the sun from her eyes. "You wish to take Mandy for a visit, a long visit at that?"

"I thought it was a sure thing."

"Criteria must be met. Mandy's shown a rebellious spirit for a while now, and..."

"She has? I..."

"And..." Lucy takes a deep breath, "and I'm worried for her soul. Satan and the Demons seem intent on pulling her from the straight and narrow. Her six months of grounding only recently ended, so she can now leave her room but still goes accompanied when shopping."

Carder was familiar with his family's style of punishment. What could Mandy have done to warrant six months of isolation? "She seems so... like such a good kid."

"All the more reason for Satan to set his crosshairs."

They come upon a shadowy figure in a confederate grey uniform, carrying a musket. It's a reenactor, someone who regularly re-lives the Gettysburg Address and Battle. The Civil War is always on his mind, even more so during the first week of July, but then, he always felt like a soldier who fell asleep and has awoken in the wrong era. Scratching his scraggly beard, he stares vacantly across the field as Lucy fumbles through various leaflets, searching for the subject she deems most fitting.

"Hello sir, here's some reading material for your break. You can read it over a cup of coffee. It discusses why God permits wickedness. That's something most of us wonder and now you have the answer to one of life's most daunting questions right in your hand."

The bewildered man shifts his eyes, making sure no one sees him stuff the leaflet into his pocket. A soldier from another century shouldn't take it.

"Please read it along with your own personal copy of the Bible," She barks back at him, but he's already given it to an older female passing by, who stuffs it into her bag. "Now, as I was saying, Carder, keep Mandy away from worldly teenagers. City kids are fast and hard and I won't have her corrupted further."

"You mean guys, dating, that sort of thing?"

"And no Rated R movies. I mean boys or girls. Both. No one who isn't in the Truth," she explains, "...which means anyone who isn't one of Jehovah's Witnesses. This school year, one girl tried digging her claws into Mandy and I had to show both girls it wasn't going to happen. They spent way too much time together. The girl was even suggesting sleepovers! Slumber parties are only parties for Satan. He never sleeps. Nevertheless, I put the kibosh on that. No, I don't want Mandy hanging with bad associations. And, brother, I'd appreciate it if you took her to the meetings, at least Sunday. Mandy's at an impressionable age. Please call me about any movies, and I'll let you know which are okay. Oh…" Lucy catches hold of Carder as if she's going to fall. She keeps her hand there. "Brother, this is serious. Amanda's on the edge." She tightens her grip. "I worry. Her trip to New York is the last resort. I'm at a loss of what to do… and I've tried so hard to teach her, and… I'm hoping the city will scare the living daylights out of her." She bites her bottom lip, pulling it inside her mouth.

"And you can't let go?"

"Oh, I'm *not* letting go!"

Her facade breaks momentarily with watery eyes. Her expressions are typically callous, thus turmoil is accentuated in high relief when it comes. If they continue like this, Lucy will return to the family in tears.

"Listen, Lucy: Rabbit's practically an adult. She's got to start making her own choices. Of course, I'll watch to make sure she doesn't do anything too crazy - no murders, no drugs."

"You're so funny." She takes no comfort, and starts murmuring private one-sided pleadings into the sky as they walk further uphill.

As an outsider listening to a foreign tongue, Carder grows fidgety. While he wishes to provide Lucy hope, he knows not to set himself up by making claims that will haunt him later. He's known Lucy for thirty-three years, knows that whatever happens, her disappointment is an eventual certainty. Whether Mandy drinks too much lemonade or slaughters kittens and launches them into crowds at funerals, he'll be blamed.

It becomes obvious that he and Lucy won't reach the summit. They turn back in the direction of their family sitting at the base of the boulders below. Haika is watching Mordecai clumsily scale the rocks, while tourists explore higher nooks and crannies. The picnic blanket is an island outlined by laughter, cameras, the stone labyrinth and the ghosts of ten thousand men.

Lucy once served as librarian to the local elementary school, and falls back on her Battle-explaining skills as they descend the hill. She tells Carder of the 44th Regiment from New York who were stationed directly in front of Devil's Den in the hill's defense. That's difficult to envision now with sparrows spinning sun-drenched song and children skipping about.

Suddenly, Lucy changes topics. "Have you seen Dad?"

"No."

"Me neither. Not lately. He doesn't write letters or call, but he sends Pups merchandise. It saves me from having to buy toys for the kids. Did you see Miriam's nursery? It's crawling with those dogs!"

Entering Miriam's nursery had made Carder's heart stop. He'd immediately seen a mural-like decal of a being he met decades before, Clove, whom Blammo toys had transmogrified into Clover. It was horrifying: they'd shaved off her horns, given her skin where she had none, and painted white blossoms on her eyes, belly and paws. Carder asked Lucy not to show Haika the nursery or mention the Pups. Lucy agreed, excited to see Carder strive to present himself well, freeing himself from his juvenile dreamscapes.

"It's all free from Dad," she says. "He's not capable of giving much more. Might as well make the most of it."

While walking across the Battlefield, Carder feels a sorrow unrelated to battle. This trip reminds him that his relationship with Lucy is what it will be for the rest of his life—*if* it remains at full potential. After joining the church, his sister thinks and speaks of little else. Her god has become an ever-present character, referred to constantly, an all-purpose helper: finding house keys, guiding her to grocery store bargains, and holding her marriage together. Carder doesn't mind her god that much, but it freaks him that this god supposedly scrutinizes everything from bath time to bedroom antics. At the core, what bothers Carder is that, in spite of her god, Lucy is unhappy. The more she focuses on evil, the more she notices it in the world, and the worse things grew, the more desperate she becomes to have wickedness wiped from the world so she and the other survivors can turn it into paradise and live forever.

"Sis," Carder says, "I'll do my best with Mandy. And I'll take her to whatever church meetings she wants."

"To be honest, it'll be good for her to get away from this setting and from that girl for a while. I can't imagine you'll be able to get her into any trouble. I hope the city scares her straight."

By this time, Mandy marches to them, carrying an empty baby bottle and wearing an orchestrated smile. Upon reaching them, she holds the bottle to Lucy as if concern for the baby's thirst has prompted her approach.

"Would someone help me?" she asks, positioning herself so Charlie Carlisle can only see the back of her head. "This is torture."

"Oh sweetheart," Lucy replies, "Brother Carlisle's a wonderful young brother who serves as a Ministerial Servant in his congregation *and* has a great job. With all the rooftops he works on, he might be able to help you start a window-cleaning business to allow you to become a full-time pioneer. Imagine how tremendous: to go preaching every single day! Brother Carlisle's exactly the type of friend you should be investing in. You never know, Mandy, it might turn into something special."

"Dirty fingernails."

"Holy Spirit," Lucy counters.

"Zits."

"A strong position in the congregation."

"Halitosis."

Lucy is shocked and offended. "A good provider."

"One brain cell."

"Don't be ridiculous! Carder, would you excuse us?" Lucy is seething, but puts her arm around Mandy and grins, waving at the Carlisle brothers. "Mandy and I are going to walk towards Plum Run."

"You mean the Valley of Death," Mandy contradicts as Lucy pulls her down the path.

"Plum Run was the original name before the war. The real name. Carder, we won't be long."

Mordecai trailed Mandy up the hill, tra-la-la'ing his way behind, and he's finally caught up. "Hey Uncle, Hi-*YAH* says she can touch her tongue to her nose. Come see!"

Hi-YAH is right.

14

RETURN – UNFILTERED, BLURRED

Driving away from Gettysburg and its farmland, they pass cornfields, silos and a field of plastic huts holding future veal dinners. Looking back, Carder originally misjudged the entire experience before it had happened. The journey into wide-open spaces wasn't as menacing as expected. And while there's no way he'd whittle away his life in these settings, he understands them better. The further away from the city he'd gotten, the more time had slowed. And maybe, the more time slows, the more secure things feel. In any case, he's ready to return to the city, where the sinister isn't blanketed in lush, green forests and polite conversation, where you know where you stand even if it's only to be told you need to get out of the way.

"I think I'm ready to make a trip into Manhattan," Carder announces as they drive over the crest of a long highway hill.

"Really?" Haika closes the Avon catalog Lucy gave her.

"No. Not at all. I should do it though. And I will. How else will Mandy see a Broadway show?"

Mandy, who's been staring silently out the back window, pipes up, "What do you mean?"

"Your Uncle Carder hasn't been to Manhattan since your grandmother died. He's stayed in Brooklyn for years now."

"Oh, brother," says Mandy, rolling her eyes. "Can we stop? I have to go to the bathroom."

Carder has dealt relatively well with the newness of the past two days, but somewhere among his sister's Kingdom Hall, Miriam's nursery and the Civil War, something atrophied inside. He's now hit with the weight of his own words. He's been trying to make himself believe he can go back to Manhattan, that his world can expand beyond Brooklyn, beyond the den in which he creates art, beyond the war in his own head, but it's a lie.

"Can we play some music that's more... chill for a bit?" he asks Haika—for her sake, of course.

"Sure." Haika then engages the teen in the backseat. "Mandy, one thing I didn't understand at Kingdom Hall: what does your religion teach about heaven? They mentioned living eternally in paradise."

Mandy thinks, but answers casually, "They believe that almost everyone will stay living on Earth. Even dead people will be resurrected to Earth, not heaven."

"What about heaven?"

"Only 144,000 people go there when they die. They'll rule over the earth with Jesus."

"When these 144,000 people win the celestial lottery, so to speak, they'll be ruling over all the dead people who've been recycled back to earth?"

"And all those surviving Armageddon."

"But how do you know if you have the magic ticket to be one of the few in heaven ruling over everyone else?"

"Holy spirit tells you."

"Well then, I hope it tells you. You could easily rule over a lot of the people I met today."

"I don't know. I'm too young. Plus, anyone I've met who says they're anointed for heaven turns out to be a weirdo. Brother Ludlow says he's one even though Children's Services took his kids away."

"The entire concept is interesting. There's a sort of class distinction even after death, even in the presence of your god. I thought everyone in heaven was equal. The same!"

"Nope. There have always been different types of angels: Cherubs, seraphs. They have different ranks."

"Heaven sounds a lot like high school. I don't know that I could ever go back to that."

"You wouldn't have to. You'd be earthbound, living forever in the promised land."

"Oh no! You're crazy if you think I'm staying in this ramshackle place for eternity. I know the earth seems grand, but it's probably one bead hanging on a million necklaces in a trillion stores. There are probably many, many promised lands. I may not know where I'm going after death, but I'm not going to be stuck here for eons." The baking car interior is hot to Haika's touch. "So you believe you're going to live forever on earth even though no other human ever has? Ever?"

"That's the point."

"That *is* the point," Haika echoes.

"Anyway, I never said *I* believed that, but yes, that's what they teach. Adam and Eve would've lived forever had they not sinned. Jesus would've as well if he'd not been killed. He never sinned."

"If we're supposed to buy that concept, shouldn't there be at least one living example of a person living forever?"

"Faith," Carder cuts in. They'd avoided religious argument thus far and he didn't want to start now. His sister used to latch on to debates for hours defending her viewpoint. "Thing is: religion doesn't have to make sense."

"Guess not," Haika says.

"Nope," Mandy says with cold stoicism, fencing herself off from the world in which she was raised.

They pull off into the next rest stop. Somehow, its bathrooms are caught in deep winter inside—though heat throttles the day outside. Carder finishes up as quickly as possible, reading graffiti, maneuvering around faintly-colored puddles on the floor and then exits the bathroom.

He runs into Mandy.

It's a different Mandy from when they arrived here minutes before. Pre-bathroom Mandy was a caramel-haired, pale-skinned girl in a long dress which could've been Civil War costuming with only her hands, neck and head exposed. But if Carder didn't know better, he might've thought that time-travel has occurred, that years have passed. The bathroom in some way transformed Mandy, wringing out all but the last of any girlhood, presenting a fully-formed woman. The paleness of her cheeks is now also worn on bare legs in jean shorts rolled above the knee. Flat black Mary Jane shoes, the style of which she's worn since childhood, are now maroon Doc Martens with thick, toothy soles. Her fitted top, while not exposing too much skin, forces Carder to recognize she'll one day be feeding children and pleasing men.

He gulps, averting his eyes. "Mandy. Where are your clothes?"

Mandy holds up her back pack, asking, "Are we going to get something to eat?"

"Would your mom be okay with this get up?"

"C'mon Uncle, there's nothing wrong with this. Please don't give me crap about it. It's hot out! Floor length dresses trap heat! Do you want me to roast alive?"

"Wait. Make-up? Are you allowed to wear make-up? And why are you removing your pigtails? Rabbit…"

"Do I look like a rabbit? It's Mandy, I'm eighteen and I look like any normal adult."

"You're only seventeen… and however-many-months."

She walks briskly to the car. Carder follows.

"Listen," he says, "I'd feel more comfortable if you look and dress like you do at home."

"Home." Mandy's tone is a devastated land. Moving forward, her pace quickens, her arms stiffen with clenched fists, the same way her mother used to do before decking Carder.

As they turn a corner, they come upon Haika who appears to be rummaging through a dumpster. Only, she isn't. She's just placed something *inside* the dumpster and now reaches behind her waist, unzipping her skirt. Within two seconds, she steps out of it, revealing long legs rich with golden skin. She too wears shorts, considerably higher cut than Mandy's, and a blue top so soft it practically begs to be touched.

As Carder and Mandy draw near, Haika raises the skirt into the air and lets go. It falls, disappearing into the dumpster.

"I didn't see those clothes as a permanent part of my wardrobe—they're so uncomfortable." With raised eyebrows, she assesses Mandy. "Hello, Love-bucket. Let's get something to eat. I'm famished."

They exit the highway for the nearest fast food restaurant. It's filled with frenzied travelers—a human goulash of wealth, poverty, age, appearance, culture and ethnicity. Carder is sure the woman at the next table—transparent as a ghost—has her wig on backwards, and her grandson or apprentice, or whatever he is, seems to have a large brain in a small head. As they come closer to the front of the BurgerQuake line, a display showcases the current kids' meal prizes.

Of course.

The Pups.

They've found a way.

But how can there be condensation inside the display case?

Carder's phone vibrates. A text message from Darren.

[*U OK?*]

It makes Carder feel ill. He needs to wash his hands again.

Haika understands. "Take your time, Doll. Mandy and I are going to chat."

Carder responds: [*I'm OK.*]

[*U get sick yet?*]

Reading that question while in the bathroom stall prompts Carder to vomit into the toilet. His knees immediately feel filthy on the tile.

[*Only when you asked just now.*]

Carder washes his hands, splashes his face with cool water, rinses his mouth out at the drinking fountain and returns to the girls.

Haika is speaking, "...but he was a pedophile."

"That wasn't proven. Oh, guess what, Haika? Prince has also become a Jehovah's Witness," Mandy says.

"Wait. *Purple Rain* Prince?"

"Yep."

"God. That just killed a part of music's soul. Damn. Gotta get those artists young before life takes over."

Mandy changes the subject. "I hear you're married?"

"I am."

"To who?"

"To Michael Harris Fiore."

"What's he like?"

"He... he assists the... he entertains the elderly. He grew up in Manhattan and... he..." Puzzled, Haika turns to Carder. "How would you describe Mike, Carder?"

"James Dean with no personality."

"Rude."

Carder continues. "He's a good guy. Grins a lot. Schmoozes the rich, constantly checks his shirt cuffs, gambles with old ladies and has an acute tendency to undervalue what he's got."

"Hey! He's good to you, Carder," Haika reprimands.

"I actually like Mike. I just think he's misplaced. If I were seeking advice about stock options, I'd hope someone like him was available. Only, he wouldn't be because I couldn't afford him."

Haika ignores that. "Mandy, do you think your brother's slow? Your dad mentioned it about four times."

"Mordecai isn't slow. He's just annoyed with Mom and Dad, but he's too young to realize why. In a way, he's smarter I was. It took me *forever* to figure it all out. Years. But then, they're my parents. I assumed they had it right. Mordecai isn't like that. He challenges anything and everything. He's a pain in my butt though."

"Mandy, you're parents love you very much."

"Yeah. I've kind of figured that out already."

Haika seems to realize that her greeting card advice sounds insipid despite her intentions. "Okay."

"Okay," repeats Mandy.

Carder goes to order food despite knowing he can't eat. His stomach churns. He returns to a table of empty cups and food wrappers between the girls. Though Mandy is too cool for many things, apparently a kids' meal isn't one of them - she's finishing it with baby carrots that would've been animal cookies a decade prior. On the edge of the table sits the toy prize: another hideous version of Clover sealed inside a plastic bag. Carder still can't get over the evolution of the Pups. It seems to have run backwards: their eyes got larger, colors more radioactive, their entire being more curved, more safe, more meaningless. He intentionally overlooks it, but feels vindicated when Mandy slides the unopened toy off her plastic tray into the garbage.

"Come on, Unc. Let's get you back home."

Carder takes some fries. He'll try stomaching them while on the road.

He had received another voicemail while in the bathroom: a cornea extraction awaits, this time at Methodist Hospital, if he can make it in time. He has to go—he'd put himself on call an hour before. It's exactly what he needs: to get away from this region of weird and back to the world he knows. His own momentum exhausted, he lets the pending extraction push the gas pedal to the floor and pull him back to the city.

Almost back home, the car idles at a stoplight.

"Why don't you drop me and Mandy at my place?" Haika asks. "You don't know how long you're going to be working tonight. Mike and I can hang out with her, and she can stay down on my level."

"Sure. Why not?" Mandy chimes from the back seat.

Carder hasn't fully anticipated the toll exacted by journeying away from New York. Time in the wilds of battle-scarred Pennsylvania and among his sister's cultish rules, though brief, has left him gasping for a moment to hole up in his cave, alone. He's not sure how Haika clued in, but whatever her reasoning, he's grateful.

"You got here a little early, didn't you, Blue Eyes?"

"I was told there was an extraction."

"They have to die first, don't they? Someone's still working with them." Nurse Grey isn't looking at Carder but at glossy magazine pages showing two celebrities, a man with large teeth and an anorexic woman with tits like cement balloons. "You can sit in the waiting room if you like."

"I'm staff."

"You have staph?"

"I'm not going to sit in the waiting room."

"Need something to read?"

"Naah. I got a lot on my mind."

Nurse Grey points her magazine at him, showcasing a spread of the anorexic movie star. "She just had a miscarriage," and then, as though seeing Carder for the first time, "Whoa! Are you okay? You look like you could use a cigarette. If you need one let me know."

Carder replies silently with shrugged shoulders. Sitting in an empty chair at the nurses' station, he wonders what Nurse Grey looks like out of scrubs. Not naked—he doesn't want to see her private property. His mind conjures mundane images: stretch pants, tube tops, tight jeans cutting off her circulation. She isn't fat, just solid, and he's used to her advances. If she weren't so attractive, the leering at him while filling hypodermic needles and the snorts accompanying her dirty jokes would be distressing. She isn't repulsive enough to deem it sexual harassment—maybe it's *sensual* harassment. Is there such a thing? Since Nurse Grey isn't hideous, Darren always encourages Carder to ask her on a date, but despite admiring her nursing skills (she can always find a vein and she has a great sense of tumor) Carder refuses.

Whoever was working on the patient is finally done.

According to the chart, the body was Mr. Grant Gaines, an old man whose wizened body inexplicably still offers the corneas of a bright young stud. Launching the blade into the first eye relaxes Carder. Its inky pupil faces him like an egg at breakfast. While one part of him performs the procedure with scrupulous care, another part processes the past few days. It's been a circus, but there's a sense of reward, mostly due to Mandy. Despite her transformation from bawling baby to virginal punk, Carder likes the Mandy which surfaced at the highway rest area. Teenage code is still her native tongue, and he constantly has to guess what's going on inside her, but at least she gives clues.

A temporary container accepts the first eye.

Mandy may be the only family member who wishes to know Carder, but she's an iron-jawed twirp at the moment. Still, Lord knows what Carder would've done were he forced into door-to-door missions pushing Bible literature in a gingham dress.

During the second eye, Carder pictures the multiple decades of light that passed through those corneas: marriage, births, television shows. They would now be joined by a second set in another body, another life, another story.

15

POTATO CHIP FINGERPRINTS, VINES & VIVIENNES

Carder doesn't mind the greasy, potato chip fingerprints on his mother's plastic-covered furniture. He loves each print, every crumb. A flock of six or seven soda cans have amassed on the coffee table, a few more joining each day, all with varying levels of cola remains. Surely this never happened at Lucy's simple, pristine home where Mandy had perpetual assignments cleaning up. Carder interprets the mess as Mandy feeling more comfortable.

Concern over how Mandy would react to Carder's home had been silly.

"I've always liked the Twilight Zone," she says, scoping out his habitat.

"You're not creeped out?"

"No more than I am back home. Less."

Surprisingly, she doesn't say much about the paintings. It's as if blank walls surround her, as if she weren't being scrutinized 24/7 by dark otherworldly beasts. Perhaps Carder shouldn't be surprised since she doesn't say much at all. Physically she's there, sleeping on the couch late into the day while courtroom TV shows buzz, brushing her teeth, sitting on the front step, reading Stephen King novels while ignoring Watchtower magazines poking from her backpack.

While Mandy's presence is comforting, it's also mystifying. Living in his time-warp, Carder had imagined Mandy younger, still fresh and discovering the world. She no longer likes mac'n'cheese the way she'd claimed in letters long ago. She's now into the few portable non-violent video games she's been allowed, graphic novels and depressing indie music by whiny, privileged boys.

Carder discusses her presence with Darren over the phone.

"Dude," Darren responds, "she's in that funky place. What's that song? She's not a girl, nor a woman. Be happy she's not running around with coke-nose and no panties. Plus, this is the first time she's been away from that Bible-life. She finally doesn't have God constantly peering through her window."

"But I can't get her to open her mouth. She has a ten-word vocabulary: 'yes,' 'no,' 'lame,' 'sick,' 'not cool' and a few others. So what am I supposed to do?"

"Nothing. She's a teenager. They float about until they hit something and stick. Like *we* did, remember?"

"I don't want her floating around and sticking to things. That's gross. Come on, you're good with girls."

"She's too young for what I usually…"

"But, what do I do? She yawns a thousand times a day. Last night she sat at the kitchen table for more than an hour doing nothing, literally nothing. Didn't read, talk, eat—nothing."

"You know what you have to do."

Carder doesn't want to know. He's made a u-turn in his goals, solidly believing Brooklyn is all Mandy needs. He doesn't reply. Why had he ever said he was ready to go to Manhattan?

"You know what you have to do," Darren repeats. "No one comes to the city without going. It will rock her world. I can get you cheap tickets to that Broadway show: The Princess Suites. My aunt went and said it wasn't horrid. It's not the Lion King, but probably still has all the bells and whistles that teens require. Aunt Mildred says the crazy black dude from that Criminal M.D. show plays the king. Hmm. Okay, I admit it sounds awful, but your niece is going to love it."

"Brooklyn's so much better though."

"I'm not going to argue that point, but Mandy wants bells and whistles. Picture Manhattan as another form of video game. It'll stop her yawning and give her new memories. The female of our species likes to get dressed up, wear the gowns and heels, fool themselves into thinking everyone's looking at them."

Silence.

"Carder?"

"Yeah?"

"Have you noticed the new shirt Larry the Whale wore to the diner the other day?"

"No."

"That's because he didn't. Don't become Larry. I'll get you tickets to Princess Suites."

"Get three."

The male voice is smooth and sounds medicated:

"Put things off for too long a time and they'll travel to meet you. Traversing shadow and bush, they'll slither their way into this world, like it or not. Hide in a cave, palace, treehouse or hovel, but you'll be found, and when found you'll face not only the original predicament, but punishment for concealing yourself."

Carder runs the bridge but without destination, fulfilling his simple desire for escape. Escaping what? He doesn't know. Everything. His skin bounces with each stride as he passes faces in an endless stream of people. Mornings don on them like ideas. They bustle unquestioningly in their execution of the day like ants. From their stammering paces and shut, paperclip mouths, he assumes many are walking to jobs they loathe.

The audiobook Carder listens to on a player Darren loaned him—*Stepping Out on You • Overcoming Agoraphobia*—seems even more tailored to his life upon the twenty-ninth listen.

"Reach out to your fear like a vine. Trust that if you let go of the vine you're swinging on, another will appear to your grasping hand, and will provide the forward momentum you need. Your other option is to hang on to the same vine for years. If you do, hang knowing that you're nowhere near your landing-place and you may as well stop swinging altogether. Remember: down isn't the target.

There are alligators below."

The words were originally encouraging, but they've begun to sound exhausted of saying the same thing over and over. During this listen, the tone becomes berating.

The symbolic vines undulate in every direction. Swinging on an unknown journey stresses Carder so much that he's re-visiting a habit forgotten since college: jogging. Long ago, jogging was his daily ritual whenever he neared the breaking point, whenever remaining inside became stifling. While running, conversations can't happen and there are too many strides to count each step. Never being in the same spot for more than a second, a runner can't be stopped by charity workers or proselytizers, can't buy or be sold anything. Constant forward movement contradicts ingrained inclinations, but perhaps that's exactly what he wants—to escape himself.

Whenever he imagines plunging himself off the Brooklyn Bridge, Carder instead jogs across it. This is the fifth day he's running the hanging pause between Brooklyn and Manhattan, high above the East River, insulated within its concrete, steel, limestone and car exhaust. As his footsteps pound the planks, sending vibrations into his kneecaps, large block letters painted on a nearby building command his attention. He's seen them for decades.

READ GOD'S WORD THE HOLY BIBLE DAILY

The sign reminds him of his brief time studying the Bible at Lucy's request. She claimed it would help him overcome the *injustices imposed* upon him by their father. Carder has seen the sign for five consecutive days now and defied it for that entire period. Nonetheless, he's amazed at his recall: *On the fifth day, God let the waters swarm forth a swarm of living souls and let the flying creatures fly over the earth—great sea monsters and every winged flying creature.* One winged flying creature, a grey seagull, glides to and fro above the cables of the bridge, but Carder has never seen the East River's waters swarm forth with any sea monsters or even fish for that matter. But surely there are monsters—the local news reported one last week—the evidence of which was a naked human body, decapitated and wrapped in a plastic tarp at the base of the bridge's Manhattan side. Darren had x-rayed the body and head separately. Yes, monsters exist and swarm forth.

Carder stops to stretch.

READ GOD'S WORD THE HOLY BIBLE DAILY

The message fills the width of a large building overlooking Brooklyn's side of the bridge like a tourist admiring the view. Its message is painted in dark green capital letters as if screaming the directive above traffic. Lucy may as well have written a billboard-sized post-note and stuck it to Carder's life.

"Do you do it?" a nearby voice asks. "Do you read God's word the holy Bible daily?"

Carder clicks off the audio book he's already been ignoring.

Her voice isn't boldfaced, green or screaming—nothing like Lucy's, not hardened or closed, but rides the air as smoothly as the soaring gull. Carder removes his sunglasses and headband, and produces a panting reply, "I don't—I do—I do read—daily—not all the time—but usually—and not the Bible."

"Me too."

"What are you doing here?" Carder asks, amused by the accidental meeting.

Claudette Vivienne points to her torso. Clean, unruffled, and breathing easy, she stands in a white tank top and matching white shorts. Beneath their translucence, a black bra and panties swim like a pod of killer whales about to surface. In combination with the velour visor bridling her ever-expanding platinum hair, she's obviously come for the same reason he has.

Without speaking, they start walking together, silently negotiating speed, sometimes briskly, sometimes lingering. Perhaps Carder's run is over.

"Where's your sister?"

"Sleeping probably. How would I know? It's not like I live with her."

"No?"

"No! I live next door. Oh, but you haven't been! You must come. It's close by. Get this: when sis and I were little, we were given miniature castles. We'd play in them all day long, a few wars, but mostly horses, fashion, princes. We pledged when we grew up we'd have real, neighboring castles each with powerful kings, and we'd stand upon the turrets and have tea together even while staying in our own castles. And..." she looks sideways as satisfaction ignites in her face, "...now we live, not in castles, of course, but in the penthouses of neighboring buildings. We can actually have dinner together, sort of, while each on our own rooftop terrace!"

"And, do you?"

"Mm-hmm!" she affirms. "Isn't that too much? Neither has a king, but part of our dream came true."

Dickens-like imagery of rotting wedding cakes near cobwebs and broken clocks push aside Claudette's disclosure that her sister's husband, Gavin, is *not* a king.

She continues, "You should come see Fardor."

"Huh?"

"My home. Fardor—in spite of its name, it's actually not far at all."

"Does your sister's place have a name as well."

"Niirdor. But her place is more like Mordor ever since she gave Sauron residence."

Carder remembers the Vivienne girls' obsession with Tolkien and all things elf, which provides a vague awareness of her cryptic revelations.

"Haika says the way we've named our homes is annoying and scary. But only twins could understand. Anyway, I love Haika for saying things like that." She slows down to a walk, "Card, I've got a question..." she waits for the affirming raise of Carder's eyebrows, "Where do your funds come from?"

"Funds?"

"Ours are oil. We weren't like Gavin's family. They have their hands in everything: television, media, toys, a couple of pickle products. They amassed so much while stretching themselves thin. Don't ever get Gavin started unless you want an earful about gherkins or action figures. But how did you get your funds?"

Carder laughs. "I didn't."

"You haven't had it long *enough* or *too* long? Wait. Are you new money?"

"I haven't had any at all—no fortune of any kind. I scrape by every month. Last time I checked, I had $537 in the bank."

Claudette is gobsmacked. Several times a week she walks the bridge among the lower and middle classes, but never purposefully alongside an *active* member. If Haika hadn't made it clear that Carder is an artist, Claudette would've immediately untangled herself from him, but art is elusive, perhaps even more so than love. It has no rules, and seems in its purest form to run amok without regard for money or rank. That places art far from Claudette's understanding, which also makes it dangerously appetizing. There's a twitch in her stomach. In that split second, her assessment of Carder travels light years, rocketing from appeal to abhorrence until it lands laser-like on the surface of adoration. She wants to eat crumpets with him atop her roof—actual crumpets—as they giggle across the way at Doe. The picture is full in her mind.

Carder observes this inner-blast-off and subsequent return to stratosphere, with no understanding of what it represents. "Does that bother you?" he asks.

"Of course not. Don't tell me you have Starving Artist Syndrome. You've got something against money?"

"It may have something against me."

"Then, that's the problem. Don't agonize over it. I'm sure you're on the cusp."

"The cusp?"

"My sister and I use visualization techniques. They'll change your life." She waits for him to ask about her about them.

Below them, traffic swarms in two conflicting directions on the bridge, cars pushing, honking, fighting in pinched stops and starts—mostly to get into Manhattan.

"Can I ask you something?" Carder ventures.

"Please."

"Haika and I recently made a trip to Pennsylvania and brought my niece to visit. Mandy and I were close throughout her childhood, even though I didn't see her much. We wrote, talked on the phone, chatted online. A lot. It felt like we were close anyway."

"Didn't you see her much?"

"I don't like leaving the city—"

"As a rule, I never even go above 14th Street."

"—and I never forgave my sister for telling everyone at my mother's funeral that mom wouldn't be going to heaven."

"You never said your mother was evil!"

"No… *no*! Perhaps she overlooked some things she shouldn't have, but there wasn't a rotten bone in her body. My sister believes hardly anyone reaches heaven. Anyway, we got into an argument at my mother's funeral. Something right out of a Mexican soap opera, only missing the humor. I'm a no-drama guy, but I was heartbroken. That experience added to the growing list of reasons not to see one another, not to leave the city. Now, my predicament: my niece is seventeen and aloof. I can't reach her the way I used to."

"You're such a good uncle." Claudette brushes her hand against Carder's as they walk, but it's so slight, he's not sure it happened.

"How long will she be visiting?"

"I thought it would be a few weeks, but she hasn't mentioned leaving."

"She'll come around. If she hasn't seen you in years, then all the letters and online chatting in the world aren't going to replace physicality. There's nothing like being with another person physically. But you're kind to care. Once I meet Mandy, I'll have more suitable suggestions. In the meantime, I know this might sound crazy, but visualize her treating you the way you want. That's what I do: I picture the people that I wish were doing things…" she pulls her t-shirt away from her torso, inadvertently revealing a small mole before it snaps back, "…doing them. Look! Here we are."

She motions to the mouth of the stairs leading down onto the island of Manhattan. They've walked the majority of the bridge together.

She continues, "You should come to Fardor."

"You live on Manhattan?"

"I do. But like I said, Fardor isn't a far door from here. I've a book to loan you—*Lip Thinking*—the one I mentioned about self-talk visualization techniques. I'm sure it'll help you. You need to come. Seriously! Take a few minutes and pick it up!"

She slides her little hand into his, making him feel like a beast in need of taming. They descend a couple of steps until Carder sees a triangle of Manhattan concrete poking out like woman's panties from a too-short skirt.

A few blocks. That's all. A few blocks away from *Lip Thinking* and all of the other modes of communication lips take. Carder senses desire swimming in Claudette, ready to break through. He could go… but can't. He hasn't been to Manhattan in years and while it's true he's going there later that day with Haika, he can't let this be his first step.

He pulls his hand from Claudette's and turns around, backing up the stairs to face Brooklyn while sweat seeps through wet ringlets on his forehead.

"I can't today. I'm sorry."

Claudette's face flares disappointment but she covers it with smiling lips which Carder won't be tasting. "Well, let me meet this niece of yours. And I want to talk to you about possible painting lessons."

"For me?"

"*From* you! Or is that beneath an artist like you?"

Carder laughs. "By the way, which do you want to be called: Claudette or *that Vivienne girl?* I want to know."

"I don't care."

"Which?"

"I really don't care! You want to package my sister and me together? Fine by me. Actually, calling me a Vivienne girl would probably make it easier all around, as everyone will know who you're referring to, seeing as that's what they use themselves."

"It might narrow it down to two, except no one will know which one I mean."

"I don't care. I got over that long ago. It's yawn-worthy. Some people believe we're robots!"

"Are you?" He almost begins regretting his decision not to join her.

"I suspect."

"Do you even care that *I* know which one of you I'm talking about?"

Claudette bites her bottom lip. "Not really. My sister and I've accomplished more as a unified pair than we ever would have on our own. I was the only one who could have helped her through her eating disorder. And I would never have gotten through university without her. You sure you don't want to come pick that book up, Carder? I'm sure things would start happening the second you start applying its principles—it might be pretty immediate."

"Not now. I'm as interested as anyone in becoming a millionaire, but I don't have time today. I'm going to check out Haika's art gallery."

"Then call me to discuss painting lessons," she says, descending the rest of the stairs to set foot on Manhattan. "I'm serious! I need your guidance!"

She's gone.

The rest of the run is exhilarating. Getting as close to Manhattan as he did, seeing that small bit of concrete, gives Carder confidence. Satisfaction makes him feel almost as though he's done exactly what he hasn't: gotten laid. He runs back across the bridge with the knowledge that he can and will return to Manhattan—the land of death.

16

A FLOWER IN THE IRON FOREST

Haika juggles eggs as if she has an audience. Their yolky contents soon spit and bubble in an oiled skillet. She does have an audience: Mike Fiore sits at the nearby breakfast nook. His stomach applauds in anticipation, but the rest of him pays attention to a small television barking highlights of a ball game. A panel of men dissects the winner's victory, expounding on what it means for all New Yorkers. Mike is ecstatic, proud of his team and feeling celebratory.

As Haika grates parmesan over scrambling eggs, she reflects on the day ahead. She'll be accompanying Carder into the city, taking him to her art gallery, then dinner and a Broadway show. Questioning why one would sign on for this mess is beyond her, yet she's done it, and hopes she'll see some small shape of satisfaction by the time it's over. If only it were all as simple as a ball game. But offense and defense are abstract in her situation. Even what constitutes scoring is muddled.

She stops to take a bite of carrot. Ah, the hated carrot—that coral-colored cone delivering beta-carotene when all one wants is nicotine—but Haika's nasty smoking-habit must surrender.

"These eggs are worth the extra money. Every bite," she says. She and Mike have been having a conversation in stops and starts, interrupted by the blathering television and Mike's short attention span. She picks up where she'd earlier left off, "Thing is, Carder hasn't been to Manhattan in years, almost a decade, I think. Since his mother died. The events of 9/11 didn't help."

Mike's eyes stay on the TV, but commercials allow him to respond while images of chewy-gooey-chocolaty diet cookies blur onscreen from six different perspectives. "Why do you need to go with him?"

"Because he probably wouldn't make it off the train if I weren't there. I'm offering support. Carder amazes me, because as stunted and scared as he appears, he actually makes changes with a little encouragement."

"You'll be missing the martini party at Jen's."

"You're kidding! What a shame," she says with biting sarcasm. "But it's kind of romantic: you're that invested in the ruination of my liver. Well, Mikey, I beat you to that long ago!"

Parties, parties, parties. Haika is sick of them. They bring together as many self-absorbed people as possible and push them into obliterating themselves with alcohol and anti-depressants to make the whole affair less excruciating.

Grated parmesan cheese melts into pulled threads. Haika stretches the stringiness with a spatula, reminding her of what taffy-pullers from her childhood did on a grander scale, slapping pastel taffy with bare hands over the wood pegs of their street stalls. Her mother had insisted taffy was dirty, so Haika had never tasted it. The next time she returns to Puerto Vallarta—whenever that is—she'll indulge and see if sweat from their hands adds to the salty sweetness. Next time—she tells herself, preparing Mike's cheesy meal. When is next time? Years away, maybe decades. When their mother passed away and left Iris to run the Inn, there was no more reason to visit. Yet, a wave of homesickness for a home long written-off hits Haika as she determines the eggs are taking too long to cook.

"I'm starving over here," says Mike—but he isn't done. "Carder's a grown man. It's not your job to be his guru."

"Are you saying you want me to stay home, or to go out with you to drown in martinis? If that's what you're asking, just say it. Besides, I like Carder. And not to worry, Mr. Fiore, you'll be fine with Carder and this entire situation once you see his paintings."

"I'm not asking you to stay, but do you think no one wonders what you're doing? Jen's going to be disappointed. Deb and Carly have already asked when they're going to meet the Unabomber. They heard about him from the Vivienne girls. Gavin said he'd worry I was being made a cuckold of if Carder weren't such a dweeb."

"That's ridiculous. Carder's the furthest thing from a dweeb. On the other hand, Gavin's a vulgar ass and—"

"He's my best friend."

"Your best friend's a crass dunce projecting his own motives. I'm not Gavin, and you should be thankful for that. And just because Carder isn't obsessed with jumping through social hoops held by circus girls, it doesn't make him the Unabomber. But then, I'd love for Deb and Carly to meet the Unabomber as soon as possible. If you only knew how much!"

"And how long can training the damn dog take? Please. If I'd known how long and laborious this process would be, I would've…"

"What?"

"…would've stuffed a cork up the dog's ass and called it a day."

Haika closes her eyes, shaking her head, and starts laughing. The eggs are now soft yellow clouds.

"What?" a red-faced Mike asks her.

"It's just…" she pauses, "…I've thought of exactly the same thing."

They both look at the oversized fishbowl goblet sitting on the counter, filled with every cork from every wine bottle of the last year.

They laugh together.

"You know I love you," he says reaching for her.

"Are you talking to me or the Yankees?" Haika says, bringing the skillet to scrape breakfast onto his plate. "I know you do, hon." And she does know. Mike loves her as best he knows how. "Now eat your eggs, your majesty."

She waits until the mix of the nutty-flavored parmesan and chives brings contentment to his tongue, then says, "Mikey, Carder is my friend. I'm going. You can take the dog to the martini party for all I care. And," she grabs a cork from the glass bowl and sets it on the table, "you can use this cork on Jen. Oh, and one for Carly, another for Deb. Stuff them in whichever orifices are most convenient."

Mike's and Haika's fights, always short-lived and unclear, dress comfortably—in elastic waistbands and sensible fabrics that breathe—anything to distract from what's hidden within. The very things Mike loved about Haika eventually led to his contempt. She's strained for years to peer behind the diversions into what the arguments are actually about, and while she's gotten better at it over the years, she cares much less than she used to. Time washed away concern. Until recently, Haika considered it a sign of a well-worn relationship and nothing more. Either way, she knows after this small exchange with Mike that if she proceeds to take Carder to Manhattan, the following week will be hell. But see, she's been to hell, knows its terrain and journeys into it regardless of the flames. And while she's there, she plans on dancing.

Carder's nervousness changes several hues as they ride the F train through the guts of Manhattan. For a while his anxiety manifests in small observations about poster advertisements. His chuckling sentences trail off before ending, pointing out artificial colors: there's Orange Peel-3, Vanilla Ghost, Mustard Gas. Even when he's quiet, he scoffs at Manhattan as though he has a personal vendetta against the city, a score to settle. Haika is happy with his reactions—they're keeping him from passing out.

Carder's hair is gelled into a mess, his eyes covered with aviator sunglasses. A plain white t-shirt hangs baggy from his broad shoulders over faded jeans and flip-flops, and a jacket is wrenched in his hands. Haika assures Carder he can wear anything he wants, anytime, anywhere, for the rest of his life as long as he realizes he's an artist. All he has to do is own it. Carder's already pale skin grows paler and the train rocks-and-shoots-and-rocks-and-shoots from station to station. The train is bloated with passengers and humid with body-warmed air.

"I hate Manhattan." Carder says as if he's in physical pain.

"I've surmised that much, Mr. Quevedo. What did—"

"Manhattan, the whore."

The hint of aggression takes Haika aback. It isn't directed at her, but she doesn't want to coddle it into becoming behemoth. This day calls for strategic caution. "That's a bit misogynistic. Care to fuck off?"

"The gender doesn't matter. She could be a male whore."

"Well, so what then, Carder? Manhattan's a whore. Who cares? Are you afraid of a city giving pleasure so easily?"

"It's not the pleasure bugging me. It's the cost." And then, as though realizing their conversation could apply to real-life prostitution, he inquires, "Don't you think they need to gain some self-respect? I'd hate for anyone I know to get mixed up in that scene. I've seen too many situations at the hospital and don't want them in my world."

"If you've seen them in the hospital or walking down the street, then they *are* in your world. Regardless of how you feel about them, they're there. And ignoring them or not walking down the streets they sell their goods on doesn't erase them."

"Crime. Riff-raff. Disease. Don't you feel that what they do is wrong?"

"Riff-raff?" She laughs at the term. "And I fail to see how the morality of the situation matters. Right, wrong, why be so obsessed? The situation exists either way, so any action to alleviate the problem by helping a person is worth a million times more than any pronouncements of judgment. Those pronouncements are usually made while sitting on one's ass, far away from the situation. Look, I'm not saying I want anyone to sell themselves and I'm not applauding it, but it happens."

The subway doors close. They've successfully passed another station.

This is good. Keep going. Almost there—she thinks. "I knew this girl, Venita Hurr, back in Puerto Vallarta who'd dole out blow-jobs on the beach to American tourists. She'd had a hard life, went from a rich, spoiled girl, to a parentless teenager on the street. If she was hungry, I fed her. If she needed to talk, I listened. And sometimes I let her wash at the Inn. What does right and wrong have to do with it?"

"Where is she now?"

"Last I heard, she was saving up to get sex reassignment surgery. She'd always felt she was born into a female body though actually male."

"That's crazy. I don't know how I'd deal with someone like that."

"Love."

"—the complications. It would be so confusing and..."

"Complicated for that person, sure maybe. Complicated for us? No. I'm thankful *I* wasn't born having to sort that out, but love pretty much answers every question."

"So she might now be a man doling out blow jobs on the

beach?"

"I don't think blow jobs on the beach were her life's plan. Last she'd told me she'd eventually change her name to Benjamin. I wonder what he's doing now. I don't even know how I'd find him if I went back."

"One question: Do you talk as much about New York while in Mexico as you talk about Mexico in New York?"

"Shut up!" She punches him gently on the shoulder.

"When's the last time you were there?"

"Eight years or so. After my parents died and I got married, I had no reason to return."

"Not even for your sister?"

"She's resourceful. Doesn't need me."

Maybe Manhattan is a whore after all—thinks Haika. Truth be told, she feels at home amidst its gunk and odor. New York City seems to operate at light speed, which is taxing, but somewhere within the constant shuffle of opening and closing storefronts, restaurants and subway doors are the elusive muses of art, theater and music—too easily missed and too soon forgotten in other locales. The City demands her residents live with dynamic energy. Sure, perhaps she drains them of money and life-force, but she drains just enough that they remain vital, stowing them away for later nourishment. Manhattan isn't choosy. She's willing to eat the goulash of the ultra-rich and the poor, of the dirty-faced man sitting on cardboard across from the posh spa and the woman in a white robe inside waiting for her massage. It's as confusing and comforting as anything Haika's ever experienced. She never fully understood it and has given up trying.

Bing-bong! It's their stop. 23rd Street. And what do you know, Carder is still alive.

The afternoon sky is a newspaper with one wadded up cloud tossed to the horizon. It's the kind of hot but dreary day that makes Southerners long for Miami and Londoners glad they've come upon such pleasant weather, a day that makes people pine for the city they consider most beautiful: that day in Denver, that month in Paris, that morning in Montreal.

Haika and Carder cross several avenues before reaching the

neighborhood with the hot-ticket art galleries. Carder deals better above ground. They walk off the beaten path, south to 20th Street to reduce interaction with crowds and cars. Haika questions her decision to squeeze so many events into one day for the toll it might take on Carder's psyche.

This day is a big one for both parties. In the back of Haika's mind, a decision awaits: how will she dive into that evening's prime task? Time is running out and she feels dirty plotting it out.

"How long have you worked at your gallery?" Carder asks as they cross 8th Avenue.

"Seven years. I've only owned it for four. It's been an interesting ride. The art world is insane. Even among creativity, bitterness and greed know no bounds. The elitism is unreal, the showiness, the..." She catches herself before launching any further into a self-defeating tirade.

With each step, a sleeker, more self-assured Haika emerges. She's at home among art and its culture. It's her natural environment. Haika has a talent for foretelling hat clients want before they know it themselves. She turns the knob on their pre-conceived notions, messes with the picture, chips away and adds to it until the viewers see something refreshing—or disconcerting—but either way, something they'll see something that *must be taken home*. If Haika has learned anything in her years selling art, it's that everyone wants a new world, though most want to stay outside the frame. Haika guides wealthy voyeurs to the most obscure parts of Wonderland, the parts that Alice either didn't know of or didn't dare speak about: the backrooms and alleys, the underbelly, the closed doors, the speakeasies, the juke joints. She shows them Wonderland's Wonderland.

Upon passing 10th Avenue, the surroundings become a flipbook of galleries. They pass the Suji Gallery which displays a conglomeration of street trash in shades of red that form an elephantine trash heap heart. Haika notices Carder looking at the woman working inside. Despite eyebrows permanently raised in consideration, the woman seems lonely, isolated, annoyed. Frown lines which were once tiny streams are now canyons.

Haika waves to her as they pass the Suji window. "Hello, Violet."

The woman inside nods and her eyebrows fly further north as her gaze sails out like a bird, dropping judgment on Carder.

Haika looks up at a simple building of concrete and glass. "The Camp Fountain Gallery is on the fourth floor."

"Not street level?"

"No. As you'll notice, the Morrow-Lemmon Gallery has that spot." Her voice slips into the refined, professional tone. Originally, she'd disdained what some call her quasi-European accent but soon found that Americans assume an exotic education comes with it and so she emphasizes it while in the gallery. While the accent is almost imperceptible, it places Haika in an automatic category of refinement and she uses it to her advantage. "Our reputation and the quality of work allows us to house the gallery in a location one can't merely trip into from the sidewalk. One doesn't come to Camp Fountain by chance."

Carder looks bewildered. "You never struck me as a salesman before."

"I like to think of it as being a secret agent for art. There's a whole association of us." She doesn't reveal the pang she feels being termed salesman, and determines that she'll kick it down a notch in Carder's presence.

Haika stripped the Knusper Gallery of its name four years prior when Mike helped her purchase it. Martin Knusperhäuschen was a sticky man whom Haika assumed bled hi-fructose corn syrup. His breath reeked of Almond Roca candies and his dandruff was sugar.

"I vant to return to Milan and find de blossoming young vermin for vife. Enough of dees New York nasty vermin," he'd say.

Haika admired that Mr. Knusperhäuschen recognized his martial possibilities head-on. Unlike the vermin in New York City, the vermin in Milan probably scurried to meet his plane due to his championing of an Italian popstar who painted blue, postage stamp-sized squares touted as "minuscule depictions of vast oceans and endless skies." Meanwhile, Haika accepted Mike's financial help in combination with an inheritance from her mother to acquire the gallery. She wasted no time washing the keys to the doors, peeling away all references to Knusperhäuschen, and burning a sage smudge to remove his energy. Her only regret was taking Mike's help.

Though she'd repaid him—with interest—she couldn't free herself from Mike's coil. He invited people to his gallery shows. It was the subject of their most raging arguments, but Mike never relinquished bragging rights and never stopped asking how things are at *his* gallery.

The gallery space is large and echoey. Sound bounces off the concrete floor to the ceiling and walls.

"I named it after a campground my sister and made-up one summer so we could make a road trip to Mexico City. We had to get Iris away from her boyfriend. He wanted to deflower her and our father loved the guy, thought he was perfect because he had money, machismo and said all the right things, but she was way too young— still in high school. Now, why don't you take a look around while I check in with Tino."

She walks to a desk where a slim young man with delicate cheek bones sits. Hazel eyes sop up the olive oil of his skin. He straightens up, manufacturing a smile.

They hug.

Kiss-kiss.

"Gargoyle-guy?" Tino asks.

"Hush up. I'll introduce you," Haika says with tilted head. "First, tell me about your date. As hot as the online photos?" She's watching Carder instead of meeting Tino's eyes. "Seriously, tell me about the date," she says through her teeth, waiting for Carder to acclimate to his surroundings.

It doesn't matter what Tino says. Haika's not listening. He rattles off something about about leather, harnesses, patty melts, space stations and corrugated metal.

Haika is in awe of Carder's swift immersion in the current show: *The Cleft House by Alex Date.* The collected oil paintings were inspired by the short eight-year life of the artist's younger brother, born nine weeks premature with weak lungs and a cleft palette not easily repaired. Alex Date spent years entertaining his homebound brother and memorialized them with paintings in which the residents' faces are fluid and free.

Carder starts his viewing at a painting of a childhood scene: a mother is literally crying her face off into a handkerchief while toys cover her feet and the living room floor from wall-to-wall. The subjects are perfect, photographic in color and scientific in rendering except for their faces.

As concerned with the method of presentation as she is with the art, Haika split the gallery's rooms into four themes representing the artist's experience: Wonder, Pain, Laughter, and Grief. At first, Alex Date was opposed, not wanting to untie emotions from one another. It isn't as if one day was painful and the other a hilarious romp. No, emotions were stranded together on an island, fending for themselves and fighting for dominance. Grief and wonder warmed their hands at the same fire, while pain chopped wood and laughter read a trashy novel, sunbathing. Alex Date didn't want the emotions separated.

"A perfectly valid point," Haika said, and thus proposed that the areas bleed into one another via subtle color changes on the gallery walls and hand-painted faux wallpaper. Its faded patterns resembled clefts here, roses there. The cleft face was a rose, the rose a cleft face.

By the opening night party, in a small way Haika felt she'd helped Alex Date represent all children leading unsymmetrical lives. Not everyone who attended the show felt the same. Some perceived the gallery's alteration as gimmicky and distracting. One critic, unconcerned with the history of the artist or paintings, called it "blank-faced, utilitarian and characterless." Haika didn't care. Those who respond to the art do so in a visceral way, and those simply investing once the artist gains notoriety, call for guidance months or years down the road.

Carder strolls in contemplation toward an enormous painting—*Jettison III*—in which a blurring, caped superhero flying into a white sky holds a suffocating blue baby. Her arms melt into the child, her blue-grey tresses spiral down into the landscape.

Carder turns to Haika with his hands stuffed in the pockets of the confederate sack coat he'd bought in Gettysburg. "People buy stuff like this?"

"It's already sold, Doll. A man from Parsippany. A judge. He had…"

Haika's vibrating cell phone interrupts them. She grabs for her suit jacket, snatching and silencing the phone. Nothing is more important than Carder's reaction to the gallery. Nothing. But the name flashing on phone screen startles her. It's one she hasn't seen in years.

[IRIS]

Haika's stomach leaps. "Carder, I'm so sorry, will you be okay while I take this call?" She taps on the phone.

"Of course." He says it as though she's being ridiculous.

Tino will take over. He always provides a flirty element to the Camp Fountain Gallery, specializing in *new money*, corralling women whose prior experiences with visual art are tied to poster shops at shopping malls. Before leaving Camp Fountain, they're making their first purchase of authentic art.

"Tino…" she gestures to Tino as if pushing him toward Carder.

"I don't see what I need…"

He can also be a bitch.

"Tino!"

She rushes out the gallery, down four floors, looking at her cell phone, rechecking the call history as the elevator descends.

[IRIS]

She lights up the cell phone screen to double-check.

[IRIS]

Any other flower would be preferable: Posey, Pansy, Lavender. Even a cactus. A thistle. But only one plant is Haika's sister: Iris. Not now!

Haika exits the building into the back alley where the gallery workers often go for breaks. She reaches into a purse so small it would barely accommodate a pack of cigarettes and pulls out a pack of cigarettes. They were purchased specifically to give her courage later that evening. Carrots won't suffice. Whatever has prompted Iris's call requires nicotine as a part of the overall experience, possibly other poisons as well. Haika can't recall the last time they spoke. Years. Their roads diverged so far it's difficult to imagine rejoining them. Miles, borders, and oceans generally provide enough obstacles to make effort unnecessary. Still, she has to return the call. There's no sense in guessing the reason her sister is reaching out.

Things with Iris are never as obvious as they seem.

She dials, waiting for the connection to Puerto Vallarta to take the extra time it always does. Surprise—no lag time. Haika envisions her sister, bent at the waist, leaning over the front desk of the Come Stay Inn, her breasts spreading across the desktop, all her weight on her stomach, in order to reach the phone without leaving the spot she's standing in. Haika can all but hear the *brr-Ring, brr-Ring* of the old, green telephone. Iris will be in a tiny t-shirt, chewing gum and fanning her chest with one of the wicker fans they keep in the front left desk drawer, along with the service bell they removed from the countertop after a guest complained about the attached note: *Please do not ring bell.* Haika prepares to hear the Mexican sunshine warming the phone it seeps through. *Brr-Ring, brr-Ring.*

Carder has conflicting opinions about *The Cleft House*. He's half-embarrassed for Alex Date, who created these oddities, parading their nakedness in public, courting misunderstanding and mockery. However, the other half of Carder is fascinated, almost to a dogmatic degree. Though he doesn't grasp exactly what the artist experienced, the paintings don't need explanation. They reach him in precisely the way language doesn't—revealing intricate riches despite the harsh circumstances that inspired them.

The gallery door opens behind Carder, pulling air. Footsteps shuffle, and a voice speaks. It's Haika's voice but stretched and sanded—as though she speaks through tufts of cotton.

"She done good for herself."

Carder and Tino turn to the voice at the same time, then to one another, then to the body emitting the voice. A maniacal laugh of disbelief pops from Tino.

Standing just inside the door is Haika, but not. It's a version of Haika who, leaving the gallery only ten minutes before, has been to Oz and back. The door closes behind her long, frizzy hair, a Haika with a triangle of three moles on one cheek and red-framed sunglasses. She takes a few slow steps forward in high, wooden heels with leather straps winding up her calves.

After a pause, Tino laughs again.

"What?" The voice asks. The new version of Haika speaks with a slight Mexican accent, acting puzzled.

Tino's professional posture melts into that of a boy standing at an ice cream truck, blown away by a new flavor. "What the 'H' happened to you?" he inquires.

"Got in from a long flight. What the *Jesus H* happen to you?" She surveys Tino. "What happen to you?" she repeats. "Look like you been dipped in lotion too long, like a fetus. You have a sister who make you play beauty salon?"

As absorbing as *The Cleft House* is, not-Haika immediately monopolizes the room. She has the strangest accent—unplaceable, straddling several countries.

"So this is what mommy's money got her? She—always the big-city girl with weird art. But you know what, Fetus?" she addresses Tino. "She never no good at art herself, so she go and marry rich. That way, she can Pimp other people's art. Where is she?"

In seconds, Tino's face jumps from hilarity to shock to outrage to understanding. "Ms. Haus stepped out for a moment. May I ask your name?"

A magnet in the floor moves Carder forward and he extends his hand. "Welcome Iris. It's wonderful to meet you. I'm Haika's friend, Carder Quevedo. I'm sure Tino here meant no offense. We just weren't expecting you. And with you two being identical twins… you caught us off guard."

Iris slowly reveals a broad smile which includes one tooth covered entirely in Trans Am gold. She removes her sunglasses and finally meets Carder's hand. Her skin is drier, rougher.

"An all-American gentleman. I'm sorry. I meant nothing by it. It's just… a man so handsome as this Tino." She turns to Tino. "You so pretty a girl just wants to ugly you up, even if just with words. Forgive me, my sweet fetus." Her eyelashes flutter. "Didn't Haika say I called?"

"When did you call?"

"Cinco minutos. Maybe ten."

"Oh," Tino chimes, "I think she went outside to return the call."

A salsa song begins to blare from the purple leather purse hanging from Iris's shoulder. Her phone doesn't doesn't just ring, it dances. "Ay! You right. She did." She ignores the call, assessing the gallery. "What the world does this kooky girl got hanging? I got to see."

While she wanders around from painting to painting, Carder attempts to explain what he knows to Tino—that Haika and Iris haven't seen each other in a long while, several years from what he's gathered. He also knows she runs an Inn down in Puerto Vallarta.

Tino whispers, "I didn't even know Haika has siblings."

"What happen to their faces?" Iris mutters to herself, absorbing the paintings.

Her suitcase, incidentally colored in Sky-Baked Blue sits towering on its side near the entrance. Just behind it, Haika approaches the glass doors, straightening her blouse and smoothing her hair before entering.

"I've never seen identical twins so different," Tino whispers to Carder as Haika walks in. "She looks like her closet suffered a bad case of food poisoning."

Hearing only the last part of his observation, Haika reprimands, "Tino. Shh!" When close enough, she tells Carder under her breath, "Contrary to popular belief it's often those dressed most quixotically that buy. Prada and Burberry buy if they bring someone to impress, but people like this…" She seems to suddenly realize Carder's calm. "What did you think of this show, Carder? Be honest."

"The longer we're here, the more I'm enjoying it. It's far more interesting than what's at the museums."

"You're witnessing art closer to the womb. Their blood has just started pumping, their hearts beating on their own."

Carder understands. These paintings, like his, are alive. Each could expand or wilt at any moment. Tremulous and ferocious, these paintings convey memories more richly than photographs, capturing layers that elude the physical world.

"How are you doing, Miss?" Haika calls, crossing the gleaming floor to the woman perusing the section called Pain.

The woman doesn't turn to Haika, but stares at the show's most visionary piece *The Patron Saint of Typhoon Brenda*.

"You would have to explain to me. I don't quite know what I see. This loco lady in the picture—what's she after?"

"Your English has gotten worse instead of better," Haika says without a hint of surprise except for the crumpled tissue she drops.

"You know I always said I only speak two languages: broken Spanish and broken English. Three if you count German, but that's…"

"…broken even when spoken properly," Haika finishes. She squeals in a way that only women can, grabbing Iris. They turn to one another, embracing and crying like distorted reflections no longer separated by glass.

"Fuck you, bitch!" Haika cries.

Iris laughs, "Bitch, fuck you!" She picks up the crumpled tissue Haika dropped and blows her nose. "My sweet Haikita, you never have changed."

They hug, one touching the other's cheek, one tugging the other's necklace. Chuckling, crying, sighing. Walking arm-in-arm around the gallery, they whisper into one another's ears as though knowing only the language of secrets. It's a sight Carder will remember for the rest of his life, and it's one of the rare times he knows that while it's actually happening. There's a happy recognition in Haika's face, one he's never seen before. They're children again, girls who smeared blackberries in each other's faces.

When they circle back around, Haika is in subdued recovery, sniffling, wiping any uncried tears from the corners of her eyes.

"Carder, why didn't you guys tell me Iris was here?"

"It was an amazing event to watch. I wasn't going to interfere."

Tino places the palms of his hands flat on the granite counter, "I was honestly worried I was having a bad acid trip. And I've never done acid."

"I know a guy who can get it!" Iris exclaims, but then realizes, "… but he's back in Mexico."

The twisted faces on the paintings surrounding them no longer seem absurd on any level. *The Patron Saint of Typhoon Brenda* hangs her oil-painted head behind them, her back to a swirling storm. She's either caught a live mosquito between her hands or clasps them in prayerful plea for the scene in the gallery before her.

17

BREAD & BUTTER

Carder suspected by the time he was seven years old, and concluded decisively by ten, that not everyone has access to multiple universes. His hunch was that most people have the skill ripped in half by some astral ticket-taker as the price of admission to adulthood. Not Carder. His ticket wasn't torn. And while he didn't exactly get the better deal, he got the more extensive one. He learned to downplay that in others' company, advertising it only with the paintings that serve as visual bread crumbs. It was neither topic for conversation nor subject of regret. People had been ruining his life in *this* world for so long, he knew far better than to invite them into another. Yet, there's a growing disquiet in *that* world, a building hunger there, for what, he's unsure—perhaps for more than death.

A woman at the table next to them wears a necklace of beads colored in Mint-Lint 1-B, diverting Carder's attention from the buzzing restaurant dining room filled with theater-goers and tourists. "Family-style Italian" is made manifest with robust voices and the passing of oversized dishes, which might have hampered the organic flow of conversation between Carder, Haika and Mandy, if there were any to hamper.

Haika clearly wants a cigarette. Her fingers search for something to hold, her eyes squint as though conjuring an imaginary flame to light her fantasy smoke, and her lips purse, punctuated as if already holding its soft weight. Alas, no prize—smoking has been banned in all city establishments.

Surprisingly, Manhattan isn't the Manhattan that swallowed Carder's mother, no longer a place seeded in a forest of porn shops and tattoo parlors. While Carder remains convinced that Manhattan is still a hooker, perhaps hookers themselves have changed. In her current appearance, she could've been drawn at an animation studio: cleaned up with a tiny impossible waist and large, empty eyes, now like a perfect computer rendering, missing the dirtiness of natural reality. The closer to Times Square they'd travelled, the more that buildings lost their edges and the sidewalks their black gum-spots. And now, here they are sitting, chewing their food in anticipation of an overproduced Broadway show. Carder wonders if live commercials are played during performances yet.

Haika exhales unseen exhaust from an invisible cigarette. The manner of her meltdown is noiseless, her mind far removed, contradictory to her usual personality. Silverware scrapes porcelain and Nebraskan women nearby snicker and whoop at Nebraskan jokes, which are funnier when ricocheting off East coast chinaware. But the third woman sitting at their table doesn't laugh. She sits, watching them eat.

Carder blinks, watching Mandy sitting in her stupor. You'd think she'd have more excitement for this cosmopolitan adventure. Aren't a person's first dinner and Broadway show considered landmarks in life? Don't they introduce women to the grand, disappointing events of the rest of their lives? Mandy spends so much time watching television, perhaps she's only used to events in other peoples' lives. She leans forward, as if searching the restaurant for anything interesting, holding on to the seat of her chair, shoulders pushed up in a frozen shrug—displaying boredom with self-important flair. The cherry lip-gloss Carder bought her, which she had loved years before, has been allowed to roll under the edge of her plate, betrayed for a twenty dollar lipstick. At least she'd arrived at the restaurant on time. While Carder didn't want Mandy to ride the subway alone, it was too hard justifying his concern, took too much energy to rail against her independence. But she arrived intact and, judging from her face, unimpressed.

All the same, this meal will have conversation. Whether Haika and Rabbit participate or Carder ends up blathering a monologue, words will come from at least one mouth.

He turns to Rabbit.

"So, Rab-*Mandy*... this is the outfit you chose? Pretty spiffy."

"Thanks for the funds, Unc. It's cool, eh? Never was one for frills."

"I guessed that from the camouflage jacket. Let me see the skirt."

"The pant leg. I didn't get a skirt."

She pulls a leg—covered in navy blue sequined pants—from under the tablecloth which matches her white sneakers. Her sleeveless t-shirt and camouflage army jacket further confuse her fashion goals.

"Would you wear this to the Hall of Justice?" Haika asks.

"I'd def not wear this to Kingdom Hall, if that's what you mean."

"Regardless, your style's totally hardcore." Without missing a beat, Haika motions to the waiter for more wine and continues, "Dollface, show him what you chose for your neck. And don't stress out, Carder, this was my gift to her."

With a finger, Mandy showcases the necklace chaining a tiny sterling silver handgun to her neck. The gun is perfectly proportioned to cockroaches, were they able to set foreleg on it. A diamond plugs the gun's muzzle.

"I hope that thing's not real," Carder says.

"If it were," Haika replies sarcastically, "it would use the world's smallest bullets." She knows he meant the diamond.

Pride skulks behind Mandy's eyes. A sign of life. "Now, I *would* wear this necklace to Kingdom Hall. Beneath my high-necked dress of course. No one would know but me."

The wine arrives again, easing everyone further. Haika allows Rabbit to sip, telling her if they were anywhere else in the world she'd be drinking her own glass.

"One question, Haika—why did you bring us here?" Carder asks, attempting to bring Haika's pre-occupied soul back to her body.

"For dinner." She lets the words fall where they will, not realizing her laissez-faire attitude conveys anxiety.

"What's wrong?"

"Wrong? Nothing. It's cold in here."

"Is Iris's unexpected arrival bothering you?"

"No. Sort of. Maybe." She tries buttering her bread, but the butter is cold and hard. She pulls the bread apart in chunks. It will remain butterless. "It's definitely cold in here. I ordered lasagna to warm myself up. For its temperature! Ridiculous!" She laughs. "Iris. God, Iris! You gotta hand it to that girl—never been dull, but, yes, I'm wondering as much as you are."

"Why she's here?"

"…why she's here. Look," Haika turns to Mandy, "and this is just between us, but I honestly never thought I'd see her again, or, I knew I'd see her again, but at a hospital or some family ceremony—her daughter's wedding."

"She has kids?"

"No—and knowing Iris that means she's infertile. Small miracle. Can we stop talking about Iris? There's something more interesting I need to address." She speaks to Mandy again as though it's only the two of them. "Mandy, what do you think of your Uncle's art?"

"It's fine."

"Isn't it? What's it like living among family history given such an otherworldly presentation?"

Mandy looks at her as though Haika's an octopus in the desert. She's slow to respond. "I dunno, it's like living in a house with a bunch of paintings hanging." She stutters, looking at Carder, "I, I—they're cool. All Unc's stuff is cool. You know that."

Lost in excitement, Haika stuffs bread in her mouth, quickly following each bite with wine as though swallowing giant pills. She continues, "They're unlike anything you've seen before, aren't they? Carder only thinks of them as childhood acquaintances, he doesn't realize the…"

Carder doesn't crawl under the table, but places his hands palm-down atop it instead. "If you get to ask us to stop talking about your sister, then I get to ask that we stop talking about my art."

Haika pulls in her lips as though she's going to slingshot the words at him. She pauses. "Have you ever been stabbed in the eye with a piece of garlic bread?" The waiter hovers around them. "Okay, fine. Here you go: I love Iris to death, but we have our issues as all siblings do. She's forever furious because my world doesn't revolve around her. I wanted to leave Puerto Vallarta. I wanted more than the beefy, teenage horn-dogs and partying tourists. I wanted out. Out to what? I don't know. But out. I didn't want to spend my life running the Inn. I left. Got an education. She didn't. She'll proudly say she's never read a book in her life. That's barely not true.

On the other hand, I pursued my passion for art while she folded sheets and cleaned pubic hair-rugs off twenty bathroom floors every day. Sorry to say that, Mandy, but it's true. Iris made the decision to stay and run the Inn with our mother after our father died, and then alone after our mother died. That's not my fault. And I don't know why she's here. I was bowled over when I saw my little-big sister at the gallery, but I'd rather not know why she's here as long as possible. Okay. Does that suffice?"

Carder and Mandy nod their heads *yes*, as the food arrives. Haika orders them two more glasses of wine and another glass of water for Carder.

She continues. "Now, Carder, I've been meaning to talk with you about something. Now that you've been to the gallery, now that you've seen the art I represent, seen that it's appreciated, revered, that its valued, accepted, and *understood* among a good number of people, I have a proposal for you."

Proposals are for loan applications, business plans and marriages. Proposals aren't something one friend makes to another, or so Carder thinks. The restaurant grows louder as the clock winds closer to Broadway's showtime. Carder can't speak, unable to turn the volume of his voice loud enough to drown everything out—right now he can't even find the knob.

Whatever's making Haika nervous has disappeared, replaced with poise and purpose. Soothing confidence somehow softens her tone even while she raises it to compete with the restaurant's hubbub. "Carder, your gargoyles are the most beautiful work I've seen in years. And I've seen a lot."

"They're private."

"I know. I understand that you're a private person. However, they're your legacy. They're your protectors."

"They're my freakin' curse."

They make the unspoken decision to pass dishes, sharing food when they're least likely to eat it.

Spooning penne onto her plate, Haika continues, "Carder, remember that day you let me come into your home? It was magical."

"What? You laughed."

"I was awestruck! It was an honor that you allowed me to see it, a privilege I'm thankful for, separate from and in addition to your friendship. It was gorgeous. Your work is precious. Priceless."

"It's—it's priceless—and now you want me to sell it?"

"I'd like you to release your work into the world. Let me use my gallery to represent you. I'll do a damn good job. No, you know what?" she briefly turns to Mandy. "I beg your pardon, but I'd do a fucking amazing job. I only say that because anything less wouldn't be accurate."

Mandy looks more and more like an actual rabbit anxiously nibbling food—her nostrils pulse and eyes dilate, ready to run.

Carder looks at Haika, who knows nothing of the Pick-Me-Pups or of the embarrassment of having one's art massacred into children's toys. First, Haika saw his circus-freak work, now Mandy, soon probably Iris, then Mike, Gavin and the Vivienne girls. Carder wants to return to his normal life: retrieving eyes from the dead and drawing maps of fantastic, nonexistent lands. He's content being left alone.

Haika places her hand on his. "Carder. Doll, you know I love you… and I'd never intentionally hurt you or open wounds, but I think showing your art will benefit you. All I'm asking is: let some of your work hang on my walls. That's all. You don't have to visit or think about them. I'd probably even finagle a way for you to get out of the opening night party if that's what you need—and that's unheard of."

Carder knows she's lying about the party, she'd let go of his hand during those words. It doesn't matter. She loves him—like a brother, or a great-uncle in a wheel-chair—but she loves him.

Haika's dress shimmers under the same lights that are cooking the room. Carder stares into Haika's eyes as wings sprout from her back. Wings aren't the only change. There's something more, something like a jewel, a pearl, something caught in her heartbeat. It hangs on the wall of her forehead: one small bead of sweat has materialized between her eyebrows like a bindi, like the flashing reset button on a computer, like truth.

"Carder," he feels the weight of Haika's sweating palm on his, "Mandy, would you bring his water closer? Carder, are you okay?"

18

PRISMS DAWN AT NIGHT

The address Darren gave doesn't match the show. Confusion quickly clears when he apologizes over the phone for not scoring tickets to The Princess Suites after all. Prices were over one hundred dollars per person, so he'd bought tickets to the next best show. Mandy is fine with it. As a child she'd loved The Princess Suites movie, but watching it five hundred times while her mother studied the Bible with Kimmy Stunnaker had gradually erased its magic. Besides, she wants adult fare.

Prisms Dawn at Night is the consolation prize. The show recently moved from Off-Broadway into an imposing Broadway theater. As is true of the recent spate of musicals, it's based on a misguided missile of a movie that's ill-suited to singing. A proud recipient of the Bradley Award, the film wasn't only known for showing the lead actor's stunning posterior, but for depicting the tale of an Egyptian immigrant woodcarver in 1904, struggling through his marriage to the crippled daughter of a pig-farmer. The surviving one of their six children goes on to become U.S. Secretary of Commerce during the 1930's and an avid cross-dresser in private. This unlikely story would have remained untold but the cross-dressing provided fantastic costuming opportunities, and Hollywood's most popular bachelor played the Egyptian woodcarver, who was poor but shirtless and as tan as a dinner roll. Courting controversy, the filmmaker chopped the movie to pieces, glazed it, buried it, dug it up, put it into a blender, and poured out an abstract, entirely confusing masterpiece. The adapted stage-version is fourteen acts, the first thirteen less than ten minutes each. After a brief intermission, the fourteenth act wanders close to an hour. Audiences are uncertain what's going on, but whatever it is, it *must* be beautiful.

Inside the auditorium, Mandy slouches in her chair. She doesn't seem to notice that, when viewed from afar, the stage resembles a giant, overstuffed pig bladder. Any porcine biologist and many butchers would easily appreciate the design. But not Mandy. She seems interested in an audience member sitting two rows away, a young woman with a stripe of jet black hair dividing otherwise blonde tresses. The girl returns Mandy's gaze, her eyebrows raised.

"Who's that?" asks Carder.

"Nobody. I think I may have gone to school with her. Nicole Cameron."

"Go say hello. We have a few minutes."

Mandy ignores him and leafs through the show's printed program.

The orchestra builds a melody of Slovakian strings waltzing slowly into the audience with sad determination before dropping bass heavy at their feet. Some in attendance feel guilty for the plight they'll see, but the suffering was ripened with acrobatic lyrics, soaring high notes and grand crescendos. At the pluck of a harp, the pig bladder splits open allowing performers—including the lead heartthrob—to gush forth on stage. The four lead characters are either living in four different time periods or experiencing collective amnesia. It's hard to tell.

The first eight acts are like this: Carder shifts continually to keep blood flow to his legs. Haika scratches the area behind her left ear. Mandy's head bobs steadily closer to her chest. Carder narrows his eyes to blur the colors onstage into indistinct shapes. Haika gasps then stifles laughter when the heartthrob onstage misses a dance step in the fifth act, narrowly escaping a plunge into the orchestra pit. Mandy looks in the direction of either Nicole Cameron or the lead actress (it's difficult to tell which). And the lead actor spins circles in a wheelchair, singing: *There must be more than this, more than peas, carrots and grits.*

During the eighth through thirteenth acts: Carder needs air, realizing the musical is based on an early episode of the Pups cartoon (hidden within the politics, pigs and poverty). Haika contemplates the arrival of her twin sister and the possibilities it will gamble away.

The heartthrob onstage feels like God—a moment he'll never recapture but spend the rest of his life chasing. Mandy's excitement rises in her chest, carrying blood, hope and certainty. The lozenge on her tongue is freedom-flavored and she never wants it to dissolve. This is the furthest she's ever been from her parents.

A swell of harmony splashes into the last lines of the show's first half: *An ever growing ladder, the swine getting fatter, does the slaughter of the liberty in our nation even matter?*

The pig bladder closes on the heartthrob and the show.

"Well," says Carder.

"Hmm," *hmms* Haika.

Mandy is silent, but nods.

The three follow the audience streaming out of the auditorium for intermission and part ways.

Carder slogs through a crowd pulling cigarettes and cell phones from pockets, touching base with nicotine and babysitters by the time they reach the street. Neon lights burn a cool summer night. Taxi brakes whistle and screech. The relief of intermission makes theatergoers jovial and interactive, wrapping their tongues around their own forming opinions. Did they like the actors? Which songs were memorable? Are the lyrics *"cloying sins"* or *"cloning things?"* Does the heartthrob's cute-factor distract enough from his lack of talent?

Carder's pulse hasn't completely settled after Haika's request at dinner. She provided him a flawless way to avoid thinking about the last night of his mother's life, in which Broadway played a key role. Nevertheless, he doesn't misunderstand Haika's admitted love. He knows it's not motivated by sex, his big hands or his riveting intellect. Her love was neither an indecent proposal nor a desire to live together, though Carder would like both. Her passing profession of love contains none of those things. It's pure. However, the Pups get in the way of everything. Carder needs time to contemplate how he should proceed.

"Oh my god," a voice calls to him, "Blue Eyes! I never would've guessed you were a theatergoer. What do you think of the show?"

Carder can't place which Nurse Grey she is, or to which hospital she's attached. Regardless, conversational autopilot takes over. "I— that music really soars, huh? You keep thinking it's going to stop, but it keeps going and going."

"I know. I wish it would never stop. I play the soundtrack all the time." She clears her throat. "Listened to it seven times in the car the other day! Of course, it was a slow day and..."

Reluctant to chat, whatever time Carder spends with Nurse Grey will be used contemplating his escape. Thankfully, the half-time festivities are drawing to a close. "Who did you come here with?" he inquires.

"I came with my sister. And we brought my nephew Tyler. He's been a little rowdy though, considering how much I paid for the tickets. My sister just sits through his bad behavior. No discipline."

Carder shrugs, asking, "And what's your excuse?" He's ashamed of the malice welling in the pit of his stomach, and doesn't know where it comes from.

"My excuse? I'm a sucker for a good musical—the concept that some of life's craziest, scariest and most exciting moments can only be expressed in song—it's charming! Life would be so much better. It would. Could you honestly bomb a city or kill someone if you had to sing about it?"

"Possibly more enthusiastically."

Doubt eclipses her face as she slides the collar of Carder's coat between her index finger and thumb. "Are my teeth okay?" she asks, flashing them along with an aroma of anchovies and marinara.

"Your teeth aren't the problem."

She slaps his chest, erupting in a sharp hyena laugh. "Oh you! We'd better be getting back to the seats. Where are you sitting?"

"First mezzanine."

"That's crazy! Me too!" She pulls Carder towards the theater entrance which is funneling people back to the auditorium. "I hope Tyler isn't bothering you. Text me if he is. He was the one yelling *"farts!"* whenever the King came onstage. I think Tyler has gone undiagnosed—I don't know what for—.but something." She retrieves a card from her purse and slips it into Carder's pant pocket.

Carder pretends she isn't holding his arm as they ascend the stairs. He turns his thoughts back to the Pups and Haika. Of course, he realizes he never fully explained them to her, but that was purposeful. To Haika, the subjects of his paintings aren't dogs, they're noble gargoyles, protectors. Carder lives in a Tupperware world to which Haika has applied a carved mahogany lid. He prefers that to the truth, to the Pups, the plastic, to the cartoon series with preschool fans. And what of the other truth? That he's escorted thousands through their last moments of life in another world? He isn't ready to unleash the insanity upon her, let alone celebrate and sell it at the Camp Fountain Gallery. A storm of failure is on the horizon and Carder wants to outrun it.

Nurse Grey giggles. "What a gentleman. I wish you'd relax like this when we bump into each other at the hospital. It's less sterile, like we're real people with actual lives." She giggles again, squeezing his arm. "Blue Eyes, this is my seat."

Something's off. Carder notices her seat is burgundy, unlike the navy blue he remembers. He looks at his surroundings and surveys the stage. From where they stand, things aren't the same. In fact, it looks a lot like the theater where he'd taken his mother. It is.

"Nurse Grey…" he begins.

"Hmm?"

"…where's the pig bladder?"

"The pig bl—Tyler stop that!" She addresses a boy stretching bubblegum from his mouth in pink strands, while an ancient woman next to him scowls.

Carder gasps. "Oh no! What show is this?"

"What are you talking about?"

"What show is this?"

She holds up the program. As he suspects, the title isn't *Prisms Dawn at Night*. The cover shows a princess in silhouette against a moonlit night.

Before the nurse can say another word, Carder flies down the stairs to the street.

Carder finds the blinking *Prisms Dawn* marquee at a neighboring theater. The sidewalks are no longer thick with theatergoers. He looks at his watch. The correct audience would already be in the dark, finding out how the secretive cross-dresser raises himself up from poverty and makes his way to the Whitehouse. Carder's dancing jog through traffic leaves him out of breath, but he draws closer to his target. As he approaches the entrance, a young woman stands outside, her long blonde hair separated by a river of black. She wears a sleek garnet-colored cocktail dress that seems to float around her. It's Nicole Cameron, Mandy's schoolmate who was seated a couple of rows ahead. Carder is sure of it. He remembers her reverse-skunk-stripe dye job, and when he follows her right arm, extended up, and focuses his sight on her hand, bent forward, then to the tips of her willowy fingers, outstretched, and the hair that those willowy fingers are combing, not her own, he finally understands. It's Mandy's hair being combed, Mandy's head being tugged. His initial reaction is one of disbelief, but Mandy's sequined pants remove any doubt. It's her. She hasn't yet seen Carder, and is typing something into her cell phone when he reaches them.

He tries swallowing the dread. Not one, not two, but three of them are now late if he counts the new girl. "You must be Nicole. How are you? Are we too late to get back inside the theater?"

The girl steps back, slyly using Mandy as a shield. When Mandy recognizes it's only her uncle, she jumps, but immediately wears a mask of coolness, slightly crooked.

"Hey, Unc! Where'd you come from?"

"A nurse from work accosted and dragged me… hasn't our show started though?"

"People headed back in a long time ago. She and I were talking."

"Let's head back in. Your hair looks fine by the way."

"What?"

Carder motions toward the girl with the floating dress. "She was fixing your hair, but it couldn't look any more beautiful." Carder studies the two of them. The girl steps away from Mandy's shielding, but still seems reticent to talk. "Did you come here with your parents, Nicole?"

"My name's Lara. You must be Rabbit's uncle." She meets Carder's hand with her own.

"Correct. I'm Rabbit's uncle. Right, Rabbit?" Using the age-old nickname feels intimate in ways he hasn't experienced lately, but he notes the protest in Mandy's eyes. "You and Rabbit were schoolmates, right? Classmates?"

"Wha—no! We just met."

"Oh."

Mandy's cheeks flush. For one second, Carder looks like he's been hit in the head with a cement idea, but he's quick to heal. "Well then, you two, we'd all better head back inside."

As he turns to the glass doors, he sees Haika exiting the auditorium into the foyer of the theater. She doesn't see the three of them outside. A tissue like the one she and Iris passed back and forth earlier is in her hand, and her face is flustered with diamond tears building in her eyes. As she's about to open the door and exit into the night, she glimpses Carder on the other side. Taken aback, she laughs and yells, calling him something awful but it's too muffled to hear. She then finds her posture and allows Carder to open the door for her.

"Thank you. God, wasn't that show awful? I'm happy to see I'm not the only one who can't sit through the second half," Haika says, stuffing the tissue into her sparkling clutch. She then notices Mandy and her companion. "Hello." And observes the girls' hands resisting their pull toward one another, eliciting Haika's toothy grin. "Guess I was at the wrong show! I should've known something like this was happening out here! I'm sure it was quite a scene, and I've gone and missed it." Then, turning to Carder she says, "Listen to me, *never* do that to me again. I thought you had deserted me." She sighs. "I need a drink. Why don't we grab desert and stroll Times Square?"

19

A REAPING: PALLIUM
Carder at 15 years old

Creep always enters their worlds through unfamiliar surroundings, making it a challenge to map and difficult to traverse. Over the years he's grown used to it, but there's no pleasure in it. Here he is again, this time thigh-deep in dark waters among cattails and marsh grasses. What can be done? Based on his previous visits, he tries to orient himself, but it never works. This is an entirely new land smelling of thunderstorms and horse manure.

Sounds of struggle nearby are hidden in the grass. One creature growls and bites, lost in devouring bloodlust, extracting life from some victim. Wheezing breaths close to death draw the young man's attention. Creep loathes the anguish of the conquered as much as the gulping delight of the unseen victor.

"Where are you?" he yells, sweeping away reedy grasses taller than his own lanky teenage height. Albino day-bats fly in circles far above, but as a child Creep had learned to ignore their harmless swoops.

Between the blades, labored breathing continues in quiet rasps.

Creep sloshes forward, bellowing again, "Where are you? Show yourself!"

No answer. Creep stops, allowing the water to settle, tuning his ear for even the smallest thrashings or resistance. The silence is unnatural. It's the stillness of something hiding. As if by radar, he spies the orb of an amber eye with long trails of rusty sleep falling from its corners. The eye belongs to someone not quite human. The being obscured in the marshy stalks is betrayed by spraying water and the scuttle of wings in his mouth. The eye belongs to Pallium.

Creep approaches through the water, gently parting grasses until they reveal a gangly beast with a sagging face, chalky and devoid of color. The fringe of its draping skin floats on the water, blood sticking to it in curds. Though still clinging to life, the bird alternates between exhausted skirmish and weary surrender. Creep wants to wrench it from the ghoul's jaws before the invisible light of life leaves its eyes.

"Release it!"

No longer captivated by the struggling prey, Pallium releases the bird, but stray feathers stick in and around his mouth as blood diffuses further in a curling dance upon water. The bird flutters away over cattails in a wobbling flight like a living airplane that will soon be wreckage.

Pallium's mournful voice pervades the atmosphere as though emanating from someplace else. "Did you hear that gunshot? It rattled the entire world, certainly rattled that unfortunate bogpie right out of the sky and into my mouth. I'm afraid it's stolen its last key."

"There was no gunshot."

The beast maintains eye contact as he casually drinks the cloudy water he's scooped with his hands, but the bird's feathers stay attached to him. Their quills have rooted to his skin, now a permanent fixture around his mouth. Creep spies four glistening, scaled wings folded awry down the creature's back, perhaps an evolutionary dead-end. They're too small and misshapen to give flight.

"On the contrary, the gunshot came from your gun." The animal's voice is deep, deliberate.

"I have no gun."

"And I've no bird. In a sense, that puts us on common ground." Pallium stands up and water droplets trickle down his body as he wades away. Creep follows. They slog forth until leaving wet grasses for spongy ground, then bedrock. Hard beneath their feet, the surface contains deep ruts. They avoid stepping on sharp jade-colored crystals that have somehow grown from the soil, striking slowly at the heavens.

Pallium mutters under his breath, "He's not as awe-striking as I'd heard, nor as sensitive, nor as filled with valor, nor as ..."

Carder stops abruptly, interrupting the mumblings. "What's that?" He motions to what he mistakes for a tower in the distance, but no, it's too slight in stature, a spindle no wider than two men together, an ornate blade of carved wood, embellished with winding, scrolling tales, jutting at least ten stories into a cloudy sky. "There in the distance. What is it?"

"A gateway. A door. Don't tell me they haven't come up with them in your world yet. It's like this: one walks through and finds oneself in an entirely new setting."

"A-gateway-a-door to what?"

A quiet chuckle fights its way from Pallium's jowls, dangling in soft reverberations. "To the Next-world."

"What next world?"

"This ridiculous game grows tiresome. As I've not been able to open the door, it's all hearsay, but it's rumored to lead to the Next-world."

"In that case, it's a doorway I won't walk through," Creep says, but Pallium continues toward the gateway. Folds of skin brush the ground as he walks and it's clear from jagged scars that at least three fingers on each hand were lost in past injury.

As they draw closer, powdery flakes drift from the sky. If they're snowflakes, they're larger than any Creep has ever seen. Some are small, but a few are the size of saucers. Another factor sets them apart from snow: they're alive. Each flake is constructed of five or six tiny horses, joined at the tips of their tails in the flake's center and on both sides at the hooves next to them.

The hound slows the cadence of his walk, asking, "If it's cold out, does ash become snow? If you have one young tongue, wouldn't two, four, six taste more? If one is in a pasture," as they'd now left the marsh completely, "do snowflakes become horses?" As he puzzles his question, the first flake hits the ground running in a fury. The connected horses manage a united gallop in the direction of the doorway. "You've no answers. I suggest you don't catch a snowflake in your mouth."

"Why are you heading to the door? I want to stay longer," Creep says.

"Then why did you put it there? It seems we have a conundrum. You desire my world, I desire yours. You desire death, yet only bring it. I desire life, but fade. You can't imagine how much I wish I could help."

"I've never wanted to bring death, and I don't know how to stay here. I usually wake up, and then have a hard time returning."

"Ah, an undisciplined mind after all this time. Pain is often solely a momentary teacher." The beast raises the decrepit nose practically dripping off him. "Did you catch a whiff of that sweet, gangrenous odor? At any rate, I suppose the bogpie wasn't all feathers and mess after all. She brought you this." With that, the jaws which had held the dying bird drop a metal key, blank of the teeth it would need to open locks. It lies on the ground, connected to the hound's slobbering mouth by one long string of beaded saliva. Creep kneels to pick it up.

It's impossible to tell from where the gunshot rings, but when Creep whips his head up the intended target is obvious. It's been struck. This time, the pool of blood isn't a bird's, but that of the encrusted old beast who now lies lifeless.

20

DUNG BEETLE DAYS

Iris situates the afghan blanket to keep her folded legs from sticking to the plastic couch cover. Haika knows this means either Iris is cold or hiding something—and it's the hottest day of the year. Before Carder left to retrieve some neighborhood coffee—non-C--ff--S--r coffee—he turned the air conditioners in his house to full blast. The sisters agreed that it's time to trade lemonade for iced coffee in hopes of jumpstarting the heat-exhausted morning.

Sylvia Quevedo had made the afghan Iris is sitting on twenty-six years prior, using leftover yarn she'd collected since girlhood. She'd hoped to finish the blanket as a small rectangle, but with no additional babies surviving her womb, she kept knitting until it would warm an adult.

"This place reminds me of la casa de Yanamaria. Remember?" Iris asks. "This place the same. The furniture cannot breathe." She rubs a squeak from the couch's plastic.

"I suppose Carder's mother didn't want it stained."

"She was right. It did not stain." Iris rolls her eyes and bites into a croissant, shedding flakes onto her skirt.

Haika adjusts her doo-rag while observing her sister. Faint wrinkles have started settling around Iris's eyes, but she's still a brazen bulldog, refusing bridles as much as Haika does.

"How is our dear Come Stay Inn?" Haika asks.

"A mess. It turn into mostly for youngs and gays." She focuses on a painting hanging near the entrance of Carder's kitchen and points to the scene therein. "Is that blood in the picture? Why the violence of... I guess you call them *animals*? Very weirdo." Iris's

English lacks confidence, concluding statements like questions, but she still shoots them as close to her targets as possible, allowing listeners to piece her meaning together.

Haika ignores her sister's distractions. "Is everything okay there?"

"Haikita, Haikita, when will you stop thinking everything falls apart when you are away? You never cared about the Inn. Don't start now, mi hermana." Her tone is the opposite of her words, like a lighthearted joke or funny suggestion.

"I do care and always have. Which leads me to the real question—why have you come to New York City?"

"Hollywood."

"Then you're way off base. That's the other coast. California."

"I know. But I want to see what is this land you live in that I see every single day on TV. Every afternoon, when I watch an American talk show, I see you in the audience. Movies too. And many, many murders need solving, all over the city, like the cop shows. And the—the forensia... err... forensics! A guest at the Inn told me that you can go stand outside American morning shows with a sign so they show you on TV. I cannot think what to put on it... *Hola Amigos and Fans of the Come...*"

Her explanation is outlandish. Morning show hosts would keep cameras as far from Iris as possible. She isn't homogenized enough for television. "Okay, Iris-my-sis, let's do it right now! We can make a sign."

"What will you have it say with no one reading it back home?"

"You tell me."

Iris thinks for a moment, and then bounces in her seat, revealing legs waffle-printed by blanket. She pushes her hand at Haika. "You will not ruin this!"

Haika tires of waiting for the real reasons behind her sister's travels. Iris will hop from stepping stone to stepping stone for ages before diving into truth. Even then, Iris will befuddle it through delivery. It's a talent she's always had.

"The youngs and gays, they are fun. I get to know them real good. They go through lots of sheets though. I'm meeting for dinner on Friday this couple that stayed there: Brian y Brian. Two Brians! Of course, neither one look like a 'Brian.'" The croissant Iris was eating has disappeared, mostly into her stomach, partly over her lap and the floor, and she's now playing with the red leather straps of her heels strewn at the foot of the couch. "Donde esta la café? Eso es ridiculo."

Haika awakes from her thoughts, realizing she hasn't listened to Iris's last few sentences.

Iris notices as well, "Tell me how you are going to make a high-mighty art show for your gallery out of this mess, out of these knick-knacks and mishmash of potpourri?" Iris recently read an article on antiquing, and proudly uses a few terms from it, correctly or not.

"Are you kidding? This isn't a mess! It's the fussy artists wearing their egos like billboards who are messes. Carder is relatively easy. If you met Alex Date—the artist whose work you saw at the gallery—*he's* a mess. Complications galore. For the longest time, no matter what I said or did, it was wrong."

"But it turn out so good, hermana."

"Sure, but it took eons to make him understand that I see the paintings as his children as much as he does. Alex gave trust as easily as most people give their virginity." She shakes her head. "Those paintings weren't only his children, they were his brother's children, his mother's children…" She trails off as though the list is endless.

"Ay yay yay, Haikita! You sound more like psychiatrist than art pimp. So, tell me his kitty's name."

"I don't think Alex had a cat." Haika is impressed by her sister's expanded English. Still, there's confusion.

"I mean Carder's cat. El gato, *his* gato, over there—what is its name?" She points across the room to a small fluff of fur sleeping curled up in the armchair. It could be a circular pillow, if pillows breathed.

Haika jumps, but soon recognizes it's the neighbor's cat, and confesses that she's grown used to Mrs. Gunderson's accusatory looks whenever she leaves Carder's house. The woman obviously thinks Haika is a prostitute. Carder assured her that Mrs. Gunderson would think that of any young, happy woman, and certainly of any woman hanging out with *him*. Haika has tried being kind, to no avail.

"Maybe she the kind that don't take to kindness. Some people want treatment like dirt," Iris says, getting up from the couch and moseying over to the cat. She picks up the animal, waking it from slumber, raising the yawning thing high above her head, then drops it into a cradled position in her arms. "You're always too kind. Always to everyone but me, anyway. Okay, so this cat is here and she's my cat now."

"What, are you taking her back to Mexico with you?"

The cat's engine purrs, and Iris pays attention to that instead of Haika's sarcasm. "This es mi gato. What will I call her?" she asks herself aloud, before dumping the cat on Haika's lap and sitting down.

"I don't know its name, but I'm not taking it back to Mrs. Gunderson. Go ahead and name it. Carder renamed *my* dog, so I think it's fair. Wait? Why hasn't Zombie noticed the cat? Shouldn't he bark or something? Shouldn't he want to eat her brains?"

Upon hearing his name, Zombie, who's been lying on the cool of the kitchen floor, lumbers into the living room without destination. He ignores the cat, ambling over to Iris, laying his head on her lap, sniffing the blending aromas of ghostly croissant and musky woman, until she shoves him away.

"I'll call this kitty 'Klaus.'"

"This cat? Klaus? But what about our Klaus back home—your dog—*our* dog? You can't go around naming everyone in your life Klaus!"

Iris sighs. "Hermana. Haikita. Our dear dog Klaus is gone. To put it nicely..." she inspects her fingernails for a moment, "he passed over."

"He's dead?" The news pushes Haika's heart off a cliff, and she pushes the cat from her lap.

"Sí. Five years ago. Bad tumor sprout on him like an ugly balloon. It made him, cómo se dice..." She taps her forehead, "...lopsided! He was lopsided. It was sadness beyond sadness."

"Why didn't you tell me?"

"Oh no you don't! Why didn't you ever call and ask '¿Cómo es Klaus?' or '¿Cómo es Iris?' You are lucky Klaus is not here telling you it was me who died! You know, Hermana, I don't want to make it more sad, but he waited for years for you to throw the ball. Years. Would not chase any ball I threw. In fact, the only way I could get him to *stay* was to throw the ball."

Silence. Haika had always planned on returning. One day.

Iris grows restless at the lack of words. She seems to equate silence with emptiness, and tries filling it however she can. "Are you okay, Haikita?"

Haika can't blame Iris for the truth, for absence, for death or for time passing. "I'm contemplating a world without Klaus."

"Then contemplate that you been in that world for five years. Plus, now we got kitty Klaus. Kitty Klaus is here to stay."

Haika turns on the television so she can think, filing away the revelation of her favorite pet's death, setting the timer to deal with it at a future date. This is what Iris does—she's Godzilla, parading into a peaceful place and eating the calm. Haika decides she can't let that happen right now. Orchestrating a show for Carder's art has to be Haika's obsession, leaving room for nothing else. Usually, shows are planned for months, but this is a last minute hailstorm that she has to turn into an ice sculpture. Carder's work is the only truly inspiring discovery she's made on her own. Ever. All the other artists she represented were already on the path, but it's *she* who paved and striped the road for Carder's work, and gladly. Focus on that—she tells herself.

The opening door wedges light into the house, revealing Darren with a bag of roasted coffee beans. It's a new label—Grounds for Divorce—a brand which won't last once its college-aged founders realize the pun isn't funny enough to entice customers.

"Well looky here," Darren jokes, "Haika moved in."

"You brought coffee," says Haika. "Carder just went out to get some."

"That's not smart."

"Don't worry, I instructed him," Haika says buoyantly.

Darren pulls the tabs from the brown bag and inhales, and then brings it forward so Haika can take a whiff. "This is the best. Smell. You may as well 'cause this is what you're going to drink. I guarantee Carder's coming back with something awful—if you're lucky."

"No. I told…"

"This is what we're having." He then sees Iris. "Hello there, Miss. You're looking *fine* today."

Iris giggles, and inhales the aroma. "It's about time," she says. "Smells good. Like heaven."

"A woman with taste, I see."

Their fermenting flirtation is interrupted by Carder's entrance. He produces a can of coffee, tossing it to Darren. Darren turns the label to Haika so she can retch at the neon colors slickly advertising ground beans. "I'll go brew us some of this," he says.

Haika grits her teeth.

"No, you're a guest. Sit down. I'll brew it," Carder says, taking both the can and the beans Darren brought.

Throwing the cat outside, Carder informs them that they need to tidy up because his Dad will soon arrive.

"Your father? When?" Haika asks.

"Gordan Quevedo—self-delusional master of the world! He should be here any time."

Vibrations from an army of small feet stampede up from the cellar—the universe below. Carder never goes there anymore. He'd probably spent years of his youth there collectively. Barbed insectoid legs cling to him, boring into his chest, pulling breath from his lungs, gnawing on his fear of preening his paintings for public consumption. He has to quell the idea that pieces of him will be consumed along with the art. Does he want his private world ending up on walls of Chelsea lofts, chosen because they match a bedspread or might provide a minute's dinner conversation? He sees the future, and it contains a partying trust-funder snorting a line of blow off one of the plates he'd painted as a child.

He looks at the kitchen clock while the coffeemaker spits, wheezing water, turning it into robust, black coffee. Since before Carder's birth, the clock's simple white face framed in red enamel had ripened from current trend to vintage piece, all the while hanging in the same spot. It still functions, but Carder senses time leaking out, and his father is coming to gather it. The clock says 11:26, which means it's 11:16, which means his father is over a minute late, which means it must actually be 11:14. Sylvia Quevedo had set the clock ahead long ago, and Carder never changed her gentle peek into the future.

For over a year, Carder has dodged his father dropping off paltry checks that would barely cover grocery bills. They're cheap insults, and Carder stopped cashing them altogether. Lately, Gordan mails the checks, removing the possibility of uncomfortable rendezvous. Carder can't understand what thread of responsibility prompts today's visit. He won't pretend the corpse of intimacy doesn't lay at their feet.

The hissing coffeemaker returns Carder to the present. In the living room, Darren's deep laughter bounces off Iris's cackles.

"Card," Haika calls from the front room, "You could've told me earlier that your father was coming to visit. This is ridiculous. What can I do to help?"

"Just don't tell him about the Gallery or the show," Carder calls back, "Nothing along those lines, okay?"

"Okay, but you and I need to have a talk."

Carder mumbles to himself, pouring four cups of coffee. When he'd told Darren about the proposed showing at Haika's gallery, Darren shook his head—that girl, the gambler. Haika informed Carder that every single show at an art gallery is a gamble. Maybe. However, this time Carder provides the chips she's playing with. He's been trying to conserve himself from loss for such a long time, but is now laying himself on its railroad tracks.

He sought reassurance online. The search results built confidence in Haika's abilities, with photos posted on the Camp Fountain website from past shows as professional and well-regarded as Alex Date's *The Cleft House*. A link to a website for a journal called *Visual Bitch* described one of Haika's shows as "a saga of time and geometry, melted down and whip-stitched into wide stretches of sweet hues and perplexing pattern." The meaning was vague but intriguing.

"Surely you can part with some of these paintings," Haika says, drifting back and forth across the creaking living room floor, a preamble to heading to the more recent work upstairs, "You've been so prolific—you can be choosy about what you're willing to lose."

"You know, I've never known anyone who has bought original art. The only original art I've seen hanging in *any* home, has been my own art in my own house. I always thought of galleries as extended museums."

"Museums are retirement homes. And believe me, Dollface,

people buy. You'll see. Just consider the appreciation one has to have in order to spend thousands of dollars on a piece."

"They'd have to be rich. And stupid."

Iris, sitting on the sofa with Darren, stops herself from nodding in agreement.

Shooting a crusty look at her, Haika says, "*Or* there could be people who appreciate windows to your lavish interior."

"I like the one hanging in the computer room," Iris says, demonstrating support. "If I had to buy, it would be that one."

"Why?"

"I don't know—it's innocent with those big eyes—only, you don't know whether it's to protect you or to knock your head off."

As someone forced to accept her own lack of artistic ability, Haika positions herself as close as possible to the Shangri-La of creativity. Watching and listening to the artists, studying the fragments they give to the world via art is like peering into a tank of vast differences, a lid often closed by the assumption that most people experience more or less the same thing. While people accept that a New Guinean tribes-girl, the President of Canada and a grandma from Duluth live differently, they take for granted that when looking at a bowl, each sees the same object. Not so. There are endless paths of experience. It's a bittersweet knowledge to Haika. Since she can't open the door to visual creativity herself, she'll at least sit outside the door and ask those passing through what it's like inside.

Haika saw Carder's worry stirring before he disappeared into the parlor. He'd started checking the time long before Darren left for his hospital shift and a twitterpated Iris went upstairs. Mandy, who had declared she only got privacy through the Public Library, should've returned home from it over thirty minutes ago.

Carder was right. The living room needs straightening up. Haika fans a stack of magazines atop the boomerang cocktail table, topping it with a recent Watchtower magazine, with a headline asking whether or not the earth will ever become paradise. She notices dried schmutz on the couch and goes to fetch a cloth from the kitchen.

While searching for a rag, Haika holds back disappointment: Iris and Darren were supposed to help decide which paintings might be shown. It was Haika's way of including them. But all they did was laze about, teasing and flirting with each other. It's nauseating. Gordan's impending visit also pauses Haika's dig for information. She had planned on further researching Carder's process, exploring the theme of gargoyles, the hope, despair and sometimes satisfaction portrayed with them. It's challenging to decipher which of her many questions she can ask. Carder's agreement to show his work was unbelievable, and Haika doesn't want anything unraveling. At the same time, she has to proceed swiftly and deeply. If she can pull the show off, it will be a triumphant landmark in her career.

She's rinsing the rag under the kitchen faucet when she hears a knock at the door. She turns the water off, and sneaks to the kitchen's entrance to eavesdrop.

Carder greets Mandy. Ah, it's only the girl—Haika relaxes and walks into the living room.

Mandy contorts her face, trying to silently convey something. Is it annoyance or shock? Is it a two-word phrase with three syllables each, or three words with two syllables? Mandy's eyebrows reach toward her hairline, but Haika and Carder can't solve her unspoken puzzle.

The charade is solved when a trench coat too hot for summer fills the doorway. The coat contains a large man. He enters, setting down a vacuum cleaner. A red face and plump neck give him the appearance of an overripe tomato wrapped in a brown paper bag. If he'd ever had hair like Carder's it had abandoned his head long ago. The door behind him remains open, allowing noon's heat to steal inside.

"Why if this isn't dilapidated," says the tomato. "Nothing's changed but that."

"Hello Dad," says Carder.

"Son," he acknowledges. He then gestures toward Mandy. "I found this little honey-muffin wandering around outside. It's not safe for a girl walking New York City streets. She's too pretty to be left alone."

"She was at the library. And she's seventeen," replies Carder.

"A gentleman wouldn't allow it."

"I'm almost eighteen and I was fine," Mandy interjects. "It's ten blocks away at most. Grandpa and I bumped into each other in front of the house."

"Don't make excuses for him, Amanda Lynn." He then sees Haika holding the rag. "Well I'll be. You found yourself a woman. Never thought that would happen—if she's your cleaning lady you should let her go." It's a joke, but once he sees that no one finds it funny, he clears his throat and extends his hand. "How do you do? I'm Gordan Quevedo."

"Haika Haus." She shakes his hand. She and Mandy exchange glances while Haika tries keeping her face from reflecting Mandy's what-now expression. She's sure they both flinch with the same embarrassment: meeting with family members who'll never see one in any role but the original—no matter how things changed.

"I'm sure you could use this. It's our old one," Gordan says, raising the vacuum cleaner a few inches from the floor. "Agnes got a new, ridiculous contraption that does everything but fly to the moon."

Knowing Carder wishes the visit quickly over, Haika offers Gordan something cold to drink. When Gordan accepts *water or brandy, or whatever else,* Mandy springs into the kitchen to get it.

"Look at this, Son! My granddaughter's more helpful than either you or your sister ever were. Tell me, Creep, whatever happened to that black fellow you used to hang with? The one you were on the phone with for hours whenever you visited? Didn't know if you were becoming a homosexual or a thug. You seemed too weak to become a thug, so I worried."

"You're talking about Darren. He was here earlier this morning."

"I thought I might've seen him scoping car windows as he passed. No matter, have you been taking Amanda to her church meetings? I'm sure your sister asked you to."

"Mandy's pretty much of age. If she wanted to go, I'd take her."

Gordan sends a hearty laugh across the room, causing Zombie to raise his head, ready to run, "You know I'm joshin' ya, Creep! I did think about it for a minute, thinking I should tell you to take her to those meetings like Lucy asked, but...no...no." The shape of his lips is a distinct 'V', as if he's buttoning down a smile. "Becoming mousier and more judgmental was the last thing Lucy needed." He lowers his voice so Mandy won't hear, "Marrying *that man* and hiding behind those church rules. I swear, she's Sylvia all over again, only in more annoying ways. At least your mother knew when to keep her… err… when to keep things to herself."

So many things.

Iris comes downstairs, passing through while pointing at the vacuum cleaner. "Oh no! Don't buy that one! Does not pick up a thing. Nada. I know 'cause I bought one years ago for the Inn. Do not be fooled." She disappears into the kitchen, singing in Spanish as Mandy returns and hands her grandfather a cold glass of water.

Gordan takes the cup as cars whiz white highway noise through the open door. In the kitchen, a radio tunes to mariachi horns and violins. Carder's father closes the front door, making sure it latches.

"This door's been doing that for at least eighteen years. Now, Ms. Haika, what do *you* do, and why in the world are you here with my son?"

Haika hesitates. She gladly withholds revealing Carder's upcoming show, but doesn't want to lie. "I own an art gallery in Manhattan."

Gordan straightens his posture as though serving in a military where money and status are General and Admiral, and begins to make eye contact with Haika as though art galleries validate communication. Haika is used to the reconsideration, but hates watching people become monkeys merely because they think she's a woman of prestige. Let them think she's a cleaning lady.

"I love art," Gordan says, "We recently invested in a Robert Clamont—limited edition."

Haika perks up—it's someone she knows about. "Clamont—he hates showers but loves cologne. You know, he carries a jar of mayonnaise everywhere he goes? Regardless, though I'd need to see it, it's safe to tell you that the piece you bought will increase in value, so it doesn't disappoint in *that* way… but who is this *we* you speak of?"

Carder steps in, "He's talking about the illustrious Agnes Pye. They worked together, and he left Mom for her. Agnes could type faster."

"Hold on, son. I'm not going to apologize again. It's Agnes Quevedo. She's been a Quevedo for sixteen years now. You need to start living in the present."

Haika pulls out of the conversation, sitting down, and begins to pet Zombie, peeved that Gordan is counseling his son in front of her.

"Have you seen the new line of Pups, Creep? It's *fourth* generation now. Can't say I've anything to do with that. They bought me out, but I'm still getting some kick back, if you know what I mean. There's nothing a good lawyer can't get you." He pulls a check from his trench coat. When Carder doesn't reach, he sets it on the cocktail table. "*Fourth* generation. Never would've thought that would happen."

Carder says, "I'd rather we not even skirt the subject."

"You're right on that count! They look absolutely bloated. Swollen-headed things. Their necks would never be able to support their noggins. Demonic eyes. They're made for toddlers nowadays because kids become adults by eight. The materials are flimsy too, not like that indestructible stuff they once used."

The room's silence soon takes Haika's attention away from skimming a National Geographic article on ancient Egypt. She notices Gordan eyeing the wall in the far corner. He's wandering toward it, feigning disinterest the way cats look in the opposite direction of food they want but can't have. Gordan's eyes dart from the cobalt candy dish to a crystal paperweight. He picks up the Watchtower magazine, flipping through it for a few seconds, before reaching his destination. He stops in front of the credenza, staring more obviously than intended at a porcelain plate hanging above. This plate eclipses others, a dominating presence. A grayish creature—closer to being a rodent-dragon than a dog—with a scaled belly and naked tail stares blindly from the plate into Gordan's eyes. The painted beast and the man peer at one another in a stand-off, but the man soon sniffs, breaking the gaze.

"I see nothing's changed," Gordan says.

"Plenty has changed," Carder counters, agitated.

"Exactly the same as it ever was. Preserved like a museum."

"Or a mausoleum."

Haika wants to ask how either label applies when the home is overrun with life. But sensing argument's edge, she tries concentrating on a picture in National Geographic: a celestial scarab beetle rolls the sun across the sky, while its earthly insect counterpart pushes its own spherical, fecal feast. Mandy sits down on the floor, leaning against Haika, crooking her neck to see pages. Her proximity is both baffling and delightful. Together, they travel to ancient Egypt.

Iris brings her brassy voice back into the room. "He's still here? Come *on!* We have much to do, no? And I am telling you, do not buy what he's selling. That vacuum doesn't suck... or it sucks, but not the right way."

Mandy suppresses laughter.

To keep from doing the same, Haika explains, "He's not selling it, Iris, he's *giving* Carder the vacuum cleaner."

"Still don't work. Why take something that don't work? No offense, Mister."

"None taken," Gordan says. "Anyway, I do have to go. Agnes is waiting out in the car. She sends her 'hellos'. Amanda, come give your old granddad a hug."

Mandy stands up and gives a quick squeeze before Gordan slips out the door.

The next few weeks fatten up nicely for Carder, but are almost nonexistent to Haika—so many things fight for attention: choosing the paintings, then cleaning, preparing them, making any needed repairs and planning arrangement. Through favors, framing happens on short notice. She commissions the creation of a website for Carder. Haika has never done so much work, nor has she dealt with such a reclusive, indifferent artist. She prods Carder into decisions.

Pricing pieces is less difficult. Carder's work will speak to people. Asking healthy prices will only snowball into greater sales. For many, surfing the latest art wave before it hits shore is a thrilling risk—and this is one Haika is sure they'll swim out to meet. She starts mentioning the elite, limited opportunity it to several clients in a pseudo-hushed tone.

One morning, as they're walking Zombie to the Brooklyn Heights Promenade, Haika mentions that she'd like Carder to brainstorm a list of possible names for the show. It needs the right fit. She offers some suggestions of her own.

"What do you think of *Leviathan Cathedral?* Then again, wouldn't you rather people discover the spiritual aspects themselves instead of proclaiming it? Leviathan *Vault?* How about a phrase using *Phoenix.*

It's the—"

"Neidin."

"—initial thing that—"

"Neidin."

"Ney-den?" It's the first time Haika's heard this word.

"Right. Neidin. That's the name of the show."

They slow to let Zombie nose a passing poodle.

"Why? Meaning what?"

"They never told me explicitly, but it's the only word I ever saw written there—spelled out on a beach peninsula with black boulders too large to have been carried. I saw it by chance while stranded."

"Stranded?"

"I woke up across from it in a faraway tree, on another piece of shore. It was dangerously high."

"*Carder Quevedo presents…Neidin*. Okay, there's nothing more to discuss. If someone or something spelled that out with boulders on a beach, we'd better take notice. *Neidin* it is."

She stops and holds out her hand until Carder shakes it. It's a deal. Carder's pie-eyes and goofy smirk broadcast his surprised pleasure.

"*Neidin* it is," he repeats, holding on.

21

EXIT DINER, ENTER RUSSIA

It's summer, so it shouldn't be raining. It's daylight, so it shouldn't be dark. It's afternoon, so the Fuller Diner shouldn't be busy. But thunderclouds brood overhead and rain delivers umbrella-less residents inside for an afternoon snack. A situation comedy laugh track roars on a small television behind the counter. Yet, it's not this that Carder, Darren and Bob the Whale—pinning a bar stool to the floor near the desert case—are watching. They're watching real life drama unfold.

Over the years, they've seen complaining customers, drunks, and old men ordering women to "shut your brats the hell up," but this is more unsettling. Their favorite waitress, Magda, is in the process of being fired. She slings words in a shouting match with her boss while removing her apron and collecting her things.

He yells, "There are reasons you came here! There were reasons you chose this place, lessons you still need to learn, things you need to do! Why did *you* come work *here*, Magda—why?"

"Because!" she screams. "It was close to my school!" She throws pens from her pockets onto the countertop.

"There are things you still need to understand, skills you need to develop for whatever comes next!"

"Like what, noble teacher?"

"Like how to make a decent God damn French Dip Sandwich!"

Magda laughs wickedly. "Screw that! I don't want to be around people who even *want* stupid French Dip Sandwiches!"

Bob the Whale, caught in goopy heartbreak over the possibility of Magda never passing him ketchup again, cuts in, "They're not that

175

great anyway. You should take them off the menu. Bread's too soggy. People want it crisp."

"I won't miss *you* one bit," Magda snaps at Bob. "And I've always felt sorry for that tortured stool you sit on. Why don't you have a heart and ease off—spread it around? This place is why your cholesterol is so high!"

"How would you know that?"

"Who do you think served you three plates of bacon while you took the doctor's phone call?"

The rainy day customers are enjoying the show. Magda rifles through her bag. Finding her keys, she marches toward the entrance.

Carder and Darren sit in a booth near the front. Having served them for several years, Magda figures it's only fair to have her say. She addresses Carder first. "You! Whichever barber cuts your hair should have his hands put in a meat grinder. And you'd better hold on to that woman you talk about all the time! You're not twenty-one anymore and even if you were you'd be lucky to find a girl *period*!"

Next, she steers her finger to Darren, almost touching the tip of his nose. "And you! You like this?" She gestures to her body as if offering it in an infomercial.

"You know I do." Darren replies, clearly loving the banter.

"Well, you better take a good look, 'cause this is the last you'll ever see of it!" Before proceeding out the door, she yells, "And dogs are a code violation! Will somebody call the fuckin' Department of Health already!? Somebody! You!" She points to an elderly woman shrinking inside her raincoat. "Call the Department of Health!"

The woman nods, gripping her purse for security.

With that, Magda departs, entering the downpour with no umbrella. Pelted with rain, she takes a few steps, stops and screams at the sky before moving on.

"All I wanted was more au jus. More broth to dip it in," Bob the Whale says, addressing the entire diner.

The diners raise their eyebrows or pretend they've heard nothing, sinking back into the usual daze of their own circumstance.

"If she were sexier that whole scenario would've been hot," Darren says. "Who am I kidding? It was damn hot! She's a firecracker!"

Magda was right. It's the last time they see her. And she lives up to her promise never to serve another French Dip sandwich. Even decades later, on the popular cooking show "Maggy's Kitchen," she refuses to feature any segments about *that* sandwich.

The diner's owner, Mr. Fuller, seems to think Magda's departure ushers in the beginning of the end.

"Get that damn dog out of here!" he yells at Darren and Carder.

Darren tells him that two more customers (the Vivienne girls) will be joining them any minute. Mr. Fuller grunts permission. He's unwilling to lose regular customers, but he tells them he never wants to see *that dog* again.

Carder and Darren are both in high spirits. Darren is elated over Carder agreeing to give Claudette a painting lesson. It will pull Carder further outside, and more so, into Manhattan. For his part, Carder is thrilled that, lately, chemistry between Darren and Iris seems to have ignited. It makes it less likely that Darren will act a goon when the Vivienne girls' arrive. Lately, he's been bent on convincing Carder that Haika and Iris aren't identical twins but fraternal.

"They look nothing alike. One twin's hot. Other's not. End of story," Darren explains.

"I'll agree with you there."

"And how is it that a hermit like you is suddenly involved with not one but two sets of twins?"

"Twins aren't that uncommon. And I know them, but I'm not *involved* with any of them. They're friends."

"How is it that a hermit like you has friends at all?" Darren clears his throat. "Oh, here they are! Move Zombie to the floor so they can sit."

The girls enter from the sputtering rain. They're dressed in a similar yet not identical manner, mixing and matching large earrings, thick weapon-sized rings, and the same rubber rain-boots in different colors.

"I wouldn't have even come out in this kind of weather, but she dragged me from Niirdor," Doe says, plopping into the booth. A small, muffled yelp from Zombie makes her readjust her position. "I'm sorry you two, but I can't eat at a place like this. How do they even stay in business? Seems relatively clean though. You must be Darren?"

"And which one are you, Vivienne girl 1 or 2?"

"At least you have the last name right. You can call me Doe." She then points to her sister. "That's Claudette. As you can tell from her geisha-like stature and flawless skin, version 2.0 couldn't improve upon the premier model."

"Damn man," Darren asks Carder, "you were serious about the weirdness?" He scoots over so Claudette can squeeze in. "Well, Ms. Vivienne, we were wrapping things up here anyway. I was telling Carder about my screenplay."

"Screenplay? Do tell."

It's hard to tell if Claudette's interest is genuine or if she's plumping his ego like a pillow she'll soon deflate.

"The premise is based on actual stray dogs in Russia. They're a huge problem. Now, this is true: the dogs have evolved social classes and unusual intelligence."

"Oh stop!" says Doe.

"It's all true. Hear me out! There are now four types of dogs: scavengers, beggars, and helpers—who actually assist security workers out of their own initiative—I suppose they're guard dogs of sorts. The fourth group is just plain wild. Anyway, to survive, the dogs have become smarter and smarter—they even ride the subway, getting on and off at specific stops. They know where they're going."

"No!" says Doe.

"Yes! Now imagine, Viv2, that you've travelled to Moscow on business…"

"Well, I don't…"

"Wait. That's exactly it. You and the rest of the world have ignored the fact that everyone's been hearing less and less out of Moscow. Maybe that's why you're going there. To check things out. Oddly, the plane you're on has few passengers. You get nervous— start popping sleeping pills and throwing back cocktails."

"I don't have to be nervous for that," Claudette says and snickers.

"When the plane lands the flight crew disappears. You wander in a haze through a quiet, seemingly empty midnight airport. Until. You hear screaming."

Doe gasps.

"You follow the screams to baggage claim…"

"Yeah?"

"...where you find a creature: part human, part canine. This mutant wolf-human monstrosity, a lycan, a beast with yellow eyes and fangs dripping blood." Darren pauses until both girls lean in, "Only twenty feet away, it's feeding on one of your fellow passengers: the man that complained about turbulence. The guy being devoured locks eyes with you and lets out one final, blood curdling scream before his head disappears. Eaten."

The Vivienne girls join hands and squeeze, shifting in their seats as though the dog below the table might gnaw their legs off.

"Oh my god!" one says to the other.

"And that's the beginning of the movie." Darren sits back, satisfied. "I'm trying to get Carder here to do some concept drawings."

"It should definitely be made into a film!" Claudette says. "Who's producing it?"

"Shopping it to several producers right now," Darren lies. He gets up, heading to the register, "Don't try it, Card, your meal's on me today."

"You're such a goon." Carder shakes his head. "*Such* a goon."

"We'll only leave you here if you promise we'll meet again to discuss this further," Doe tells Darren as they prepare to depart. "It's important to find the right financial backing for your film. Will you be directing?" Her tone is serious.

"Why don't we have the painting lesson at Fardor?" Carder asks Claudette. "It's your lesson, not Doe's. Plus, we're right next door."

"Because I don't have an easel. And won't it be fun if we have Doe pose? She has the best tea, a Chinese oolong called..."

Doe tries to supply the name. "Tie-guan-yin. The leaves can be brewed repeatedly without losing strength."

"It will literally detoxify the shit out of you," adds Claudette.

Carder enjoys Claudette—she's intelligent, strange, appreciates his humor and—he'd recently found out—has a taste for raunchy Pulp novels. Carder's wry refusal to join what would've been a two-member book club to read *Bombshells in Fifty-buck Bomb Shelters* cemented Claudette's demand for painting lessons. He agreed to them, but why should it require Doe's inclusion? While the Vivienne girls are distinctly different, together they become a freakishly unified third party.

"Welcome to Chez Niirdor," Doe chirps as the elevator opens directly into her home on the twenty-fourth floor. "I have to warn you, Sauron's here. I've been trying to get him to go away on business, on *anything*, for weeks now. Look here," she says in a higher, even chirpier voice as she scoops up three small dogs, one by one. They look like they've flopped out of 16th century oil paintings. "Thoth, Moth, and Roth are King Charlie dogs. We breed them. 'Rilla does most of the work in that regard. I'm sure you'll see her cleaning up. When the puppies don't sell or aren't show quality, we donate them to a foundation for the ethical treatment of... dogless people... or something. We don't just throw them away or..." She wisely stops.

They proceed into the belly of the home, then up to its toupee, a paradisiacal rooftop terrace garden, lush with exotic plants. Upon their arrival, a soil-covered gardener finishes pruning several Brugmansia plants. Carder praises the pendulous, tropical blossoms dangling like orange trumpets and the lemony aroma of the jagged leaves. Doe asks the gardener to make cuttings from them for Carder to take. After giving a few instructions in a clunky Spanish accent which Carder doesn't understand, the gardener disappears behind vines and pillars.

A man sitting behind an open newspaper addresses Carder, "It's apparent that the conjoined have conned you into joining them, Quevedo." The newspaper drops to the man's lap revealing Gavin Daguerré in reading glasses with frames so black they could've been drawn on with permanent marker. His legs are crossed at the knee, and he sticks a half-eaten crust of toast in his mouth. He looks even older than before, more like a father who would disapprove of Doe's form-fitting clothes, rather than the husband who encourages them.

"My Sauron!" Doe greets him with a weak peck on the cheek.

"Don't call me that ridiculous name in front of company," he says, keeping an eye on her. "It makes you seem common."

"I'll call you 'Sauron' until you give me the ring I want."

"What's wrong with the rings you already have? Oh, blimey. Forget it. Go buy a ring. Quevedo, I suppose you ran out of things to discuss with your therapist? It's our duty to refresh your supply."

Carder isn't sure how to react. "Thank you?"

"My wife and her sister were recently telling me that you're going to show some art at the Camp Fountain Gallery?"

"Oh God." Carder awakens again at the petrifying reminder. "Yes. It's true. I am."

Gavin sets the newspaper aside and gets up, directing them to a wood easel standing near a wrought iron chair and a table holding a basket of fruit. Doe's floppy-eared dogs are obsessed with random objets d'art lying about, fighting over them. Gavin watches them but continues, "It must feel good to get a sudden career boost—and the attention of Haika's art-minions throwing fistfuls of money at you. Doe, dear, would you be so kind as to bridle your fucking dogs. Now!? Thank you. Moth just swiped the mummified cat I asked you not to bring out."

"But Claudette and I thought it would be a great artifact to hold in my portrait." With that, the Vivienne girls and the gardener chase the dogs, which seem to think it all a magnificent game.

Gavin's attention isn't yet diverted from Carder. His gaze is knowing and perturbing. Carder tries to dismiss that.

"The entire show is Haika's doing," Carder says. "I couldn't care less if the paintings were *never* seen. In truth, I'd prefer it."

Gavin looks into Carder's eyes for a few speechless moments. He allows the wordlessness to expand. His mustache makes all expressions look more or less like a twitch, but perhaps he'd grown it as a testament to testosterone. Without it, he'd look like the den mother of a troop of ballerinas. Carder can almost see the tights hanging loosely on Gavin's scrawny, Nutcracker-hopeful legs as he demands shaky pliés from the girls.

Gavin drinks a piss-colored liquid from a glass goblet. "Have you ever been to Hong Kong, Quevedo?"

Being addressed as Quevedo transports Carder back to junior high school gym class, standing in tight shorts while Zeke Ehret puts him in a headlock. He refocuses and replies, "No. Can't say that I've been." Carder hasn't even been to Chinatown.

"Ahh—the things you've missed. If you go to Hong Kong, I guarantee you'll be friggin' impressed. They manufacture miracles—things you can't conceive of become extraordinary, physical objects.

Ideas solidify into products for relatively little money. It's a business owner's wet dream."

"I've heard." Carder's experience with the Pups made him far more familiar with foreign factories than he'll admit. He hasn't been to Asia, but something tells him Gavin's view of the situation is skewed.

"Places like that aren't celebrated, yet it's within those borders, those buildings, that most of the work takes place. Entire empires of product take material form outside of U.S. boarders to guide American, and then International, culture. The dreams of every child in this country are born in Asia—every game, doll, raygun, even bibles. Some would say that art shapes minds. They're mostly wrong. I mean, who but a handful of people will ever interact with your paintings? However, find the simplest product, the most cheaply made appliance in America, the video games, shoe laces and bedding sets that follow—and you'll have linked into millions of malleable minds. And those minds won't know it's happened, not deeply."

"So you're telling me that we can thank shoddy goods for the ugly state of the world affairs?"

"Come on, get real. If it weren't these things, the same thing would just happen some other way."

The Vivienne girls are tired of waiting.

"Carder, come on!" They yell in unison. "Business later!" Except for the few punctures it sustained, they've rescued the mummified cat from the jaws of the dogs.

"Listen, Gavin, I'd better go earn my fee."

"Okay," says Gavin before heading indoors, "Enjoy your time with the girls, but remember… people can spot fakers."

Many cocktails and brushstrokes later, the canvas has become a muddy panel attacked by a schizophrenic kaleidoscope of paint. Nonetheless, the two things Claudette depicts well are Doe's sad, sunken eyes. Carder explains to both sisters that he *expected* to see her skin as grey, lifeless splotches in the portrait. Lifelike skin isan achievement.

22

KIN

Brody Sutcliffe has a vague memory of Maeve setting down her cereal bowl that morning to stuff a shining card into his messenger bag. Later at work, beneath long, fluorescent lights and pea-green cubicle furniture, he examines the postcard announcing a gallery show for the art of Carder Quevedo. Certain angles spotlight Maeve's fingerprints.

"It's important," Maeve had said. "Let's do it. Let's go."

Brody will attend the show for her sake: Maeve is the one who loves the visual arts.

"Plus, if you have an artist in your family, I want to meet him."

"The artist isn't in my family," Brody tells her. "Not blood anyway. He's on Lucy's side—Stan's brother-in-law—so it doesn't matter either way."

"Still…"

They kissed goodbye without finishing the conversation. Brody's lips are prone to being chapped, and his girlfriend is living lip balm. Japanese lineage covered her with soft skin flowering in two lips like petaled promises. Her eyes are orchids.

Brody has mixed feelings about seeing Stan, but he's happy he'll see only two family members before tomorrow evening's gallery event: Stan and Mordecai. Certain that his older brother will notice Maeve's skin, Brody gloats. He recalls that, back in the day, the darker Stan's girlfriends were, the happier and—later—more heartbroken Stan was. How that trail of Asian girls created a path leading to Stan's flat-assed and bone white wife Lucy, puzzles Brody. Perhaps both extreme happiness and gut-wrenching heartbreak are too much. Maybe Stan simply prefers being comfortable. Brody wishes he could taunt Stan with details of Maeve's oiled skin, the same way Stan used to tease him with tales of his own girlfriends, but it wouldn't be considered funny anymore. Brody misses *Stan B.C.* He'd been cool, able to laugh in the moment, not critiquing every second as it happened.

"Lucy and the baby will stop in briefly to see Carder's newer paintings," Stan tells him on the phone, "She doesn't want the baby exposed to city pollution for long. Anyway, we're here to pick up Mandy and bring her back home."

If he cared, Brody would be hurt upon finding out that his only niece has been in the city for the majority of the summer without contacting him. But over the years, he's grown used to the deliberate distancing of his family. Feelings for them gradually dissipated into a numb observation of reality. They were like a song playing through the walls of an apartment down the hall. Why pay attention? You'll never be allowed inside to hear the nuances or know the lyrics. That's what it comes down to: his family is muffled bass—that's all. A shut door. It is what it is.

In actuality, Brody knows he's fortunate to have *any* contact with Stan, their mother or Stan's family. It all boils down to baptism. Irony would've spun things so that a two-second dunk under water, bleaching sin in swimming pool chlorine, would've later transformed him into the Antichrist once he realized he no longer believed Jehovah's Witnesses' church doctrine. He would've been subsequently disfellowshipped and shunned, preventing any relationship with his family—a *"we love you so much that we're going to pretend you don't exist!"* sort of concept. But by the time he was thirteen, Brody had already developed a fear of commitment strong enough to resist his family's pressure to get baptized—it was Brody's chickening out that saved him, preventing irrevocable consequences later. At least now he hears from them occasionally, even if the phone still transfers the tears in his mother's eyes.

Save for a few straying strands, Stan's moussed hair refuses late summer winds, the opposite of the thick curls running amuck on his little brother's head. It's another reason to wonder how they'd come from the same gnarled family tree, when it appears they wouldn't have even come from the same genus. If Stan were an oak, Brody thought himself a willow, better yet, a streetlamp. Regardless, only two things provided clues to their brotherhood: the Sutcliffe family name and their deep, identical, midnight voices. People said they should become radio DJ's, sports announcers or audiobook readers, but Brody hates sports and Stan's reading time is devoted to the church's Watchtower magazine.

Both brothers stand shivering on the roof deck of the Circle Line Ferry, the first time they've seen one another in sixteen months, since Miriam's birth. Another baby, looking the same as the one before the one before. Copy #3.

The air taps post-nasal drip from Stan, but he ignores it while extolling Lucy's demands that he carry a blanket so Mordecai won't catch cold in the wind. She was right, the air off the waters is chilly, and the blanket ensures they can endure a spot atop the boat. Wrapped in the khaki-colored blanket, Stan resembles a teepee and Mordecai a little Indian poking out from between his knees. Brody is in a long sleeve t-shirt and shorts, not the least bit cold.

"Yeah... so do you have any job prospects?" Stan asks, wrapping his arms around Mordecai.

"I'm fine with jobs right now," Brody replies. *Not this conversation again.*

"Oh. Wait, what *is* it you're doing now?"

"Gee, I'm not sure I can make rent this month, Stan. What, you think I'm destitute? I'm catering, temping, playing gigs—mostly at The Knotted Café in the Village. I play the occasional Sunday brunch at a French restaurant on the Upper West Side, but they like their music in the background, more aloof—so I wear sunglasses while performing, sit further away from them and never smile. Works every time. They're a bunch of pigs who never listen to the lyrics."

"Bro, I wasn't implying anything. At any rate, Lucy's been teaching the kids music at home lately. We're thinking of having each play an instrument. They just watched *The Sound of Music.*"

"That's wonderful." Brody is thankful the subject has changed. As the Statue of Liberty grows closer, he fantasizes about the Sutcliffe kids dressed in uniforms made from their rose-colored curtains and screeching out wild, apocalyptic songs on a rag-tag assortment of kazoos, recorders and cymbals. Luckily, Stan only brought Mordecai this time. It *is* a business trip after all. The visit wouldn't have happened otherwise. Mordy had happily announced he was ahead in his home-schooling, so he got to go with dad.

"Homeschooling's the best decision we ever made," Stan says. "We were too late for Mandy. Can't believe she even made it to graduation, but this guy isn't going to have to put up with degenerate, worldly teachings."

Fellow passengers shuffle toward the front deck to get a better view of Liberty's flowing robes. The commotion brings Mordecai out of a trance. His wide eyes soon scope the massive statue of a green, torch-wielding Amazon woman.

"She's so big, Dad. Big! Look!" He runs out of Stan's arms, hopping towards the oohs and ahhs of the tourists. Though she's a statue with incredible posture and presence, Brody has successfully ignored Lady Liberty for years. It's not like she's going anywhere.

"Says here they finished building her in 1886," Stan yells out from a tourist guidebook, then assures an unconcerned Brody, "No worries. Mordy's all right. The whole world's so huge to him. He's a modern Christopher Columbus. Think you'll ever get married and have kids, Brody?"

"Eh. I don't worry about it."

Brody recalls Stan's and Lucy's *Thank You* card ages ago for his wedding present—an engraved brass doorplate which made it no further than their first apartment's door. The card's message, in Stan's heavy handwriting, read: *I always pictured our children playing together, growing up hand-in-hand.* Their first child clawed her way into the world eleven months later - fat, proud and reckless. Copy #1: Mandy. Brody's thoughts jump to Maeve, the way she'd kept stony-eyed despite a stationary tear on one cheek while revealing that childbirth might be difficult. Small hips. Small rips. She'd cut her hand that day.

"You'll change your mind about children." Stan twists puzzled lips and takes a breath as if to continue, but instead looks at the Hudson River spraying from the ferry's hull.

"I'm so excited that you're coming to Club Soda tonight," Brody says, pulling down his long sleeves. His tattoos are burning to meet his brother's scrutiny, migrating as close to the edges of his sleeves as possible, taunting. "I made sure Mordecai can come too. Don't worry—it's not a crazy environment. Just beer."

"Beer? I thought it was a coffee shop."

"It's *like* a coffee shop. I mean, there's beer, but it's not the type of place people go to get drunk or crazy. It's a first stop in most people's night. They get the party started there and then move on. Calmly. They move on calmly."

"At 10 PM?"

"Things are later here. It means a lot to me that you guys are coming."

"Of course we are! So…" Stan says, "…Mandy hasn't contacted you since she's been here?"

"Nope." Brody says it without disappointment. She and he had never hit it off, even when the little piranha had made her life's debut. The newborn cried every time he'd held her. "Have you seen her since *you* arrived, Stan?"

"Nuh-uh. She's become a bit of a brat. She and her mother do nothing but fight. Mandy's actually refusing to see us until tomorrow night. And Lucy's excited to bring her back home, but she gets too pushy with Mandy. Women are supposed to be so naturally caring, but the whole mother-daughter dynamic makes no sense. They end up stepping on each other's toes, on purpose sometimes. Nabbing and nipping at each another. We've spent so much time raising Mandy the right way, protecting her from depravity, and she acts like we've done the exact opposite, to keep her from enjoying herself, you know?"

"Nope. Sorry, I don't. What about Lucy's brother?"

"Carder? We'll see him at the show. It's his show. Lucy's not too happy with him. He hasn't been studying the Bible with Mandy or taking her to the meetings. We want her to keep connected to a congregation. The book of Proverbs says that a person who isolates himself will seek his own selfish longing; against all practical wisdom.' That's Mandy."

"I guess home schooling's the way to go then." Brody doesn't hide his sarcasm because Stan's ears automatically sift it out anyway. "But Mandy's approaching adulthood. Isn't she eighteen?"

"Not eighteen yet. Soon. Don't rush it."

Close up, Miss Liberty is bigger and bluer than Brody

remembers. She isn't looking at them, unaware of the hundreds of tired visitors huddling around even though she asked for them. The Sutcliffe brothers had been there as kids, but Brody remembers little about the experience: the big sandals, the long winding staircase inside her, and a sweating red-faced Polish woman with a cushiony ass who kept bringing their stair-climb to a halt with demands for an elevator.

Mordecai runs around in circles, hitting Brody once in a while, then running off again. He accidentally hits Stan in the balls, leaving Brody to support his wincing brother. Stan promises with clenched eyes that he's okay, it was an accident, and what does he need testicles for anyway? Apparently, there are no plans for Copy #4.

Mordecai reaches up to touch the statue as if she isn't nearly a hundred feet above them. "Whoa! She's a queen—see the crown?" He then addresses the Lady herself. "Hello, Mrs. Giant!" Her lips are pursed shut. She stares ahead without blinking.

"We'll come here after Armageddon, Mordy. I'll bring you. And I bet Liberty will either be lying in the river or obliterated completely…like in that movie *The Day Before Today's Tomorrow.*"

"You mean *yesterday*?" asks Brody.

"Tell your Uncle Brody that you want him to be there with us after Armageddon."

"I want you there," Mordy says, and starts spinning.

"I get that," Brody replies, seeing halfway through his statement that Mordy's attention fizzled, "but your grandma isn't expecting I'll survive it. She called the other day, warning me that I'll probably be getting my eyes eaten out by birds after God kills me."

Stan shakes his head *no* and slides his reading glasses halfway down his long Sutcliffe nose which is lost in the New York guidebook. "Yes, those are mammoth toes, Mordecai, but did you know that the French gave us the Statue of Liberty?"

"The *French*? The French are good for nothin'. They're against freedom," Mordecai squawks.

Brody can only imagine where he got those ideas as he knows his brother's religion claims political neutrality. They won't even vote.

"That's not true, Mordecai," says Brody. "That's why the French gave her to us, to show that they believe in freedom too. In fact, if you went to Paris, you'd see that the Statue of Liberty has sisters—statues that look a lot like her. So she's a French-American. And we're not as diff…" but Mordecai skips away, closing in on a woman whose fuchsia purse contains a quivering Chihuahua.

Will this experience be as exhausting as Brody's last trip to see Stan, Lucy and the kids? An hour-and-a-half was spent getting ready that morning before they'd poured into the mini-van, practically coasting in neutral to the Museum of Natural History. Unfazed by the life-sized skeleton of the Tyrannosaurus rex, Mordecai and Mandy pulled Brody and the rest of them into the gift shop where they picked through three dollar geodes and tiny snow globes containing a few flakes with nowhere to go. Mandy broke the handle off an *I want my mummy* coffee mug. Hushing her, Brody paid an annoyed cashier in silence. After perusing nature books and fool's gold for forty-five minutes, Lucy rubbed her pregnant belly and said, "I'm tired. Need to sit. Plus, there's no sense in going through the museum *now*, we've seen all the highlights right here." The rest of the day was covered in Chuck E. Cheese, children's music and a toy ambulance on which some smart-ass toymaker had installed a siren.

"Hush up!" says the woman to the Chihuahua barking inside her purse.

Stan corrals Mordecai and his probing hands away from the woman and ushers him into an elevator. They're soon at the pedestal observation level, ten floors up.

Outside, Mordecai points up, "Whoa, the toes got bigger!"

Where did Mordy get the foam Statue of Liberty crown he's suddenly wearing? They haven't even been to the gift shop. This day makes Brody comfortable with the prospect of *not* having children.

Walking halfway around the observation deck, they join the statue in viewing the jagged Manhattan skyline. Brody doesn't understand his life anymore now than when he first moved to New York, maybe less, but he's closer than ever to what he wants: his music and Maeve. On the other hand, he still mourns the loss of relationship with his mother and brother. At this point, it's hard to remember the times when the three of them stayed up late in their pajamas, crunching caramel corn and watching vintage Hitchcock. Brody is no longer even sure they're memories. Maybe they're impressions, maybe they never happened. In addition to his fading family, Brody hates his office job—phony people unsuccessfully concealing their dullness. Perhaps fulfillment will only ever be found in the cracks, not the whole.

"*But*...we're on the path, Brody," Maeve had recently said over a glass of wine in their tiny apartment in Astoria. "That's all that matters. If we can just get through these years it'll all gel. Your job sucks, school's killing me, but we're on the path. Once you release your first album and take this sexy psychologist with you to the Grammys, we'll then see how important these years were." She squeezed two of his fingers.

"They don't give Grammy's for my type of music. I'm not commercial enough."

"They will. They better—I'm already looking for the right dress."

"I wish he could see your nipples. Is that wrong?"

"Who? Your brother? Stan? My nipples?"

"They're perfection. Can I at least tell him about them? They deserve mention."

"Ew, that's wrong! And gross! And creepy. And off-limits!"

Stan motions with his chin toward Manhattan, "Do you remember how much sky the Twin Towers took up? It's a shame."

"Do you know what mom said when I called her on 9/11?"

"What?"

"She said that she was glad I was okay, but that I was already dead in God's eyes."

"Oh, bro. I'm sorry. Don't take that in a bad way. Try thinking of it from her perspective. She wants you to come back to Jehovah. She shouldn't have put it like she did, but if you're not living according to his standards, you're as good as dead. You can't be happy in this wicked world."

"I am happy!" Brody looks away at the sun. "Stan, you didn't call me *at all* during that time."

"I heard you were okay from Mom! Of course I was concerned. What kind of person do you think I am?"

Silence prompts Stan's sigh, and brings his attention back to a restless skyline. How can anyone choose to pack into such a grimy city, like cattle or those ants that build bridges with the dead bodies of their brothers to reach their destination? And did Brody see that filthy woman singing *Jolene* on the subway? Her hair was cut like a man's and she had rough, truck-driver hands. He suddenly jumps. "Dang it! I left that blanket on the ferry. Lucy will kill me. Oh well," he mutters, then asks, "So, this is it?"

"This?" It takes Brody a second to realize Stan refers to their current experience. "I suppose it is. I couldn't get us the tickets to actually go up into the statue. You know, they only allow so many, and it's a chaotic mess. I'm sure it's caused a lot of claustrophia. People come from all over the world to get into her. Kind of like your ex-girlfriend, Pamela, eh?" He elbows Stan.

"It's probably better that way. Mordy seems like he's ready to go. And waiting in all those lines to get *here* was excruciating. Plus, you probably didn't want to go up into her anyway, did you?"

"Why not?"

"When we went as kids, you threw a fit the entire way. And when we got to the crown and looked out, you said, 'That's all?' like you expected more."

Brody laughs. "All those stairs and then all we could see from the windows in the crown was a puny patch of sky. It didn't feel all that… liberating." He laughs again—what a twerp he'd been.

"But remember the breeze coming in?"

"No."

Stan puts his arm around Brody, just as he had when they'd stared out from the hundred-foot woman twenty years before. A chilly wind blows a sense of loss through Brody. It's a wind his long-sleeved t-shirt can't keep out.

Club Soda hums. Heady dark beers and golden ales are strewn out along the bar, their glass beading with the nectar of humid air. The small space will only grow warmer as weekenders trickle into the cramped Lower East Side bar throughout the night. By the time Unity hands him a second round of Rheingold, Brody feels at home.

Tuning his guitar becomes easier.

"Honey, it's okay," Unity says, setting her bangled hand on his. "Your brother won't be able to help but be impressed. You're impressive! You're going to sing *Tower of Nothing*, aren't you?"

"Oh yeah, definitely going to sing a song ode to my oppressive church-upbringing. Stan would *love* that. No. Then again, maybe if he doesn't show up, I'll intro with it."

Unity smiles. Aside from Maeve, she's his only fan. Then again, there's that petite boy who shows up every time Brody plays, but he's peculiar, hanging on every note, every word. He knows the lyrics and, after the performance, shoots out dinner invitations like missiles. The guy wears scarves year-round and fixes Brody's collar whenever they meet.

"Be yourself," Unity continues, "You're good at it. Remember, your brother's on your turf. If he's truly as white and religious as you say, he won't understand a single song anyway."

"I didn't say he was *stupid*. I said he was *religious*." Brody had been not-so-gently helped to realize the difference by Maeve who makes 'Christian' look good. At first, he thought her religious proclivities would make dating difficult if not impossible, but she shocked him by being reasonable, loving and tolerant—three qualities he'd never equated with religion.

"If you say so." Unity raises her eyebrows and walks back to the bar.

Brody is drawn to Unity's bouncing runaway curls and the freckles settling only on her nose. In another world, one in which Maeve didn't exist, he would pursue her, but Unity wants his music, not him. On the other hand, Maeve loves Brody and would stay with him whether he was a janitor or simply content being soul-raped by the corporate world—as long as Brody was satisfied. Maeve is reassurance. She's mashed potatoes, the Sunday paper.

The first musicians of the night, a guy-girl duo calling themselves Bear Children, open with a chord-happy song. "*Don'cha kiss past six?*" they sing in harmony. Brody knows the pair and doubts either has ever been awake before six as he's never seen them in daylight. On the other hand, he's sure that his brother does *not* kiss past six and begins to wonder if Stan and Mordecai will show at all. He wrote extensive instructions for their cab ride and pressed a twenty into

Stan's hand, but he knows he invited them to what Stan considers a den of iniquity. Brody looks around the bar, attempting to apply Stan's mind to the scene. Paintings of sad-eyed children on the bar's walls become vulgar and overdone instead of funny or charming. The floor needs sweeping, the jukebox is scratched to hell, and odd odors of rotten bananas and a men's locker room fill Brody's nostrils. A few barstools away, a girl in a low-cut spandex top laughs and shouts "Oh you *fuuucker!*" to a shaggy-haired hipster who'd put her purple prayer beads around his neck.

A few songs later, Bear Children transfer from the slice-of-pie corner-stage into the world of brew-chugging patrons. It's now Brody's turn to play. Carrying a tray of drinks, Unity tells him not to worry, she'll watch for his brother. Brody worries, but has to perform, and goes on stage. His nerves demand he forego his usual skittish chitchat with the crowd. Closing his eyes, he finds and fingers the guitar strings, clears his throat and waits, internally begging his voice to rise to the microphone. There's always an instant when he wonders if it won't come, if he'll produce a sound so monstrous he'll never outlive it. But his voice eventually emerges, and after only a few verses he gets lost in the song without restraint. He sings about his relationship with his mother, though most assume it's about an old girlfriend or boyfriend. He wishes Maeve was there with her comforting, almandine eyes, her black-indigo hair glossing at him through all else. She always pretends it's the first time she heard the song, and told him to imagine her in tonight's audience. For his part, Brody plays the song to an image he knows well, one of Maeve lying naked in bed, reading a novel. As he reaches the final verse, he opens his eyes, allowing the audience in.

Stan came! There he is, sitting on a barstool next to the eerie, petite guy. Little Mordy stands wide-eyed, holding his chin the same way Stan sometimes does. Brody sings:

> "...*Standing in a glass dress,*
> *A shattered mess,*
> *Shards of delicacy,*
> *split shadows and dark matter.*"

At the song's conclusion, the bar floats a few seconds before those with hands free of beers applaud. Stan claps the same way he would after a sermon, with weight and seriousness. Mordecai jumps up, flashing a grin of teeth yet to know life's stains. He wears his foam Statue of Liberty crown and holds a cigarette lighter provided by Unity, which Stan begrudgingly allowed knowing the kid would never get it lit.

Brody introduces his brother and Mordecai to the rest of *Club Soda*, resulting in Mordecai running up to the stage, saying too loudly into the microphone "Hello, New York!" He then bows. The bar chuckles and sways, a few roll their eyes, groaning, and someone shouts "Get that boy a beeee-ER! On me!"

Brody calls Bear Children back to the stage so he can say a quick hello to his brother, to make sure he and Mordy are all right. The duo jump at the prospect. Performers fight for any stage time they can get.

The creepy-petite boy approaches and says with hands clasped, "Very moving tonight." Brody ignores him for once and squeezes through to Stan.

Unity pushes curls behind one ear and hands Mordecai a Roy Rogers in a plastic cup. "That'll be six dollars," she says putting out her hand to Stan.

"Wha?" both Stan and Brody say in unison.

"I'm joking! You two are plenty alike." She then asks Mordecai what he thinks of Brody's playing.

"I wanna be a rockstar, just like Uncle Brody! Dad, I want a guitar!"

"Isn't he the sweetest boy?" Unity asks no one in particular. Her silver skull ring sparkles under hazy blue lights. "It was wonderful to meet you, Stan. We love your brother. And his music. Brody's got the heart of a Buddhist monk in the body of a hippy-soldier. What a combo, eh?"

Stan looks less than pleased. "Brody's quite the guy. It was nice meeting you too, Unity." As she walks away, he mutters into Brody's neck, "Doesn't she have a real name?"

"Um, oh my God, I think her name's actually Gertrude or something."

"Well, her mother must be proud, huh, Brody?"

Brody feels so good that Stan showed up, he starts relaxing and tries to decide which song he'll play next for his brother—*To Be*

Cowboys or *Paper Veins?* Thus far, Stan's only heard half a song.

Stan slaps Brody on the back, tells him they always knew he was a fine guitar player and sticks a rigid twenty in the palm of his sweaty hand. "You know, I think it's actually illegal for Mordecai to be here. We should probably get back to the hotel. You understand."

Brody understands.

He accompanies them to the door. Stan is now an older version of the boy Brody once wrestled in the backyard, a grown version of the punk who taught him how to flip the bird and explained to him that pubic hair wasn't fur, that its appearance didn't mean Brody was slowly turning into a werewolf from the crotch up. Now, Stan is a man walking with a smaller version of himself, Copy #2, that wears a foam crown with its spikes ripped off and scattered throughout the bar. It will be a long while before he'll see them again after the following night's gallery show. How much more will they change before the next visit?

On sparkling nighttime sidewalks, Stan announces that tonight is their little secret, which Mordy's mom doesn't need to know anything about.

Mordecai nods his head in agreement. "I love secrets! I'm good at them, ask Mandy! Hey, Uncle Brody, I get to see my sister tomorrow!"

"I know! That's going to be exciting!" Brody scoops him up for a goodbye hug. The kid is annoyingly adorable.

A cab screeches up beside them and Mordecai climbs onto its spotless black seats.

"Hey!" Suddenly, Stan seems to feel rushed, as though he didn't call the cab of his own volition. "Bro, you're real good. Truly. You ain't got nothin' on Led Zep—not that I listen to them anymore—but you're good. You need a band though. It's the music industry: girls go solo, guys need a band. If you're gonna keep doing this, you gotta get one. Okay?" He hits Brody in the chest, while the taxi driver yells at them to *get in or get out!* Stan repeats himself, "Okay?"

"Okay."

The man and his son are then swallowed by the taxi cab. It leers a few feet to leave, but stops. Stan's window rolls down, "Hey, Bro!"

"Yeah?"

"Your song about mom?"

"Yeah?"

"Spot on, Brother, spot on."

Brody swallows a sigh as the car drives away. The summer night slaps his face and tells him to get back into the bar where six more songs will be born.

23

OUTSIDE LOOKING IN

The eve of Carder's show sneaks up and sits on his chest. It's heavy enough to leave a mark, but doesn't. His lungs are tight. Breaths short. *Being here now* doesn't help. *Now* is the last place Carder wants to be, but he's trapped. *Sixty-five steps. Sixty-five steps to the car.* Driving aimlessly, racing whoever is next to him at traffic lights—grandmas, families, even teens. It solves nothing. He doesn't need a car to change the situation, he needs a time machine. But what would that accomplish?

For Carder, the evening holds on to minutes like they're babies or beers, but the thing it doesn't hold is Haika. Mike's social calendar has them attending a benefit dinner for childhood leukemia, an obligation that annoys Haika, largely because one of the guys assigned to their table left his wife when she was diagnosed with leukemia herself. Haika couldn't stand the thought of sitting near him. He'd pretended that Ann no longer existed long before she'd actually died. Apparently, only children get his help. Mike argued that the event is a way to network *and* help sick children, a truth which Haika said she understood but loathes. It's probably better she'd gone—it means Mike won't later ruin Carder's Camp Fountain event out of spite. Plus, Carder and Haika are jointly stressed. Carder rations information and withdraws like a sullen twit, and Haika—to whom curating the show is vital—dives for information until she turns blue. Still, her absence that night leaves Carder on edge.

A bassline thumps from Mandy's headphones as she stands in the doorway. Carder wishes he could hold her above the pain she's experiencing, to remove any worry over her family. Unfortunately, his arms aren't large enough to offer the solace they once did. She outgrew them.

Mandy removes an earbud. "I'll be in my room, packing."

"Okay, Mandy. If you need help let me know."

"I'll be fine. G'night."

"'Night."

"Unc?"

"Yeah?"

"If *you* need anything tonight, let *me* know too."

"I'm fine."

"Me too." With that, she pushes the earbud back in place and vanishes from the doorway. The evening is tense - not only will she soon see her family, but will also return with them. Gettysburg. Her mom. Dad. Miriam. Mordy. The Battlefield. Each is taxing in unique, dreadful ways.

If thumping pop music drives Mandy's apprehension away, Carder envies her. Nothing does that for him. Wandering back and forth from television to refrigerator with a gurgling stomach, he's the volleyball in a match between crime shows and junk food, but his heightened nerves leave him too raw to watch violence and his appetite turns away from the few greasy snacks in the cupboards.

Mandy's love of grocery shopping had tapered off. It will be missed, but Carder pushes that thought away while fumbling through the cold contents of the refrigerator in search of light fare. Not much there. Scrounging several types of lettuce and greens, he fixes himself a makeshift salad that accompanies him to the den. The space there expanded when his paintings and most recent sculpture were removed. Carder shuts the door and flips through TV channels until settling on a nature marathon featuring meerkats. He turns off the lamp, leaving the room lit by a flickering band of meerkats in a state of agitation. Like the nearby wildebeest at the same watering hole, he watches their alarmed antics: running around helter-skelter though they're safe. Sitting in a dingy armchair, Carder chews his cud, trying not to think while watching.

For some time, he doesn't know where his mind goes, or that he's even there. If he could maintain that state, he would, but it ends abruptly when the lamp buzzes and flashes the room, popping its filament. Carder jumps in his seat. Meerkats scatter. He sits up and turns off the television. The meerkats leave in a blue zip of electricity. Darkness. Only the pale hush of moonlight steals in. But darkness isn't the sole difference. The room's climate has split into harsh borders meeting down the middle of Carder's body. Tropics jut against arctic regions. His left leg sweats. His right freezes.

Different sounds fill each ear: melodic echoes, ancient, beatific, fast, red, golden, square, heady, primeval, close but from another plane—sounds that make little sense.

In his right ear, a curious holy choir sings from somewhere on the streets outside. Angelic high notes enter, muted by the home's plaster walls, windows, wires and brick. In his left ear, a familiar song begins from somewhere inside the house but outside the room—one he's heard thousands of times: Rachmaninov's Prelude in C-sharp minor. It's delivered in ominous musical bellows, some heavier notes fall close to Rachmaninov's styling, but then merge with new instruments—discordant brass, disjointed strings, broken woodwinds and percussion—all played in ways most orchestras would consider blasphemous. Both songs fill Carder separately but simultaneously, disparate parts join in an amalgamation of multi-colored melody, puzzle pieces that shouldn't fit. Carder tries convincing himself that Mandy must've dug through his music collection and found some obscure, warped Rachmaninoff. It can't be, but perhaps she played it in place of her sorrow for leaving.

Yeah, tell yourself that. You should be so lucky.

A light appears around the doorway like a celestial picture frame, more intense than anything in Carder's home. He ought to, no, he *will* get up and check on Mandy.

Though the windows are closed, the blinds begin battering against them until something pushes forth. Standing knee-high, four fully-formed otherworldly nude women emerge, two on each side of the windows. Once they materialize fully and walk several paces, four perfectly proportioned men of the same stature move forward, followed by four more women and on and on in a ritualistic manner, sauntering forth in rhythm. The Adams and Eves of this procession, of every shape and relative size, of foreign and familiar features, wear no fig leaves. Women's breasts roll, nipples point freely, the men's scrotums and penises are framed in curls of natural hair on oiled bodies. Above their heads, they hold tropical blooms of various flowers—blossoms that are giant in proportion to the small beings. With arms raised, the bowls of their armpits catch and cradle light. As the procession moves forward, the blooms change, morphing geometrically, architecturally into manmade objects like forgotten pieces of machinery—cogs, toothy key-like pieces and sharp square blades. At this point, Carder figures he's crossed the line to certifiably insane. However, once certified, why not sit and watch the parade? The first group of women walk like apparitions in a long line right through the closed door. Without warning, the last one disappears and the music stops.

"Space is so limited here." The voice fills the same ear in which the sacred choir sang. It isn't Mandy's voice. Deeper and more penetrating, it must emanate from a body far larger and less ordinary than hers.

"Has he grown deaf?" another less forceful voice asks in Carder's other ear.

"Not deaf. Possibly mute."

"Are you sure this is the same misanthropic…"

"…fop? Yes."

"I was going to say… humanitarian… psychopomp."

This back and forth chatter helps Carder acclimate to the situation. When he closes his eyes, he doubts he did for he still sees his reflection in the mirror across the room. The reflection's eyes are closed. He wants to ask who's there, but words lodge in this throat.

"Come now, you know us." The deeper voice brushes the walls from floor to ceiling. "You do."

This is a first. Carder had never before met creatures of Neidin outside their own land. All reaping took place within that land's borders. It's been many, many years, but he thinks he knows them, though never in this manner, never here, not of this world. Once he recognizes the voices, he knows Mandy is safe and unbothered in her room. It also helps him find his own voice. "Dyrak, if that's you and Everett, I don't have time for another labyrinth. They're too difficult. My time's full now. Besides, you bested me long ago."

Carder's previous time with them was the only visit to Neidin which ended safely for all involved.

"What's this? No!" says the smaller voice—Everett. "You've bested us since then. Your labyrinth has greater difficulty than ours.

We're here to… what's the word… exacerbate… exaggerate…"

"Congratulate," says Dyrak.

"For what? Congratulate me for what?" Carder asks.

"For what you did, what you're doing, what you're about to do."

Carder considers the garbled pronouncement as a sign to do nothing, and he does exactly that. He leans back in his chair and stares at the ceiling, trying to feed his senses on its endless blank white, to send himself into the gauze of the universe and forget turmoil. He contemplates the ceiling's ivory undulations and decides they're variations in his sight rather than paint caught in the act of fading.

"I'm still not sure I don't have regrets." Everett says.

"You always have regrets," Dyrak replies, then ventures an explanation to Carder. "Before you, we'd almost settled on a songwriter in Angel City back in the 60's. Talented, but addicted. Kept pressing heaven's buzzer until he was allowed in. A waste if you ask me."

"How do you know he went to heaven?" Carder is suspect of these two creatures. They've deceived him in the past. That's why they're still living.

"He had a weakness for providing food and coin to the needy. Heaven loves the poor—streets of gold still need their urchins, right?"

"Yee-OUCH! Motherfucker!" Carder yells in response to what feels like biting electric shocks on his left foot, right hand, and the back of his neck.

He springs from the chair and raises the blinds to see if a choir of robed boys stands outside crooning lyrics of a long-dead language. There are no choirboys—only a white sky with motionless pink lightning suspended mid-strike, and a sun eclipsed in black and haloed in red. The black sun suddenly jets across the sky, rolling to the center of the windowpane. Carder jumps. It isn't a colorless sky filling the window. It's actually the white of a giant eye focusing on him.

"You've gotten hairier." The voice and eye are Dyrak's. "Uglier."

Then Everett's. "All humans are like that. They only start out cute. Still, Creep's firmly maintained his endearing hesitation."

Carder is partly soothed knowing this apocalypse is likely

occurring only to him, but equally dismayed that the experience is an anomaly he can't share.

"What do you want?" Carder directs his words to Dyrak's framed eye.

"Who said we want anything?"

"You're at *my* window."

"Exactly, Creep. Open the window, so I can speak more softly. I don't want to wake the entire neighborhood. There was a female, one with bi... bin... bi-nocks?"

"Binoculars," Everett offers.

Carder knows exactly to whom Dyrak refers. "You mean my neighbor, Mrs. Gunderson."

"A female-woman wearing a tattered blue housecoat covered in flat, farcical flowers? I say—if you want flowers, then grow the damn things. Hers are chintzy and insincere."

"Yup, that would be Mrs. Gunderson."

"She's currently eyeing my anus—it's staring into her window as much my eye is staring into yours. Yes, currently. She's on the other end, and thinks it's the pink puckerhole of Time. Wants to be swallowed by it."

"Your puckerhole? I doubt she wants anything to do with it."

"She already believes it's a wormhole. Worms are pink. It's a hole. The connection's simplistic but understandable. Regardless, she's a ghost of a woman desperate to cross over. *Too* desperate to cross over. But I'm not here for her. You can thank me later."

"Now you're a Grim Reaper?"

"Temporary, part-time work. You people have such incredibly short life spans. It's amazing that some deliberately shorten them even further. Don't look at me like that! I needed a change and always admired your work. But you know, you think it's going to be different, less stifling, more independent, more autonomous, powerful, savory, and respected, but the politics are the same everywhere. I've never been an ass-kisser like your neighbor... Mrs. Underskin."

"Gunderson."

"Mrs. Bungholeson isn't going to open the window willingly, but you aren't her, and I'd like to box-step your attention back to my request, if you will, back to opening the window."

Carder sees no harm in opening it—the two creatures had never hurt him—but no sooner has he unlatched the lock, raising the window a fraction when a tarry, green limb slithers through the crack, shoving it open the rest of the way. Then the limb moves back, settling in repose on the windowsill, leaving a trail of slime dripping from the frame. A wet, black nose fills the window.

Inhales.

Exhales.

Inhales.

"Don't push me," says Dyrak, apparently addressing Everett. "By tomorrow, Mrs. Cumbersome's going to think there's a crop circle where her garden was."

"Relax," is Everett's response. "I've almost got what I came for. Besides, I wanted to smell him again. I'd tried recalling human odor for such a long time. Do they all smell so savory?"

Before Carder could address him, the voice disappears along with the snout. Carder has an innate sense that Everett's presence is altogether gone, so he opens the other window blind, showing more of the still-present Dyrak. Sharp teeth protrude from Dyrak's body in strange hit-and-miss patterns.

"Where'd Everett go?" Carder asks.

"Traveling, or I absorbed him, or he wanted a new place to ruin, or he's dead. What do you think? He's gone. Wanted to see more green than that on his limbs. Personally, I prefer faster beings. Plants live in such a slowed down state."

A sudden sound comes from the bedroom door. The doorknob turns a bit, only to stop. It's locked. Impossible. There is *no* lock. It jiggles lightly, then more firmly. Then, the door vibrates with a few solid knocks. It should burst open as the rumblings grow harsh and desperate. Someone or something wants inside, but for some reason can't enter. Carder looks at the golden light pouring in around the door frame. Shadows on the floor tell him something waits.

"Card, would you let me in? It's colder on this side."

No. It can't be. His mind plunges to his feet. It can't be—but it is—the voice of his dead mother. Sylvia Quevedo. Carder's toes pulse like they were stepped on by an elephant. How does one collect one's heart upon the return of a dead loved one? Though he hasn't heard the voice since her death, it's Sylvia's. It has the timbre of molasses, a melodic filigree that shepherds calmness within him. Only, now it doesn't. Tears that have been building for years twist back to their source without falling. Carder turns to see Dyrak's eye in the window and feels a gentle, tarry limb petting the crown of his head.

"Go on," Dyrak says.

"Come get a glass of water, my little Creeping son," says his mother's voice as it often had.

Carder's mouth is too cottony to reply. He looks at the base of the door, and where he would expect to see the shadows of two feet, he sees the rippling grey blur of infinite oscillating shadows. The door vibrates as though objects are being pelted or rammed against it. He'd give anything to let his mother in, whether ghost, goblin, angel or vapor. But he's frozen. Can't speak.

The suction of Dyrak's green limb kisses the middle of his forehead until he plucks it off.

"Go on," Dyrak repeats, leading Carder to reconsider the prudence of doing so.

When Carder turns to peer out the window and assess more than Dyrak's pupil and limbs, he hits the desk next to the door, overturning a jar of pens, knocking over books stacked chaotically for years. They fall, covers creasing, pages splay, worlds bend and open. The door jostles and shakes. Weight leans against it, causing the hinges to sigh. Disoriented, Carder bends down to collect the books and notices something sticking out from the space below the desk. He feels for it, expecting the burnished handle to end in a long-forgotten screwdriver, but when he brings it out from under the dresser, it's a woodcarving tool of which he has no memory. It could've been there for decades.

In an instant, whatever is on the other side of the door grows quiet and the light is now unbroken by shadow, leading him to believe Sylvia, or whatever it was, has left. Desperation explodes inside him. He pulls on the door, but it won't budge and he doesn't have time to waste. Looking at the newly found chisel in his hand, he determines it will prove a fast, toothless key to the sealed door. With abandon, he shunts the chisel into the wood around the doorknob. The old wood is dry—it could've been kindling—quickly shattering into beveled smithereens while an array of rhythms bound up the stairs. The doorknob falls to the floor among splintering chunks and the door bursts open, knocking Carder backward to the floor while a hissing, yowling cat bounds into and across the room as though being chased. Clawing its way up the curtains in terror, it leaps out the second-story window which is now only inhabited by night.

How long has he been lying there? When Carder turns his head, he sees bare feet and a perspiring glass of cold water lowering into view. Ensconced in diffused streetlight, it's held by a saint chewing bubblegum. Mandy.

"Here," she says. "Drink this."

Night tightens and swallows Carder whole.

24

CREEP CRAWLS TOWARD WHITE LIGHT

It's easy visiting an art gallery, standing at the reception desk, studying the top postcard in a stack announcing the show. It's not feasible to Carder that he's forefather to the surrounding creations, the supposedly robust artist responsible for them. A crease ripples down the card as Carder bends it and resists the urge to sign his own guestbook.

NEIDIN

by Carder Quevedo

The card's fold pleats the title, ruining it and the landscape behind. Though a difficult decision for Carder, Haika had convinced him to place the painting of Briar on the postcard. It seems a curious choice at first. Briar was a tiny thing, a sunspot, a speck. Maroon footprints trail behind him like clown noses dropped in the snow. He heads to a destination out of view, denoted by the retreating perspective: a long, trodden path leading into a distant tunnel of darkness. Even as such a small point in the painting, Briar's sickle teeth clamp the handle of a satchel. Whether carrying serum, message or money, the contents are hidden. The frozen moment in that land had been painted inaccurately, like a photo negative. What looks like snow-covered countryside felt false even when Carder was there. Paying attention with his peripheral vision, rays from the suns of Neidin lit the ground at different angles, and the ground had blackened in sharp carbon-like cuts not depicted in the painting. Carder bends the postcard again in the opposite direction. Briar is oblivious that he's trapped by the printed announcement pimping his world.

"Unc, this is a slick gig!" It's Mandy in a small, cotton dress that a breeze could rip in two. This is the first time she's worn one since leaving her prairie home. Lara, who Carder recognizes from their run-in outside the Broadway show, accompanies her.

"Thanks," he replies. "I'm not so sure about the sculpture though."

"It's one of the best parts! You and Haika nailed everything."

"It was mostly her."

"Whatev—like Haika said, the work is yours. She just tied a bow on it."

Haika's footsteps drum across the concrete floors, amplified in the immense room. "Everything's in order," she says. "The wine's ready..." She checks her watch, "...and people should start arriving anytime now." She turns a crooked mouth to Carder. "This is the beginning of..."

"...the worst day of the rest of your life," he half-jokes.

"...a wonderful evening."

In an attempt to distract himself from anyone trickling in, Carder walks around the gallery. He starts at the sculpture of the arctic spider-wolf which holds an ominous glamour multiplied in eight glossy eyes, as motionless as gleaming cherries. The majority of the art chosen is from the past decade. His painstaking attempt at sculpture was only a recent endeavor. Artistically, the spider-wolf was his most difficult challenge in years.

Four people enter. Then, three. Two. A resistant cork pops from a wine bottle. Haika retrieves two glasses and walks to Carder. One more person arrives.

"The wine's a Rioja, smooth with a mushroomy aftertaste and hints of chartreuse, minerals and money." She looks around the gallery and raises a glass. "Mr. Quevedo, you done good."

"Is it normal to feel like an alien is going to burst out of my chest?"

"More or less. Just keep smiling. No, not like that! You look like you might slaughter everyone."

"You know, Mrs. Haus-Fiore..." he starts.

"Ms. Haus. Call me Ms. Haus."

"...Ms. Haus, I've come to terms with the actual show itself—

just not the *experience* of it."

"Sheesh, that's good to hear, my friend."

"But, it's strange letting go. I can hardly remember a time in my life when they weren't playing a major part."

"I know. Letting go is always strange, no matter what one is releasing. But don't fret, your relationship with your creations will continue. You'll always be tied to them. I've seen it a million times. There's an invisible connection, a web that neither you nor your art can break. A psychic link. I promise you, Carder, *I promise you*, you'll feel good about this show down the road, and, you know what? I want you to stop denigrating your work. You *are* your art, and it tells a damn interesting story."

Carder raises his hand to ask for a moment. He starts walking away, mumbling.

"What?" Haika asks.

He's turned pale. "I think... I might get sick. I'm going to go get some air."

Claudette is determined to be the first of Carder's widening circle of devotees to arrive, setting out for the gallery early on her own. It's a thorny undertaking. She has a lot on her mind, but tries shoving her crises behind the exciting discovery of Carder's *inner* inner-sanctum. She's waited too long for it to manifest, and now that it has, she wants to pour over it like barbecue sauce to baby back ribs.

But Doe.

It's difficult to relegate Doe to the back of her mind when she's the brightest star in Claudette's sky. Unfortunately, that star has been dimming lately. Being realistic about her sister's eating disorder forced Claudette to accept caloric management, however distressing. Doe said she wants to recognize her own disorder pragmatically, but what she calls recognition seems more like reverence. Claudette wants Doe to not only control but overcome it. However, Claudette had to compromise: she will live with her sister counting grapes as long as full-scale anorexia never again becomes her body-snatcher.

A doctor recently informed them that Doe's internal organs of a sixty-five-year-old.

"Oh no!" Doe joked. "My organs have gone ahead and retired to

Boca Raton!"

"Ms. Vivienne," the doctor replied without amusement, "your organs may have retired to Boca Raton, but I'm worried the rest may not live to meet them there."

Doe assured the Doctor that neither she nor her organs have any intention of living in Boca Raton. Ever. Perhaps Paris. Doe's body is a temple—and fried donuts aren't allowed access. Whoever heard of a temple serving cheesecake or sopapillas? No, Jesus was on track when he chose unleavened wafers instead of something fattier—even if they *were* still carbs.

When they were teenagers, Claudette followed suit by developing her own disorder, though she set herself apart, favoring bulimia over anorexia. It took years of work to change her behavior from depriving herself of nutrition altogether to a simple obsession with health food and exercise. With that accomplished, Claudette turned her attention to getting food through the door of Doe's temple any which way she can. Lately, Doe's sickness has become noticeable. People who once lightheartedly yelled for someone to give Doe a cheeseburger, soon politely requested she get a healthy meal, and now meekly beg for someone to get that girl a stick of celery with a light smear of low-fat peanut butter. A peanut? A cracker? White rice?"

These thoughts run the treadmill of Claudette's mind due to her encounter with Doe that morning. She dropped by Niirdor only to find that her sister had been manically trying on clothes since dawn. By the time Claudette got there, Doe was overtaxed, hardly able to dangle her ruby earrings and ask if they made her face look fat. She looked gaunt and exhausted. X-rays aren't needed to see Doe's bones.

Overcome with excitement, Claudette exits the car two avenues too early. The driver speeds off, leaving her to walk. In her mangled mental state everything blurs like the background of a cartoon world. Only the blaring horn of a taxicab flashing by inches away makes Claudette realize the impact of her sister's situation.

Claudette's path to the gallery has been traveled enough times that it draws her. She spots the correct scaffolding across the street, a permanent reminder of construction that's supposed to happen but never does. The usual homeless man appears beneath it, holding a cardboard sign. The message is hard to read. Claudette assumes it denotes hunger and the willingness to accept cash and all major credit cards.

Standing on the opposite sidewalk, Carder notices Claudette and waves, crossing the street to meet her.

"I had to get some air," he tells her.

"Trés sexy," Claudette says. "Did Haika pick out your outfit?" He's been cleaned up, contained in navy pin-stripe pants, orange Van sneakers and a grey, collared shirt which an auto-mechanic might wear.

"Nooo... These are my clothes—she didn't dress me. I'm not a doll."

"I am. If you pull the string on my back, you'd be surprised at what comes out of my mouth."

"And do both Vivienne dolls say the same thing with strings pulled?"

"Most don't get to pull either string."

"Then most don't play the right way."

Claudette feels a rush through her cheeks. Carder's ability to decipher the girls' code gives her goosebumps.

"Where's Viv2?" Carder is toying with her, using their codenames.

"Out of commission. Her gears have been slower as of late." Claudette's gaze drops to the ground as she imparts the knowledge, but she swallows her distress with a weak smile. "She's malfunctioning. It seems somehow Claudette's self-destruct button was pressed. Red alert! It's exhausting. Tonight, I just had to hand over the oil can, reboot her and scram so I could attend an esteemed artist's debut show."

"I'm sure your esteemed artist is grateful for your friendship."

The word 'friendship' buzzes Claudette. She hasn't heard it applied to her for longer than she can recall. It also buzzes someone sitting on the sidewalk: the homeless man, Denny Ford.

"You can't afford the sun," he says, sending up a raspy voice.

Claudette looks down at him, trying not to inhale the cooking stench of peppermint and feces. To ignore or not to ignore. Usually, there's no question. She doesn't like being harassed, let alone stoking the situation further. But this man saw her wealth so plainly—how did he know? Does he assume anyone *not* living on the streets is affluent?

What Claudette doesn't know is that in the 1950's, Denny Ford worked for Delia Davidson Design, a couture fashion house taunting all but the most opulent women. Thus, he'd heard Claudette's swishing chiffon from miles away. Denny silently admires the well-executed corseting. He wonders what fabric lines the dress, but is also stung with recollections of the fashion world destroying his life and refashioning him into the curmudgeon he's become.

Claudette mistakes his staring for lust. "Excuse me?"

"You can't afford the sun! It's not for sale."

She cringes. "You're right, I suppose. The sun's…"

"…not your personal spotlight! So how 'bouts you two *esteemed* oxygen pirates get the hell out its way?"

Carder takes charge. "Of course! We're sorry."

Claudette is incensed. "Don't apologize to him!" she says as Carder nudges her away.

"It's okay. He could use a little help. Here…" Carder pulls the wallet from his back pocket, retrieving two dollars and then addressing the man,"…one from me and one from her."

"But he's just going to buy alcohol with it!"

"So was I."

Denny Ford grunts at the measly bills.

"And give one from Doe! We can't leave her out." Claudette instructs.

"I would, but I only had two," Carder replies.

"Of course. Allow me." Claudette opens her bejeweled clutch purse with swift timidity and pulls out a hundred dollar bill. "This is all I have. Please sir, go get yourself a good meal. Here: *from Doe*," she says as though reading it from a gift tag.

"I'll do that…" the man yells as they walk away, "…if you go get yourself a dress with some decent stitching."

That seals the fate of Claudette's dress—destined for the Housing Works thrift shop.

"Are you kidding? You look abso-fab." Haika says exactly what Claudette needs to hear.

"I spoke outside to our artist," says Claudette. "It doesn't seem he's doing well."

Down the hallway, muffled hacking wanders from behind a closed door, drawing attention to a stomach's undoing. The sounds call for comment.

"It's ninety percent nerves, but he thinks he's going crazy as well, or perhaps it was food poisoning."

Mandy overhears and tables her glee over having successfully convinced the cater-waiter to serve Lara champagne. As the Vivienne girls provided the night's libations, Mandy thanks and greets Claudette, then addresses the circumstances of the previous night.

"Last night was awful for Uncle Carder. I've never seen him that way—crazy—but not the type of crazy *he* thought. He practically broke down the door to his den. When we talked this morning, we tried pinpointing what caused the episode. He hardly ate anything yesterday—very little—fixed himself a small salad from the Farmers Market and mixed in that weird stuff you gave him, Claudette. Maybe the salad dressing was too old. I don't know, maybe he just has the flu, but he was delirious. I was up all night… watching him talk in his sleep. He kept saying 'she's gone.'"

"I'm not sure I understand," Claudette says. "I've never given Carder lettuce or salad dressing." Her mind swims until it finds the only island upon which to land, and when it does, that shore is sturdy and certain. "Oh no! No, no, no…"

"What?"

"Don't tell me—he ate the Brugmansia!?"

"Ate what?"

"Brugmansia. It's a tropical plant our gardener grows on the rooftop in summertime. During Carder's recent visit to Doe's place, he admired it and we gave him several cuttings to start his own plant. It's extremely poisonous."

"Carder went to your home?" Haika asks.

Claudette douses her smile. "Just the other day. Our gardener warned him not to eat it. I would think its bitterness would've been the second warning. Brugmansia should never be ingested. It's a powerful hallucinogen, and a somewhat mean one. It'll do a number on you for sure. And on the eve of his show! I'm shocked he's functional enough to have shown up at all tonight."

"Holy crap!" Mandy blurts. "Well, I'm sure he'll feel better knowing he isn't crazy after all."

"Dollface," Haika says, "in most cases, crazy's an insane concept." She motions as though stifling a yawn and turns to Claudette. "Speaking of the eccentric, Vivs, where's your other half?"

Being used to Haika's sarcastic manner, Claudette smiles. "She's not feeling well either—but for Doe it's due to what she *didn't* eat. Brugmansia would do her some good if only by virtue of filling her stomach. She sends apologies for not making it. Don't tell anyone, but I'm going to purchase one of Carder's paintings for her so that she'll have a piece of the occasion even though she's not at its opening gala. I'll pick out exactly the painting she would—I can see through her eyes."

"And Gavin? Where is he?"

"He'll certainly make an appearance. He's excited about the whole thing—to the point of idiocy…though he usually operates at that point anyway. What about Mike?"

"He's never missed one of my openings," Haika says and laughs at her faux pas of sexual innuendo, for Mike hasn't visited any of her openings, physical or otherwise, in months. They've become sexless. Lately, it's more common for her to dip into her lingerie drawer for the sleek serpentine vibrator than to hold onto her husband's broad shoulders. Haika tempers questioning what she's staying faithful to with knowledge that many friends' marriages have also become nearly celibate. Making love? From nothing? It's a good form of birth control, though as a highly sexual creature that's little comfort to Haika. It's like having a cellar full of wine one never drinks.

With the approach of a lean young man in a fedora hat, Claudette excuses herself so that she can experience Neidin fully before crowd-size poses obstacles. There's something familiar about the young man approaching, but Haika is incapable of saying what. He engages Mandy instead of Haika.

"Don't tell me! Mandy! Mandy Sutcliffe! Is that you?"

Of course. The velvety voice and deep-set eyes are a Sutcliffe trait, but his energy favors a more suave, relaxed side of the family. Haika enjoys watching his oafish surprise at Mandy's transformation. He probably last saw her wearing a dress which might set sail, with bows pulling braids down her back.

"Hello Uncle Brody," Mandy responds glibly, with a loose hug and pat. "I didn't know you were going to be here."

"Me either, really. It's Maeve who insisted," he says motioning to a woman sparkling like sunlit honey. "Is your family here yet? I saw your dad and Mordecai yesterday. They came to watch me sing."

"Mordecai?" Distress trembles through her voice upon hearing her little brother's name. "No, they're not here yet. They're in New York, but obviously not here. I've been in the city for a while now—visiting my Uncle Carder." A look from Brody prompts Mandy to add, "I'm sorry, Uncle Brody, I should've looked you up, but…"

He cuts her apology short. "How do you like the city?"

"S'cool, but my parents have come to herd me back to Gettysburg."

Brody inspects the necklace on her neck. It's the silver-and-diamond pistol which Haika gave her and a rearing horse charm which Mandy added herself.

"Your parents have loosened up, eh?" Brody asks.

"Not at all. They've gotten worse."

The metropolitan sky passes into dusk, drowning cricket song with the rush of passing cars. Illuminated shop windows and neon signs defy budding darkness while an increasing flow of people stroll into the gallery. Among the mix are Iris and Darren who walk hand-in-hand in comfortable affection.

Iris found her victim… it serves him right—Haika reconsiders the second half of her thought for it really has nothing to do with Iris. Haika is confused. Why does Darren fawn over Iris but show her such derision? She sees the pair laboring through the thickening crowd. The pride Darren exudes for his best friend's paintings—is balanced by Iris's perplexity over them. Iris would prefer trashy romance novels and explosive action movies—she understands those. Still, here's Iris, holding onto Darren's arm, chittering into his ear.

Carder returns to Haika's side. "It's strange," he muses, "No one came to my high school or college graduation, and I never had a wedding—but this…" He loses the words.

"This is closer to your being. It means more. And it isn't only loved ones attending. Some come for the spectacle, some for the art, and some for the liquor." She sighs. "Actually, a lot come for the liquor."

"Like a wedding."

Haika hopes telling Carder about the Brugmansia will calm him. While admitting he's happy his home doesn't need padded walls, the wine glass still shakes in Carder's hand. Stammering and sweaty, he reveals that when he awoke at noon, he ate a few more bites of the noxious salad without thinking. Preoccupied with surviving the day, he hadn't paid it any mind, wolfing down whatever sustenance he found. This time, however, his nervous excitement and the tart leaves successfully prevented more than a few bites, but it was enough to flip simple anxiety into a heavier, psychotropic experience. Carder doesn't reveal that his vision occasionally blurs or that he's confused about which of last night's events actually happened.

"Feeling better?" someone asks in his ear. If he didn't recognize Claudette by her voice, he would by her platinum hair engulfing his head like a pac-man on a power-pellet.

"I'm still standing."

"You know what I want to do?"

Carder does. Even in this shifting, clenching crowd, Claudette's engine runs hot.

She continues, "A friend of mine recently sent me a batch of Pot Tarps from Cali. And I…" She sees the confusion in his face.

"Pop Tarts?"

"No. *Pot Tarps*. They're like those rolled up sheets, the fruit snacks, but they include a special ingredient. At any rate, I want you to come over one evening, eat some with me and sit back. Then, I want to hear all about the world of Neidin."

That won't happen. Carder has never expounded in detail about Neidin to a soul—and doesn't plan on changing. He lets it go, relieved he can joke a little. "I'm still recovering from the other plant you gave me!"

"Oh my God, Carder, I'm so sorry about the Brugmansia. Weren't you listening when Lorenzo instructed you not to eat it?"

"Alas, no. I was distracted by a crotchety old man, gourds, and two cloned sisters chasing dogs carrying a mummified cat. Not to mention, I was teaching one clone to arrange colors into a likeness of the other."

"Well, when you put it that way! I'm glad you didn't end up in a psych ward and that you're feeling better. And it *was* ridiculous the way Gavin insisted on gourds being situated around Doe, wasn't it? I'm surprised he didn't have Doe sit atop a television with board games and a stock ticker spread below. He didn't want a painting of Doe. He wanted a portrait of his accomplishments—and she's only one of many."

"She's an investment—I've seen her jewelry. Church bells have fewer rings than Doe."

"Have you seen Gavin? Watch out for him, will you?"

"Sure. If I see him I'll tell him you're on the look-out."

"No, no. *I* don't want that icky little eel. It's just that he's been in a foul mood. I don't know what his problem is, but he's been especially mean. Don't take anything he says personally."

"I barely listen to anything he says anyway."

"Good. How are you? You're looking a little pale." She says it as if seeing his heart tremor through his skin.

Carder doesn't answer, but nods, rushing back to the bathroom.

Having cleared his stomach and mind, Carder exits the bathroom to an utterly changed gallery. The difference is vast. It's as if he slogs through Kafka's *Metamorphoses* turned inside out, imposed upon the entire world, stripping away all pretense, plasticity— missing the soap-sudded smell of a world that won't be cleaned. The entire space is fuzzy, covered from wall-to-wall in a motley stew of fluorescent-colored hair—nuclear oranges, rancid pinks, gassy greens and antifreeze blues—though no one else seems to notice the variegated disaster. Pale light bloats the size of the crowd, only this time Carder sees through human costume. He groans. So, this is his experience. Perhaps the previous evening's weirdness was purely the beginning. He clears his throat and determines to surf this hallucinogenic mishap.

Only a few yards away, Claudette is now an ancient Aztec android wearing knife-sharp antlers and eyes blackened à la Día de los Muertos. As if dipped in circuitry, she now drips with fiber-optic decoration, her skeleton face glows with naked teeth surrounded by other scrolling cobwebs and flourishes. Where's Mandy? He sees only the shadow of a black rabbit on the walls. Before Carder can reach her, someone stops him. What would've been a young woman holding an infant in her arms is now a pulsing creature: an enlarged flea or a gnat under an electron microscope. She hurls out a wide, jagged grin and turns to Carder with eyes ready to explode from her head.

"You're the artist! I saw your picture on the information-sheet." She then addresses the infant-sized maggot in her arms, "Look Muffin …this man created all this. What do we call this?"

"Goo," the maggot replies.

"My husband loves this type of work. He's a tattoo artist at Permanent Markers. Anyway, he's always looking for inspiration. I've absolutely got to bring him here."

Carder walks on. With cockroaches and rats everywhere in this city, why not allow maggots to enjoy this visual feast? Among the wine, maggots, monsters and memories, he searches for Haika. She's easily spotted standing in the corner, easily spotted but in the form of an ivory being, layered like an onion and emitting light. Her features have a gauzy transparence. Pearled feathers, almost scaly, curl around her phosphorescent eyes, rounding their sleek softness about her head. Traveling down her back, they gradually turn darker, black by the time they reach her feet. Haika is a diamond no matter which world filters her.

"Are you okay?" she whispers when Carder reaches her.

"Kind of tired of that question, to be honest." He refuses to tell her that she looks like the Las Vegas Strip under ten feet of snow. No reason for alarm. He'll bridle the situation, making sure he comes off no wackier than usual.

The light within her pulses once. "And I'm tired of asking it, but right now, Love, how are you?"

"Alternating between dying and… wonderful."

"Here, take my hand. Come." But she doesn't have a hand to offer. Carder takes hold of something resembling a fire hose—only it envelops his hand as if he's plunged it into a vat of pudding. "Tino will work the room for a minute. Tino!" She gestures to a blue badger armored in a coat of mail, rolling its eyes and raising a paw. It offers Carder a mint.

"Where are we going?" Carder asks.

"Just come into the office with me for a second."

When they arrive in the back office, it's grown to the size of a warehouse. The creature - Haika in layered lights—closes the door and wipes Carder's forehead with a cloth. Unlocking a cabinet, she pulls out a bottle of tequila with half its contents remaining.

"Take a swig."

"I was just sick in the bathroom."

"So I heard."

"You did?"

"I've got my eye on you. Did you drink any water afterward, Hon?"

Carder nods.

"Then have some of this." She shoves the tequila bottle to his chest. "It'll do you good."

"No thank you," Carder declines, mesmerized by the flickers of Haika, human Haika, shimmering through membranous layers.

"Fine!" she says, unscrewing the cap. She takes a look at the bottle and kicks it back, taking a swig, then begins unlocking a door on the opposite side of the office—leading to the hallway, an alternate path into the gallery. Haika pauses before opening it. "Aw, hell - one more swallow." She drinks from the bottle again while Carder watches the liquid burn an amber trail within her quivering translucence.

If there were a battle between all the images of Carder's life—from his mother's soft arms reaching into his crib, to Darren's smug grin during their first joyride upon getting driver's licenses, to baby Mandy sleeping in this arms, to every single setting in Neidin—if each vied for the prize of Most Beautiful Moment—the contest is over, the winner defined. This is by far the most stunning thing he's ever seen: the tequila-drinking angel.

Haika clears her throat. "Much better."

Observing the resplendence of the moment between Haika and tequila, and wanting to stretch it as far as possible, Carder changes his mind and grabs the bottle, taking three chugs before handing it back.

When Haika sets it atop a file cabinet, a few of her feathers drift to the floor. "Now, Carder, we're going to re-enter the gallery from its front entrance. It's starting to fill up, but here's the thing: I want you to mentally step away, remove yourself from the history of your work and try seeing it for the first time."

"Impossible."

"*Pfft.* You've been doing impossible things from the second I met you. So… impossible? I don't know, but that's irrelevant. It's necessary, beyond necessary in your case. So grab your spear, your cowboy hat, put on your armor, bring your squirt gun—whatever it is you need to see your work differently!"

"I don't think I can."

"Force yourself, godammit! Carder, you're in so deep that you can't see your art for what it can be or what it *is* to other people. If you did, you wouldn't worry so."

"I—"

"Just try. Trust me."

"I—"

"Try." She demands, and then offers a glowing hug to which he obliges.

Once Haika opens the alternate door to the hallway, everything—including her—has miraculously returned to its usual state: sparse, boxy architecture, concrete floors and white walls. People are human again, with another cluster entering the gallery. The last of the group is a prim woman in a skirt so stiffly starched it could be concrete. She looks like she's lost in the woods and holds the evening's second baby. This time it isn't a maggot.

The woman speaks to a tall man.

"This place isn't baby-friendly."

The man is Stan Sutcliffe, who asks, "You mean this gallery?"

"I mean this entire city," clarifies the starched woman—Lucy Sutcliffe. She holds baby Miriam in her arms.

Walking next to Stan, Little Mordecai exclaims, "CooooOOOL! Uncle Carder made all this stuff?"

"He did, little Bug. It's—it certainly is interesting, isn't it?"

Carder and Haika re-enter the gallery behind the Sutcliffe's, too close not to say something.

"Lucy!?" Carder's glad she appears human—not even he can imagine what he would've beheld had she arrived shortly before.

"There you are, Brother. Good job on the art. Hey Stan!" She calls to her husband and hands him the baby, then turns back to

Carder. "Can't say you didn't surprise me after all. Say, I want to talk to you about some things. Can we go somewhere? Is Mandy here?"

Haika cuts in. "It's so good to see you Lucy. I'm glad you're supporting Carder tonight—Jesus would *definitely* do that." Though she's sincere, Lucy doesn't seem to receive it as such. It was a poor choice of words. Haika disregards Lucy's askance expression. "Being the artist, Carder needs to stay here throughout the reception, so it'd be best if you two don't run off, but I do want to say: Mandy has been an absolute doll. A gem. You should be so proud of her. She's running around with Lara somewhere."

Lucy is about to reply, but stops. She stares into Haika's eyes, which are no longer phosphorescent, but have brightened to the color of ripe limes in this well-lit room. She readjusts her focus, in realizing that this is the same woman who came to Gettysburg, who attended Sunday Kingdom Hall Worship with them. Taking another breath to say something, Lucy reconsiders, and instead faces Carder and reaches, twisting the skin of his chest between her fingers. The last time she did that was decades ago when Carder pestered a guy she'd brought home. It smarts. Storms swirl in her eyes.

"Carder." She takes a cancerous tone, but readjusts it to sweetness. "Brother, where's my daughter?"

"You know where—she's staying with me."

"Of course I know that! Where. Right this moment. Is she?"

Carder's skin remains pinched between her fingers. She twists his perception: is it he or Lucy who's confused? Are they both? Already nervous from the jagged journey through this epic night, when Carder's path comes into conjunction with seeping family issues, everything compounds. His sister, with flaring nostrils and puffed, Pennsylvanian bangs, stands before him with a false smile, titty-twisting him to death. In front of everyone. His sister, whose face is melting, whose jaw crumbles. Here is his sister with skulls in her eyes.

Though his nipple pulses with pain, he notices Mandy watching. Only in that moment do the cumulative changes since he'd boomeranged from Brooklyn to Gettysburg and back hit Carder in the head. Mandy's hair is shorter, blonder, almost white, her eyelids lined with a lush forest of black licorice lashes. Her body, once hidden in full-length Kingdom Hall costuming, now shows blue veins beneath the paper-white skin of her arms and chest. And her personality has gone through an even greater but more relaxed version of these changes. The Mandy he knows now: Rabbit / Mandy / *Amanda Lynn Sutcliffe: 6 lbs. 5 oz.* / the infant he'd held / the little girl who'd written letters stained with grilled cheese / the announcement that young Lucy once whispered into a napkin at a forced family dinner: *"We're going to have a baby!"* / the plucked off plastic head of the doll which tiny Carder handed back to his big sister / the Mandy he thought he'd known—it was all slung to the horizon in these past weeks. The Mandy he now knows is *Mandy*, the real Mandy, is *Rabbit*, the real Rabbit. He opens his mouth to tell Lucy that her daughter is right here, right next to her, but nothing comes. Lucy's eyes go berserk searching the room, not recognizing that her own daughter stands close enough to touch.

"Where's my child? Where's my child?" Lucy asks, finally releasing Carder's nipple, now purple with broken blood vessels beneath his shirt. She turns, with no logic, to a stranger on her left, a figure she'd previously blocked out. "Have you seen my child?"

The stranger shakes his head—no, he hasn't seen her child.

The crowd is crammed with competing noises of conversation, mellow beats of DJ'ed electronica and clanking glasses, which allows few to notice Lucy's commotion.

Lucy freaks, turning to her right, to a young woman in a short dress, a teenager wearing a mawkish mess of blonde hair and a necklace pointing a gun at whoever comes close. Mandy. But Lucy doesn't see that. "Excuse me, have you… seen…," and as the last words are spoken, Lucy knows it is, "…*my daughter*?"

It isn't Amanda.

It is.

It can't be Amanda.

It can. It can't be—but it is.

If Lucy straightens her posture any more, new vertebrae will have to grow. Wordless and alert, she observes the girl she once knew, unconvinced it's this person she once held in her womb. Looking the young woman up and down like a scientist discovering a new species, she examines every detail. The girl looks common, loose, no longer pure, possibly like she *never* was, dirty in ways that bleach and a pair of rubber gloves are powerless against, that a squeegee or sandblaster can't purify. A wave of revulsion arises in Lucy, higher and higher, until she tastes it in the back of her throat. To see this image before her, her daughter but mutated, this antithesis of everything Lucy ever taught, this rejection, this once godly girl now godless and fleshly. It's like being hit by a train.

Behind Mandy, a girl wearing a beret casually checks in, "You okay, Mands?"

Mandy doesn't look at Lara, but nods, watching her mother's mouth swirl with appalled insight before it finally opens.

"You're Lara, are you? Amanda, we always knew you had it in you. We're not stupid. But we hoped you wouldn't choose this lifestyle."

"Mom…"

Lucy stops her daughter's speech with her hands. In sudden awareness of the crowd, she lowers her voice, hissing out the words to lessen any spectacle.

"Look at you. You're now of this world—no better than Judas Iscariot. The kingdom of God is no part of this world, Amanda. Remember? That's the first Bible verse we ever taught you: John 18:36. You had it memorized within two days. You were a smart child, but you're now like the harlot herself: Babylon the Great."

"Mom. Mom, listen! I'm… happy. For the first time for as long as I can remember, I'm happy. I never even knew what that felt like before. I no longer wake up every single day wanting to kill myself because I'm not who you wish I was."

Lucy's eyes water defiantly. "You only think you're happy. Do you think alcoholics think they drink too much? You can't be happy. Not like this. Now, you listen to me. You have a choice: leave with us right now. Go get in the car and we'll take you back and help you through this, help you gain favor in Jehovah's eyes. Or stay here amongst this *trash*. Oh, to lose my precious…" She takes a moment. "No. We can't support this. Not at all. We must be strong. If you stay here, Amanda, you won't hear from us again. You'll be disfellowshipped. We won't even be able to speak to you. Go to the car, Amanda, go now!"

"I won't."

"You won't?"

"I can't."

"You can and you will." But as soon as she says it, Lucy knows that Mandy *can* but won't. She pulls herself back, overcome by a force of strength she'll forever label as Holy Spirit. It's the only thing that gets her through it. Her own strength is gone.

"Goodbye, Amanda Lynn. Your heart will change, I just hope this world doesn't rob and rape you before that time. Goodbye. Send your dad and the kids outside." She turns away and quotes scripture while pushing through the crowd to the exit, trying not to cry: "*Don't think I came to put peace on earth. I didn't come to put peace, but a sword. For I came to cause divisions, putting a man against his father, and daughters against mothers...he that has greater love for either son or daughter than for me is unworthy of me.*" For a moment, she stops, but doesn't turn around. "*Remember the wife of Lot,*" she says and exits.

The Sutcliffe family's drama doesn't command the gallery space for all attendees. There are enough people in attendance, enough drinks and chatter to allow the lopping off of an entire family member without overtaking the event. After all, babies cry, mothers brood over their teenagers, husbands lose their tempers, families fight. Unhappy families pay attention to their own unhappiness, and happy families fill their attention with other things.

Finally, champagne and wine washes away barriers—good and bad—pickling the hearts of those in attendance, peeling back scales from their eyes, opening their vision to another world and if that isn't possible, at least opening them up to one another. When executed well, a gallery's opening night party gradually spins away from mere selling. The art no longer cries for attention and the ego of the artist no longer needs stroking or derision. The occasion becomes a full-fledged celebration. Even the critics, some as Haika's friends and some who would enjoy seeing her barbecued at a luau, rest from thinking up snarky comments, allowing themselves to enjoy. The evening reaches a point when strangers chat without qualm.

Three such strangers have become an inadvertent trinity standing before a painting entitled *Zeitgeist Sun*. A large porcelain platter holds its scene. One of the few earlier pieces hanging, it shows a rough-skinned citrusy creature sitting in a foaming grey landscape that wavers between mist and dirty dishwater. The perspective has viewers looking down on the beast, while the beast peers up out of the painting toward the group's last third—Iris Haus.

Another third of the group, Brody Sutcliffe, speaks up. "I'd never have guessed! The artist is a relative of mine, but no one told me it was like this. It's—it's—"

"What did they tell you?" asks the middle individual, a woman named Mimi Manchester. Her pony tail is slicked tight. She holds a zipped portfolio and wears a business suit fit for a libidinous librarian.

"You see," explains Brody, "My family vehemently loathes communication. They implied that the guy was some sort of sideshow freak. If I hadn't met him at my brother's wedding ages ago, I would've expected a bearded lady. They think he's strange, but then again, they think human government is strange."

"Imagination *is* strange." Mimi Manchester says. "While the paintings aren't what I expected, they help me understand the Pup universe better. They give me—I don't know—a more expansive view. I hadn't known the extent of their richness. Or terror. Previously, I took it all at face value. This, this is a virtual phantasmagoria."

Brody is unsure what Mimi means. He's also uncertain whether they're waxing the painting with bull-shit pronouncements to impress themselves or if they're sincere. He almost walks off, but observes Mimi staring intently at the painting, as if wanting to touch the human toes of the yellow creature and jump into the frothy waters to save the miniature dolphins dying belly up at its feet.

Brody loves passion, passionate people, and people who passionately apply that passion to the arts. He can't resist. "What do you mean?"

"Well, I'd only ever seen Lemon Pie as sweet and light."

The hinges of Brody's jaws aren't loose enough to ask what in tarnation the woman is talking about, at least not fast enough to beat the jaws of Iris, who only adds to the shifting conversation.

"I love cherry pie," Iris says. "Now Carder—he think everything taste too sugary, but what's anything without sugar? Lord don't give us sugar to sprinkle on sidewalks."

Brody is officially lost, and ready to remove himself from the trio, when Mimi continues. "Originally, they planned more natural-

looking dogs, but the vivid colors took everything to another level."
She raises her chin as though her knowledge stands on a ladder, with
better views, and says to Brody, "I apologize. I derailed your point.
You're right, the artist is strange. I should know. I dated him."

"How long were you together?"

"Two hours and thirteen minutes. I didn't know who he was at
first. He seemed intent on keeping himself from me."

"I don't know him to date anybody ever," Iris says, pushing her
sense of authority forward, reassessing the woman. "See my
boyfriend over there? The hot chocolate?" she waves to Darren
who's standing with Carder. "He's best friends with the artist. He
worship him like he's the god of a tiny people."

This astounds Mimi Manchester. "Then you're a part of the
inner-circle! How is it?"

Iris massages the exposed part of her chest before answering, "A
lotta dirty dishes."

As is common in the Sutcliffe family, Stan is too slow to herd
the children out to the car without Mandy. He stands wordless next
to her, lingering. That boyish haircut—he thinks. While he has
nothing to say to his daughter and knows that as long as she no
longer worships like the rest of his family the consequences are
irrevocable, Stan is in no rush to leave his girl behind. However, as
far as Lucy is concerned, the gavel has fallen. She briefly returns to
speed things up and walks in on Mandy standing next to Mordecai.

"Amanda, what do you think you're doing?" Lucy rages at her
bewildered daughter.

Stan intercedes. "Come on, Lucy, let her say goodbye to her
brother. She can at least have that. No. No, stop! We're giving her
that. Here, take Miriam from me. Now—it's okay, Mandy, take your
time with Mordecai." He pulls Lucy forcibly by the arm to the other
side of the room, instructing her to change Miriam's diaper while
they wait.

Mandy leads her little brother behind the counter near the
gallery's entrance. It's clear the boy is confused. The mix of art,
grown-ups, loud music, a crying mother and a new version of his
sister is jarring. Still, any fear is diluted since nothing dreadful has yet
happened in the boy's life.

Amanda doesn't want Mordecai's confusion to grow. She kneels, putting herself at eye-level with him, while waging war on her own tears.

This is it.

Mordecai speaks first. "You should've seen Uncle Brody last night. He just told me that he's starting a band called, um, Flavor Crystal? No, Flavor Pistol! Shh! Don't tell mom though."

"That's cool," Mandy says. She then whispers a jingle she'd made up when he was born:

> *"Mordy-man, Mordy-man,*
> *The boy who runs without a plan,*
> *Go fast as you can*
> *Fast as you can, little man."*

"What's wrong, Rabbit-girl?" he asks.

Mandy smears tears away the moment they escape—only a few. She'll one day feel proud she contained most of them. She doesn't want Mordy's last memory of his older sister to be one of her crying.

"Mordy-man, I'm not going back home with you. I'm staying here in New York City."

"To be with Uncle Carder?"

"You got it. So I won't be seeing you for a while, okay?" At the earliest, she'll probably see him again when he graduates high school. Or if someone in the family dies. Her mother won't want Mandy's worldly ways imprinting onto him. "I won't see you for a lot longer than I want, but I need you to know that I'm always thinking about you."

"I'll come see you!" Mordy claims, trying to approximate confidence and comfort.

"I hope you can." She already sees his memory of her being erased. "I wish you could." Pragmatism tells her that Mordy is so young that her absence will fade these proclamations of love. Words don't make up for not being there, regardless of their sweetness and intention. Still, she tries. "Brother..."

"What?"

"It's time for our game, Promise and Secret, okay? I know how good you are with secrets."

"Dad says I'm to be trusted."

"He's right. You are. You always know when *not* to say something." As she says this, Mandy unclasps the necklace Haika gave her from behind her neck. The diamond pistol remains on the chain, but she frees the pendant horse, sliding it from the links into her palm. "Two things, Mordy. A Promise and a Secret for two things. That's all."

"Em-kay," he agrees with quiet voice and glistening eyes.

"First, promise me that you'll always remember this moment. Can you do that? Like we did in that field the night we kept the moon in our heads? Remember its blue light, the lightning bugs and the smell of fireworks? How we dropped our burning sparklers and kicked mushrooms from the ground? And how we chose to remember it all on purpose so we could go back whenever we wanted?" Mordecai nods, remembering. "Let's do that again now," she says.

"I can do it."

"And can you also remember what I'm about to tell you?"

"Yeah."

To prevent her parents from seeing it, Mandy refrains from dangling the horse pendant before Mordy. Instead, she presses its pointed ears and metal equine shape hard into the boy's palm.

"Feel this horse in your hand? It's a special horse. Not just special to me, but special because... it's a unicorn."

"Liar," Mordy says playfully, gently touching his sister's cheek. "Unicorns have horns! I can feel—this don't have one. It's just normal."

"No, it's a magic horse with its own secret, a unicorn in hiding. I promise you it's a unicorn, no matter what anyone else would say. I can see it. Will you keep him for me—as a secret?"

Mordecai nods again.

"Good. Now, keep him secret and if you bring him back to me some day, however long from now that is, when you can visit, I promise he'll turn into a unicorn."

"Really?"

"I promise. But it can only happen if it's kept hidden. Our forever secret?" There's one wayward tear Mandy can't coral. She has to leave. Pushing the horse into Mordy's pocket, she hugs him harder than she has in all four years of his small life and lets go.

The trinity of Brody, Mimi Manchester, and Iris moves from one painting to another with its back to the madness, while Maeve and Darren chat and drink on the sidelines. Brody ignores his brother's family saga, not only because he's tired of it, but because he's enjoying the banter of the two coincidental critics delivering vastly different perspectives. Much time is spent listening to Iris announce that she doesn't *get it*, followed by Mimi's explanations to help Iris edge closer to understanding. At the moment, they stand before a painting called *Cut*.

"Do you think I'm estupido?" Iris says, brushing fly-away hair behind her ear.

"Not at all. Never!" replies Mimi. "I don't know what the title on this one refers to, but I believe the animal's an early form of Teeter-totter. Yes, I'm sure."

The word won't form correctly on Iris's tongue. "Tader-toader? Tater-*totter*? Like potato-snacks? French fries?"

"No, no. Like a see-saw on a playground. ¿Cómo se dice en español?"

Years of college Spanish class supply the answer to Brody, who is elated to use vocabulary he'd assumed would waste away for the rest of his life. "I believe it translates: *balancín*," he says.

Iris nods in recognition. "Oh. Balancín." She studies the painting while finishing another glass of champagne.

Mimi gloats. She's rarely able to provide her expertise. "Notice the way his tail—I know it's a mile long—splits into three objects: a pair of scales, a gavel with blades coming from each side, and a lock? I believe it may have led to his being used in the School Daze line."

"Teeter-totter. Teeter-totter." Iris turns the word over as though repetition brings focus to the long-forgotten wafer on her tongue. She shuts one eye as she considers the painting, repeatedly sounding out each syllable.

A few feet away, Lucy returns with a freshly changed Miriam on one arm and on the other an overstuffed diaper bag that looks like it's been sideswiped by a rainbow. She reapplied lipstick, hardened her hair with spray and tightened her resolve. She stands next to Brody, the only familiar person nearby.

"Where's Stan?" she drones at Brody, who missed the drama.

"He said he'd wait outside on the sidewalk with Mordecai."

Brody despises the forced interaction.

Mimi Manchester continues with Iris. "You know, I think you might actually be able to help me with something."

Iris eyes her with suspicion. "Go on." At the Inn, when guests start speaking like this they want discounted rates, 7am check-in times and extra towels.

"I came for a lot of reasons tonight. I haven't been able to approach the artist myself yet, but perhaps if you accompany me, I'd be more successful. You see, one reason I came was to ask if he'd speak at an upcoming convention."

"¿Que?" Iris is only half-listening, as she's transfixed by the baby in Lucy's arms, the way little Miriam looks as though she'll roll away if set down. Miriam squeaks, grabbing at the strap of the colorful diaper bag. Her fat little fingers direct Iris's gaze to it.

Mimi Manchester persists, "If it's not too presumptuous, I'd like to ask Mr. Quevedo to speak at a convention."

"What type of convention?" Iris asks disinterestedly as she notices a cartoon character embroidered on the diaper bag. It's a white dog, with a tail that transforms into a world globe at its tip, standing atop the center of a playground seesaw. Iris looks at the painting, then at the diaper bag, again at the beast bearing teeth in the painting and then back at the grinning dog on the bag. All the while, she's half-listening to Mimi Manchester.

"It's a convention for Puppers—they're fans of the Pick-Me-Pups, of course," Mimi says.

Iris looks Mimi dead in the eye, then at Brody. She looks at the diaper bag, then the wall. Then, like a flash flood bursting down a mountainside, Iris leans her head back and begins cackling at the top of her lungs, an abrasive laugh, one well-acquainted with whiskey and heartbreak. It bounces off the ceiling, raining down on the crowd, capturing attention and pausing conversations. She cackles on for several moments.

"Pick-Me-Pups! Haikita, it's the Pick-Me-Pups!" Iris yells across the room at a volume Haika hears without effort. "Haikita! Haikita! Look!" With great excitement at having solved a riddle percolating since she'd first set foot in Carder's home, Iris grabs the diaper bag hanging from Lucy's shoulder, points to it and then to the painting to cinch her realization. "Oh Dios mio! I love those pups when I was little. It's tater-todder. Balancín! Haikita, es Balancín!"

A light murmur makes its way through the crowd as Iris connects the dots for everyone, drawing a picture between two worlds of which the attendees had been largely unaware. The dog on the diaper bag, which Carder's father mailed to Lucy about a year prior, corresponds to the creature in the painting. Simultaneous recognition ripples through the crowd. Low murmurs become well-formed chuckling.

The Pick-Me-Pups!

Of course!

You know, the little, plastic, animated dogs! Remember Dazzledrop and Slate?

Yes!

That's them!

Carder, who was caught up in Mandy's heartbreak, feels punched as the world of Neidin is dismantled—replaced by a blubbering, slapstick galaxy of cartoon dogs. Someone elbows him in acknowledgment.

Neidin is gone.

In an instant, the fortress built from the paintings which helped Carder endure years of solitary confinement, which had forced him to embrace a world even if it wasn't this one, becomes nothing more than a diaper bag, nothing more than a way to deal with the most inconsequential shit of family life.

The embarrassment is too much.

Despite Haika's calls, Carder instantly parts the crowd and runs out the door, with Mandy following behind.

25

HAPPINESS FOUND
WITH MULTIPLE STAB WOUNDS

They've become one creature—no longer Carder and Mandy, uncle and niece, male and female, adult and teen, nerd and sinner, straight and gay, freak and butterfly. Together, they're one—alone, disowned—the same shared soul spread between two bodies, winding down four flights of stairs like a snake coiling an escape. Everything that's happened to Carder has happened to her, and the rejection and grief staring at Mandy looks his way as well. Her tears well in his eyes, but Mandy no longer holds on to them, shedding them freely on the stairs they descend. Tears of anguish. Of ecstasy. Alternating. Mixed.

Neither knows to where they run. There's no need for navigation. All that matters is that they go jointly. Each walked an isolated path for so long that their combined experiences now surpass heartbreak. By the time they hit the street, they gulp in hilarity. They laugh like animals howl, to the center of the universe in their stomachs. Their arms, empty of loved ones and imposed histories, stretch and reach, moving freely. Extinguishment from the respect of those who purported to love them means there's no more loss to fuel the burning. Abandonment lets them proceed *with* abandon. They pass through hell's gate only to find an uncapped fire hydrant cooling its streets on the other side. They run as if propelled through its waters, letting it pummel their legs in gushes. Their eyes are opened and they see: bright, hazy graffiti on brick walls, remnants of spent firecrackers in gutters and a summer night containing only them. The sidewalk goes anywhere they choose. And so they run on,

231

run, run, run, laughing in gasps. When they reach 8th Avenue, Mandy clamps a warm hand on the back of Carder's neck—in recognition of big black Buick close by. They pause, out of breath, looking at one another and decide to run again.

"Ahem!" It's a pronouncement rather than the clearing of phlegm, but it stops Carder and Mandy before they can break away. A figure exits the Buick, slamming the door.

"Where do you two think you're going?"

The booming voice emanates from someone close to the core of the Quevedo family tree. It draws Carder and Mandy, turning them to meet Gordan Quevedo.

Carder wakes from his trance. "Dad?"

"Don't tell me you're leaving right as I arrive!? Why, why you're the artist! That would be ludicrous!"

From inside the Buick, the hypnotic bassline of a Rhythm and Blues song cranks louder. *"This is no ordinary love,"* sings a sultry voice, as the mechanized window rolls up. From outside, Carder and Mandy glimpse the bowling pin fingers belonging to Agnes Pie.

"Does she ever leave the car?" Mandy asks.

"No," Carder answers.

Gordan answers as well. "Her angina is acting up, but she downright insisted on me coming to see your show. I'm headed up there now, while she waits in the car—*if* I can find the place. Listening to Sade is about the only thing that calms Agnes." He inspects a piece of paper containing written directions, pulling it forward and away to focus.

For a moment, Carder questions leaving the Neidin show. Responsibility starts dragging him back, undoing their escape.

Mandy sees this and wraps her arm around him. "We're leaving."

Her resolve emboldens Carder. "Dad, we're going."

"You're not!"

Before Gordan can raise his head, the Carder-Mandy monster tears away. One head tips back and yells, "Enjoy the show!" The other breaks into laughter. Both disappear around the corner.

Having watched two generations of neighborhood thugs apply slow torture to his corner-deli, Hanif has an eye for what his wife calls *potential situations* and he calls *shit storms*. Trouble comes in a cacophony of spices and right now its aroma is as pungent as his father's vindaloo. A seemingly crazed man and teenage girl approach his shop from across the street. Hanif turns off the portable television next to the cash register.

Carder pants, bending over, holding his side. "Stop! Stop! We have to stop. I'm old."

"But you're a jogger!"

"And you're still a baby!" Carder's eyes meet the shopkeeper's through the window of the deli before they enter. "Let's get something to drink."

They decide on chocolate KoolMoo drinks, because memories outweigh the need for hydration, and Mandy reminisces on a time when Carder impractically sent her some KooMoos in a back-to-school care package.

"It was when you gave me that Pick-Me-Pups backpack. It was ill!"

"Oh, was that the year they were cool?" He twists the cap, opening a bottle.

As shopkeeper, Hanif crosses his arms, with his eyes on them. Common sense says that ownership transfers when money changes hands. One doesn't chew bubblegum before inserting coins in the gumball machine. It's a simple concept.

"Yeah... that year. Everyone at school loved it. I was popular for a few minutes." It's obvious those minutes were centuries to Mandy.

Carder drinks the rest of his KoolMoo in one gulp and sets the empty bottle atop a stack of boxes, dropping his head into his hands as if washing his face. "God, oh god, those stupid Pups! God oh god, they're the bane of my existence. Have you ever felt like you live in several worlds at the same time, yet none of them make sense?"

"My entire life."

Carder feels it from across the store—a stab like a long needle. He doesn't see it yet, but bounds forward, grabbing for it as much as it reaches for him. Its colored plastic is familiar—Yellow Fever 3. It turns out, it's a Pups knock-off. Rumor was that molds of the original Pups were smuggled from the factory and used to create a cheaper line to poach business. It's kind of like making fast food with cheaper, more fattening ingredients.

Driving his hand deep into a row of hanging toys, Carder plucks out the dog, ripping the cardboard from a metal peg on the wall. He then vaults forth, grabbing a cigarette lighter from next to the cash register, and exits the store.

"Hey! You pay," the shopkeeper yells.

But Carder had paid. His entire life. He paid with a childhood shut away in the dark, with sleepless nights, with the role of lonely geek in high-water pants, and failed savior to an agoraphobic mother. He keeps walking, not consciously leaving Mandy to deal with the aftermath, but the petroleum dog he has taken begs for punishment, and Carder has the means to dole some out without hurting anyone.

Half a block away, he raises the lighter, setting flame to one corner of the packaging, while, in the distance, insults volley between Rabbit and the shopkeeper.

The victim's lidless eyes are permanently open over a frozen smile of silent pain. Gradually, the flame takes over, gnawing on the bottom corner of the package as if luxuriating over the opportunity. Carder holds the box by its far side as the outer bubble of clear plastic whimpers and sighs, folding in, curling out, melting in indecision. What form to take? Where to go? How?

Mandy soon appears at Carder's side, watching the smoldering until the blazing flames lick Carder's fingers. Heat forces him to drop the burning box into a dented garbage can on the street. The fire grows, lazy then gluttonous, devouring the package and its contents, but not without releasing fumes that draw a coughing fit. When he recovers, a gleam of exhilaration glasses Carder's eyes.

"I always wanted to do that," he says.

"...to leave someone to convince a shopkeeper that you weren't stealing?"

He tries breaking his attention from destruction and smoothing it back into that of a conscientious adult. "Did you pay?"

"Yeah, for our drinks and the stuff you took, but..." Mandy bumps him with her shoulder since her hands are full, "...but I didn't pay for these."

She drops three more plastic dogs into the fire below. Carder allows the dogs and any remaining concern to melt. Both he and Mandy laugh again, whooping, mesmerized, lost—until they hear a yelling shopkeeper and a metal baseball bat pinging against a mailbox. Looking at one another, they toss money into the air and run.

Wandering the streets of Manhattan, they arrive at a drugstore. The windows are brightly lit, holding curling, yellowed posters depicting jaundiced consumers hugging each other—their relationships are deeper, better, stronger because they fill pharmacy prescriptions and buy hairspray here. Junk food calls to the city's citizens, shampoo fights for shelf space, gadgets sit at attention. It's now late. Few people walk the aisles.

Carder and Mandy enter the store, continuing their warpath to find anything Pup-related. Instinct parts them. Carder comes upon the greeting card aisle. Usually, the Pups make a few spasmodic appearances in the children's cards, offering congratulations on birthdays, as if completing three years around the sun is some great feat.

A large, silver-haired woman wearing coolats stops fingering the cards, pushing her eyeglasses back on her nose to observe a gruff man with pit stains perusing the cards as well. That man is Carder, and his appearance is enough to delay the woman's sympathy card search (death is everlasting, anyway). Carder is unbothered and wears the woman's judgment like the sash of a tweaked-out beauty queen.

There!

As suspected, a pie-eyed Pup peeks out from the birthday cards. It's a new dog with no basis in Neidin. At best, it looks like the shell of a rind of an air-pocket of nothing. He yanks the entire stack, three cards deep. The Pup holds a golf club with poor form. *"FOUR!"* reads a poofy dialogue balloon.

Carder rips the entire pile several times over and drops them back in their slot.

Guilt is immediate. Even in his drunken stupor, Carder questions what a dick he's become. It bothers him, but he stuffs the emotion until it's under his feet and soon behind him. Mandy's sharp whistle signals him from another aisle. Carder finds her in the toy aisle, which is nothing more than a ragtag collection that even the Velveteen Rabbit would sell at a garage sale. Her eyes are bloodshot, her nose is flush and runny. Her hair has lost its coiffed-but-messy perfection, replaced with the manky locks of someone woken from bed. She meets Carder with raised eyebrows and jiggles a small box encasing a duck-like toy dog whose maniacal expression matches her own. The dog is fresh, unborn, begging to be freed from its cardboard-and-cellophane womb, to be taken home.

"I see you found the genuine article: an authentic Pick-Me-Pup. As authentic as they are, anyway," Carder says.

"Yep." It's the detached response of someone living far from her current situation.

"I've no idea which one it is. It doesn't resemble anything I ever painted or drew."

"*Buddy.* Mordecai has one."

"Buddy? They've got to be kidding. Why not paint it white with black lettering that spells a generic D-O-G? Buddy. Why not call it Spot, Bandit, Chico, Smokey? Wait, let's see how bad it gets—if you turn the package over there should be a small story describing our little amigo. Let me guess... Buddy is friendly, loves everyone and everyone loves him, hugs are meted out in limitless supply? Something like that?"

Mandy flips the box over, staring down at it. For a second, Carder wonders if the Pup's story is more complicated than predicted, but he then sees Mandy's falling tears. They strike the box. Her hands. Her dress. The floor. Her shoulders shake, almost in the same manner as when she laughs. Whistles peep out as she struggles to speak.

"I—I've known this day would come ever since I was a kid," Mandy says. "Knew I'd lose them. Everyone. Everything. I knew it every moment, every second, every day. They didn't see me at all. Never. I was a hologram. They loved the hologram of me, loved who they wanted me to be, but not *me*. They couldn't see me. I—I was invisible. I've been invisible since I was ten, probably before that, but that's..." her voice falters until it's a whispering squeak, "...that's when I started noticing." The box drops to the floor. She almost does as well.

Carder catches her.

He knows he isn't only holding Mandy but all the past years, holding the newborn baby with knowing eyes. It's only now that he understands what that baby knew, why it wailed upon meeting the world. He'll hold Mandy for as long as she'll allow.

Angry, she screams an ugly cry of frustration sent up among the hanging lights and bloodless shopping music. "I—I shouldn't be doing this. I wasn't meant for drugstore crying. Feels cheap." She sniffles, "...on discount."

"Mandy, there's something I want to tell you: you can live with me for as long as you like." He thinks for a second. "Even longer."

She sniffs again and rubs her nose. "Thanks, Unc, but one thing?"

"Anything," he says. Her loss hurts him, but part of him is thrilled with this present moment, and vaguely ashamed of the simultaneous existence of both emotions.

"You don't have to call me Mandy. I don't want you to. That girl's gone."

"Okay. Amanda?"

"Unc! Come on!" She looks up at him with a half-baked smile, tear trails drying, drumming his chest with playful fists. "Rabbit, of course. Rabbit!"

A piece of white light, brighter than any star, whiter than any lab coat and hotter than desert sand melts the block of ice around Carder's heart. He gulps it back before water overflows. "You *are* a rabbit." He tempers the glee of his own ridiculously sincere tone. "You're the tiniest rabbit."

She pushes him gently away. "Uncle?"

"Yeah?"

"One condition," she says, regaining her breath and scornful voice. "Call me Rabbit—but no cooing or saying stuff like that. I'm not your toy to squish, okay?"

Carder gulps again, ready to agree, but another voice supplants his.

"Excuse me sir. I'm going to have to ask you to step away from the girl." The voice comes from a man in dark blue. Next to him stands a store clerk in a striped vest, and encircling the two of them like a shark is the woman from the greeting card aisle. She fingers the elastic of her waistband, then motions toward Carder, careful not to point.

"That's him, officer," the woman says. "Look, there are two of them, and they've destroyed more merchandise." She wipes her hands on her pants and pushes her eye glasses close to her face.

Carder looks around, searching for the destruction of which she speaks, and sees two plastic legs poking out from a mangled box beneath Mandy's foot, bearing the brunt of her weight.

Buddy.

So close to breathing open air.

Buddy.

The officer turns to the clerk, whose tired anger spans many levels, saying, "How would you like to proceed with this?"

The clerk shifts her hips to one side.

26

A REAPING: MUSÉA
Carder at 18 years old

"Remains inside. Every side remains inside..." The words trail off listlessly.

Hot.

Dim.

Somewhere nearby, water trickles. Creep is as dazed as someone awakening in a hospital from a fever-dream. Odors of rotting plants or animals—or both—are overpowering. These peeling walls, are they organic or manmade? Irregular architecture blends into this cave-like dwelling: rocky then smooth, angular then shapeless.

A weighty sludge of rubbery leaves bigger than his body is stacked atop him at least three feet high. It makes breathing small and difficult.

"Oh, those," says the same frazzled voice from before. It's restless. Female. "Why? For warmth, of course, young man!"

The vegetation's gravity becomes less oppressive as it's pulled away in whooshes, the leaves thrown haphazardly around the room.

"Where to put them? Nowhere to put them. Put them there—or there. There! Feel better? Better, but you'll soon be cold!"

Creep cricks his neck to see as far as possible in both directions, but the figure remains hidden. Night vision gradually pulls blurred shapes apart, rearranging them into crisper, individual pieces. He asks himself what each object is: the legs of a chair, a group of shelled insects hiding beneath a cabinet, damp newspaper clippings and—is it, yes!—a hairless, python-thick tail coiling in ashen skin.

"I know. Such beautifully pale skin can only be attained by

smearing Carsom oil all over—that, and straining the stars completely from one's day. I suppose you won't be suns-tanning, then?"

Once the leafy pile is completely removed, Creep's blood surges. His veins pulse like an accordion. He looks down at his naked body, his grimy skin, his penis. Vulnerable and exposed, he ignores his parched mouth and attempts speaking. "I—," he clears his throat, "I—I don't—," and then again. "Why wouldn't I want sun?"

"Treasure remains inside. Safe. It sits away from corrosion. Here, let me inspect your eyes." She places cold fingers, as slender as pencils, above and below his eyelids, widening their slotted aperture to expose his eye. "Yes, the pupil's coming along nicely. Nice dark holes in that head of yours. Someday, you could see a great deal."

For the first time, he sees her face. Her jaws are inches away. Parts of her are still hazy to his adjusting sight, but this is no earthly animal. Points on her body—the bridge and tip of her nose, her fingers, the apples of her cheeks and her eyes—are hardened, transparent, glasslike. At certain angles, they seem filled with moving milky substances. Any reaction to her form takes a backseat to the growing suspicion that she can read Creep's mind. Instinct tells him to worm away.

"You don't have to—" she responds to his thoughts. "You're not a worm, are you? More of a maggot. A maggot bent on flying. I set aside an article just the other day about that condition from an issue of Rational Pornographic. Where'd I put that?"

His head throbs.

As she bends down to rifle through mountainous piles of clippings, he sits up. On nearby shelves, glass containers of various sizes sit filled with unearthly creatures, many resembling fetal versions of her own kind, others very different. A few seem freshly trapped, exploring their cell for escape, many are lethargic or dying, and most are nothing more than dried carcasses. Shells.

"I need to go outside," Creep says aloud.

"Save your voice," she responds with indifference. "It's all been decided. I don't know why anyone would want to venture there. Outside remains outside. From the looks of you, you've lived your life swimming in a vat of acid. Here's a blanket."

"I haven't." Creep ignores her instructions for silence, but takes the dingy too-small blanket. Still finding his bearings, his host's uncertain manner tells him he should resist. He says, "This is how my people look."

"I've never seen a nastier ram. And no horns! Can't figure out what variety you fall under. Don't suppose it matters. It's not as if you're tied down, boy—do whatever you will." She yanks down his bottom lip, examining his gums with petrified fingers. It smarts, as though she's cut him, but it's probably the pressure or the clamminess of her hands. "Mm-hmm. You must be parched. Shall I serve up a cozy tumbler of Shift-flower tea?"

Creep wonders what's in the concoction. Can he stomach it?

"It's made of Shift-flowers, obviously," she answers, "though I'll add some knob-wing to mine, mostly antennae. And some Summer salts. Oh, calm yourself. If I were going to murder you... wouldn't I?" As soon as she asks this she holds up a small orb. "The wooden eye of my absentee partner. It's all I wrestled away."

Sitting up again slowly, so his aching head won't pop, Creep tries to control his thoughts while the glass demon muddles around grabbing for this and that. Who is this creature?

"Muséa's my name. Today, anyway."

Muséa plucks antennae from a struggling beetle. The insect is reminiscent of an old army helmet—and about half the size. Dropping the quivering antennae into her tea cup, she turns the beetle over and grates flakes from its shell into the steaming liquid. Then, in deep consideration, she lingers over a celadon shaker with mist rising from its pinprick openings, but tosses it at the wall behind her. Disregarding the breaking shards, she drops a pinch of blue powder into Creep's cup and pushes it to him.

"There you go. Never mind the Summer salts. They might make you sprout hair...or worse. I added bruised sugars to yours as I'm wont to think you can't handle salts."

The drink's rising vapors carry the musty odor of forgotten dreams—what he remembers of them, dreams that sleep late and miss appointments. Creep drinks and his energy begins re-inflating. No, the tea isn't so much forgotten dreams as plummy security. Muséa has only filled the cup a third of the way so that his shaking hands won't spill it. Still, after taking a few sips, he sets the cup down, uses his strength to stand, then hobbles toward the source of light across the room. The encrusted table, slimy as toad skin, serves as support. The distinct urge to go outside arises in Creep—whatever that desire means, whatever is outside—but as soon as the tea surges fully through his stomach it fades.

The glassy parts of Muséa fill with a jaundiced, moving liquid below the surface. "Danger seems succulent to the knob-wing…" she says, referring to an escaped beetle crawling across the tabletop to feed on stray sugar granules. After a moment of hovering hesitation, Muséa slams a fist down on the bug to no effect, then again and again and again until it's a puddle of reaching legs slowing to a stop. "…but that's only the taste of death."

The room jumps and she screeches. "Listen!" She repeats it in whisper. "Listen."

Booms braid together overhead. Thumping that could be a battle outside vibrate the walls and shake the floor. A few jars fall from the shelves, shattering with creatures and corpses inside. Muséa cries at their loss, scooping their remains into her arms.

Without being able to verify, Creep pictures the seismic knocks as giant beasts—roaming, attacking, decimating one another and their environment. Color-changes in the diffused light echo like missiles striking.

Creep sits back down on a tree trunk-stool.

Months pass.

Jars fill.

Tea grows cold.

Escape dozes off.

He pales.

Years fall between his toes.

At some point, the explosions stop.

"We're safe," Muséa says.

Safe suffocation.

Creep's fingers look foreign, like black fingers on a corpse. The determination to get out of this dank hovel awakes in him again, but this time he clings to it, shoving himself up until he falls against the wall. Stumbling toward the only passageway, he makes the decision to deny any lulling he'll feel and heads in the direction of the undulating light. He's grown tired of the blight of his companion's lightless world.

"Go then," Muséa says, "but I'll tell you: you're ruined. You're not the needle you could've been and it's more than cloth out there, it's armor, and you'll never puncture it. But it will puncture you."

Creep can hardly remain conscious, but continues throwing himself forward down the passage in a series of step-fall, step-fall, step-falls. He doesn't have the energy to look back when the baleful shrieks behind him break into quiet weeping.

"Remains inside," she sobs. "Remains inside."

The sounds behind soon stop. All is still.

When he's certain she's gone, Creep turns back, collecting the jars that still hold life.

27

GODS IN CAPTIVITY

Cheap disinfectant and remnants of dog poop delivered via shoe sole overpower the concrete-cooled air, but otherwise the jail cell is clean. It certainly isn't as atrocious as anticipated. Gavin Daguerré will never again feel sorry for anyone in American jails. The police officers were almost sympathetic to Gavin's plight, becoming more so while riding to the station. Upon Gavin bragging about his family's involvement with broadcasting 1955's The Honeymooners, they even apologized for tasering him. Officer Pulle perked up, telling Officer Kelly that he and his granpop had always watched that old bastard Ralph *Right-in-the-kisser* Kramden. From that point on, the officers ignored Gavin sans the usual fuck-with-me-and-you'll-wish-I'd-shot-you demeanor. Gavin assured them it was all a huge misunderstanding, listing off all his accomplishments since college, promising to give their families DVD's, spicy pickles and packs of lozenges. Gavin doesn't have time to spend a night in jail—as he's preparing for an annual business meeting in Asia.

Two others are in the same shared space where docile offenders spend time. One man sits dozing with mouth agape, a thread of drool stretching in a vertical tightrope from his mouth to his knee. The other guy stares ahead with bloodshot eyes, groaning every now and then. Gavin sits down, shutting his eyes to block as much of this experience as possible. Even later, when the door opens and shuffling footsteps introduce a new cellmate, he pays no heed.

"Oh my god. Gavin? What the hell are you doing here?"

It's a familiar voice emanating from someone with whom Gavin least wants to share this experience.

"Who called you? Surely you're not here to pick me up?" Gavin says without opening his eyes.

"I wish that were the case, but if it were I suspect they wouldn't have locked me in. What are *you* doing here?'

"Me? I'm not the one who has an evening full of people celebrating my art. I have more of a right to be here than you."

"But... why are you here?"

"It seems I've become a bit of an arsonist." He opens his eyes to catch Carder Quevedo's baffled expression.

"Arson? You? Wha—how?"

"Doesn't seem plausible, does it? But it was thirty years in the making. Do you know the difference between people like us and the rest of the world's lemmings, Quevedo?" He waits in vain for an answer. "We actively *create* our reality. We construct it."

"We?"

"Don't play coy, Quevedo, that mask doesn't suit you. Emasculates you. Then again, how can I criticize your plan of attack? It's worked wonders. Either way, you and I make the difference. *We* change reality. Most people readily accept the changes we impose without any of their synapses connecting. They want their world served to them on a plate. We serve it. They don't want to change it themselves, don't even know they can, but you and I—we know better, eh? We take the ropes, tying their world up however we want. Don't turn away, Quevedo! You did it. You may be a dope in many lights but you've accomplished a lot. More than your father ever did."

"My dad?"

"Yes, your dad! Gordan Quevedo—a chump of Olympic proportions. He always was a prick—jealous of others' achievements. Every day was an all-out war. The man has no bedside manner or finesse. You look a damn mess, by the way."

"Me? What about you?" Carder asks, looking at Gavin's swollen lip. "But forget about that. How do you know my dad and why didn't you tell me earlier?"

"Your dad... your dad. Wish he and I had never crossed paths. Eh, maybe I would've let him shine my shoes. You know what? No. He's not even worth that. Anyway, I did see the dirty Mexican tonight."

"You saw him tonight." Carder states, skeptically. "And he's Spanish, not Mexican."

"Briefly. He's responsible for this." Gavin pulls on his bottom lip, revealing a ruby-colored split oozing blood. He would stop talking to let it heal, but it still pulses for revenge. Carder's entry into the evening furthers that sensation, even if he's entered in a backward manner.

"Stop it, Gavin. You truly expect me to believe my dad did that? He hasn't exercised in..." he considers, "...actually, he's *never* exercised."

"I know. You're surprised your old man can do anything more than eat sardines and chorizo, right? Nope. When he throws a jab, it has weight. More so, nowadays. Don't get the wrong idea, though. I clocked him as well. Probably broke a few more blood vessels in that nose of his. Maybe a black eye. It felt fuckin' good administering it, too! Better than sex." He enjoys watching Carder's confusion swim like fish in an overcrowded tank, and wants to sprinkle food flakes over it until all inside are dead.

"Where did this happen? When?" asks Carder.

"What, why, how?" Gavin mocks, causing one of the other two cellmates to waken, shift and spit.

Carder leans forward, pushing close to Gavin without concern for violating personal space. "Yeah. All those. See, I just saw my dad tonight. He was fine. My niece and I ran into him while leaving the Camp Fountain Gallery."

"Then you just missed me as well. I attended your show! 'Course you weren't there when I arrived. Haika looked like a million bucks—and her sister like a hundred—but I've never seen Haika so crestfallen. Absolutely defeated. Between her and Claudette, I pieced together that you'd stormed off in a pageant of angst just because a few people concentrated on the Pick-Me-Pups instead of..." he takes on a taunting tone, "...on your multi-layered, fantastical work."

"It was far more complicated than that." Carder fidgets, sitting on his hands, then crosses his arms over his chest, frustrated. "How did you know my dad?"

"Excuse me, but I'm telling *my* story. Not everyone has a hall of paintings to do it for them."

Carder looks around as though he might change seats to the

furthest corner, but that's only a few feet away.

Gavin continues. "Wait. No, seriously, wait! Let me fuckin' finish, will you? I'm your elder and all that." Gavin gloats when he sees his words working on Carder, has begun settling down, leaning back to listen. "And you, Quevedo, weren't a cute kid. Snot-nosed, scrawny and timid, walking around like you were gonna break. *'God,'* I told Aggie, *'what a careful kid.'* I even remember meeting you. It was after a blizzard applied white-out to the entire city. When we returned to the office, you'd come for a visit in a red sweater with snowmen knit into it. You were dinky for your age. At first, your visits weren't bad—you certainly weren't spoiled rotten like your sister. She stole things from my desk drawers: for one, a Crystal Gayle album. Anyway, you were different—even in your nerdiness you were a sponge soaking up everything. You'd barely reply to anything I asked you, right?" Carder doesn't reply. "No, you're still the mute brat in the red sweater."

"You really knew my father?"

"Maybe you're not soaking up as much as I'd thought. I'm a little shocked you didn't recognize me months ago. At least you could've remembered my name. When you were a runt, you ate enough of my lozenges to have a whole mouthful of cavities. I'm offended. I earned the right to a spot in your memory."

Carder looks at him blankly.

"Dammit, I hear the crickets chirping in your head. Wait…" Gavin searches his person for something and laughs upon finding it. "Haha, they let me keep these for a reason." Cellophane crinkles. Gavin waits for Carder to meet his extended hand, and drops a small piece of hard candy into his palm. "Put it in your mouth. I'll wait."

Whether it's the crackling wrapper, the sickening sugars shed onto Carder's tongue or that he's ingesting the only calories he's had in hours, a cavalcade of memories instantly unlock. The television screen in his mind plays an animated commercial he's seen a million times, though not in several decades: two wrapped lozenges, complete with arms and legs, walk, kissing and pulling at each other's wrappers. Jumping out of their shiny packaging, they march off while a jingle plays: *Olden Tyme Minty Hums: when you're old in time, you'll still want some.* The imagery of that ad is burned into Carder's mind, and brings memories of Gavin: cardigans, slicked hair, breath smelling of bourbon and candy canes.

Gavin perceives the recognition, and smiles in triumph. "Ahh? Uh-huh! I knew I was somewhere in that shriveled brain of yours."

"Olden Tyme Minty Hums?"

"Of course."

"They're gross." Carder pulls it from his mouth and sets it on the bench next to him. "Too sugary. Didn't anyone ever tell you?"

"I beg to differ. There are at least 42 million tongues on this planet that have dissolved them and felt nothing of the sort. Your taste's off. There's a name for that condition."

A cellmate picks up the discarded mint, quietly placing it in his mouth. His glare dares both men to say a word.

"I remember you now. You were Mr. D. Too bad for you I'm not the little punk I was."

"Oh, please! We're already in jail. What do you think you're going to do? A shit-load of nothing!" Gavin doesn't like Carder scanning his saggy skin for the square jaw and taut cheeks of a younger man. He's always been younger and cooler than Carder's father, still is, but despite treatments his face hasn't weathered well. Yes, this is him: Mr. D, Gavin Daguerré, multimillionaire, husband of one of the two hottest women in the world, owner of every vital company in existence. Except Blammo Toys.

"You worked with Dad at Blammo?"

"I didn't just work with him. For a couple of years... I owned him. He was my employee, gopher, slave, whipping boy. Couldn't even smear a good bagel. Paperclips confused him! But that's before..."

"The Pups?"

"...The Pups. If not for you, I'd still own your dad. You're lucky I'm a tired man because it should've been you that I gave the black eye to tonight, and I would've if your dad hadn't claimed it first."

"Gavin, you're seriously making no sense—though at this point, I'm not sure I care. Is my dad okay? Living? He's not paralyzed or anything?"

"Unfortunately not. That fucker can still punch like a Kodiak bear."

"Then can we just let everything be and move on?"

"Clearly, you moved on long ago. Don't think you fool me,

Quevedo. And no, we're not letting everything be! God or the devil sent me to jail tonight. Then, he sends me a singing telegram in the form of the creepy kid responsible for every mess in my life. So you keep your ass firmly planted. You're a captive audience and all that, right? Be that. You've given me a criminal record, so just be *that*."

Carder groans. "Go ahead. What?"

"I'll tell you what. You're the fuckin' ruination of my life, godammit. No, hear me. I know you were a little pinprick of a kid—probably had a dick the size of an eye-dropper at the time, but you may as well have pissed in the holy water sprinkled on me 57 years ago. *So what*, you say, *it's the piss of a six-year-old!* That might be true, but piss is piss."

Carder looks at the walls as if deciding his reaction. "You have millions of dollars and a beautiful wife who adores you, and you're going to hold something against me—I don't know what—from when I was six years old? Are you hearing yourself?"

"Don't go there, Quevedo. Don't fuckin' sass me! You might fool Madame Tussaud herself, but I saw you for the freak you were before you even had one curl of pubic hair. You think all I wanted in life was a girl like Doe?"

"I never thought about—"

"No. Sure, I'd always wanted to marry a set of twins, but I once had someone much more impressive than Doe. You ever met a woman whose tits realign like missiles aiming for your cock no matter where you are?"

Carder clears his throat at the vulgarity. One of the cellmates wakes upon hearing "tits," and rolls his head closer.

"But then, Aggy didn't only have the tits. She had the beauty. Smart, but not too smart. She was, she was…" Gavin realizes that he's tying himself up in tangents. "…a bitch! Aggy. God damn that woman to a hell without mascara or Motown!"

Aggy? Agnes Pye? Carder has only heard her called Aggy a few times, but there's no doubt that's who Gavin refers to. She'd met his dad while working at Blammo. Carder remembers how mean she was. Her put-on compassion upon meeting him had faded quickly. "We don't unscrew light bulbs and lick them," she'd said. "Gordan, is he retarded?" Those were the only words she ever spoke to him. She'd spoken *at* him occasionally, but never *to* him.

Carder has had enough. "Okay, Gavin, I'm saying this respectfully—whatever you're trying to tell me, tell me on one condition: Don't mention that woman again."

"Aggy? She wormed her way into our lives, didn't she? But okay! I moved on to many hotter women anyway, the last of which was Doe. Doe may be a neurotic mess, but she's supple. And insatiable. That woman would fuck four times a day if I wanted to. Still, she's lucky I'm not King Henry VIII."

"She actually might wish you were. Anyway, I hear she's not so hot right now. Claudette says she's sick."

"Tell me about it! But don't let's deviate. Women are distractions. When you meet a truly good one, tell me."

"I've met many."

Gavin sighs. "We're not going to get along well if you don't shut up. No more talk of women." He readjusts his posture. He's used to surfaces built for comfort by entire teams of Scandinavian designers, not jailhouse benches. "Okay, I'll start cutting to the quick. Your father was an ignoramus and he knew it. Always skulked around the office, listening, forcing himself into meetings. See, he'd had success with one impoverished idea—the Bubbly Ball—it blew greasy bubbles when thrown back and forth. Remember? The bubbles were so artificial, almost impossible to pop."

"Never heard of it."

"Figures he wouldn't have mentioned it. It resulted in law suits and a major recall. Couple of Wisconsin kids gagged on the bubbles. But if you go to the fuckin' stinkiest dollar store in Jackson Heights, you'll still find them, renamed. Anyways, your father was obsessed with redeeming himself. Still, it was *my* dream he stole, my destiny. You see, taking candy from babies is as easy as… taking candy from babies. Small, blank minds beg to be filled. *That's* the time to write as much as you can on them. Scribble whatever you want. You could write: '*Someone ate a shit sandwich and you're the resulting bowel movement,*' and it won't only stick in their memories forever, but they'll believe and celebrate it whether they know it or not. Parents rejoice when you offer something to fill their kids' minds, because parents are after their own kind of candy—and it's easier to grab if their kids are plugged in or pacified. It's an altogether human circumstance begging to be steered. You're giving them a gift and they're willing to pay whatever you ask. I had an entire line of toys poised to storm the market."

"How?"

"I told you to let go of the coy act. It makes me hate you more."

"How?"

"Fuckin' dogs, man. What else do whiny brats on five of the six continents want? Kids want sugar, give 'em candy, want something spicy, give 'em a pickle, want something to love, give 'em a dog. Wanna give kids something to love that doesn't bite, shit or shed? Give 'em a plastic dog that'll take all the love they can dish!"

"You're... you're overthinking something simple. You're bastardizing something pure."

Gavin belches. Twice. "Don't get all moral on me. You're no better. You're the one who gave me the idea! Every once in a while at the office, your father would bitch about how much his kid wanted a dog. Then, your mother, Sally, no—Sylvia..." When Carder shifts forward in his seat, Gavin jumps back in his. He enjoys pushing, but is sober enough to tell that he's skirting the limits and changes direction mid-sentence. "...your mother was a sad but good woman. All mothers are good. Quevedo, day after day, months and months of your father's endless yammering about his dunce kid pining for a dog, something clicked. I conceived of them in one night."

"The Pups?"

"No, but same thing. Dog Day—stuffed dogs of all popular breeds, realistically rendered and ready to become chew toys to infants everywhere, but the entire line failed miserably. Miserably. You know how long it's taken me to be able to say that? That word wasn't meant for me. Anyway, that's when Gordan marched in with a revamp of colorful designs, dogs from another world with fuckin' personalities, ready to teach kids, be the friends they never had. I'll tell you, I was floored. Didn't know how your father squeezed such focused concepts from his ass, so sure of exactly what kids want. But I do now. I do now, Quevedo."

Carder's shoulders drop.

Gavin thinks he's turned the knife in sufficiently varied ways, enough so that even if Carder doesn't fall to pieces, he'll transmogrify back into the sheepish child. He's wrong. Carder only sits numbly. If

Gavin could've conceived he would encounter Carder this way—in jail—he would've imagined a surge of power, of dominion. But it feels like nothing. Not only does it *not* fill him, it takes something away. *Quevedo* takes something away from him again, something more, something unnamable, something he'll never have no matter the time wasted, plans drawn or money spent. Only, Gavin can't name what *that* is. Gavin tried crossing Carder out, but the universe had circled him.

There's a long silence.

Carder is caught at the intersection of ridiculous and unbelievable. Ever since the evening before the show, when visited by Dyrak and Everett, he's expected weirdness might leave its stamp at every step. Now, Gavin sits before him, a messier, swollen-lipped old man racing through the same quicksand as Carder. He raises his head, looking into Gavin's eyes, peering deep inside a damaged mosquito wanting to drain blood from the world. Carder remembers enough tidbits to believe Gavin's story, and is actually thankful to have a *where-are-they-now* update. Has anyone involved in the Pups' creation ever moved on?

"Gavin, you still haven't told me how you ended up here tonight, or how you assaulted my dad."

"It was stupid, I know. Doe and her carbon copy kept warning me, as if I'd ever trust their judgment. Their café hasn't been doing such great business. The Kung Pao Prosciutto Wraps and Ostrich Eggnog didn't go over. Not that I care. Sorry, I digress. So, I could've confronted you about your pilfering of ideas when we met up again a few months ago, but I wanted to do something with impact, give a little gift to Gordan. Mike told me of Haika slipping into her bird-with-a-broken-wing syndrome toward you—I swear these women are way too bored—how she started going on and on about your authentic, untainted, gorgeous art. Then, Claudette buys into it, acting like you're some sort of divine Madonna, and she wants to suckle at your teat in holy bliss." Gavin looks at the floor, shaking his head in revolted laughter, then sits up. Seething resentment replaces amusement. "Friggin' stupid attitude. She acts like money's the problem, but do you see her giving up her riches to live among the leopards?"

"Lepers."

"She'd be devoured in a second. Doe wouldn't even have energy to run. And Haika. You know, if I'd seen Haika for who she was at the beginning, I'd never have let Mike marry her. I'll admit her beauty's distracting, and I recognize that she has an eye for which art sells, but ..."

Carder grabs Gavin's legs just above the knee. Hard.

The cellmate who's been sleeping opens his eyes and says, "Don't make me step in. I work the door at Cleaving Peaches and I've broken the noses of poodles bigg'r and tough'r than both'ya. Back to your corners."

Both Gavin and Carder lean back, miming relaxation.

"Sorry." Gavin brushes imaginary dust from his lapel. "I'm starting to see what a fuckin' joker I look like, setting fire to the gallery and..."

"What!? Setting fire to the gallery?"

"Put yourself in my shoes. You have this ember of burning vengeance giving you ulcers and spreading diarrhea over three decades—and you've a chance to vanquish it, expunging it completely. Do you do it? Of course you do, don't say fuckin' otherwise. You do! You get a hold of a blow torch and—*POW!*— watch it in flames."

"You're disturbed, Gavin! Tell me you didn't torch the gallery! Is everyone okay? Did anyone get hurt? Haika?"

"Course not, calm down! Everyone's fine. Do you think I'd wanted to ruin my present life getting revenge on the past? I quickly realized carrying a blow torch around a large group of people wasn't the smartest thing—utterly moronic. *They'd* get hurt. *I'd* get caught. However, I did have several bird cocktails at Café Beryr earlier tonight—they have a new flaming drink called the Firebird which, like the restaurant, probably won't be around much longer—and I decided stupidly that a cigarette lighter would be less obvious. I'd fry up a few choice paintings without getting caught and no one the worse. I almost got away with it."

"Hey, you think I could get another one of those mints?" asks the cellmate who'd previously pilfered Carder's. He and Gavin negotiate a back and forth. Gavin proclaims the officers only allowed one lozenge, and only due to a medical condition called Dry Throat.

Gavin doesn't have to worry. The cell door unlocks, and an officer appears.

"Yo, Gavin Dagur-whatever... Mr. Honeymooner! Someone's come to pick you up."

"Of course! Who is it, who is it?"

"A 'Mr. Mike Fiore.'"

"Completely expected. He's overdue."

Carder perks up. "Great! Can you tell Mike I'm also here? I'm sure he already knows."

Gavin takes his time standing up, and dusts himself off. "Mm-hmm. I'll tell him."

The officer leaves with Gavin and doesn't return.

After Mike's snub, Carder no longer expects to be beamed out of his prison sleepover. Under normal circumstances, Darren might reach in to *set things straight*. Carder hopes that Haika won't swoop in, breaking her halo over everyone's heads, transfiguring the police station forever. She must have spent the night recovering from the gallery fiasco on both practical and psychological fronts.

Alone, Carder finds his restraint from society—albeit short—a wondrous thing. He'd grown used to isolation long ago. It can become comforting to have interaction wrenched away—as though life's pause button was pressed, and he's forced to sit and reflect.

The cell door unlocks.

With neither antlers nor robotic accoutrement, Claudette Vivienne steps forward to claim Carder. She apologizes to him for the behavior of *asshole-Mike* and her sister's *pygmy husband*. After the necessary paperwork and formalities are completed, they walk from the precinct into an early morning steadily being drained of darkness. Light and mist enters the scene at leisure while the two stroll to the car she'd ordered, driven by a stocky man. She couldn't bear to call her usual driver, Ekon, in the dead of night as he has a wife and family. Claudette looks at Carder as though he's a Viking wandering home with battle-wounds. That tells Carder how he really must look.

"I suppose I've a lot to explain."

Claudette is especially beautiful in the dissipating moonlight. Without make-up, she looks pink and alive, as if hidden electricity surges beneath her skin.

"You've nothing to explain, Carder," she says. "It was a messy night. Be thankful you left when you did. Things got a heck of a lot... sillier. Anyway, talk if you want to, but only for yourself, not for my sake. I was there."

The words float from Claudette's mouth like spiderlings riding the winds on silver threads, satisfied to land wherever they will. But they don't, so she warms Carder with a quilt of silence, allowing him to pay no mind to that night's events or to the coming consequences. They simply settle into their ride.

The hum of the motor buzzes like jungle nights which only the driver has experienced. The car cuts the dawn, leaving brightening pieces of it on their faces and arms, and Carder rolls his window down to find the breeze heaving promises of autumn. So much has happened over the summer. The past few months had left him grabbing at whatever rocks or branches might stabilize his trajectory. Carder doesn't want that struggle anymore. Closing his eyes, he wishes a wave of tears would flow. He wants to cry, would give anything to have that relief, but whatever tank supplies them is empty.

After they pass several blocks, Carder says, "I'm a horrible parent."

"Since you're not a parent, I don't mind agreeing with you."

"But do you know how my niece is? I left her behind, hauled away from her like a serial killer. She could've gone to jail."

"She didn't. Card, you underestimate Mandy. She's perfectly fine, back at your place with Haika, wearing those awful baggy boy-pajamas. Sweetie, don't torture yourself. You're not the only person who cares about her. Goddammit, I'm furious *for* her. Your sister is jacked up. How did you ever come from that family?"

"And yet, Lucy loves Mandy more than anything."

"Hell no! Anyone who disowns their child like that doesn't get to claim love. There's no excuse! Did you know that Mandy believes they'll never speak to her again?"

"That's no exaggeration. They won't."

"Surely they'll soften as they realize she doesn't believe lock-and-step with them. They can't expect everyone to believe like them."

"They can. And do. Lucy will probably be bedridden for a week with a broken heart."

"But she'll never speak to her own daughter again? That's sick. Mandy is the heartbroken one and she might be that way for the rest of her life. If it weren't for you, where would she go? The streets? Drugs? Drinking? Suicide? I can't fathom what life would be like with one's friends and family ripped away—and by their own choice."

Carder sighs. "You're right. It *is* jacked up. But Lucy thinks Mandy is causing this."

"Except, Mandy's not shunning her mother." Claudette sighs as well. "At least she has you and a place to live, to get a new start. Still, do you want her working at that dingy diner where we met you and Darren?"

"Is that what's happening? That's the first I've heard of it. As far as I knew, she was going home with her parents. I guess that's why she didn't mention it." He shifts on the car's leather interior. "I don't have much to offer Mandy."

"What!? You've given Mandy more in these past few months than she's probably had in a lifetime. It takes incredible strength to rip up one's life and create a new one. I can't even fathom the level of loss she's going through. We weren't meant to mourn the living."

With these words, Claudette looks out the window.

Carder thinks of Doe.

"Carder, without you, Mandy's road would've been prolonged, or at least much rockier—and she knows that. Don't expect her to write it in a greeting card. But Mandy thinks the world of you." Claudette pulls a stray thread from his sleeve. "Many do."

Carder senses that Claudette's tug of the thread, which breaks, is her first step in undressing him. While her words touch him a great deal, he isn't ready to go further. He changes to topics they can wrestle without unfastening buttons or zippers.

"Can I ask you something?"

"Anything." Claudette's reply is wet with hope.

"I don't know what happened at Camp Fountain after I left. Gavin's tirade was cut short by Mike's arrival, and it was hazy at best. Would you fill me in?"

She looks at the passengers in the taxi next to them. They appear sloppy drunk on love—or lust.

"Card, I'm glad you didn't stay at the gallery. You escaped two stupid men. Of course, one was the numskull mayor of Mordor and the other was... your father. Oh, you knew that much? I hadn't met your father before that. You do resemble one another, but he's missing your mojo. A hardened man." She pauses. "How should I proceed?"

"Tell me everything you saw."

"Okay. Though I assure you, I knew nothing of Gavin, dabbling in the Picky Pups—"

"Pick-Me-Pups."

"Yes, those! I didn't know them as a child. Doe and I weren't allowed to play with plastic. And I had no idea your paintings were used in their design. It seems Gavin knew about them the entire time. He worked at some point for a toy company in an effort to show-off to his family, a kind of I-can-do-anything act, but then again, his hands were always in everything. At first, I thought he just didn't like you—he generally only likes ass-kissers. Doe says his inchworm causes insecurity. Did you know the fool has a latex fetish?"

"A latex fetish? Okay. What's wrong with that?"

"He's allergic to latex. Regardless, it's now obvious that his jealousy of you is ravenous. I think it's because you built upon your art, you took it further, all the while not even flexing your muscles or controlling people, or having to prove your worth. He can't understand that. You progressed past those dogs, while he—despite making a quadrillion dollars—couldn't." Carder leaned his head away. "Am I not right?" Claudette asks.

"I think you overestimate me."

"Wow. You not only underestimate Mandy, but yourself too. Where was I? So... you and Mandy left the gallery. I don't blame you. Iris acted ridiculously. She didn't mean to. God gave Iris too much volume and no mute button. I have one though. Be good and I'll show it to you." She gets no reaction. "After that, I helped calm Haika. However, right as things started to settle I saw Gavin schmoozing around like a weasel. He's good at fooling people, but I've been around him long enough to see through his veneer. He was practically spinning circles, conducting seventeen conversations at once. I watched him from across the room and knew it was all a distraction, but I didn't know why." She stops and addresses the chauffeur, "Excuse me, Driver… please take the Westside highway. Less stoplights." Claudette places her hand on Carder's leg, preparing him for the rest of the story, wanting to make it as painless as possible. Her eyes linger. "Card, Gavin set your work on fire."

"Oh god, that wasn't a joke? Gavin never finished telling me the story. How bad was it? No one got hurt?"

"Not badly. I don't think Gavin had well-laid plans, which is unusual. He couldn't have or he would've thought of something better. Perhaps Iris's revelation threw him off. Regardless, if your father hadn't stepped in, there's no telling what might've happened. We all could have burnt to a crisp while stampeding out. Oh, God, can you imagine the colors? Hold on now, Card. Whatever you feel about your father, he truly did help. I was standing across the room, watching Gavin pull out a cigarette lighter. He got close to the white-furred spidery sculpture, of which the sheer gorgeousness will never be matched, and held a flame close until the creature was literally ablaze. Your dad saw this at the same time as I, but he was closer. There was yelling. Commotion. People rushed toward the door. Your father caught Gavin by the back of the neck, flung him to the wall, and kicked the lighter away when Gavin dropped it."

Carder throws his head back against the seat and stares at the car's ceiling. "I, I—I don't know what to think anymore, what to say, how to feel. I… I…"

Claudette is at a loss as well. Delivering bad news isn't her strongest suit. She decides she'll try something new. "Have you ever seen two old men fight? It was an odd dance between two lumbering oafs." When Carder laughs, Claudette allows herself to do the same. "I'm not joking. It was almost slapstick—and if there weren't a fire to put out and some semblance of decorum we were trying to regain, we probably would've let them duke it out until it was impossible tell whose wrinkles were whose. Oh, no mistaking it, your dad would've won. He was throttling Gavin. You know, I think I might actually like your dad."

"Ugh."

"Card, he saved your art."

"He's done a lot of things to me besides saving my art."

"I hear you, but if he hadn't been there, at the very least the sprinklers would've gone off and ruined your pieces. At worst…"

"He shouldn't have. He liked but hated my work. When all this was happening, did my dad and Gavin speak?"

"They were yelling at each other like two old Sicilian women fighting over a loaf of bread. Your dad was spitting, screaming for Gavin to keep his hands off your work. Gavin said your dad was a thief and had... I'm sorry...."

"Had what?"

"Exploited you your entire life."

"Well, not my *entire* life."

"Card, I'm so sorry the way things turned out. But we saved everything—except the sculpture. It's stored in my memory though."

The city spins as the car circles onto the Brooklyn Bridge. Carder needs silence to process the details Claudette revealed.

"One thing," She says, amused. "Someday, remind me to describe what Haika looks handling a fire extinguisher."

They cross the bridge and Carder grows restless. He's numb and needs to lie alone on the sands of isolation—wherever those might be. Claudette has been nothing short of amazing, but he needs to regroup on his own, without expectation or social obligation. Many times as a child, he'd tried willing himself to transform into an inanimate object, usually a smooth black rock on the furthest beach of the most distant land, a land that never felt another human's footsteps. Instead, and against his will, he's become the foundation to a small village of demanding residents: Haika constantly prodding him to expand. Darren always fighting her for that prod. Rabbit will probably write a memoir about becoming the adopted lesbian daughter of a sycophant toymaker. Claudette wants intercourse. Iris is always hanging around, bleating like a psychotic sheep. Mrs. Gunderson wants him to watch her cat—the one that flew out the window, chased by his dead mother's ghost and whatever million creatures she'd brought with her.

Zombie.

Zombie is the only one who doesn't bother him. Zombie walks around in his dogness with nothing but a gurgling stomach and limitless love.

The car finally pulls up near Carder's house. The windows are lit like bars of gold, matching the Trans Am parked off to the side. Carder thanks Claudette profusely, asking if she minds dropping him off without coming in, though that means the driver will escort her back across the bridge to Fardor. She understands.

"Promise me you'll get some sleep," she says.

"I promise. Ms. Vivienne, you're an amazing friend. Thanks for understanding."

As the car rolls away, Carder imagines the next few hours. Haika will need an exhaustive discussion. After all, he'd ruined her career in the span of one night. Rabbit might still be awake, waiting for her uncle to return from jail—which will require another apologetic monologue he isn't up to delivering.

The moon is unsteady in the sky, like a wobbling marble glimmering in weak reflections of sun, producing no light of its own. Carder's steps pound their cadence toward the house, but the rhythm grows slower and slower.

Twenty-two more steps—he figures.

Twenty-two steps.

They're twenty-two steps he doesn't take.

28

THE FURY, THE SOUND,
THE WINE COUNTRY

Mildred White wraps her 87-year-old hand around Carder's to give him the keys, but inadvertently passes him a wig as well. She'd probably grabbed it upon hearing a knock at the door—but either she'd seen Carder and decided it wasn't necessary or she's altogether forgotten about it. The keys float between them in strands of synthetic hair until detangled. Darren's Aunt Mildred shushes Carder's apologies for having come to her doorstep so early. Darren's asleep, but *she's* up all the time, and no longer needs sleep or dreams. Despite Carder's hurried countenance, she ushers him inside, seating him at the kitchen table.

"You're having orange juice," she says.

In the few moments it takes for the juice to rise to the glass's rim, years are shed. Carder becomes a gangly teenager again. Aunt Mildred has been old his entire life. On the other hand, he's been young and foolish the entire time. Still is.

"Mister," she says, "You're still in jail. Maybe there are no bars or policemen..." She knocks lightly on Carder's forehead, flapping a terrycloth sleeve in his face. "...but it's in that noggin. Then again, you never would leave your head, no matter how we'd entice you. But don't see how that matters now. People do as they will," she pauses, losing her train of thought. "Ah, yes. The cottage. There's not much in or around Mattituck to comfort you, but you go do whatever it is you're going to do, Mister."

Darren's Aunt Mildred always imparts Yoda-with-cancer-like wisdom. She's called Carder *Mister* for decades after a summer of applying Jason, Thompson, Carson and Godfrey—two of whom were her brothers, now dead.

"You're such a dashing gentleman. You certainly deserve a break," she says as though courting romance. She looks deep into Carder's eyes before noticing some old toothpaste spackled to the collar of her robe. "Well, hell…" she says, shuffling away. "But, remember, the heat don't work there. Don't have to—no one's usually there after July. It's getting cold though. This winter will be an early one. There's no air conditioning either—Lord decides the thermostat. And no shower. Only a 'tub." She examines the flake of caked toothpaste she's pulled from her robe. "But make sure to baptize yourself in the Sound. The water's not deep. And… wait one moment. I've something for you to take."

Carder promises Aunt Mildred he'll take the small brown bag she gives him, and thanks her for the gift of being unreachable. Silently, he's also thankful for her nonchalant approach to life. She's been in a better mood ever since a black man became President, and is certainly happy to help a downtrodden young white man by offering up *her* summer home: a small cottage in Mattituck, a couple hours outside the city on Long Island's North Fork. She acquired the place from a man she'd once cleaned for as a young girl. He didn't give it to her, she bought it outright! My, how the world has changed!

The day is new. Sun still hasn't penetrated its chilly air, but the thread holding off autumn has broken. Summer is over. Driving the highway, Carder decides that Aunt Mildred is right: he's still in jail, locked within the sticky syrup of his own thoughts. He looks down at a stack of paper on the passenger seat. It's one of Darren's screenplays, a familiar one Aunt Mildred passed him in addition to the bag. "Be gentle on him," she told Carder though she'd only ever read the synopsis. "I suppose awful movies are the only kind they make nowadays."

Carder has read previous versions of *Perpetual Hump Day*. It's a sort of *Freaky Friday* meets *The Matrix*, the story of a suburban white man from Kansas and a black teenage girl in Harlem who simultaneously wake up having traded bodies for no obvious reason—she, in white-bread Kansas working to support the man's alcoholic wife, and he, now dating the star shooting guard of the basketball team at Phillip Randolph High. It's a promising start: two worlds bleeding into one another. About once a year, Darren revisits the story with Carder over dinner, always full of ponderous questions about his own story: do the two lead characters know each other? Do they meet and fall in love, spending the rest of their lives enthralled with the person inhabiting their former body? Darren explained that he'd added a magical ambassador to move things along, the film's ethereal-but-gritty spiritual guide. The problem with this project is that the screenplay itself has been Darren's own perpetual hump day for the past five years. Despite being his hands down favorite story, he's never been able to resolve what happens. Carder told Darren that the prior year's edit was the best thing he'd written yet.

That excited Darren. "Really? Wait, then! In this newest edit, the man from Kansas has been in the girl's body for seven years. He's pregnant with her second child and pursuing a degree in Child Education. The Harlem girl stuck in the man's body has become a multi-platinum white rapper, popping Adderall and attending red carpet events with an entourage of women. Problem is—I can't finish the story."

"Does it have to be finished?"

"You ever been to a never-ending movie?"

"A few."

Reviewing the script again will be the perfect diversion for Carder while he's away. Even if it's awful, its messy fiction was far more successful than Carder's actual life.

A week flies by in the drafty emptiness of Aunt Mildred's cottage. Local vineyards are becoming barren fields of black, leafless vines reaching toward blank skies. Early autumn winds blow in off the water and wander the hallways at night, preparing the house for another winter. Dust. Mothballs. Dried-out paneling. Rice Krispies with an expiration date in 1986. Hangnails. Baths with barely warm bathwater cooling further as it falls from the faucet. Silence. Push-ups. Crunches. Pull-ups. Jacking off. Silence. The stars. Looking out the kitchen window at any passing car while eating pretzels—here's a blue MINI Cooper, there's a station wagon filled with schoolchildren, now a *Baltar's Meat* truck brandishing a picture of a cow, chicken and pig, mirthfully hugging each other. Old romance novels in a nightstand drawer, with grandiose smut. Carder has little in common with their lusty heroes. He's had sex, but never "driven his maleness into her hot cave of want" nor "tasted the honey-pulsed window of womanly soul."

The sounds of nature would normally be anomalies to Carder. Darkness should be accented by night life fraternizing at local bars, people ought to be milling about, cars honking and sirens flashing. The absence of those things at the country cottage leads Carder to believe it's a place one comes to die, that perhaps *he* could die there. Before the first week is over, he meets a tight-lipped Mandy for a non-eventful lunch, a visit he asks her not to reveal, and almost considers abducting Zombie, but knows it would result in unwanted interaction with Haika. He has to find better ways to thaw into life. To do so, he ends up breaking the one rule Darren made about his stay.

"You can go there," Darren said when offering Aunt Mildred's summer home for a getaway, "as long as you don't do any art projects. I don't want to walk in there, or even worse, I don't want my aunt walking in to find a sculpture of found objects taken from her garage, or a mural of mating sasquatch on the wall, or whatever your crazy brain conjures."

When Carder asks a local storekeeper about the high prices of art supplies, she tells him it's the cost of importing from the city. Carder groans and pays with his credit card. Imported indeed.

The dark circles beneath Haika's eyes mean nothing. They're permanent as far as she knows. The gurgling of her empty stomach is a welcome distraction, as are hangnails, the anime movies Lara has loaned Rabbit, and random visits from Doe. She changes the color of her toenails three times in one day. Though she possesses the ability to cook delectable meals that once pulled Mike away from desks, sheets and ball games, her lack of motivation to do so in the week since the catastrophe convinces Haika she's right to resist motherhood. She knows the type of mother she'd be: the type who burns all of her clothes and shaves her head, the type to join the Peace Corps or move to another country to start anew—but it would have to be an enchanted country, a country with less pain and nicer weather, less stairs, brighter stars. She would be the type of mother who young children love but then grow embarrassed of until they're ten years into adulthood with one failed marriage under their belt. That's when they'd see how cool she'd always been.

Haika doesn't have that kind of time.

Getting out of bed is nearly impossible. It's her accomplishment each day. That, and trying new wine. Sadness enhances her taste buds so she can enjoy the cache of wine she's built in Carder's kitchen as a lone sommelier. The Nero d'Avola, a Sicilian grape, currently holds pole position, though a Greek chorus of bottles sits in judgment—mournful bottles, goading her into an impromptu wine-tasting for one. Four more bottles are soon open.

Dammit, now she'll have to drink them all before they spoil. She'd better get started.

When Haika knocks over an open bottle of Bordeaux early one afternoon, reducing her *waste-not* goal by one, it's not discussed. Neither Haika nor Rabbit rush to clean it up. They both stand, watching the wine expand its form across the floor, taking on the shape of a foreign country with changing borders. It's a nation stained with burgundy landscapes, peacefully expanding its territory without hurry. They let its shape travel the floor, through the wood grain and between boards. Haika figures that if it's to spill, let it spill thoroughly and spectacularly. Even having the time to contemplate it dries and cracks the mud of her sadness.

Rabbit takes the threadbare dishcloth from her while Haika stands frozen, simply letting Rabbit clean the floor sloppily. Wine will be forever trapped between the floor boards.

"I keep reading it," Haika admits to Rabbit.

"I get it," Rabbit responds, "but it says he's okay."

Haika pulls out a note which she's kept close. The paper is soft from wear. She unfolds and reads it again.

I'm ok—need some time.
Thanks,
C

It's difficult to read between the lines when there are so few. Everything about the note bothers Haika, from the blank, pressured scribble to get ink flowing, to the crude handwriting, to the method of delivery (Rabbit had found it taped to the front door on the morning after the Camp Fountain debacle). She'd thought she heard a knock, but the note appeared, not Carder, and the Trans Am's spot was empty. There's nothing more to say about it, so Haika bends down to help clean the floor, though it amounts to spectator sport. She traces a groove in the floor's wood grain with her fingernail, following its fluttering tide of growth rings. The sleeve of her blouse rides up, revealing a mole.

"I made an appointment to get it removed." Haika says of the mole, for it's as irregular as the wine spill, smaller but irregular, a tiny, distant island.

Rabbit nods, still sopping up sticky red residue.

Haika wants to tell Rabbit so much—about her unwillingness to return to the gallery, her disinterest in everything, her fear of becoming a cynical pariah, of permanently wearing the equivalent of sexual bug spray. "…and I signed up for a sewing class."

"Why?"

"Why not? Clothes don't appear from thin air."

"Making clothes? Interesting." Rabbit says as though it's the least interesting thing on the planet.

It is.

Though Haika is doubtful of her own interest in sewing, she signed up for the class when she passed a new fabric store on Montague Street. Surely local sewing classes are in dire need of support, though she fully expects a cabinet of lidless containers to dump needles over her during the first class. Remember needle-girl?—they'll say forevermore, transforming her into a tragic anecdote—beware becoming a pin-cushion! She already knows she'll hate everyone in class. Her goal is to muster the strength to sew a pillow, possibly to simply lift a needle. If they sew letter shaped pillows, she'll sew a lowercase 'L.' She won't use the pillow. In fact, she'll probably leave it in the classroom unfinished and never return. It already fills an imaginary trashcan.

"Who am I kidding?" Haika asks. "Never mind. I don't know if I'm going to sewing class." She doesn't even know in which direction she'll next step, perhaps to the couch. Her sigh becomes a yawn. "Where's Lara been? I've not seen her around. And I'm sorry I'm such a gloom-pop."

"It's okay. She said that I'm changing and she's already got enough drama in her life. She can't deal with mine. Oh well. Guess she's not getting her movies back. That's okay, now I don't have to buy *Princess Mononoke*."

"You've known each other for what, two months?"

"I've changed a lot during that time."

"For the better, Rabbit. For the better."

"You think?"

"Are you kidding? You're closer to the mark than you've ever been! At least someone is."

"Thanks," Rabbit says gruffly.

Haika recognizes the appreciation, though the girl's withdrawn countenance still drives her crazy. She'd recently dreamed that the only way to get Rabbit to talk was to smack the words out of her.

They both stand up. The floor is as clean as it's going to get.

"Have you seen him?" Haika asks, expecting to get little information.

"Not much, but someone's been feeding the neighbor's cat. Seriously, there's a bowl of food outside on the windowsill. I haven't seen that cat since before the show's opening." She pauses. "How's Mike?"

"Gone. With Gavin to Asia. They're working on some new way to rip-off the world. They're set on building another factory, to provide a grander platform from which the factory workers can throw themselves. 'But not to worry' Mike says 'We're installing nets at the base to catch any jumpers.' That's who *I* married."

"It must be hard on you not to have him here."

"You know what, Rabbit? I actually prefer him away," Haika says with delightful shame.

"That's not who I meant." They stand, blinking at one another. "Anyway, I wonder where the cat's food is coming from."

The appearance of cat food could mean everything or nothing, but Haika will take any small sign that Carder might return. Her heart is too sore to pretend things can possibly be repaired. She isn't even sure in what ways they're broken. Sure, she'd pushed Carder into showing his art, but he had allowed it. Haika is hurt and angry that he didn't tell her about the toyline. She *should* feel absolute fury. It's something that should've been disclosed, and if Carder were any other artist, any other person, she'd be happy to very publicly cut ties. She wavers. While she'd never embarrass him as he has her, she considers whether or not they'd both benefit from moving on, closing the chapter, perhaps burning the book of their friendship altogether. Their relationship has Frankenstein features— complicated but alive. Carder's angst is sewn up with her hope. The pulse of her life is stitched to his shadow. If whatever they had is over, Haika will wear the wound, but she at least wants her last memory to be something other than watching him rush away from her, from his art and the gallery. She at least wants a goodbye.

She suddenly notices that Rabbit is in the kitchen rinsing out the dishcloth.

There's a rapid succession of five knocks at the door, their rhythm is a song which she and Iris loved when they were fifteen. They'd listened to it a thousand times that summer and Iris had adopted it as her knock ever since.

The look of happiness on Iris's face makes Haika want to vomit. Iris challenges the cool weather with bare legs and a straw sun-hat. The hat's white brim and yellow crown resemble an egg in the process of cooking, with fat yellow ribbons trailing down each side like runny strands of yoke. It's too ridiculous to have been designed with breakfast in mind. Probably only Haika sees it.

"This city is the difficult one," Iris says, pulling the hat from her head and scratching her scalp, her hair frizzing. "You run an errand and a half-day is gone. Still, looky I got here."

She holds up two rooster-shaped keychain bottle-openers with jagged cap-removing combs. They're identical except in color: one burnt orange, the other neon green.

"You choose whichever cock you want."

Haika won't.

"Haika, do it. Choose. I can even give you the green." But Haika doesn't reach for either. "Fine, here… orange for you." She tosses it at Haika. "Why so quiet, hermana?" Iris throws her bacon-esque red and white striped jacket at a chair a few feet away, revealing short shorts and a sleeveless t-shirt. "Always dress like the sun is out," she says before sitting down.

Haika ignores the question, the key rings and the fashion tips. She's deciding how to force Iris to reveal why she's come to New

York City. It's clear Iris won't be forthcoming without pressure. "I'm sure I know the answer to this, but where have you been staying?"

"With Darren. It takes less money, gives more love." She laughs. "And you are here."

"Takes less money? I've never charged you anything to stay with me!"

"Sí, but it's too far from there to Darren's place. Plus, I was afraid Mike might sneak down and mistake me for you since you're here so much, Señora Quevedo. Nice ring to that sound, eh?"

"I'm pretty sure you would've been safe. Anyway, you know Mike's away."

"Puhhhlease smile, hermana. Your smile could fill a cathedral with men. I know, 'cause I see it whenever I look in the mirror at church. And, Sis, we gotta get you out for a night. One thing I'll say for Nueva York—los hombres son más calientes que infierno! What are you doing tonight? There's this lounge on…"

"I'm not remotely interested."

Iris sighs, dropping her shoulders. "Games. Okay, Haik—you tell me. You tell me."

"I haven't seen Carder since the night of the gallery opening…"

"I'm sorry."

"…Mike will only speak to me about money…"

"Yikes."

"…my career's in who-knows-what state…"

"ehhh…"

"…the dog won't eat." Haika's voice breaks from laughter to tears. "He shat in my shoe this morning."

"Is that the smell?"

In an instant, Iris leaps up from the couch. The sight of her sister's tears always makes her cry too. She grabs Haika.

"Hug."

Haika doesn't reciprocate, but stands as Iris squeezes. It's more like being fenced in than hugged. She has loved and hated Iris for as far back as she can remember. How can they possibly share every strand of DNA?

Haika finally speaks. "…and I'm angry at you. Furious."

"Wha—me? Que?" She won't let go of Haika, squeezes harder. "You are, as you say, bat-shit crazy."

"*I'm* bat-shit crazy? Babe, you blew in with the winds unannounced, shacked up with Carder's best friend, ruined one of the greatest friendships I had going *and* my career in one foul swoop… and I *still* don't know why you've come."

"Why I came? You have always tried to kick me off your life!"

"Yes, why you came, Iris. Why did you come?"

"To see you, your life and the way you pound out the road in front of you while you go. Everywhere is a construction zone to Haikita! You always hated my—how you say?—vicinity! Papi always said your shit don't stink."

"Sis, the last time I saw you was at my wedding! Do you know what I thought while you walked down the beach toward the minister? *This is the last I'll see of Iris unless I come back here.* I knew you'd never leave Puerto Vallarta."

"But there I was, and here I am. See, I always knew you *would* leave. Always trying to create a new world, a new world you can never be satisfied with. I'm satisfied. I love it at home. The sun is different there, cats baking on sand, the iguanas, the surf, the constant state of happiness—*that's* what you cannot stand: the constant state of happiness."

"Laziness isn't happiness."

"No, the rat-racing you do here is not happiness. They say people here so driven. Maybe so. But they're bad drivers and don't know where they're driving *to*! No, the refusing of your land and tongue, *that* is not happiness. Always digging your way to freedom will keep you dirty and in the dark. And in a hole. And probably eaten by birds! You say you saw the last of me, but here I stand in the stench de mierda del pero."

"Lo siento, hermana," Haika whispers. "It must have just happened. The smell wasn't here before…"

"But I'm still here. Standing in the smell. Here I am. For you. With you. Yet you hate me."

"No I don't." Haika grabs Iris. "Hug," she says.

Iris won't. She stands stiffly as Haika holds her.

"You hate me?" Iris's eyes are pleading and irate.

Haika doesn't have the energy to hate her. Besides, though Iris smashed Haika's life with a Mexican mallet, the cracks were already there—a light breeze might've resulted in the same outcome. It's difficult to rage against someone applying destruction so innocently, maybe without the best intentions, maybe with no intentions at all. Haika had set forth to create her own identity, but now sees her own reflection retreating in the mirror. Iris is all she has. Thus, it isn't compassion or valor staving off her hatred. It's the fear that if she pushes Iris away she'll have nothing. How is choice involved?

"Yes, Hon, of course I love you. Mis ojos, mi espejo. Of course I do." Haika kisses her.

Iris softens. "Remember *Through the Looking Glass*?"

Haika quotes as though reading it. *"It's no use now to pretend to be two people! Why, there's hardly enough of me left to make one respectable person!"*

The streams of Iris's tears run dry, her body loosens and she returns to it. "Together maybe we can be one respectable person."

"Yes. Add us together and it's a hell of a world."

"And maybe bat-shit crazies find the best caves to shit in."

They laugh in harmony. To anyone else it would seem peculiar, but they'd shared a womb, they'd been the same embryo before it decided there was too much for just one person.

They sit on the couch, one on each end, their feet touching. Haika missed this bond with her sister for years. It's the oldest, most comfortable feeling she's ever had.

"I still don't know why you're here."

"Shh. Don't ruin it. Let me tell you a story about a beautiful black man that found a pink beach-pebble on a city sidewalk. He picked it up and put it in…."

"I want to hear this, but two things…" Haika says, turning her head toward the kitchen. "Rabbit? Would you brew us a fresh pot?" She turns to Iris. "Okay, and the other thing—Iris, can you try to use an indoor voice from now on?"

Iris laughs. "I am so loud, mi hermana. Forgive a girl, eh?"

Haika tries to laugh as well. "Probably. My life's destroyed, but probably."

"And you too, Rabbit!" Iris calls out. "Forgive a girl. It's the Christian thing to do. Jesus would love it!"

"I've nothing to forgive you for!" Rabbit replies from the kitchen.

"But when you do!" Iris says in her loudest voice yet.

The coffee grinder's screeching drives the dog from the kitchen into the living room.

"Sis, you gotta paper towel? Someone has to clean up the Zombie shit. And let's dry us up too. I don't wanna cry no more. Sí?"

"Sí."

"You sit. I'll clean it up. Then, I tell you why I came to America."

Music becomes Carder's friend and lover, accompanying him during breakfast, bathing, jogging and painting. Though he skips songs that Haika overtly gave to him, he begins listening to, digesting and connecting to albums she's been nagging him about. Some he's heard before, but they'd never reached him as they do now: *OK Computer, Blue, Disintegration, The Madcap Laughs, The Doors, Little Earthquakes, Never Mind the Bullocks, Two Suns.* Though Carder has no musical reference points, he deems it possible that Rachmaninoff was ancestor to the Chemical Brothers who are fourth cousins to Coltrane but only through marriage. Under the influence of song and cannabis, Carder philosophizes that he's found the most logical reason he'd come to this planet: to experience the sacred combination of song, weed and art. The music mixes into the painting process, which mixes into everything.

He develops a friendship with Aunt Mildred's mammy cookie jar: a big, black ceramic woman wearing a headscarf and a white dress so long it dusts the countertop. Having a racially insensitive cookie jar is scandalous, but feeling scandalized by a cookie jar is ridiculous. Passed through generations of Aunt Mildred's family, it symbolizes freedom and recognizes history changed. Carder respects that the cookie jar has seen half a century of life without cracking. One drowsy morning, he sits at the kitchen table with the wise, old woman in front of him. The pleasure of being indoors wears thin, and he wants more than putzing around looking for things to fix while Nine Inch Nails rips through the house. He doesn't have the discipline to delve into Darren's screenplay and he's used the last tube of Prussian Blue. Thus, painting is paused.

This morning, his head is still floating in the sedation of sleep. *Coffee*—the cookie jar advises—*coffee and cookies.*

Damn Haika for getting him addicted to caffeine.

The cookie jar has been empty and Carder knows she'd love to be full again. He asks her in silence what cookies she'd liked, grabs his coat and gloves and heads to Sullivan's Grocery, a small store with few choices. He'll also stop by the art store to pick up paint.

The roads are wet with the last night's rain. Sidewalks don't exist in Mattituck. People are scarce, but wildlife is everywhere. A city-dweller from birth, initially the lack of advertisements and fluorescent signs of life is disconcerting, but Carder begins seeing that modern cities mirror nature's cities, and nature's cities exist at every step. While lonely traffic only motors by occasionally, birds dive and scoop, and insects chirp and whir like televisions, radios and car alarms. Remnants of paw prints provide evidence of unseen creatures zipping back and forth through soggy soil. Cats peer from windows of homes offering smoke signals from solitary chimneys. Ultimately, life is pervasive even when it isn't flashing neon.

Carder muses at the headstones in Luther Cemetery, which he uses as a shortcut. The winds of death play peacefully in the grasses between graves, and an animal peeks from behind a headstone, breaking Carder's stride. It's a common rabbit with ticked brown fur, eyes pulsing, hunching in its fluffed coat for warmth. Unlike red-eyed lab rabbits, it's confident in its ability to escape, unaware of its relatives being shoved into Easter baskets or pulled from magician hats. A true playboy, this bunny is buttoned up in stillness, yet ready to throw it off and dash away. Carder digs into his coat pocket for a granola bar he'd found in the kitchen cupboards. Breaking it into pieces inside his pocket, he's cautious not to make sudden moves. He brings out his hand little by little, as though retrieving a cornea, carefully throwing granola close to the headstone obscuring the animal. The rabbit breathes at him before taking a few hops to the food.

In the distance, a car hums closer, the road buzzes wet beneath it. When the car draws closer, the rabbit darts to the shrubs. At about ten yards away, a car window rolls down and a familiar voice emanates from inside.

"Creep! Carder! Is that you?" It's the unmistakable voice of Gordan Quevedo, which then turns to the passenger whose mouth is visible, covered in clownish coral-colored lipstick. "It's him."

The engine turns off, the driver's door opens, and Carder's father awkwardly finds his way into the frigid air. He seems displaced among nature, wearing a dark brown corduroy jacket and pleated dress pants which smack of poor attempts to update a failing frame. His nose slants like a mishung meathook—the same crooked nose Carder has known his entire life—a nose meant for hovering over cigarettes or French onion soup, not over tombstones in Mattituck.

"What god-awful thing are you doing here, Son?" Gordan holds a black leather briefcase he's had for decades. The handle broke long ago, replaced in mismatched tan.

Carder kicks at the ground, irate but silent, trapped in the open with nowhere to escape but shrubbery—and he's not a woodland creature. "How did you find me?"

"I went over to black fella's house. At first he wouldn't say where you were, but I told him I wasn't leaving until he did."

"I guess you weren't there long."

The awful shape in the passenger seat is pushing her presence toward them without moving. No wonder the rabbit ran. Every forest animal, flying creature and insect is probably in manic search of getaway. The world wilts in her presence. Wow—thinks Carder—what wonderful phrasing for Agnes's future gravestone!

Gordan pulls a cigarette from his jacket, which in turn pulls an invisible ripcord of memory in Carder's mind: an image of himself, the little Creep, carrying the crayon-filled cigarette packs Gordan had emptied. Creep was cool then—filling himself with color instead of smoke.

"Look, son," Gordan says, "Agnes made me come here."

"That's a laugh. Don't keep saying things like that."

"Why are you in this graveyard, Creep? We're lucky we've found you. What would we have done if we hadn't chanced upon you?"

"You could've called."

"You wouldn't have answered."

"Can I have a cigarette?"

"You shouldn't smoke," Gordan says, pointing the pack to his son. "Here."

Carder resents the intimacy implied by his father lighting him up, and diverts his eyes to the closest headstone until his puffs are full and independent. He hates cigarettes, but right now cancer seems easier than conversation.

"I came here, Dad, because I wanted to honor Raymond Shankle." He refers to a headstone before them. "He was only with us for thirty-one years."

"You knew him?"

"Not while he was alive."

"My condolences. You still working, making money, paying bills?"

"Vacation days."

"I'm sorry about your gallery show. A real pity."

Their conversation spits and swallows in stops and starts, a meandering creek of words without direction. It will dry up eventually, but not soon enough. Carder wants to take a wooden stake and drive it deep into the conversation—to make it bleed bright, make it cry and find life. But trying to talk with his father had died long ago. There's no reason to pretend they'd shared anything but a few memories, a frail woman as mother and wife, a bloodline and a toy brand that wears them like costumes. Gordan likes the costume. Carder doesn't.

They stare at the headstone before them. No flowers memorialize it and the grass is unbothered.

Raymond Shankle
1940—1971
God had need of gardeners

Carder ponders silently that he's chosen the wrong life-path. He can't imagine god needing failed artists or cornea collectors. But gardeners! Gardeners beckon and raise the smallest things to life, causing their environment to twist and flourish in endless variety. Heaven's gardens are likely full of young horticulturists harvested from Earth to landscape and coddle celestial plants. It seems earthy folks are most heavenly, while people like Carder, with their heads in the sky, seeing *only* sky, are the furthest thing from it.

The two men stop talking and apply their lips to the act of smoking—an experience unruined by communication. They both exhale while the passenger door of the Buick opens and slams shut.

Footsteps and mutterings rush forth with the smell of a perfume-doused walrus. The voice is too high-pitched for her body and has the same effect as a dog whistle. "All this hemming and hawing. It's too much. It's ridiculous."

"Can you show some respect? We're mourning a gardener," Carder says in the direction of Agnes Pye. He doesn't look at her, trying to avoid damaging his eyes with her image. She's now beside them, breathing in-and-out, in-and-out like a wheezing ICU ventilator that needs shutting off.

Agnes is confused by Raymond Shankle's headstone. "Was he a relative or something?" she asks.

"Relatively," replies Carder.

She ignores him, addressing her husband instead, "Listen here, Gordy, if you think we came all the way here to… Gordan, *Gordan.*"

A fly-sized feeling lands on Carder's shoulder, cleaning its wings before whizzing off. It's gratitude. While it's there, Carder realizes how lucky he'd been whenever Agnes Pye wasn't present. Memories of every dinner he's ever eaten without her grow more succulent, every bad movie is less bad, B-movies ascend to A's and better movies become cinematic masterpieces. On the contrary, in Agnes's company, Carder longs to be trapped by high tide in an overflowing cave, or wading happily into the boiling soup of an active volcano. Is this woman really Gavin's lost love and Gordan's mistress? Is this the woman who had supplanted his mother and whom Doe Vivienne has replaced?

Gordan meets Agnes with silence. Perhaps her years of yellow teeth and teased hair have finally become too much. Finally, in order to speed up the whole experience, Carder glances at her. Whatever her allure was in youth has faded into wrinkled pillows of flesh. She's gained more weight. Her polyester slacks are the casing to a hot dog cooked swollen, ready to spray its juices into the stratosphere. Her grabby hands pull on the briefcase in an attempt to paw it away from Gordan. Carder takes a puff of smoke, then flips the remaining butt to the ground, extinguishing it underfoot.

Agnes unleashes her tirade. "He's always going on about the little genius. Well, the little genius got just what he deserved, didn't he, trying to pull one over on the public like that? People aren't stupid and, Gordy, I hope this makes you realize how damaged and deceitful…"

She talks around Carder, on top of him, about him, but never to him. The entire scenario becomes surreal and out-of-body. Carder stands next to himself while he, his body and his father watch the woman rant, spitting as she speaks, tugging at the briefcase. Gordan won't let go. He wears a fallen face, exhaustion fills his catalog clothes. He's a tired man, a man trying to figure the best move— Carder sees it in the way Gordan bites his lip and raises his chin mechanically like the bucket of a human backhoe. It's then that Carder knows there's something his father is holding inside, something that won't come out, a sort of paternal constipation. Words were always Gordan's enemy, making life a combat zone of misshapen terrain even during pleasant times. But no one drives so far from the city without reason. They haven't come to drink tea and look at Aunt Mildred's old photos.

Gordan's strong hands grip the briefcase handle, not pulling against Agnes but not releasing it. Carder remembers what Gavin told him about fighting with Gordan, but there's no black eye, no physical signs. His father couldn't have punched another man. His father has no adversaries. No, it didn't happen.

Agnes Pye is still yapping "…and if you'd give it to me, Gordy, we can get it all over with and go home."

Carder knows he'll never hear whatever it is his dad came to say. If any words come, Carder won't understand them as intended anyway—they'd shoot from the bow of his father's mouth, wobbling arrows missing their target. The two men stand wordless, peering into one another in the only real connection they've experienced since Gordan left Sylvia.

Unable to gain response from her husband, Agnes raises her head to Carder. She's so wound up her head scarf has fallen, revealing her hair. It's a black not found in nature. The color contradicts her intentions, accentuating thinning hair rather than hiding it.

"See how you make your father suffer? There's nothing genius about you. I always told Gordan as much and now there's proof. Do you know what you're father has done for you?"

Knocked teeth out? Broke a foot? Tied up a boy in the cellar, leaving him there for hours alone in the dark? Caused weeks of missed school? Left a boy's mother with no skills or job, no beauty or dreams—and left her son to comfort her? Letting it all remain unsaid is Carder's gift to his father, because he knows the man is weak and old and ashamed.

Agnes continues, unaware. "All those years you holed up in that dingy house, churning out that stuff, thinking you'd be famous, while your dad's blood pressure rose to non-human levels. If your mother could…"

"Stop." His father's voice is hard.

Agnes is big-eyed and befuddled. She and Gordan are still connected by the briefcase. "What?" Her voice soaks in shock.

"Enough." Gordan's tone is solid. "Stop!"

"Gordy, you're not going to defend him! He's the reason you've been sore for days… and stressed for years. It makes me heartsick. It's *you* who should check yourself, Gordan!" It's clear she's unused to Gordan constructing walls that take any effort to get around. "I'm hungry, and I don't want to be at the Outlets all day. Let's get this over with." She jerks at the briefcase again.

Gordan turns to her, lowering his eyes to hers. His lips are pinched thin, whitened. "I told you: I'll do this. Leave it be."

"We're wasting time. Do it already!" She seems a spoiled child trying to surmise how far to push.

"Leave it be!"

They stand as though handcuffed together.

Pulling.

Resisting.

Yanking.

Clutching—at first in slow stops and starts, but as frustration grows, so do their efforts. Huffing and puffing, Agnes uses her free hand to pry at the case, but the more she scrambles the stauncher Carder's father stands. Carder wonders how many centuries this moment can hold, it neither progresses nor stops, an everlasting spectacle in limbo.

Finally, there's a few seconds of struggle—it's a one-sided scuffle for Gordan never moves, but Agnes slides on the grass, pulling the case in every possible way.

Heaving.

Pullling.

Tugging.

Carder expects her to swing one leg over the briefcase, making it appear that her ass is eating it. She throws her weight against it in one massive pull.

The handle is weaker than both Gordan and Agnes.

It breaks.

The case splits from an 'I' to a 'V', unfolding like a book, throwing its contents into the air. There's only one object inside, and that object pops into the world like a rising moon, up, up, up, up, until it's no longer eclipsed by the case. It's a painted porcelain plate rising quickly against the wall of sky, as if lifted by an invisible hand searching to hang it.

Momentarily, the plate hovers in one spot. The imagery on its face is as pure as the day Carder painted it. As if looking from inside a giant porthole is a grey dragon-like beast, replete with a scaled belly and pink, hairless tail. The tips of its ears, nose, mouth, throat and belly are ashen. Carder hadn't mastered depicting their glassy transparency at the time he'd painted it. During the suspended animation of this hiccupped moment, Gordan Quevedo and the animal stare into one another in silence.

Its trajectory sprang forcefully from the case. Gravity executes its fall, and the plate's center meets with a corner of the headstone next to Raymond Shankle's, the grave of Raymond's mother.

Myra Shankle
1922—1994
Devoted Mother and Wife
Ye hath broken the heart of thee world wyth ye abcense.
Ye shalt now clean God's house.

A thousand high notes should scream obliteration, but only dull cries of breaking porcelain puncture the day, scattering shards across the ground like tiny pieces of wedding cake no one has eaten. Carder's childhood story has become a constellation, a salt spicing Myra Shankle's grave—another mess for her to clean up.

No superglue could've returned the plate to its previous state. Carder can't even focus on a cohesive image in what now seems a puked-up mix of seventeen-year-old color.

Agnes gasps, throwing her hand over her mouth. Gordan doesn't react, but stands watching as though it hasn't happened. Carder stands in the sticky scene, numb. Long ago, he'd realized how quickly things leave this world, but he's struggled ever since to make it more difficult for things to leave than to just sit and stay.

Agnes jumps in. "I'm sorry!" she says, in theory to both men. "Obviously, that was an accident." She discretely pockets the case's broken handle.

The blood of the fight leaves Gordan's face, his eyelids sit heavy. He releases a long sigh, letting the open briefcase fall against his leg and slide to the ground. Emptied, Carder's father shoves both hands into his pockets.

"Godammit, Agnes. Look what you've done."

Agnes straightens her jacket, pulling up the zipper as far as it will go. "It *is* done. That's it. It's over. Let's go."

Gordan stays in his spot, but pivots to her. Unclenching his teeth, he says, "What you don't understand, Agnes, is that we didn't return the plate."

"What? We most certainly did."

"No, we gave him back *pieces* of the plate."

"Well, I… we'll…"

"Get in the car. Now!"

The last time Carder heard that low guttural timbre in his father's voice was the night before his father left his mother. It's a savage sound, barely holding shape. When it passes through Agnes, she turns on her heels, making for the car, grimacing, shepherding her pudginess to the Buick. The car door shuts softly with intentional anti-slamming, and muffled music starts playing a R&B song: Smooth Operator.

Carder and his father wait.

Neither one gathers the pieces.

The wounded briefcase, crippled again, has run its race and lost. It lies on the Shankle plot, its toothless mouth agape.

Gordan clears his throat.

The father and son behold one another.

"I'm sorry, son. She'd already lost so much. There was nothing more I could do to help her."

Carder is a statue. There's nothing to say. No reason to clarify. Gordan isn't speaking of Agnes.

Carder hears his father's steps whooshing away through the grass until he too disappears into the car. It rolls away in the distance, taking the jazzy, sunbathed song with it.

Sullivan's Grocery offers only the worst coffee. Haika would be appalled. The cookies which Carder set out for weren't on the shelves and he refuses to settle for less. However, at the art supply store, he softly squeezes a new tube of Prussian blue paint in his hand. He unscrews the cap, relishing the dusky, unmixed hue. As always, it reignites a feverish hunger for canvas.

29

WHAT'S WASHED AWAY

"Movies aren't bad," Rabbit tells Darren as though she's the authority. "All I'm saying is your stories would fly well as graphic novels. You can do both, right? Plus, with Uncle Carder at your disposal, he could easily pencil them."

"Thing is, he's *not* at my disposal. It seems as though he's gonna hole up at Aunt's place indefinitely."

"You think?"

"No signs otherwise. I'll probably have to go pull him back into society."

"When?"

"We'll give it some more time," he says, looking at his watch as though he might go in hours though he means longer.

Darren and Rabbit have become an unlikely pair. Haika watches their friendship from across the living room. It hurts a bit, but Haika is well aware that she's become a junkyard of emotion—not exactly attractive to budding friendships.

"Heya," Iris interrupts, speaking to Darren and Rabbit. "Speaking of comics, why don't you two walk down and get the newest issue of Wonder Woman for Rabbit's brother. Sweet to collect them for him. I'll even pay. Here's a couple dollars."

"I'd need a couple more," Rabbit replies.

"You supply the rest, Darren. Or you two could go hang out with the Elvis twins."

Haika laughs. She sits near Iris, with an awful sewing magazine unfolded in her lap. "The Vivienne girls speak *Elvish*, not Elvis."

"So they're in Elfland not Graceland. You think the King did not have elves? Meh. Either is fine and both are loco. "

"Doll, we're all loco. It might seem to you like you're not, but you're simply on different floors of the same asylum."

"Now, Darren, go on and take the Rabbit with you. It's time for me and Haikita to talk."

Darren shrugs at Rabbit, and kisses Iris on the forehead. They're soon out the door, leaving Iris, Haika and Zombie alone.

"Depressed dog," Iris says. "Don't even know the last time his tail wag."

"Heartbroken. And lethargic. He finally found someone worth caring about and—*poof*—gone." Haika yells to the dog, "Get used to it, buddy!"

"Happens to everyone, so why not to a puppy dog?" Iris asks. "If happiness is a warm puppy, then this dog is freezin' cold."

Zombie lies on the floor next to them, unmoved except for occasionally redirecting his ears. It's his only sign of life.

Haika wonders what strange mix a child of Darren and Iris would be—a parallel to chocolate-covered bacon or salted caramel. She flops the magazine onto the coffee table. "Iris, stop beating around the bush already. What's going on?"

"Okay, okay. You know me too well, Haikita. I have news."

"I already know what it is."

"You do?"

"Yeah. I almost think I felt it the moment it actually happened—which is…" Haika searched for the concept, "…*disturbing.*"

"You did?"

"Yep."

Iris's face falls into open-mouthed horror. She palms her chest, clutching ice-cube sized turquoise beads. "Oh, Haikita. I'm so sorry. It was the only way."

"Darren isn't that bad, Sis. He and I get along much more than we used to. I think he had to warm up to me, to see I wasn't trying to take advantage of Carder. I don't know exactly when I passed the test, but I think I did. Anyway, I'm not the least bit surprised. I'm ecstatic!"

"Ex-tatic?"

"Utterly, Babe! You always said if you weren't pregnant by age thirty, you'd find a stud."

"That's what you think? That Darren is my stud and…"

"Well, yes, but not in an offensive way. But please tell me you don't already know you'll be breaking up with him at some point in the future?"

"Pregnant? Dios mio! No estoy embarazada!"

"You're not!?"

Iris swallows her courage in realization of Haika's mistaken belief. "No, no. Haikita…" She takes a deep breath before exhaling in a rush of explanation. "I came here, to America, to see you, and because, not for a baby, but because of the Inn. Haika, the Come Stay Inn is closed. I know it's a surprise, but I have no more money to run it… and no desire. And anyway, I don't want to have the desire. Well, I want more money, but don't want to use it on the Inn."

Haika bolts up from her chair. Willful disbelief crops up only to be immediately beaten down by truth. She had always suspected conditions at the Inn would degrade with Iris at the helm. Images of dilapidation, peeling pastel paint, nude chickens running amok—fat and featherless—weeds, grimy bathrooms, ceilings with circles of water damage like rippling rings in a dirty swimming pool, a dirty swimming pool, lumpy mattresses long expired, fraying artificial flowers and broken terra cotta—they all became Haika's expectation for the Inn on the day she'd stepped away. Yet, that didn't prevent her from leaving. She trusted that the Inn's charms were as constant as the Pacific Ocean, hoped the Pacific Ocean would constantly distract guests from any developing faults at the Inn, and that any developing faults wouldn't become an earthquake under her feet. The Inn was their parents' joint dream, their means for leaving Germany—how can Iris and she give it up? Iris's words are poppycock. Haika *wills* them into poppycock. She clears her throat. "Is no one running the Inn?"

"It's been closed. I closed it about a month before I arrive here. It's okay, a man named Jorge is watching it. It needs too much work. You were right to leave it behind, Haikita. We will share the profits from the sale, but I'm selling it as is. No remodeling or painting—that would take a million dollars and years. Ay yay yay! Don't freak, someone will buy it."

Haika sits down again as though she doesn't know what she's

doing—she doesn't. She feels she isn't sitting but falling, not resting but losing motivation to do anything but conserve what's left after this bombshell. She can't fault Iris for walking away from Puerto Vallarta—she'd done it herself—but Haika needs time to contemplate a world that washed away while her back was turned.

"Iris, I'm not mad, but so much has happened lately, I just need to go on a walk. By myself."

"Of course, Haika. And I'll start washing these walls. Es ugly to see where dust built up now that the paintings are down. Go on, Haika! Go think!"

When Haika hobbles away with a leashed dog slow to follow, Iris grabs pen and paper and writes: *Prueba de embarazo*. Translated, that means: "It's possible Haika's right about a baby. I sure as hell better find out." She folds the paper several times, placing it inside the cup of her bra.

30

A REAPING: KYYTH
Carder at 33 years old

For some time, the human and the beast sit wordlessly at the bottom of a stone wall rising endlessly above. At its base, a lip curves out, allowing them to sit precariously upon the sheer cliff's narrow ledge. Silence hangs suspended.

"You have come."

"I was brought."

The ancient creature, once possessing the stealth of sudden lightning, doesn't move. Perhaps he can't.

He can.

He slowly raises one spidery arm to the human's face, cupping the entire skull. His gentle grasp quickly becomes tighter, raising Creep from the ground.

The creature continues in a dry voice, "This is not how I envisioned ending."

"Kyyth, you're not ending. Only this is ending. You're simply moving on."

The creature's burnt orange exo-armor no longer shines. His scales are pitted, a collection scratches from skirmishes, from seeking shelter or from destroying it. Eight blinkless eyes of varying sizes sit in its semi-human face, like round, red skies with miniscule white moons. Their form is foreign. It's impossible to know how or what they see, but it's obvious they've seen many things from many sides—and judging from the creature's appearance, they'd possibly seen millennia.

"Do you know how long I've watched you?" asks Kyyth. "Since

your head was soft, since your jaw sprouted its bone garden, since your dawn. When you were bruised, I was broken. When you were held back, I was stopped. But confinement never conquered you, and I was pleased to see you grow within your world. There's no other like it. Still, it was not easy waiting to see you in full form. Even more so as of late."

Creep believes the creature's claims. He wants to take comfort in them, but it doesn't come. The gesticulating barbs along the length of the beast's limb, the curve of its abdomen and the unending body along the ridge holds comfort away. Creep reminds himself that Kyyth is soft inside. Old. Whatever the recipe of the innards within the monster's chitin armor, they must've withered and withdrawn for the beast can barely shift itself, and yet still possesses far more strength than any human. It's this deformed animal, this harsh conglomeration of armored dog and black-widow-snow-centipede, which had spied on Creep. How could that be comforting?

"It wasn't meant to be like it was," Kyyth says.

"Well, what is?" Creep has been beyond expectation in both worlds for enough years to know that. He now dangles by his head from Kyyth's claw at least twenty feet in the air, held over the chasm. His speech within the grip is labored, his breaths shallow.

"This battle wasn't intended, not at this level of pain, emotionally or otherwise. Your people heighten things until they become sickening. Some have said that to err is human, but no. No, to ravage and ransack is human. To warp things is human."

"Would you please set me down? You're wasting away in delirium. I can help you."

Kyyth's choking laugh is like a million insects chirping in different tones. "Help me what? I can see you more clearly from afar."

"Help you find your way from this precipice."

The creature lowers his barbed limb, lined on one side with white, hairy quills, and Creep obtains relief on the ground. Beside him is a roaring bonfire, a welcome respite from the cold. The flames lap at black night air but can't illuminate it enough to make things feel less deserted or dangerous. Only the crackling fire separates Creep from Kyyth whose segmented body stretches along the precipice like a centipede for as far as light carries and beyond.

However, by his slouching, almost injured pose, it appears Kyyth didn't rest by choice, but collapsed.

"I'm dry inside. A husk," Kyyth says, as large scales fall from his belly, revealing what seems to be hollowness inside.

Creep has no food or water to offer. There's nothing to be done about Kyyth's suffering. He wants to help him, but he knows how this proceeds is solely up to the beast. He peers out into the gulf of darkness before them. There's another stone cliff far away on the other side the canyon, almost too distant to see.

"I'd always lived gloriously. Royal and savage. I've leapt across wider chasms without care. I've raged and fought wars for the thankless, and loved with voracious love. I've breathed needles and broken daylight in two. Now, I sit, unable to move."

"I know."

"Do you?"

"I do." Creep sees glimmers of grandeur, of times past, nesting in the beast's words. "And I'm here. Do you think I didn't know you were watching? Do you suppose that I've not felt your energy rippling through me every day of my life?"

"It makes the nature of this even more tragic."

"How so?"

"I'm alone. Stripped of my consort, lost in the wilderness, dry and hungry but too old to care. I'm alone."

The human's anger flares. "Alone? You? Never. Me? Never! Not even if we wanted to be so."

"Not even if we wanted to be so," the creature repeats with a sense of gentle reverie amidst the clicks and quivers of his fangs and mandibles. Its antennae reach as if feeling the air for new sensations, and it turns toward Creep with red-ink eyes reflecting fire. "You," Kyyth says, then pauses. Without reaction, he stretches a limb over the flames until it blazes, then thrusts its searing heat to Creep's face.

Creep wants to jump to extinguish it, but that would portend certain death over the cliff.

"I have finally seen you whole," the creature continues. "Now, you will see me." With that, it labors until its torso rolls onto the bonfire, immediately engulfed. Burning, the creature stands up, powerful and vigorous, with a stature it might've had when young. Pops and sizzles curl and peel its outer armor, dropping it. Dusty blue-black scales fall from his face. For a moment, stands a creature of glowing, burning liquid. Its boiling colors bubble their changing hues like hot grease.

Creep feels Kyyth's howl in his own spine, as the beast, now a glowing fireball, leaps off the edge. It seems to hover, its brave last moments on display, hanging from the night. Then, it falls, singing the surrounding air. Gravity follows, pulling the remainder of Kyyth's serpentine body through the fire, separating the thick radiating thread from its casing. The canyon below is illuminated as the burning creature plunges into the void.

The path is cleared.

31

FINDING GREY

Following the cemetery bedlam, Carder falls into a hole for the better part of a week. The first hole is his art. In a paint-covered t-shirt Claudette gave him (imprinted with *NORDIC ELVES DO IT FOREVER!)* and with skin spotted in acrylic colors like a Dalmatian with gay pride, Carder holds a paint brush in his mouth. He's surrounded by emptied honey jars and plastic cups filled with water-diluted paint which hadn't made it to canvas. The smell of two-and-a-half days of unshowered man blows around the cottage, but Carder doesn't notice. He's deep in the chambers of creativity.

He paints for two hours despite a parched mouth, and after a quick drink, for two more.

The cell phone on a nearby tabletop curses at him, vibrating until it falls facedown on the floor. Carder forgot to turn it off that morning. Several days before, he'd sent texts to Darren, Rabbit and Claudette notifying them all not to worry, he hasn't filled his pockets with rocks and swum into the Sound. He expects this is another text from Claudette, who's taken to leaving him dirty texts in Elvish. Nonetheless, it's not her. It's from an unfamiliar number.

[*Aileen here. Went to the re-opened gallery—amazing art. Wanna C U.*]

Aileen Grey. Nurse Grey. Aileen was the first, the queen, the original reason Carder applied the name to the group. The rest are only subsets. They pale in comparison.

Carder replies: [*In Mattituck on Long Island for a while. And begins typing another: See you at the hospital*]—but Nurse Grey's response appears too quickly.

[*I'll cum there. Need to talk to a friend. Send ur address.*]

And a second later: [*Please?*]

He already typed a solid NO, but the musk of his armpits prevents him from sending it. Carder reeks of unhealthy seclusion, which doesn't bother him per se, but convinces him that a visit might be beneficial. The crick in his neck tells him to take a break from painting. Finally, a pang in his stomach and a stare from the mammy cookie jar leads him to believe he should see someone *non*-ceramic. It's been so long. Besides, he needs groceries—the cupboards are now merely siphoning off space. Leaning against the kitchen countertop, he stretches in a yawn, knocking a small paper bag to the floor—the one Aunt Mildred gave him. A sugary scent wafts up. He picks up the bag, unfolding it's creased, brown paper. Inside, sit seven cellophane-wrapped black and white cookies. Carder looks over at the mammy with her arms crossed wisely on her stomach. Though it's been a week, the cookies are fresh and soft. He takes a bite while studying a framed photo hanging on the wall. The snapshot is colorless but for its yellowing age. Young Aunt Mildred stands arm-in-arm with a grinning man resembling Darren. Both wet subjects wear modest bathing suits and are caped in towels. *Make sure you baptize yourself in the Sound*—says Aunt Mildred, possibly Milly then—*the water's not deep.*

Carder looks at the photo, the cookie jar, his phone, and texts: [*Ok. Come over. Address to follow. Might be at the water. Will send you directions there too.*]

The water of the Sound sears Carder's hands and face. If he hadn't fetched an old wetsuit from the shed he wouldn't be swimming at all. The freezing waters wake him from his stupor, slapping him with jovial waves. Carder's relationship with fish had previously been kept to pet stores and dinner plates, and he's leery that the few small fish swimming near him could multiply into jumping schools of thousands. But he chooses to trust the old woman who lived through similar encounters for close to a century. She was right. The waters aren't dangerous.

In the distance, a hopping woman waves from shore. Carder waves back.

As he leaves the waters, he sees her fully. He's seen her in many incarnations in many hospitals in many situations, but this is the first time Nurse Grey is truly in focus: a petite, thin woman. Her creamy skin seems bloodless, her black hair clipped with kinky, rotini curls, her branchy arms swaying as she bounces. Dark eyes flutter above her cheeks like black-spotted moths over snow-covered hills. Having traded frumpy hospital scrubs for a fitted top and blue jeans, the topography of her curves mesmerize. Where's her coat?

"You brute! Not even the cold stops you!" she calls. "Until you waved, I feared the worst. You know that old poem?" Clearly, she was jumping for warmth, not as a seductive Irish jig.

"Hello, you," Carder says.

"Hello, Blue Eyes."

She shuttles Carder back to the cottage, where they engage in deep conversations over the course of two days, conveying them only with their bodies in carnal communication.

"Can I ask one thing?" Aileen asks, brushing her hair while Carder turns his phone back on.

"What's that?"

"Can you act semi-normal when you see me at the hospital now? Don't let this make you act stranger than usual."

"*Right now*, I think can do that. Hopefully, I'll feel the same way at the hospital."

Aileen begins picking up her clothes from the floor, taking a few steps to her panties, several more to a lone sock, as if following a trail left by naked children captured by a witch. She returns the items to her body, refilling the double catapult of her bra.

While Aileen leads her zipper back into a tightlipped, metallic smile, something like disappointment heads toward her—but she fights it. She's learned to accept life's experiences *as is*. Life has no obligation to hand her things in the form she wishes. Sometimes a connection she hoped would last a lifetime compacts into a few seconds, or months— days in this case. She's stopped forcing things. Thus, while it's obvious that thirty years from now, Carder won't be helping gather her things while their grandchildren wait downstairs, he's there now—*not* helping her gather her things—and she appreciates that. Kind of. She's trying.

Carder is oblivious, checking his cell phone. It lights up with thirteen new messages. Scrolling through texts he hasn't checked for days, he sees: Rabbit wanting to lunch, Darren telling him to get his ass back to Brooklyn, Claudette needing him.

Carder then listens to his voicemails, mostly hang-ups. In one, he hears Darren cursing under his breath.

The final voicemail worries him—Darren again: "Carder, this is an emergency. It's not a fucking joke. Whenever you get this, pull your hand off your cock, get in the Trans Am and haul-ass back here." He sounds awful. Shaken. Angry.

Carder picks up a remaining sock, handing it to Nurse Grey. "Something's happened. I have to go."

32

ONLY GLASS

Sun whispers through the blinds of a somber room, where twins stand observing each another in wonder and admiration. With identical movement their hands hesitate, then reach to one another in synchronized gesture. Their fingers meet, pressing against their joint existence. After a few moments their faces shift in recognition: they're separated by something—a slight barrier, some kind of film. In the next instant, reality fills the room. Their jaws quiver with shellshock: it's only one woman, one twin, one life standing before itself. The barrier is a mirror smudged with fingerprints. But she swears she saw movement separate from her own! A slight twitch! Embarrassed eyes flashing away! A forced smile! No. It's only her own image alone.

Her world has been halved, her sister lost.

In a dangerous operation performed by life, the two twins were successfully separated. The main device used was a tool with a sharp, thin blade—a tool called death—an instrument dividing quickly, easily if used efficiently.

The twin stands in front of a fireplace, looking into the mirror at her own eyes. It's difficult to look away. Funny—she thinks—this must be what it's like to visit a loved one sentenced to life in prison. The glass would separate them like this. If only there was a phone to pick up. Tears fall in duplicate. The mirror is a screen playing exactly what's happening as it happens. She wants it turned off, and starts raging in search for—she doesn't know what—something to stop it. On overload, she lifts a heavy vase from the mantle to… to…

"No!" says someone rushing into the room, putting an arm

around the struggling woman, "let me help you! What do you need? Can you tell me?"

At first, she can't say anything but tries until gulping out, "Please. Yes... cover the mirror! I can't see her like this!"

"Of course," her companion says, realizing the mirror contains a ghost. "One second." She springs into the next room, ransacking the closets, returning with a bed sheet and awkwardly hangs it over the top of the mirror. Her grieving friend sits down in a wingback chair, rocking herself with legs in skewed support. With the reflection gone, screams and tears appear in many forms and frequencies. It's several minutes before they speak, and when they do, it's Claudette's voice that breaches Fardor's dead air.

"She's gone, really gone."

"I know, I know, Babe. I'm sorry. So, so sorry."

Haika is helpless. The unexpected loss of Doe Vivienne is immeasurable. Doe now lays at the mortuary awaiting burial. There's no comprehending it. It makes no sense. Haika knows that the likelihood of twins living and dying in synchronicity is unrealistic, but their lifespans should overlap in some kind of harmony. Isn't it implied, almost promised, by the nine months they share in the womb, wrapping their arms around one another before they're even fully formed? It's expected, taken for granted—and in many cases, doesn't happen. Now, two mismatched twins sit on the second level of Fardor. Its queen wears robes of mourning which, to be precise, are only a t-shirt nightgown.

At times, Claudette speaks through sniffling and tears. "Haika, can I ask you something?"

"Of course."

"Why did you always discount her?"

"What do you mean?"

Dabbing fresh tears hidden in the corners of her eyes, Claudette gathers herself with surprising lucidity. "Why did you discount Doe? I understand why you sometimes ignore me—I'm a ditz, the men blather on like idiots around me, my feelings for Carder probably don't help, and I'm as weird as a zillion dollar bill. But Doe—Doe was a true innocent, helping every creature she crossed paths with, bleeding money into every charitable organization in existence. Hell, if someone founded The Greedy Mother Fuckers of America

Organization, Doe would throw thousands at them like confetti. She... she did a lot of good."

"Claudette... I didn't have as much interaction with Doe. I've always known you better."

"By choice, Haika. I never understood how you saw through Carder's force field, but not Doe's. Was it because of your attraction to him? Or because he's male and she's a..." Claudette chuckles sadly for a second, "Well, she would've said 'fembot.'"

"Doll, I wasn't ignoring her. Apparently, I didn't demonstrate that very well, but I'll continue to see Doe every time I look at you. I'll never forget."

Claudette whispers, "Thanks."

Though Haika feels her response is meaningless, the grieving woman's observations are a knife to the gut. Having always prided herself on seeing beneath the veil, Haika now quizzes herself—why did she push the twins away when they clamored for attention? Had the breasts preceding them blocked her from seeing the rest? If they'd been male, would she have striven to understand them, excusing the faults and foibles she deemed unforgivable in other women? Although the Vivienne girls could never have approached the same affection she feels for Carder, she recognizes the truth and it smarts. She painted the girls with the same broad brush everyone else had. It's rancid but it's reality. She had put them in frames *she'd* chosen instead of allowing them to present themselves as they wished.

Claudette gasps. Since Doe's death, she continually has realizations of small details now erased. "Oh my god, there are no Vivienne girls. The Vivienne girls are gone." The statement ends in more tears.

"It's hard to imagine a greater loss," Haika says with true understanding.

"If only I'd been there when she went. I was there earlier that day."

"Heart attacks are random, Sweetie. There's nothing you could've done. You know that. You can't be by someone's side twenty-four hours a day."

"But if only Gavin had been here instead of abroad. He's her husband. He might've noticed something."

Haika hugs Claudette again. From what she understands, Gavin and Doe operated on separate floors of the house anyway. Separate floors, separate continents. What's the difference?

"I told Gavin, if he dares to show himself before Doe's memorial service, I'll nail his scrotum to the floor and push him out the window."

There's a nail gun sitting on the nightstand.

Aware that Gavin will show up for the service to save face among friends and colleagues, Haika convinces Claudette to let her step in when he does, but also agrees that no additional interaction with him is necessary.

Grave concern had grown over Doe Vivienne's return to what she called a calorie-restricted diet, and what everyone else called anorexia, but no one imagined the swiftness of this outcome. Youth is the antithesis of death. But anorexia robs youth, erasing it inside and out. Claudette lamented the appearance of her sister's ashen skin and thinning hair, soon covered by wigs. Doe's disease reapplied jumper cables to her already weak organs, shocking and starving them into nearly automatic shutdown. Only four nights prior, she and Claudette sat atop Doe's Niirdor rooftop, watching a sunset spray the colors of carrots and cantaloupe, of lavender lace and purple haze over them. They structured the next day: shopping, lunch, movie. Claudette planned on leading Doe into producing film. Since they'd never *star* in them as they'd originally intended, it would've been the next best thing. Producing films was costly, a venture prone to flop, but the Vivienne girls felt the rush of sailing into a storm of risk. Gavin be damned! It was something that might've jolted Doe from wasting away and allowed her to outrun her illness.

After Claudette kissed her sister goodbye, Doe walked to her bedroom like a robot low on batteries. Tired and a bit out of breath, she sat down to remove her wig, admiring its immaculate perfection. She turned on a television show: celebrities were hosting tours of their homes. Doe was annoyed. Her home triumphed over every one shown. She missed recognition, but three dogs vied for her attention. Moth, Roth and Thoth basked in her warmth - though without much body fat, Doe had chilled considerably. They licked her hand, whimpering in delight when she called them, when she rubbed their bellies. Her dogs gave gifts that money, men, parties and people never had. And they were there when her heart blipped its final arrhythmic bleep.

When Doe's door went unanswered the next morning, Claudette used her key. Only the smartest dog, Thoth, greeted her, nipping and running in circles, gently wrangling her through the home. Claudette called, wandering until she heard the television-chatter from Doe's bedroom, quiet in case her sister was sleeping. But intuition told her something was wrong. She called, moving forward into the room to find Doe sprawled facedown on the floor. Two dogs lay against her, and though wagging their tails upon seeing Claudette, they stayed at Doe's side, providing warmth to a body turned cold. Niirdor would be in deep winter forevermore.

When Carder arrives at Fardor, Claudette looks like an apparition. Her mascara is blotted like bruises, rubbed, smeared with her fists, her nose as red as if she'd returned from a run in the snow. Carder has no words. With Haika lurking in the shadows, Claudette stares at him. She can't provide a path for the pronouncement. She won't say it, won't say that her sister is dead. Carder sees through to every cell in Claudette's body. Every muscle, every fiber, every organ, every bit from toenail to pituitary gland vibrates with loss. In his arms, she howls and whoops, writhes and rumbles like a thunderstorm until there's no more rain and the sky is mud.

"I must leave both Niirdor and Fardor," Claudette utters in a weary voice. "Fardor's a disappearing kingdom. And without Doe, Niirdor's already gone."

"I know," Carder says holding her, asking Haika with his eyes exactly how crazed the loss has made Claudette. Does she believe they're in The Lord of the Rings? Haika shrugs.

"No. No, I'll no longer live here. It's over. I'll never go to Niirdor's roof again. Imagine the emptiness I'd see. Never again."

"Nothing's the same without Doe," Carder says.

"She was so gorgeous. Sparkling," Claudette whispers, thrilled by the thought. Although anyone else might've mistaken her words for shallow epiphany, Carder knows Claudette speaks to levels well beyond physical appearance. "I—I tried helping her. But Doe was deep in a hole, never able to find her way out. We tried, but our hands were too weak to pull her up." Then, she turns to Haika. "We couldn't pull her up." She turns to the empty room, "We couldn't."

Carder holds her while Haika places a hand on her back.

"I waited for *years* for Doe to arrive at anything close to happiness. I tried everything, but she always had an illogical hatred of her life. Hated it. Hated her husband but wouldn't leave him. He treated her horribly. I told her that if she wanted to be happy or content she must leave him. She wouldn't. Doe had the means to do *anything* she wanted, *anything*, but she refused to recognize it. She was comfortable with unhappiness, addicted to it. If we brought her to the light, she edged to the dark, transfixed. The sad part is that she left this world never seeing her own beauty. It was as though she thought there was a missing piece to being whole, a secret key to society, a code she'd never figure out." She blows her nose into a tissue. "Doe. I couldn't help you!" With that, she throws her head into Carder's arms again, sobbing.

Forced re-entry into society is dizzying, but with Claudette in need, Carder has no time to question. The death of a loved one transforms the rest of one's life. Doe's death knocked Claudette to her knees, and whenever she's finally able to stand again it will be as another person. While Claudette is trapped in that feeble state, her friends can only approximate the largest, most abstract gifts: love and friendship.

Carder stays with Claudette and Haika the entire day, joined by Darren, Rabbit and Iris later that evening. He and Haika support Claudette through a day of arrangements, of acquaintances showing up and periods of debilitation. They make sure food is eaten, naps are taken, that whatever needs to happen does. Darren is radiating over his own life despite Claudette's situation, but Iris doubles over in screaming banshee heartache whenever Claudette cries.

Trapped in sticky grief late into the night, when normal circumstances would have everyone leaving, most of them stay. Only Carder steals away back to the Mattituck cottage he'd left abruptly, returning to clean it so that Aunt Mildred will find the place as she left it. His mind is nothing more than grey jelly as he drives there, straightens the place up, retrieves his things and drives back while night becomes dawn. He might've stayed and slept, but no, it's time.

The golden car chews the black miles, its motor purring like an electric cat. Carder's interaction with Haika had lingered shyly in the day's periphery. Whatever they would've said when reunited had to be tabled so they could rise up as two people devoted to a third. Haika had looked almost as disheveled as Claudette: her eyes vacant, her hair in unwashed chunks, clothes wrinkled. And her manner had matched her appearance. Though both she and Carder hadn't spoken at any length, they rubbed shoulders, with their own issues in the background. Having addressed harsh realities with Claudette all day long, they silently agreed to leave their own concerns for a later time. *That time* is at 6:30 AM on a morning wanting nothing more than to be allowed to sleep in bed for five more minutes.

33

DAWN OF THE UNDEAD

The closest one can come to seeing past the barbed wire and fearful pageantry that being male usually requires, is observing a man with his dog—a sport Haika used to enjoy. However, her life is in shreds and between homes. Coping strategies develop: Buddhist books are read and yoga becomes regular.

Ever since the chaos at the Camp Fountain Gallery, Haika has had time for all the things people are meant to: reading the Times, styling and re-styling her hair in the mirror— punk/soft/pixie/mussed—and flossing her teeth. These things can be done whenever, and right now she's doing them at six in the morning. Done showering, she reads the instructions for *Bright White Bite:* a product promising teeth five times whiter after only seven treatments applied three times daily in a two-step process taking ten minutes each. It's math she's too tired to figure. She edits the instructions to two steps: suffocating her teeth haphazardly with bleaching liquid and hoping for results lighter than mustard. People should be glad she's not paving roads or mixing medications.

Lately, Zombie is a slug, doing little more than plopping down in whichever room Haika's in. Lying on the bathroom floor, one paw touches the toilet's cold porcelain. A mild case of gas migrates through his digestive system, perhaps eventually prompting a roll to his other side, but he'll deal with that when it comes. When Haika drops a wrapper, Zombie takes half a whiff of its wintergreen without even reaching his head to inspect the crinkled foil. He's busy staring at a crack in the wall behind the toilet.

Errf?!

Like a furry bolt of lightning, Zombie's ear shoots up. His melt-away posture becomes machine-taut. Hearing faint but familiar footsteps and key-scrapings unique to one person—a swell of excitement moves him before his canine mind can catch up. Springing off the floor and out the bathroom, the dog trots down the stairs so fast he almost rolls head over tail, squealing the entire way.

"What the hell?" Haika says at the dog's startling reanimation.

But she knows.

She splashes water on her bewhitened teeth and swiftly follows the dog.

They both know.

The stairs seem crooked, each step a different width, but Haika doesn't care if she falls. If she does, the stairs will cough and deliver her. Whatever transpires, she's surging and ready.

For some reason, a pause occurs outside. The individual on the other side stops. Zombie begins barking at the top of his lungs, scratching at the door and then bolting around the living room, throwing himself from couch to floor to chair to door again, flipping over, using one leg to push himself across the room on his back, then standing up again, barking the entire time.

At last, the door opens. On the other side of the threshold is Zombie's *one person*. The dog drops to the floor, squealing and rolling, exposing tummy until Carder Quevedo crouches to greet him. Zombie jumps on him, not knowing whether to lick or be held, not knowing how to choose its action and trying to choose them all at once in flustered, sloppy joy. Let fur fly, slobber slob, and his body fall as it may. His man is home! There's a definite, fanged dog grin, a bright white bite closer to mustard, and a tail slashing air like an Olympic fencer.

"I missed you too, boy," Carder says, tugging on the tips of Zombie's ears.

Though Haika and Carder had seen one another only hours before, he's changed. While with Claudette, Haika tried not to notice it, but it's unmistakable now: he's different. Not in obvious ways. His expression isn't as tired as one would imagine after recent events and at this time of the morning. He looks the same way vacationers at The Come Stay Inn do settling into true relaxation on the fourth day.

Haika wonders, however, if all forgiveness and love will be spent on the dog, leaving her standing in the middle of stairs, on neither the first nor second floor, with peroxide and peppermint on her tongue. She will go no further until Carder looks at her.

Carder sits Indian style by the open door, with the dog wriggling on his lap. The man's eyes are jubilant slits when he looks up. He's already smiling when he sees Haika. Thus, she assumes she hasn't provoked it, but is simply seeing his amusement with Zombie.

"Haika." His eyes open in recognition.

She walks slowly down three more stairs until only a few steps from the living room floor. Her hands search for places to put the dental floss she'd inadvertently brought, twisting it around one finger.

Will she sit down or stand? Where is she walking to? Will she touch him? She wants to fix the wisp of hair sticking out from the side of his head. But she's reticent. She's stone.

At last, Haika speaks. "You okay, Carder?"

"Yeah. Where's Rabbit?"

"She went to a late movie with Iris and is staying overnight with her. She'll be working with Tino for the first time later today."

"With Tino? She's working at the gallery?"

"You got it. The gallery. She needs the money and I'd love to see her quit working at that dreary diner ASAP."

"Thanks."

"For what? I did it for *her.*" Haika's soul starts slipping to the back of her body. Carder is giving nothing, nothing she needs. Even an obligatory hug or nod, any sort of signal to what lies ahead, would keep her from receding.

Carder scoots Zombie down to the floor.

"How've you been? How's Mike?"

"Didn't anyone tell you? Mike and I are over."

"Over!? *Over* over?"

"Over."

"Damn, so much happens when a person's not around."

"It's been a slow-motion break-up over the last three years. He's been relatively decent thus far. He'll turn me into a whore in his mind and to his friends, but he'll be okay. The world has women and he's got money. He's humiliated, not heartbroken."

"And you?"

"Me?" She's loath to admit, but being the topic of conversation feels good. "Me. Well, I have to make some decisions…"

"My dad visited me."

And like that, Haika is no longer the subject. That's okay, she knows Carder by now. It's his way of dipping a toe in. He always has to do that first. By sometime next year, they'll get to the crux of things.

"Haika." He gets up to bring something into the house. He keeps talking while carrying a canvas inside, backside forward. "My time out there was definitely needed. Helped me figure out a few things." Walking toward the stairs, he turns the canvas around: a new painting. "Here. This is for you."

Haika can't speak. The painting captivates her, trapping a gasp within and freezing the fear she'd brought downstairs. The piece is more fluid and abstract than Carder's usual work: a flourishing scene in billowing colors, dark and muted, broken by a milky apparition, a luminous otherworldly being radiating from within. One tawny, glowing thread coils down through the middle of the woman. She's ingesting it, caught in the act of drinking from a glassy object tilted to her mouth—a bottle raised high. Hints of the room behind the maidenly figure are shrouded in shadow.

Carder shifts his stance, attempting to elicit a reaction.

Haika can't look away from the painting. "Why did you paint this?"

"How could I *not* paint the most beautiful moment of my life?"

Haika turns away, rubbing the crown of her head to prevent a schmaltzy, tearful mess. She sighs.

"Do you know what it is?" Carder asks.

"Of course I know what it is, Carder! I was there!" She's confused as to why she sounds angry when she feels the exact opposite. If ever a portrait of her was to be painted, Haika never would've believed it would contain her swigging tequila, or that it would be depicted with such ethereal mystery.

"But—but…" Carder starts mumbling with growing discomfort, "…but …so, what do you think?"

"What do I think? It's the most gorgeous-mother-fucking-wonderful thing I've ever seen, okay? Are you happy? I love it. I want to inhabit it. Hell, I *do* inhabit it. It's too much, Carder. I'm stunned—unable to put into words what it means. I want to go blind looking at it."

"Good." He exudes newfound satisfaction while Zombie reaches for him, stretching furry legs.

Haika breaks into reality again. "But you must be tired. Do you want some coffee?"

He reaches out, grasping her wrist.

"No."

"Something cold?"

"No."

"So what do you want?"

"You." His tone is new, one Haika has never heard. It holds no question and startles her. Carder walks up two stairs and pulls her close to his breath. Haika doesn't know what's happening, but realizes how much she's missed Carder's smell. It's nothing unusual, a hint of skin and his cheap bright-bottled shampoo.

"I want you," he repeats.

An invisible explosion occurs, revolving the universe around them. They are the core, raw ingredients—skin, fluids and emotions—pivoting into things higher yet animal.

Carder kisses Haika while leading her backwards up the stairs. She'd never fully entered the living room after all. Easily, without looking, they pass through the hallway, the bedroom, then the bed, feeling for it with their legs and ignoring the dog dashing around them. There are still many matters to discuss, so many questions stored up, but the answers will be searched for first with their bodies. There's no more reason to wait.

They come to a cruising speed, kissing for a while. Crisscrossing his arms behind her, Carder breaks their fall onto the rough blanket below. Haika pulls at Carder's t-shirt, but the shirt holds on, stuck at his head, revealing a pale, hairy torso, but bagging his face. The neck of the shirt is too small. Haika tugs and laughs. One way or the other, she'll get him naked.

"Will you just take this thing off?" She wants her breasts against his chest. She pulls. "Take it off!"

"Are you sure? Are you sure you want it off?" He masks his

chortles behind the cotton T before it pops off.

Whichever future will happen will happen, right now they'll create present warmth together.

When Zombie whines for attention, Carder hops out of the bed, leading the dog out the door...

"You gotta understand, boy. You caused this."

...and slams it shut with his foot.

While everything's occurring, Haika is setting up a permanent display in her life's museum. She systematically works through her senses to feel the pressure of Carder's supine body against her own, their mixing sweat which makes the sheets chillier in some spots, warmer in others, the grayish walls—now bare of any art save for the patterns of dusty circles where plates once hung—the taste of skin-salt, the bitterness of pre-cum, the sound of a ticking clock, garbage men outside screaming their way through streets, an occasional barking dog. Breathing. Bed springs. Breathing.

Afterward, they realize that sex solves nothing. It never does. Maybe it isn't meant to. Sex holds so much within its own event that maybe it can only be itself. They are at the head of a comet with life's fragmented issues trailing behind for thousands of miles.

They lie separate, as though they're two halves of a split city, wreckage. Only their ankles touch as their heartbeats settle.

Surely none of this has happened. Surely they still stand on the stairs, hugging friends starting a clumsy discussion. Maybe she's grinding up coffee beans. He's kicking the floor with his shoe. But no.

Awkwardness pokes into the room along with sunlight to see if there's a place for it, but it finds no resting spot.

"Dude," Carder says, baffled.

"Dude," Haika replies, perplexed.

"You."

"No, you."

Haika is gorgeous naked, soft as the hush before a thunderstorm and bright like dawn. Carder kisses her pink belly, not Salmon Belly, but a pink impossible to reproduce: Haika-pink. Carder smells their sex and settles into the afterglow, knowing they still have much to discuss.

"The reviews weren't that bad. Many were shockingly positive. Honestly. Kevin from *Art Lust* said that the pieces showcase the foundation of a house built on profit, that in a reverse trickle-down effect, the Pups are the furthest trickle from the spigot. Even then, many feel the Pups were one of the more richly creative mainstream toys ever to strike."

"Doesn't sound like art. Sounds like an invasion."

"From what I've surmised, they *were* an invasion. They reached more people than the Bubonic Plague—and didn't do as much damage. I must say, your designs dealt their coup de grace with precision."

"Look, I'm sorry…"

"It was kind of gorgeous in a way. If it hadn't happened to me, I'd say on some levels it was positively delicious. Warped but delicious." She says it as though savoring the taste, but pulls her legs from his and rolls over.

"Haika, I'm sorry the way things happened. I never intended any of it."

"Why didn't you just tell me about the Pups?"

"Lots of reasons. First of all, my art isn't the Pups, the Pups are the… evil… caricatured… carnival copies. You know like… hidden twins, or…" he searches for the correct term, "They're like vanished twins!" He motions to his side as if a stunted, lifeless body hanging off him.

"I know what a vanished twin is. Anyway, the origin of your art, or the Pups, or whatever—that's not what gets me. It was obvious you weren't forthcoming. I let it happen because I care about you and wanted your experience to be as painless as possible. What gets to me is all the months you led me to believe they were gargoyles or gods. From what you'd said and what I pieced together, I thought they were guardians, your own personal mythology. I don't know. I guess I'm still stretching to figure them out."

"No, Haika, I never led you to believe those things. You arrived at those concepts. You were always saying things like: '*This universe you created…*', '*The peaceful monsters…*' How could I stomp all over that?" he asks, still resisting shedding any additional light on his time in Neidin.

"Carder, I'm one of your best friends *and* the curator of your show. We spoke about your art incessantly. Couldn't you have explained it, let me know that some of the paintings had plastic figurine versions released for the world's five-year-olds—*spanning the last twenty-some years*? Do you know what a fool I looked like?"

He's glad she said it. He knows she'd taken a chance on him, but he doesn't know if he wants blame for the truth: that what she saw in the paintings might not be there.

A shaft of light through the curtains now cuts across them, throwing a bright border between their bodies.

After some consideration, Carder sputters, "I apologize. I never would've put you in that position purposefully, but Haika... you were the first person in my life to see past the Pups. I absolutely love what *you* saw. You took the liberty to see a world no one else did. You wanted the rest of the world to see it too. And all along, they were just cartoon dogs."

Haika leans forward in anger. "Stop that right now! Whatever they are or were, they aren't cartoon dogs! Stop denigrating them. Your father might have done that, the factory spitting the toys out might have, half the fucking girls and boys on this planet may have done it, but you sure as hell better stop it! You and I both know those paintings aren't caricatures and it's about time you showed them some respect. Pick-Me-Pups my goddamn fucking twat."

He's never seen Haika like this. Rebellious tears ride wet trails on her cheeks and her body shivers with wild energy. Pulling her knees to her head, she wraps her arms around them as if gathering herself. Carder is taken aback with the new understanding that she isn't simply defending him but championing the creatures and world at which she's peeked.

She continues, "Did you get the plate back?"

"I'm not sure what I want to do with them yet." He nods to the room, assuming she speaks of the plates in general.

"No, I mean from your dad. Did he give you that plate back, the one he purchased at the show?"

"He tried to."

"Well, Carder, it's my turn to apologize. I had no right to sell it to him. I'm sorry, because I knew even then you probably never would've let him have it. But it was sacred to him."

"Sacred? That's ridiculous!"

"You should've seen him at Camp Fountain. He approached me after his run-in with Gavin, after the police left and Darren was fetching a bag of frozen peas for your dad's face. I didn't give the plate to him easily. But your dad was impossible. Worshipped it. At first, he thought that saying the plate was important would cause my bleeding heart to let him have it. No way! I told him I'd rather hang it on the walls of hell. Then, he tried a bull-shit story about it being your grandmother's favorite..."

"She died before I was born..."

"I figured. Finally, when he saw I wasn't about to hand over your work. The color rushed out of his face. He was fussing and wringing his hands, saying he had to have it. I asked him why, playing the role of Napoleon with vigor. Looking like a cornered animal, your dad used one last resort: the truth. His entire countenance changed—told me it represented the happiest times of his life. He actually took my hand and said that the painting was from a time when three things had briefly coincided: a gifted child, a sweet wife, and a guaranteed living."

"You gave the painting to him?"

"Hell no, I didn't *give* it to him! I told him it was the most expensive piece in the show! And only let him buy it after I said every single thing I wanted to say—about you, your art, and him. Looking back, it was an enraged and rambling monologue, but he withstood it. I said a lot of things. I'm horrified in retrospect. I chewed him out for calling you Creep. Who in their right mind calls their child a creep? It's borderline abusive. Hon, I know he hurt you far more than you let on."

"And what did he say?"

"He stood there, solemn. He took it and said he probably deserved my derision."

"I'm surprised he just stood there taking it."

"Why?"

"Because my father did many cruel things, but only called me Creep at my own request. He wasn't the one that gave me the label, it was the creatures of Neidin. I think it's because as a child in a foreign world, I'd crawl around trying to remain hidden until I became more at ease with my job there. Dad was the only one who originally paid attention to my stories until he realized I was serious. I was a little fart at that time, but he listened to my demands and called me Creep. Looking back, maybe it developed into a term of endearment."

"Well, damn. Makes me the schmuck, doesn't it?"

"At least he got what he wanted. He walked away from the gallery with the plate in hand."

Carder stews, staring at nothing.

"What?" Haika asks.

"It's not in hand any longer," he replies, recounting his experiences at Aunt Mildred's cottage *sans* any references to Nurse Grey. Haika provides the perfect audience and moves closer to him, with her head on his chest while he paints the tale of the cemetery experience as best he can. After that, they don't review it any further. They're done.

34

PARASITES & CHLOROPHYLL

The past hour has been spent reading the latest draft of Darren's screenplay *Red Dog*. Haika sits wearing Carder's old *Beavis & Butthead* t-shirt tied in a knot at the side, her belly-button exposed like the socket of an eyeless Cyclops. Her baggy corduroy pants are rolled, advertising space to ten electric blue toenails painted with the same polish Haika wore the day she and Carder first met. While the polish is the same, the rest of her world has changed.

After a scrubbing, the far wall in the living room is no longer stifled by a decade of dust. Iris abandons her bucket, taking a break, focusing on a bag of plantain chips and using Darren as furniture. It's a rare bum-around do-nothing day. They channel French cafés, conjure the spirit of cats, and don the mental state of pasta: soaking in life. The gang was meant to join up later for dinner, but chance has gathered all but Claudette early. Having dragged out a television and video game console, Rabbit is reveling at Carder's cyber-guts which she's strewn across the television screen with a pick axe.

"This script is a lot to chew on," Haika says. "Darren, are you sure you want to set it in Moscow? Have you ever been there?"

"Nope, but Claudette's trying to force me to go."

Iris cuts in. "You *are* going. Don't sad-schoolboy me, Darren. As Claudette said, if you are going to be a serious writer, then you have to write seriously."

"I get it," Darren says, "but I'm suddenly regretting not setting the story in Fiji."

Haika takes him seriously. "I understand that, but Moscow has that bleak, sinister cold. I can picture the breath of these human wolves set against the onion domes of Russian churches. Humid noses, dripping fangs, frost. That can't happen in Fiji—they'd be drinking, swimming and sunning."

Iris holds a salted chip to the light. "Plus, Darren have to bring the bacon."

"What?" Carder stops playing the video game. "Why's that?"

Darren closes his eyes, shaking his head. "Iris! You couldn't wait until tonight?! Claudette isn't even here."

The moment for plantain chip silence has passed. Having been shut up, Iris tosses one chip in her mouth, crunching it loudly.

"What's going on?" chimes Rabbit, still watching her avatar standing over Carder's freshly decapitated digital body.

Haika's face doesn't change, but she throws the script at Iris. "I knew it!" she exclaims. "I knew it! I knew it! I knew it!"

"You knew before I did, mi Haikita."

"Ha! I knew it! But never mind, Iris, go ahead... tell Carder and Rabbit the news."

"The news." Iris hides her face in Darren's neck. "Maestro?"

Darren takes cue, leaning forward to Carder's chair, Haika perched on its arm. "We were *going* to wait until dinner, standing on a chair with a glass of wine in hand to tell you, the restaurant, the world..." he pauses, "but I suppose we may as well say it." He speaks as though he's alone with Carder. "Brother, I am, we are, Iris and I, we're going to have a baby!"

Carder is silent.

Darren hits him on the knee, squawking at his own statement. "This chick right here, the most beautiful woman in the world and I are creating someone together." A look of stupid delight crosses Darren's face. With an unzipped grin he turns to Rabbit. "I'm going to have my own mini-me." And he lets out a whoop of joy.

"You and, and Iris? A little baby human?" Carder asks.

"A baby human!"

Carder eventually settles down enough to congratulate Darren and Iris, to hug them and everyone else repeatedly.

"How far along are you?"

"Tres meses," Iris says, raising three fingers into the air. She pats her belly as though she's eight months into her term.

In an instant, Carder declares it a day to celebrate, to get ice cream, to raise a glass of champagne, to buy lottery tickets and balloons.

And that's exactly what they do.

After his second glass of champagne, Carder settles back and looks at his best friend as the rest laugh in conversation. Darren is no longer the coolest punk-writer-geek he's always known. A slow metamorphosis occurring for ages has transformed him into a man, soon a father, possibly a husband.

With reproduction now in the mix, they discuss the facets of lives readjusted. After all, wherever Darren sees the Deathstar, Iris sees a mirrored disco ball. When Darren sees lasers shooting death-rays, Iris sees club lights meant for dancing. Then again, the life they're negotiating together is somewhere amid those things.

Darren declares he doesn't want his son's first name ending with an 'o.' His point is taken, but only after Iris declares other names off-limits: Luke, Leia, Han and *Opie-Juan*. Regardless of the chosen name, she won't have her child left out of its culture as she and Haika were, even if that culture is as an American-Mexican-Black-German swirl.

"American," Darren clarifies, as if he's in control.

"Maybe, but su niño will know Puerto Vallarta."

"We can't live there amidst all the drug wars."

"It's not like that. But I need to return soon. To finalize everything at the Inn."

"Like what?"

"Haika told me to clean it up for the sale. Fixing. Repairs. A little landscooping. Es verdad, it will save us many thousands."

"Nothing doing. You aren't lifting a finger!"

"I'm pregnant, not dying," says Iris, though her gap-toothed grin shows she loves the attention.

"You can't! I'm not having my knocked-up girlfriend and our illegitimate lovechild working to remodel Mexico!"

Haika interjects, "He's right, Iris, it makes no sense. But you know, I've been thinking: what if we were to operate the Inn through one more season. For mom and dad?"

"Mama y Papa are not caring at all. They're in a better place—a place so good they haven't sent postcards!" She points to the ceiling as though their parents are merely on a higher floor.

"For me, then?"

"*Now* you care, Sis. You care? Then, you're turn! And welcome to it."

Haika taps on Carder's arm. "Can you imagine? Living in Puerto Vallarta? At the Come Stay Inn?"

"Sure, I can *picture* it." Carder replies. He imagines living in swaths of green, with jeering tri-colored birds in palm trees, the sky bleeding into the sea.

"You're kidding!" Darren exclaims. "Haika, you'd do that for us?!"

"Sure. I'd live there—or at least go for a *while*."

"Well, that's it then!" Darren reanimates with excitement all over again. "You can stay here, Iris. Haika can go down and take care of the Inn. Oh my God, this is amazing!"

"How in the world?" Carder asks. He can already see Haika falling far into a primeval jungle thousands of miles away.

"I *do* want to get away from the gallery and the art world for a bit," Haika confesses. "And I don't want to sell the Come Stay. It's history. It's home."

The color leaves the room. Thoughts of being separated turn the world grey. Tropical storms brew between Haika and him. Nameless hurricanes await christenings.

"…but…"

"But?"

"…but what'll *I* do?" Carder asks.

Haika falls into his lap from the arm of the chair. She's so little, so female, kicking her legs up like searchlights. The feeling of loss blowing into Carder hasn't crossed over to her. Instead, she smirks while looking into him, producing a quiet chortle only he hears.

Pointing a thin finger at him and touching the tip of his chin, she asks, "You?"

"Me."

"You, Carder Quevedo?"

"Yes, me."

"You'll be the bartender."

It takes a second. "I can't bartend. I've never."

"It's easy. I'll show you. Oh Iris, the boys will love him down there."

"Es verdad. Your cute face will mix good drinks no matter how bad. I'll give you the best caipirinha recipe. That will show them you know something."

Carder is still baffled—Haika is letting him drift away gently instead of with crashing waves.

"How?" he asks. "How would this happen? I can't work down there, I'm sure."

"Okay, don't bartend. But I promise you'll be fine, especially once you hear how much your father paid for that plate I sold him. I know haven't told you, but you didn't ask and I was saving it for the right time," she says preemptively. "You won't have to worry for a while. I played hardball. I wasn't lying when I told you I whipped your dad's ass." She then addresses the girl at the video game console. "What do you say, Rabbit? You're a little late to rush college applications for schools you haven't had time to consider anyway. What's say you come south to the Inn? It's in Mismaloya off a little cove. You've never seen anything like it."

The game controller falls from Rabbit's lap. "Don't know. I need to think about it."

"It would be nothing short of sizzling sun and sand. Be assured, we'll return here several times. We've an upcoming birth, and these guys will come see us—and Claudette has to come down with Darren. They've a script to write and any good writer knows margaritas and sunshine ignite creative flow! Next spring, we'll come back for a few music festivals. We'll research your college options, and after Burning Man next August we'll deliver you to whichever school you settle on."

"Well…" Rabbit looks equal parts excited and confused. "Unc?"

It unfurls up from the floorboards, throwing its hooks out to the world, clawing its way forward, using the coming baby, using them, using Rabbit, using anything it can to become reality. Carder watches it in the middle of the room, until he knows with certainty that Puerto Vallarta will happen regardless of his struggles. Thus, he drops his resistance before it blooms, he reaches for the vine before him, ready to swing.

Carder looks at them one by one: Rabbit, Iris, Darren, and next to him, Haika.

"I think it could work. Let's see what we can do."

315

35

AN UNEXPECTED PARTY

Nature infuses itself deeper in Carder's psyche with each passing day. His relationship with the outdoors is lopsided and organic, with as many facets as there are shapes of leaves. Steadily, he grows used to the sounds of growing vegetation, plants baking in their expansion, stretching toward their favorite star. They open their solar panels, participating in loose rituals of heady, wanton photosynthesis, clamoring to rip carbon dioxide from lungs. Competing, they try to outdo one another with shades of astonishing greens. The brightest. Most burnished. The roughest. Rubbery jade. Viridian. Olive. Emerald. Pea-sprout. Peacock. Fronds stand like stained glass, like paint, like living road signs. Carder walks the hill's spiraling maze of paths with a dog following. Palms reach for him, brushing against his arms when he treks down to town or ascends back up the slope to the cherry atop his jungle sundae: The Come Stay Inn.

Time in Mismaloya remains free and unmeasured, providing spectacular displays of growth and decay.

What time is it exactly? He looks at the spot on his arm where a wristwatch would sit. It's naked except for a mosquito bite.

In the midst of relaxation, Carder has learned to carve wood—its bulges, curves, supple spots that want artistic release, osseous parts rejecting it—but as usual, he's at a loss for what it is he's sculpting.

A whistle sounds from downhill. Not far. Zombie bolts, disappearing into the bush.

Carder mimics the call of a yet-to-be-discovered bird, telling the hill's whistler he'll arrive momentarily. Before setting out, he places another piece of wood on the ground, reuniting it with the shavings. Then, reconsidering, he picks it up and tosses it high into the enveloping brush, opposite the direction of the whistling. It hits something with a knock—not guests, for there are none. By now the hill is sprinkled with Carder's whittled abstractions: miscarried mandrakes and half-carved wooden half-lives strewn about.

He traverses the wobbling paths south, carrying his woodcarving chisel. He didn't think to leave it behind. It gives his hands something to do while he works his way through the labyrinth, listening for the hybrid whistling, following its high notes like landmarks.

A lofty ficus tree stands thick in his path, looking as though it governed the area long before tourists ever ventured up the hill for picturesque vistas and spiced margaritas.

"Hey you!" Haika calls to him from a spot on the other side of the tree. Carder dives into greenery, taking the tree limbs in his hands like they're partners in a square dance.

"This guy's a hearty fellow," Carder says of the old ficus.

"He watches over the others." Haika shields her eyes with one garden-gloved hand as she sets down clippers.

Initially, Carder thinks she means all the other trees of Pausa Hill, but no, she's motioning to a particular grouping. He approaches Haika from behind, pulling her to him so they gain a similar perspective looking at the same things. The taste of her neck is salty—she's glistening with perspiration. From the pile of thistly weeds, she appears to have been clearing an area.

"Stop it!" she squeals, wiping her neck.

"What? Does madam prefer the sun's poison tongue?"

"Simmer down."

"What did you mean? Which *others* does that tree watch over?"

"Those trees. There."

Three trees of more or less the same height sit close together.

"My father planted them sometime around our birth: the lemon tree for me, the lime for Iris. They've withstood a few decades, many harsh summers and a bad infestation of thrips."

Haika's tree is straighter and more rigid than Carder would've guessed, encircling itself with slender, leafy spokes.

"They're beautiful," Carder says, incapable of attaching old memories, yet trying to appreciate what the branches hold for Haika. "And what about that one? The third?"

"The third. The orange tree. Iris and I have surmised that the third tree was for my father's son, a boy named Danilo, a half-brother born in secret. He died in an accident as a child. We weren't supposed to have any knowledge of him. It was a different time then."

"I didn't know."

"Of course not. I hadn't said. I wanted to wait until I could give the ground something new." She motions to a tiny ficus sapling. Delighted at finding it on the other side of the hill, Haika had carefully uprooted and relocated it. "I want this to grow as sturdy as its guardian, without the pressure of constantly producing citrus."

Carder could almost get lost in the moment if not for a beast peering from their kitchen window in the distance. A small window frames the pink blur. It's no use trying not to notice. Still, Carder looks at the horizon supported by curvaceous, tropical hills. It's no use. The creature in the window emits a high-pitched screech followed by the voice of Benjamin, their all-purpose housekeeper.

"Sí, es su mama!" Benjamin calls out so Carder and Haika will hear. He's far off, but the winds haven't come, so his words reach them easily. Speaking in a high-pitched baby voice as though it's not him but the pink infant talking, Benjamin says, "Hola, Mama! Hola, Papi!"

"Hola, Dollface!" Haika sails her voice to the top of the hill, then turns to Carder. "I'd better go get our little Salmon Belly and bring him down."

"I'd like to stay here for a bit."

"That's fine." Haika presses a quick peck onto his cheek and disappears into the flora. "Come on, Zombie."

The dog looks for permission from Carder, then trots off.

Carder stands, doing nothing, thinking nothing. Drinking it all in. The crickets of his mind mix with the songs of jungle insects. Haika's three trees shimmy their lemon, lime and orange leaves like sleepy, blinking eyes.

Until.

If it weren't impossible, Carder would swear the sky flashed several colors. It's so fast the passing hues are difficult to pinpoint.

Abruptly, the ground vibrates with the bounding walk of something large. Images congeal in Carder, impossible things: rhinoceroses, guerillas, panthers, murderers, elephants, psychopaths. What if it's thieves? What if it's thrips? Is he about to be accosted?

Leaves shuffle and bustle, branches snap and sway, limbs spring back as something passes. Silence again.

"Haika!?"

No answer.

Finally, the leaves of the old ficus tree rustle. Carder swivels, preparing to use the chisel as a dull, two-inch weapon.

The being stands at least twenty feet high and leans indifferently against the tree as though casually waiting at a bus stop, with one appendage wrapped around the ficus in cool calm. Its black eyes are so glossy that Carder sees bubbled reflections of the trees and himself. He wants to speak, but can't. He wants to run, but he's frozen. Besides, the being's willowy countenance seems lithe, nimble enough to stop him cold.

"Difficult geography," the being says in approximated English, devoid of any facial expression. "But brightness is great. Here. Your fault-weapon." It tosses a woodcarved object at Carder's feet, the same one he'd flung into the foliage before following Haika's calls.

Carder explores the chisel he brought, pressing its sharpness against the center of his palm until it hurts like it will bleed.

1. Carder is described early on as someone who "might have been a surfer, a playboy, the man whose girlfriend wears his t-shirt as a nightgown, or the vacation lover one hooks-up with for two incredible weeks," but that he "...is darker. And lonelier." Despite his misfit-leanings, he has many interactions with women. What is it that makes him appealing or relatable?

2. Did our knowledge of Carder's past (which many characters in the book didn't have) make him more or less sympathetic? What information do you think he should or should not have revealed to others in the book?

3. Despite being Carder's mother, we never experience Sylvia Quevedo while she's alive. What can we surmise about her character and her influence in Carder's life even after her death?

4. What significance do the residents of Neidin have in the novel? What purpose do they serve in Carder's life? How do they correspond to events taking place in the "real world?" Are they real themselves?

5. While reflecting on the Vivienne girls, Haika realizes that "she painted the girls with the same broad brush everyone else had... She had put them in frames *she'd* chosen instead of allowing them to present themselves as they wished." Is this accurate? If Carder had been female or the Vivienne girls had been male, how might things have been different?

6. Carder, his father –Gordan Quevedo– and Gavin Daguerré all had a personal history with the Pick-Me-Pups. How did each deal with it differently and how does this demonstrate how much our circumstances

are influenced by our reactions to them?

7. Mandy's family is complicated. How do you feel about her parent's decision to disown her? By doing so, what tangible or intangible things are they taking away from her? What are they taking away from themselves? How is this different than Carder's reaction?

8. The novel moves back and forth between myth and "real life." What do you think of the juxtaposition of otherworldliness and gritty day-to-day living, and what purpose does it serve?

9. What meaning does the presence of death have in this novel? Which deaths —and the way in which the survivors dealt with them— felt familiar from your own life experiences?

10. Of all the themes in the novel —family, religion, death, myth, self-preservation— which one resonated the most for you?

ABOUT THE AUTHOR

Elias Barton has lived on the edge of an active volcano, worked in a Bible factory and was a semifinalist in both 2011 and 2012 for the Amazon Breakthrough Novel Award. He currently resides in Washington DC, painting, dodging zombies and feeding unicorns. while working on his second novel "The Circadian Ladder."

For a soundtrack playlist to the novel, to make contact, and for other various sundries please visit:

www.EliasBarton.com

Elias Barton is available for select readings and lectures. To inquire about a possible appearance, please make contact through www.EliasBarton.com.

ACKNOWLEDGMENTS

The author would like to thank many who were instrumental in bringing this book from inkling to ink. Gratitude and a glass of wine to the ever-present editor, Peter Couchman, whose eyes see everything, and to the editing skills of Carolyn Goldhush, Rebecca Jaycox and Ann Votaw. Warm regards and cold salutes to Scott Tamblin and Rebeccah Campbell for medical insights (and to Rebeccah for oodles of '*twin*formation'); to Dereck Romero for musical guidance; and to Ronald Couchman for education on the Battlefield, friendship and belly laughs.